CHAOS DEALS IN DEATH
THE CHAOS COVENANT ~ BOOK TWO

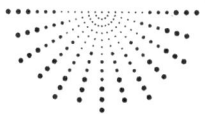

KATE CRAFT

CHAOS DEALS IN DEATH

Book Two in The Chaos Covenant series

Copyright © Kate Craft 2022

First Edition: September 2022

The right of KATE CRAFT to be identified as the author of this work has been asserted by her in accordance with the Copyright, Designs and Patents Act 1988.

All rights reserved. No part of this publication may be reproduced, transmitted, or stored in a retrieval system in any form or by any means without permission in writing from the copyright owner, nor otherwise circulated in any form of binding or cover other than that in which it is published and without a similar condition being imposed on the subsequent purchaser.

This is a work of fiction. All characters in this publication are fictitious, and any resemblance to real people, alive or dead, is purely coincidental.

Paperback ISBN: 978-1-7397349-2-3

Hardback ISBN: 978-1-7397349-3-0

For enquires, please visit: www.katecraft.com

When we read, do we truly become lost? Or have we simply found our true place? Step inside and see.

— KATE CRAFT.

To Mum,
I'd do time for you, let's leave it at that…

CONTENTS

1. Visions — 1
   Eastern Outlands – Etiyan Vale
2. An Intrusive Guest — 18
   Eastern Outlands – Etiyan Vale
3. Shelter from the Storm — 33
   Eastern Outlands – Kavakin Desert
4. A Devil in the Details — 48
   Eastern Outlands – Kavakin Desert
5. Trouble at the Port — 65
   Eastern Outlands – Kavakin Desert
6. Hunter Becomes the Hunted — 82
   Eastern Outlands – Kavakin Desert
7. Prophecy Unveiled — 96
   Danika
8. Mischief Makes a Mess — 114
   Danika
9. Deception and Deals — 131
   Danika
10. Friend or Foe? — 147
    Danika ~ Esterbell
11. A Secret Between Friends — 162
    Esterbell
12. Maelin's Bridge — 174
    Southern Outlands
13. Shadows Amongst the Herd — 185
    Southern Outlands
14. A Devil's Den — 203
    Southern Outlands
15. A Phoenix Rises — 219
    Southern Outlands
16. Plans and Dreams — 230
    Southern Outlands ~ Esterbell
17. Frosted Fire — 243
    The Bloodywood – Esterbell
18. Shaded Exorcism — 257
    The Bloodywood – Esterbell
19. Smokey Deceit — 270
    Esterbell

20. Divided *Cantor*	285
21. The Voices Will Tell You *Esterbell*	293
22. Walking Nightmare *Cantor*	298
23. Death Summons a God *Esterbell*	315
Afterword	335
Also by Kate Craft	337
Acknowledgments	338
Street-Team	340
About the Author	343

1
VISIONS

EASTERN OUTLANDS – ETIYAN VALE

Am I dead?

Maya woke to the soft sensation of something small and gritty flittering across her face. Sand carried by a light wind had half-buried her in the dunes of Etiyan Vale. She shot up, displacing the sprite that had been sitting on her chest, diligently awaiting its master to wake up. Loki, a high level Finkel sprite with a long, furry coat as white as crisp snow, purred in response and disappeared in a puff of wind. Dust coated the inside of her mouth and Maya swallowed hoping to clear it. Reaching up, she touched her neck. The skin was sore and swollen, and the events of what had happened came flooding back.

Maya had spent the last few days mostly confined to her bed, recovering from the Esterbellian attack…and Elkin's betrayal. She could only suffer Thelic and her grandmother hovering and fussing for so long before insisting she take a walk by herself. Well, Loki had tagged along. There was no denying the little Finkel, and Maya could tolerate the silent companionship. The sprite gave a whispering whine as he reappeared, floating up to Maya's shoulder to lick her neck. She chuckled, the sound closer to a cackle with her sun-parched throat as she stroked Loki in the space between his two tall ears.

Glancing around, she noticed she had made it as far as a small cluster of desert trees just on the outskirts of what remained of the ruined city. She froze as a sharp wind whispered along the sands, and Loki lifted his head in response to scan the dunes.

A soft voice drifted along the breeze, barely audible against the rustle of fauna. Maya recognised it. She touched her throat again. Whoever, or whatever had conjured that whisper was no friend. Why it seemed intent to harm her, she had no clue. But Fatari might know.

"If you wanted to rest, you should have stayed in bed."

Maya smiled at the sound of Thelic's teasing tone. Even against the soft wind, she could pick out his breathing, quick and shallow, betraying how long he had wandered the sands in search of her. Maya turned at the waist and covered her eyes from the glare of the Avalonian sun as she peered to the top of the dune. There he was, spear strapped to his side and arms crossed. Though she couldn't make out his expression with the sun directly behind him, she would have bet half a lung that it harboured at least mild disapproval.

"Why didn't you answer when I called?" he asked, sliding down the sands.

"I didn't hear you," she managed to croak. "I don't suppose you brought any water?"

Thelic stopped at her side and crouched. His eyes, a brilliant clash of grey and blue, scanned her body from her feet, to her legs, to her waist, his gaze stopping abruptly at her neck. "Those are new," he said quietly, indicating the fresh bruising.

Maya attempted to swallow. "Water?"

Without looking away from her neck, he removed the small pouch from his side and unscrewed the top before giving it to her. Maya drank hungrily from the purse and wondered just how long she had been lying there. She supposed it was likely longer than she had promised, seeing as Thelic had come looking for her.

"Tell me what happened," he said.

Maya glugged the last of the water before dropping her hands into her lap and taking a breath to clear her throat. She shook her head before answering. "I'm not sure. One moment I was walking with Loki, and then the next I heard a voice and someone...better yet, some*thing*, started strangling me. I guess I passed out."

Thelic's only response was a shadowy scowl as he raked a hand through his dark hair and scanned the surrounding dunes. The Finkel, seeming to sense his concern, hopped onto Thelic's shoulder before slathering the warrior's cheek in quick-fire licks that Maya was sure were meant as kisses. Thelic sighed and allowed some of the tension to leave his body, though his right hand remained firmly on the hilt of his retractable spear. Maya was ok. Though, she was never safe, and Thelic was beginning to get the sense she never would be.

"Have you seen my grandmother today?" she asked. "I need to talk to her about these voices. The fact that one of them manifested in a way that could touch me is a little…disconcerting."

Thelic bridled at the understatement but nodded. "Last time I saw Lifaya was this morning. She was heading to the caves with some of the children."

"What about Kadhim and Zarina?" She hadn't seen their gypsul companions all day either.

"They should be about. I think I saw them tilling one of the sand fields."

Maya chuckled at the thought of the very stoic Kadhim tolerating the local folk's directives on farming matters. "It baffles me how they manage to grow anything in this kind of environment," she said, dipping her hands into the soft silica.

"I suppose the same could be said for the cold climate in Cantor, which is highly regarded as a farming nation," Thelic mused.

"It's wonderfully bizarre. Two territories totally divided, and yet thriving despite the extreme elements."

"It's because of the elemental sprites that crops grown in both Etiyan Vale and Cantor are able to thrive." Holding both hands out to Maya, he helped her stand and brushed what remained of the dust from her thin, linen clothes. "You're sun-parched," he said, pointing to Maya's hands turned red in the sun.

"I'm fine, they aren't sore. I'll just have a terrible tan-line."

"BB can take care of that."

"The tan-line?"

"No, the dehydration that comes with it," he muttered.

Maya scrunched her face at the idea of summoning the temperamental Water Finkel – a sprite she had contracted at Batshari's temple – for something as benign as moisturising her hands. Batshari, the grumpy God of water, would almost certainly be unimpressed.

"It's a good chance to practice," Thelic offered, not bothering to hide his grin at Maya's reluctance.

"He bit me yesterday."

Thelic chuckled at the reminder. "I know. I heard you curse like a bordello madam."

"Little devil. He's lucky he doesn't come with a return address, or I'd ship him straight back to Batshari–" Maya paused at the sensation of something wet dribbling down her leg. Already cringing with a sense of dread, she looked down and was mortified to find a large wet patch slowly forming on the crotch of her trousers.

"You know, if you needed to relieve yourself–"

"Don't," Maya warned Thelic, before sighing in defeat at the water sprite, otherwise known as BB, and his funny idea of a prank, before taking a seat on the hot sands to dry herself.

As Thelic and Maya crossed the dunes back to the small town of the Vale, they discussed plans for leaving. It wasn't a particularly happy topic. The dangerous trek from Danika, through the territories to the Outlands had almost killed them on more than one occasion. But from what Fatari had told them, the group had little choice if they were to find the Gouram shrines, obtain the seals and collect the scrolls before the next alignment.

Maya sighed as she touched Batshari's mark across her chest. It was only the first of the four Gouram seals she was to collect to safeguard her life during the ceremony to close the gateways.

"That's a lot of sighing for so early in the day. Why have you gone quiet? Is your throat giving you trouble?" Thelic asked with a nudge to her shoulder.

"No, my throat is fine. And I'm not sure I should say what I'm thinking out loud," Maya admitted.

"Well, that just makes me all the more curious."

"Naturally. Sorry, I shouldn't have said anything, it's nothing really," she assured him, plastering her best attempt at a smile across her face.

"I doubt that. Come on, out with it."

Sighing again, Maya stopped beside the first building on the town's outskirts. With corners crumbling from lack of maintenance, the old home had been abandoned many years ago when the first of the town's inhabitants had moved on. Maya glanced around for any potential prying eyes and stepped closer to Thelic once she had determined they were alone.

"Why hasn't anyone asked if I even *want* to be the next saviour of Avalon? Everyone just assumes I'm more than willing to throw my life on the line for a world that hasn't been particularly welcoming." Maya wasn't sure what she expected Thelic to say. But what he *did* certainly took her by surprise.

Grabbing Maya by the shoulders, Thelic closed the gap between them and crushed his lips to hers. She relaxed in his grip, leaning deeper into the kiss and taking the moment to step away from her enforced responsibilities.

"What was that for?" she asked breathlessly as he broke away.

His silver eyes bore down into hers for a moment longer before responding. "It's a reminder. I have no expectations of you, Maya. In fact, if I had a say, I would take you deep into the Outlands where nobody could find you."

Maya chuckled. "Ah, but then who would save Avalon?"

Thelic scoffed before pushing her back against the crumbling stone wall of the decrepit home. "I'm not the hero you think I am. I couldn't care less about this world. I'm more concerned about you, about keeping you alive long enough to actually *live*."

Trapped with her back against the wall and Thelic's arms either side of her, there was no hiding from the sheer intensity of his words. He wasn't joking, that much was easy to tell. He would see Avalon burn before it took her life trying to save it. She shivered at the thought; both thrilling and terrifying her. This was the man she was falling for. The man who would kill to keep her safe without a second thought. She reached up with both hands to cup his face, allowing her body to convey what she failed to conjure in words.

"Miss Maya?" a small voice called out.

Thelic suppressed a growl at the interruption, stepping back as a young boy approached. Belatedly he realised it was the same boy who had been trapped under the rubble during the battle against the Esterbellian soldiers. Thanks to him, they had won with ease when the boy had gathered the other children from the caves to fight alongside them. Thelic smiled at the memory of little etiyan shapeshifters charging across the dunes to their aid.

"Miss Maya, do you have a moment?" the boy asked hesitantly.

"Of course." Maya pushed back from the wall and took a knee on the dry sand. "How are your wounds?" She stared at the crude bandages around his wrist and both knees. It was her fault the boy had nearly been crushed to death the day of the battle; her power – bolstered by raw emotion and the planets' alignment – had broken loose uncontrollably.

"Fine, thank you. Me and the other children were wondering if you might come to the Telling tonight?"

"The Telling?"

The boy nodded his head excitedly. "Fatari will be dealing prophecies, as she does after every alignment."

Unsurprisingly, this was the first Maya had heard of such an event. Did she even want to know her future? Every other fable, both from Thelic's late father and that of her ancestors, all seemed to end in death. The boy continued to stare hopefully. "Of course, I'll be there," she promised.

"Great! I'll save you a seat next to me," he assured her, before skipping off to inform his waiting friends.

"You didn't have to say yes."

Maya turned to Thelic, her mouth pulled in a tight line, one eyebrow raised. "Did you see that kid's face? Plus, I sort of owe him after very nearly crushing him to death." She raised a hand to halt any half-attempts at a protest from Thelic, instead taking his arm to lead him into town.

Sure enough, Kadhim and Zarina were working hard in the sandy fields, laying seeds and raking the silica back to cover them. In the adjacent plot, children pulled at the roots of fully bloomed flowers holding ripened red fruit ready for harvest. Maya stopped to wave at the two gypsul who were quickly becoming friends to her and Thelic, but decided to leave them to their work.

Before long, the couple grew bored of walking the short paths between dwellings and made their way towards the town hall. Young gypsul boys and girls crowded the entrance, each of them eager to get inside.

"What's going on?" Maya asked a girl who stood at the back the group.

"The Seer is having a vision," she replied, boredom lacing her tone. She looked up then at who had asked the question, to see Thelic eyeing her quizzically. "Oh, sorry! I didn't realise it was you," she exclaimed nervously.

Before Maya could respond, the young girl began barging her way through the group, telling the others to make way for 'the Blessed One'.

The Blessed One? Bloody hell, Maya thought, forcing a smile for the small, expectant faces as she passed.

Inside, the town hall was cool in comparison to the dry heat of the desert sun. Pots filled with water and reeds were evenly spaced along the walls of the circular room, acting as an old-fashioned air conditioner. At the centre of the room stood a long and low stone table. More children crowded about its edges, their attentions focused on the Seer, Fatari – otherwise known as Lifaya, Maya's grandmother.

Sitting at the table, Lifaya held her head in her hands, both elbows on her knees as she shook with concentration. Seeing what she thought was her grandmother in a state of distress, Maya broke forward and placed her hands on the old woman's shoulders.

Lifaya mumbled in response – not to Maya, to the flash of images racing through her mind as the vision took hold and propelled her into a storm of prophecies.

"Get her some water," Maya instructed the closest child, a boy no older than ten. He gave a curt nod before pushing through the group to do as she asked.

"She's fine, Maya. She'll come out of it soon," Thelic said. Hearing the mumbled whispers behind, he turned to address the children. "Right, the Seer will need her rest when she emerges. Go on, scoot." The whispers quietened as he spoke, but nobody moved. Placing one hand on the hilt of his spear, his eyes narrowed as he squared off against the young gathering. "*Now*."

The sound of scuffling feet and giggling filled the confines of the domed hall as the younglings fled. Maya couldn't help but chuckle at Thelic's gruffness; the seasoned warrior more accustomed to intimidating thugs and assassins than children.

Lifaya shot to her feet, sucking air through her nostrils as she snapped back to reality. Dark spots crept in to crowd the corners of her vision, and she threw out a hand to steady herself. With help, she sat back down on the cushions and leaned against the stone table. She looked up at who had helped her and found Maya's olive-green eyes staring back.

"What are you doing out of bed?" the Seer asked, tuts of disapproval coming with every second breath.

"You said I was okay to walk round today," Maya replied with a shrug after handing over the cup water.

"Not all day. Spirits, Maya, you must give your body time to recover, or it *will* break down." Taking the cup in her hands, Lifaya drank thirstily.

"Yes, I've gathered that much. Anyway, less about me. What happened? Are you okay?"

Lifaya threw up a hand to wave off her granddaughter's concern. "Just another vision. It was a big one though, the longest I've had in a while."

"What was it about? Did you see anything about our journey?" Thelic asked. He had taken a seat on the edge of the table and regarded the Seer curiously.

"I did. It seems your timeline will have to move up. You must all leave tomorrow."

"WHAT? What is so damned important you had to pull me from sleep and through a bloody sandstorm?" Keela demanded as she stepped over the town hall's threshold. After shaking off the sand that had gathered in the folds of her clothes, she brushed at the dust coating her lightly tanned face.

Night had fallen, and with it a storm raged through Etiyan Vale. The sight wasn't uncommon in the barren desert of Kavakin, and the townspeople rallied to baton down the hatches before returning to their homes for the evening. When the winds raged, there was little to be done. The Telling would have to wait, the children disappointed; but this was a way of life amongst the dunes of the Outlands.

"Lifaya had a vision," Kadhim offered in explanation, smiling at the perpetually frustrated woman.

Abandoning the impossible task of taming her windswept

hair, Keela glanced around the confines of the singular domed room that formed the town hall, registering that the Seer was missing. "Brilliant. I thought she wasn't having those anymore," she said as she took a seat at the stone table. "So, who dies? Better yet, who is *supposedly* going to die? The old woman's visions seem to be getting a little muddied over the years."

"You're in a pleasant mood this evening," Maya stated dryly, crossing her arms to stop herself from thumping her half-sister. "We thought you might want to know that we're leaving tomorrow morning. Though I'm not sure why, Lifaya hasn't told us yet. All we know is that something has changed, and it requires an earlier departure than we had originally intended."

Right on cue, the door burst open and Lifaya rocketed through. Her silver hair whipped furiously with the gale as she turned on her heel to force the heavy wood back into place and block out the elements. Once the latch was secured, she faced the rest of the room, taking in the five waiting faces.

"Good, you're all here. I've got the map," the Seer said excitedly, hurrying her steps across the stone floor to stand beside Maya.

"You wasted your time," Thelic said as he watched the older woman unroll a large piece of parchment across the table. "We already have a map of Avalon."

"Ah, but this one marks the locations of both the gateways *and* the Gouram temples. It will save you scouring the lands."

Maya watched as her grandmother pointed to small circles dotted around the territories and the Outlands, each with a triangle at its centre. She touched the pendant Thelic had purchased for her on their travels through Fortus. Each of the elements were represented by a symbol, a triangle that differed slightly by its position or a small line drawn horizontally. Her pendant was an amalgamation of the elemental symbols, all connected by the circular sign for spirit.

"Now, there is one temple where I know you can contact Ragashi, the Gouram of earth. I am bound to him as he is to me," the Seer said confidently.

"Oh. I figured you and the Gouram Batshari were besties after conjuring that castor circle during the battle," Maya said. She knew Fatari was powerful, but she had no idea just how far that power extended.

"I am contracted to both. That is the reason for my gift of far-sight. Though, it comes with a price." Stepping back from the map, Lifaya turned and motioned with her hand for the others to sit down. "There is something you must do before seeking out the Gouram."

"Here we go," Keela muttered, placing her back against the cool stone of the tower wall.

"You must go to the territory named Danika, first," Lifaya began. "The leader there plans to align himself with one of the other territories, Fortus, in preparation for war. This is what the humans have been waiting for. With Danika stepping into the fight, it won't be long before Transum is forced to take a stand as well." She turned squarely to face Maya. "If you do not convince Carnass to stay his forces, this war will ignite before we've had a chance to quell the chaos."

Maya swallowed the small lump forming in her throat. "What makes you think I can convince him?"

"I saw it. Well, as is customary, I saw two paths etched in fate. Either you succeed and the path is cleared to carry out your search. Or…"

"Or we fail and life is made ten times more difficult?" Maya guessed. If the Seer's expression was anything to go by, she was right.

"Either way, Maya, war will happen," Zarina said, shifting

along the hard floor to sit closer to her side. The young gypsul's white hair, tied in its signature braid, fell delicately over her shoulder as she leaned her body to the side to touch her head to Maya's. "All we can do is try to delay it."

Maya got to her feet. "Surely that can't be it. We could try and convince the Keepers and the gypsul that war isn't the answer."

Everyone in the room remained silent, humans and gypsul sharing a look with the same thought occupying their minds.

"They won't listen," Kadhim said with a tired roll of his eyes. "Each side has too much to lose. In our case, the gypsul will be wiped from existence in this small slice of Sythintall. If the humans fail, they either die, or they are banished to return to their world."

"That's what I mean. It doesn't *need* to be that way," Maya insisted. "Neither side must die for the other to prosper. If there's peace, why can't the humans remain here and live out the remainder of their lives amongst the gypsul?"

"Would you ask a djinca to lay down with a rasicus, Maya?" Keela offered in comparison.

"And who, exactly, is the rasicus in that metaphor?" Kadhim asked, one eyebrow raised in unspoken challenge.

In this world, a rasicus looks like and holds a similar status on the food chain as a rabbit would on Earth. And Keela would never put herself in the same boat as what might be considered prey, which answered Kadhim's question.

Maya stepped between the two, wary of things getting out of hand before their discussions had even begun. "That's not helpful, Keela. It also doesn't help that the humans are unaware of the true cause of the chaos, perhaps we could educate them on that?" As Maya had come to learn, the chaos was a deadly leak of elemental power from the five gateways of Sythintall. Humans had been taught that this was born *purely* from the third realm; the realm where contracted sprites from Earth were banished when humans made the crossing to Sythintall. While in a way that was correct, it was the power of the foreign sprites themselves that caused the deadly fog; a veil that slowly encroached on the territory, suffocating it.

When the great Majors had crossed over from Earth to Sythintall almost three thousand years ago, they went back on their word. They promised the Gods of this realm, the Gouram, that they would never return after soliciting help with the chaos on Earth. Instead, the Majors created five gateways and sealed off the five territories with a deadly boundary void from the rest of Sythintall, as a safe haven for humans. They believed this would protect them from angry gypsul, and it did, for a time. But now, the world was choking on the bleed between realms, and Maya – half human, half gypsul – was the only one capable of stopping it.

"The humans already suspect the gateways are somehow to blame, surely they would appreciate the need to close them?" Maya asked, searching the faces of her friends for a flicker of understanding.

"Not likely," Thelic muttered. "With the gateways closed and the boundary void eradicated, they will expect the gypsul from beyond to come in waves of retribution, with no way to get back to Earth." He sighed picking at the grains of sand lodged under his fingernail. "I would expect the same."

"That's not strictly true," Fatari said, speaking for the first time in a while. She had been listening to the discussion, marvelling at something she hadn't seen for a long time. These warriors from both sides of the coming war were willing to sit and discuss these problems. It was a start. "One gateway, the original, will remain open as it always has done. From there, any humans who wish to return to Earth can do so, once stripped of their contracts to the sprites from this realm."

Thelic's gaze snapped to the Seer. "You can do that?"

"Yes, I can."

"How? And if so, why hasn't this been made known to the younglings dying from overuse of their contracts?" Thelic asked. He rubbed at the leather cuff around his wrist as he spoke, thinking of his own contract with the Vasibas of wind and earth.

"Because nobody knew how, exactly. Not even me," the Seer explained. "That was part of my vision. I saw the Gouram Stone being used to draw the sprites from their hosts. I'm not sure how, yet. But as you search for the other seals, I will do my best to find out."

"Would you part with your contracts, Thelic?" Maya asked.

Thelic looked up from his feet to see Maya staring at his wrists, and quickly dropped his hands to his side. "No. At least not anytime soon." How could he? He needed the contracted power for Maya, to protect her.

Maya nodded her head in understanding. She didn't like it, the unknown. Under the leather cuffs on Thelic's wrists lay the marks that determined his lifeline. Thick and black at the birth of a contract with a sprite, those marks slowly faded and shrank, until they became no more, and the host died. She hated it.

"Okay, what's the plan then?" Keela asked, standing to brush the dust from her trousers. "We head to Danika to try and convince Carnass to wait before joining Fortus in the war preparations? Then follow your map to the temples and hope one of the Gods responds? Some plan," she muttered.

"I'm afraid that's all we've got," Lifaya said with an apologetic smile. Taking a seat on the edge of the table, she regarded each of the remaining members of the group. She watched Keela, Maya's half-sister, amble around the circular room as she flicked her blades in both hands. The woman was stubborn-willed and brash with her words, but Lifaya had misjudged her, misjudged the vision she'd had of Maya being betrayed. Keela would be tested in the coming trials in a way the others simply would not understand.

Next, the Seer looked to the two gypsul, Zarina and Kadhim. Zarina stood at Keela's side, helping her untangle the long, brown hair that flowed down the Esterbellian's back. Zarina would do well to calm the natural tension between species, an easily lovable and kind woman. Kadhim, however, would be a little trickier. As his feelings changed and developed, so would the dynamics of the group. Had he realised? Did Maya notice his growing attachment to her?

The thought prompted the Seer to look next at Thelic. Sat on the edge of the table beside her, he held a large stone in one hand, his spear in the other; sliding them together to sharpen the spear's deadly tip. This man was trouble, in more ways than one. But he was also Maya's best chance at making it through this alive.

"Okay then," Maya said, breaking the silence of meditative thought. "We leave for Danika tomorrow. Who's coming?"

Everyone looked at her as though she had grown a second head, each with their eyebrows raised and head tilted.

"We're all going, idiot," Keela answered on the others' behalf. "We wouldn't have half a hope if you went by yourself."

Maya opened her mouth to object, pent up stress and frustration at the brink of exploding, then stopped. Keela smiled at her, no sarcasm or jest in her eyes or in the soft curve of her lips. It was understanding that Maya saw there, and a fondness that was slowly blossoming. She let out a long breath and smiled back. Maya didn't say thank you, she didn't need to. They weren't going for her, they were fighting to save their world and their people from a common enemy, the chaos.

Maya turned to Fatari. "In that case, I need another prophecy from you."

2
AN INTRUSIVE GUEST

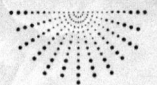

EASTERN OUTLANDS – ETIYAN VALE

Maya smiled as she packed her canvas bag with the clothes gathered from their travels – trousers, a coat, shirts and boots from Brijid, the healer in Danika; lighter and more sheer variations from Wilix, the tailor in Transum; a robe from the Ragashian Tribe at Slitter Ridge; and desert attire from Etiyan Vale's Pavinicum encampment.

So many had helped Maya and the others along the way so far. Though, admittedly, just as many had tried to kill or waylay them. Maya reached forward to grab the last piece of clothing on the bed to pack – a worn pair of leather gloves, far too big for her small hands; designed for colder climes and rough, working hands. Elkin's gloves. He had given them to her as they had traversed through the Shadow Mountains to Slitter Ridge, her hands bleeding from the scraggly rocks…

"Can't have your blood conjuring castor circles around here, Maya. Knowing my luck, you'll dislodge a boulder right above my head!"

That's what Elkin had said, giving her the gloves under the gentle guise of protecting himself. She had known he was lying, then. What she hadn't realised, was that Elkin had been lying the whole time; about why he really wanted to join them...about everything.

"I'll kill him for that."

Maya's hands froze at the deep and rumbling tone of Thelic's voice, the leather gloves still clasped between her fingers.

"Kill who? For what?" she asked, bending down and tucking the gloves deep into the side of her bag.

"Elkin. I'll kill him for putting that look on your face."

Maya finally turned, disturbed by the way his voice grated in low fury. Thelic's expression only served to worry her more, his teeth clenched together and hands balled into fists so tight, the blood had completely abandoned his fingers. This wasn't him. While their initial meeting in the Danikan glen and their subsequent journey through the territories had proved this man was a warrior, he never sought out the violence – though it always managed to find him.

"Don't say that," Maya whispered. Abandoning the chore of packing her bag for travel, she crossed the room to stand in front of him, placing one hand around his white-knuckled fist as the other traced the sharp line of his bristly jaw. She smiled as the tension left his shoulders and he leaned into her palm. "You remind me of a German-Shepherd," she said with a laugh.

"Do I want to know what that is?" Thelic rumbled.

Maya pulled her hand from his chin and leaned back to tap the side of her face in a dramatic pause for thought. She knew Thelic wasn't easily insulted, even if he *was* being compared to a dog. It was his nature; the primal need to protect; the animal ready to attack, but so easily subdued by the touch of a gentle hand. Well, it was that, and the soft and subtle tones of blonde amongst the brown of his lengthening stubble.

"No," she said, smiling cheekily up at him. "I think I'll let you ponder that one for a while. Maybe let it curb your mood from fury to curiosity," she finished with a wink as she pulled away to move back to her task.

A hand reached out, grabbing the back of her shirt and loosening it from her trousers as she was pulled backwards. She smacked into Thelic's hard chest, his hands releasing the worn material of her shirt to wrap around her stomach. He held her there as he dipped his forehead to rest against the curve of her collar.

Heat blazed along her back where his breath came in deep, heavy waves. She squirmed against his hold, the motion only resulting in a low growl as he tightened his grip. The heat from her neck moved down her spine and along her stomach, everywhere he touched burned like a fever.

She pinched the skin on top of his hand and he loosened his hold, just enough let her turn and face him. He leaned in to touch his lips to hers – and instead met the palm of her hand, one placed firmly across his mouth, the other touching his forehead.

"You're really hot," she murmured.

"As are you," he said in a jovial daze.

"No, you're burning up. I think you might have a fever. How do you feel?"

In response, he made a move to lift the shirt over her head and groaned with annoyance when she batted at his hands. He tried for her trouser button next and growled when he was met with the same result. "Woman, will you cut that out?"

"Seriously, Thelic. You're swaying." She put a hand out to steady him then nudged him towards the bed. If he collapsed on the floor, he would be staying there for the night. Maya was strong, but Thelic was almost twice her weight and about a foot taller, she wouldn't have a hope of moving him.

"Come on, into bed. Did you sleep at all when I was recovering?"

He hadn't. Maya had slept for three days solid after the battle with the Esterbellians. Too much power used all at once had completely drained her reserves and almost killed her. He gripped his forehead and stumbled over to the bed, flopping down onto the hard, straw mattress with a resounding thud. What if Elkin returned with more soldiers? That's all Thelic could think about. About how his best friend in this world had betrayed them. And for what? A Keeper's promise? Elkin should have known better.

"Oh...hmmm...yes," Lifaya mumbled to herself, feeling Thelic's forehead with the palm of her hand. He had broken into cold sweats not long after Maya had left the room to fetch her grandmother. The Seer continued with her assessment, feeling along his legs, his chest, his arms.

Thelic let out a vicious hiss as Lifaya's palms brushed the tattooed marks along his bicep. The sound was cause enough for everyone to take a step back from the bed, but it was his face, contorted in a rage they had never seen before that stopped them in their tracks.

"What's wrong with him?" Maya asked her grandmother, stepping forward once again to touch his hand. The skin beneath her palm was hot, too hot for a mere human's body heat. "His fever is getting worse."

"He has a guest, it seems," Lifaya declared with a muttered oath, offering no further explanation as she hurried from the room.

Maya tried to follow, but Thelic's hand clamped over her wrist, his strength considerable despite his weakened state. "Okay, I'll stay," Maya promised. She worried her bottom lip between her teeth as Thelic nodded his head slowly, the small movement sending ripples of pain across his body.

"Move aside, Maya. And stay back," Lifaya instructed as she hurried back through the open door with Kadhim at her side and a small, leather pouch in her grasp.

"NO," Thelic roared. "Get the fuck away from me, old woman," he snarled vehemently, throwing out an arm to strike her.

Kadhim was there before the blow could land, catching Thelic's arm and wrenching it back down into a straightened position on the bed.

Lifaya's shock quickly dissipated, and she reached into the folds of leather. Inside was the Gouram Stone, a jewel akin to an opal, smooth on its surface with spectral-coloured lightening in its veins. The Stone glowed as she held it in the palm of her hand, the coloured tones exploding with a light that seemed to emanate, originally, from Lifaya herself.

When the strength of that light seemed ready to set the Stone aflame, Lifaya thrust the pendant to Thelic's chest, and he screamed. That sound didn't entirely belong to him. His scream could be heard but it was quiet in comparison to the guttural roar that seemed to echo alongside it.

He has a guest, it seems. That's what the Seer had said. Maya thought back to earlier in the day, when the voice she had heard, a harmless whisper, had moved corporeally and strangled her. Something else – perhaps the same being – was now attacking Thelic, *using* his body instead of trying to break it.

Thelic's back arched on the bed, the angle unnatural for anyone but a seasoned gymnast. His fingers dug deep into the mattress, scratching at the thin cotton sheet and ripping the underside of his fingernails.

Maya raced forward and clutched his hand once again, trying to stop him from tearing his nails loose altogether.

Lifaya's head snapped up at the movement. "No, Maya!"

Thelic's hand was ripped from Maya's so fast she barely had time to blink before it wrapped around her throat; Thelic's nails, already bloody from clawing at the bed, now sharp and ragged against the skin at her neck. He let out a roar and his fingers opened slightly, releasing some of the pressure. But not for long. A cold, cruel sneer washed across his face as whatever possessed him regained control.

Fatari continued her chants, holding the Stone tightly against Thelic's chest, straining with the effort to maintain the power flowing through her, into the Stone and then onwards into Thelic.

A shift happened, the power no longer pumping into Thelic, but pouring out of him. A billowing stream of ethereal fog was sucked from his writhing form like a vacuum, and he fell limp against the bed.

"Fuck!" Maya croaked, grateful for the breath returning to her lungs as she put one knee on the bed at Thelic's side. She didn't have to get any closer to know he was alive. His breathing came in quick, shallow draws as his body began to relax.

Lifaya fell backwards onto the floor, clutching the Stone tightly in her hands, strands of silver hair plastered against her forehead.

THE OTHERS HAD LEFT while Maya had tended to Thelic, carefully ensuring she dried his skin and changed his clothes to make him more comfortable. Once he'd slipped into sleep, she made her way to the town hall where she was sure the others would have convened after what had just happened.

"What the hell *was* that?" Maya asked as she came barging through the door of the town hall.

As expected, Kadhim, Zarina and Lifaya sat at the table,

each with a goblet of wine in their hands as they talked in hushed tones. The moment Maya appeared, their whispers died, and they each looked to one another.

Maya paused in front of them and waited, resisting the urge to tap her foot. It wasn't anger that drove her, that stole her breath and seemingly took over her body; it was fear. "He looked like he was possessed."

"I've been meaning to ask, what happened there?" Zarina pointed to the light bruising on Maya's neck.

With everything that had happened, Maya had completely forgotten to tell them about her own visitor earlier that day. "Something attacked me," she said. "It didn't take over my body, like with Thelic. Though I suppose whatever *that* was felt keen to strangle me as well."

Kadhim stood from the table and closed the short distance between him and Maya in less than a second. His hands flew to her throat, checking for any sort of swelling or broken skin. No, just lightly bruised, though that was bad enough. "Why didn't you tell me?" he asked.

Maya stepped back, holding her hands up between them. "I'm okay, really. I just never got around to telling you all about it."

"Never got…" Kadhim tilted his head to the ceiling, the layers of his medium length, wavy black hair falling back from the corners of his face as he let out a deep groan of frustration. He held it there for a second, calming his temper, before bringing his head back down to face her. "We need to know these things, Maya. How the fuck are we supposed to protect you if you're not willing to share information that might help us."

For the first time, she realised Kadhim's eyes weren't the dark black she had always assumed from a distance. They were a deep shade of blue with a lighter violet edge. She met those eyes with her own burning determination. "It wasn't a matter of willingness to share, Kadhim. I was going to tell you, I just hadn't gotten around to it."

Kadhim cursed under his breath before returning to his place at the table. "The sooner you realise your own importance, Maya, the better."

"How could I forget?" she muttered in response as she took a seat next to her grandmother.

"Tell us what happened, Maya," Lifaya prompted, taking her granddaughter's hand and squeezing it gently.

With that small gesture, the tension in Maya's shoulders released and she recounted the event on the dunes outside of the Vale.

"What were you doing out there?" Zarina asked, her intonation expressing curiosity more than the irritation clearly displayed in the tight-lipped Kadhim.

"I just went for a walk. And I made sure to stay behind the stones. It's not like I was expecting trouble," Maya said softly. The locals of Etiyan Vale had placed small piles of stones around the borders of the Vale as a marker – venture much further and you were fair game to any passing grokusi, large snake-like creatures that dwelled beneath the sands of Kavakin.

"Okay, then what?" Lifaya asked.

"I'm not sure. I heard a voice, but nobody was there." Maya touched a hand to her neck, the skin still sore and mottled with light blues and browns. "Then, it strangled me."

"We're too close to the boundary veil," Kadhim said, clenching his fists on the table. "The spirits have been getting restless, they sense her power."

Lifaya nodded her head slowly in agreement, releasing Maya's hand to rub a tight spot on the back of her neck. "You're not wrong, but there's little we can do about that.

She will need to travel south to source a ferry back to Danika."

"She can't–"

"Hey!" Maya barked, interrupting Kadhim and Lifaya's verbal joust. "I'm right here, so how about speaking *with* me." She angled slightly in her seat, facing Kadhim. "What does any of this have to do with the boundary veil?"

A deeply tired voice behind them answered in Kadhim's stead. "The spirits, those trapped in the veil...one of them possessed me, didn't it?"

Maya turned at Thelic's voice and sighed with relief. The feeling didn't last long as she took in the ragged exhaustion evident in the shadows under his eyes. "You should be in bed," she said, standing from the table to help him over the door's tall lip and into the town hall.

"This is linked to what happened to Maya, isn't it? It's what happened to the adults that lived here, the so-called shaders," Thelic said, accepting Maya's help as he took a seat at the head of the table. "What are we missing?"

Kadhim, Zarina and Lifaya held their silence for a moment, considering where to begin. Maya and the others needed to know. The Seer was right in that they would need to travel south to source a ferry to the Danikan territory. Unfortunately, this would eventually bring them all closer to the veil, and they had to be prepared.

"Do you understand what happens to those who touch the boundary veil?" Lifaya asked the room. When no one responded, she continued. "Well, as far as we can tell, it sort of dislodges the soul and sucks it from the body. These souls are then trapped in the veil, with little means of escape and no way to return to their bodies that continue to age and decay. For those that simply venture too close, a spirit can latch on and feed off their essence. With so long spent in such a desolate place, the spirits' souls are corrupted, they're darkened. The spirits' raw emotion and need to punish the humans responsible for their misery is what leaks into the shaders."

"I see. That's what happened to the adults here," Maya said, considering her grandmother's words. The shaders she and the others had met at Slitter Ridge, and those who had attacked the houses near Brushkin Break. Those gypsul had been possessed. "The veil was created by one of the Five Majors, right? How does it have that much power, I thought it was just meant as a barrier," Maya asked, looking between all those at the table who might be able to answer.

"That's right," Lifaya said, interlinking her long fingers and leaning forward on the table. "It *was* one of the Majors. Danika created the void to prevent gypsul from the outer regions attacking the humans who were crossing over. What she didn't realise was that the boundary she was creating was borrowed from the third realm, its presence – like the gateways – a foreign entity that got out of control."

Kadhim shook his head. "She was playing with a power she didn't understand. They all were, and we still suffer for it, three thousand years later." In their short time together, Kahim had made it abundantly clear of his thoughts regarding the Five Majors, predominately his utter loathing of the historical founders.

Zarina placed a hand on Kadhim's shoulder, her ability to calm a rising storm not to be rivalled. He leaned back, brushing a hand through the dark waves of his hair before holding out a hand for the Seer to continue.

"These souls, the spirits ensnared in the veil as a result of venturing too close, they can sense your power, Maya." Lifaya explained. "They want it, they believe it will set them free from the cold world they're trapped in."

"*Would* it set them free?" Maya asked.

"In some ways, yes. Just like your power can close the

gateways, it is also the only thing capable of tearing down the boundary veil and reuniting the territories with the rest of this world, with Sythintall."

"And so, the end of chaos will give birth to blood and vengeance," Thelic muttered. "The moment that wall is torn down, it will be a bloodbath. The gypsul will lay waste to the humans for what their ancestors have done."

"That's why your quest comes in three parts," Lifaya said. "Retrieve the scrolls and gather the seals, close the gateways, then unite the humans and the gypsul. The humans will be in a position that forces them to either get along with this world's inhabitants, or return to their own world. The gypsul are a peaceful race. We have never sought war or political unrest. That is a human trait."

Maya leaned froward and placed her forehead on the cool stone of the table. Scrolls, seals, gateways, veils. It was a lot. A hand gripped her knee under the table and she rolled her head to the side. Thelic's face was contorted, brows pulled down in a mixture of pain and frustration. His eyes dipped to skim over the bruising across Maya's neck and he squeezed her knee again, harder this time, his jaw tightly clenched at the thought of what he had done.

Maya placed her hand over his and smiled. Something had taken over his body. He wasn't to blame. But he was a warrior, one that had been powerless against a force he couldn't see or control. Raising her head, she briefly shut her eyes, willing the pressure behind them to subside with the impending headache.

"How do we defend ourselves from these attacks?" Thelic asked.

"You can't. Your best bet is stay as far from the boundary veil as you can," Zarina said softly. "Though, that won't be possible the farther south we get." She pointed to the map of the region, and trailed a taloned finger from Etiyan Vale, down the length of Kavakin to the southern tip. Sure enough, the land thinned to a point where the boundary was barely a mountain away from where the ferry point was marked.

"I see, then we'll just have to look out for the signs," Maya said with a weary sigh. "Can you teach me how to use the Stone to draw the spirit out, like you did for Thelic?" she asked Lifaya.

"Yes, it's simple really. You charge it with your power, and then, using the Stone, you command the host's sprite to expel the foreign element. As Thelic has two Vasiba sprites, the process was quicker than it might normally be. From what I can tell, it's a similar process to the one used to extract elemental sprites from a host, but I will consult with the other Elder's to make sure."

"You need zingan root," Zarina said, pointing to Thelic as she rose from her seat. "Little pinch of that and you'll be good as new."

"Zingan root?" Maya asked.

Thelic groaned beside her, clearly unhappy by the young gypsul's suggestion.

Zarina chuckled and stopped by his side, patting his head like a mother would a grumpy child. "If we aim to leave tomorrow, it's the only thing that will sort you out in time. You know that. I'll go and grab it and leave it in your room, then you should get some sleep." Leaving no chance to argue, she skipped to the front door of the town hall, silver hair bobbing behind her, and disappeared into the darkness.

~

BACK IN THE ROOM, Maya tucked the covers around Thelic, propping his head slightly and making sure the blanket reached his feet.

"Stop fussing, I'm fine," he growled, unaccustomed to the attention.

"Well, considering the amount you've had to take care of me, you can lie there and take it, Thelic Anthon," Maya said sternly, hiding her smile at his sour expression.

As promised, Zarina had left a small parcel on the bedside table. Maya retrieved it and returned to sit by Thelic's side. Beneath the packaged layers of fabric was a roughly cut chunk of vegetable root about the size of Maya's little finger. Maya held the ginger-like item up to her nose and breathed in. The air turned sour with the smell. She dropped her hand and turned her head, swallowing the bile conjured by the pungent aroma.

"Oh god. That's disgusting!" she cried.

"The taste is worse," Thelic said, eyeing the vegetable like a convict would a noose. He leaned over and plucked it from her palm, then shoved the entire root into his mouth. A bitter, sticky foam coated his tongue as he broke through the skin into the hollowed centre. He gagged; his body desperate to expel the second unwelcome visitor of the day.

Though the vegetable was firmly locked between Thelic's lips, the smell seeped into the rest of the room. Maya's hand flew to cover her nose as the scent grew worse. Unable to help herself, she backed away, heading for the door and the fresh air that lay just beyond.

"Don't…you…fucking…dare," Thelic ground out between chews. "You…made me…do this."

Maya hesitated, her fingers clasping the handle. She grinned. "Sorry, it's not you, it's the smell." She bolted from the room, the cool, night air a welcome relief. Never in her life had she experienced something so repugnant. Once again, this world baffled and awed her. She looked up at the three moons, their light broken amongst the clouds that speckled the sky. A small gust of wind swept between her ankles before coming to rest on its usual perch on her shoulder.

Loki, the Air Finkel, was a welcome companion. Though, he hadn't always been. Their first official meeting had been in a glen. He had saved her life that time, but as they continued their journey, his playful ways of testing Maya's abilities had almost killed her. Thankfully, since then he'd taken the hint and opted for gentleness.

Still wired from the day's events, Maya walked beneath the low canopies of the town, weaving between the courtyards and the dusty, unpaved paths. A sound akin to crickets chirped in the background, accompanied by the low hum of the desert's night-time critters scurrying across the sands. The desert storm had passed quickly through the town; Kavakin's temperamental weather a mystery and seemingly impossible to predict. The canvassed canopies dipped beneath the weight of the sand, some ripped in places and the grain falling through like a desert waterfall.

"Maya?"

Maya turned to see her grandmother sitting alone in one of the courtyards overlooking the mountains to the east. "I thought you would be in bed like everyone else," Maya said, surprised to see her.

"Ah, once the storm had passed the children were insistent we continue with the Telling. It was short and sweet this year, a single prophecy meant for their ears, regarding a future of unification. We've not long since finished, believe it or not."

Maya chuckled. The children here didn't necessarily have a difficult life, but they faced challenges, both physical and emotional; challenges some of the more fortunate youngsters couldn't even imagine. She made her way across the courtyard to kneel on the sand beside her grandmother. Beyond the eastern mountains, the glow of dawn crept over the peaks. "Who did you see unifying in your vision?"

The Seer glanced from the mountains to Maya with a somewhat sad smile. "Their parents," she said, taking a sip from the steaming cup in her hand. "Now that you have the Gouram Stone, when you return, we can finally dispel the spirits that have shaded their hearts, and bring them home."

"I suppose that's a start," Maya said softly.

Lifaya turned to face her granddaughter once again, noting the lines of tired stress across her forehead. She leaned slightly to the side, wrapping her arm around her stiff shoulders. Nothing was said. What was there to say? Maya had a burden to carry, a whole realm depending on her. Of course, the young halfling always had a choice. But not really. Who would damn an entire world just to save themselves the trouble of reviving it?

3
SHELTER FROM THE STORM

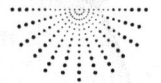

EASTERN OUTLANDS – KAVAKIN DESERT

Keela had been waiting since dawn for Maya and the others at their agreed meeting spot near the palm garden. As the sun crept higher through the day, she had done what all soldiers must – she had slept under the shaded trees, catching as much sleep as she could while she was able. She woke to a boot roughly catching her ankle and looked up to see the less than pleased Thelic.

"What did I miss?" she asked.

"Not much," Thelic grunted, offering a hand to help Keela to her feet.

"Actually, he was possessed by a spirit caught in the boundary veil's chaos and then tried to strangle me," Maya said. "Zarina made him eat zingan root as well."

Keela burst out laughing while the rest of the group shuddered at the thought of the vile vegetable root. Picking up her canvas pack, she slipped both loops over her shoulders and let it settle comfortably against her back. "That would be believable if we were anywhere near the boundary veil–"

"It's true," Zarina said, stepping up behind Keela to help

readjust the pack. "We're close enough to be affected by the spirits' reach."

"You can't be serious?" Keela groaned, all humour dying out as she looked to the others.

"Afraid so," Maya said, her grimace joining the tired nods and further darkening the group's mood.

"Brilliant. One more thing that wants to kill us then," Keela muttered. With this new knowledge of a more difficult to see enemy, she stood idly for a moment as the others passed then followed on, keeping to the rear of the group where she figured she was less likely to suffer a dagger in the back.

Progress along the dunes of Kavakin was predictably slow, their feet sinking with every step. Better protected from the scorching sun with their long-sleeved desert attire, they were able to travel by day in the hopes of avoiding the predators that sought their prey in the coolness of night. According to the map and the Seer's knowledge of these parts, their journey south would take a little over five days, assuming they made it to the southern ferry port at all.

Much like their trek to Etiyan Vale, the sandy hills were littered with the ruins and remnants of old towns, long since abandoned with their proximity to the veil. Only substantial ruins were carefully marked on the map, a statue of some-sort or a peculiar patch of craters spouting an effervescent mixture of gas and lava. It was these craters that attracted those who worshipped Pavinic, the Gouram of fire. Stories had passed through generations of the gypsul that the old God continued to reside in these craters, swimming through the long, underground tunnels, keeping an eye on the surface dwellers.

Maya jumped back as one of the craters bubbled and

burped, spitting gas and molten rocks into the air. Despite what may have been suspected, the air wasn't entirely odious. Instead, it was oddly metallic, like a blacksmith's forge had been built into the depths of the crevice.

Understandably curious, Maya approached one of the smaller holes that appeared less active than the others. Inside, the fiery liquid didn't reach the top. You couldn't lean down and dip your fingers in. It was the entrance to a large cavern beneath their feet, the tunnels easily reaching the height of a small church or a house in some parts. She moved back from the side, suddenly wary that the floor beneath her feet could give way.

"That's why we travel near the craters where possible," Thelic said, walking over to stand beside her. "Grokusi can't pass here. Despite their hard scales, they are as likely to perish in the fire pools as we are."

Maya nodded her head in understanding but felt inclined to state the obvious. "Isn't it safer against a grokus, rather than the possibility of falling through a crack to our deaths?"

"She has a great point," Keela said from behind them as she nudged the sand before every step. "I would have mentioned it earlier, but you all have a tendency to ignore my perfectly reasonable suggestions."

"Look around you," Thelic instructed the two sisters. He waited a moment, searching his peripheral for movement. "There." He pointed to a spot barely twenty feet from where they stood. The sand pulsed, like something buried beneath was breathing.

"A creature?" Maya asked, instinctively reaching for the dagger at her side.

"No. The movement is too erratic. If it were an even rhythm – up two three, down two three, up two three – then we would know it was something alive and sleeping beneath."

Maya regarded the spot again. Small puffs dislodged the sand every few seconds. "It's a crack, another hole?"

"Yes. That's what we look out for. No pulse, no problem." He considered those words for a moment. "A bit like with the living."

Maya and Keela smiled agreeably. He wasn't wrong.

A squawk from above caught their attention – Kadhim, urging them to keep moving.

"Anyone feel like poultry for dinner tonight?" Keela asked as she regarded the black, red-winged shapeshifter above. She shielded her eyes from the sun's glare, tracking the bird as it moved through the cloudless sky. Her fingers twitched towards her back, where four throwing knives lay dormant and ready for use.

Perhaps it was how close they were to the chaos of the boundary veil, but the slowly darkening humour and each members' hands dangerously close to their weapons was not lost on Maya. Even she could feel it. That tug towards the darkness, like an invisible string pulling her closer and closer to the chaos. A choking desire to take those steps further east, to where the spirits waited.

~

As the sun crept slowly down to hide its light below the horizon, the group had made it to an old, deserted village in good time. Zarina and Kadhim had spotted the litter of stones in flight, noting the broken but tall walls that might shield the group from the harsh desert winds, and a functioning water-well to replenish their supply before moving on at dawn.

"Let me get this straight," Keela said, waving a leg of meat rudely in Maya's face. "You're immune to the spirits' possession? I thought they wanted your power?" She pulled the meat back as Maya swatted the air in front of her.

"According to my grandmother, yes, I'm immune. The Gouram essence is too powerful for the spirits to overcome, they would just as soon be expelled from my body before being allowed to take control," Maya explained, echoing Lifaya's words the morning they had left the encampment.

"Well then, what's their goal? You say two of them tried to strangle you. Why would they do that if they meant to use your power to free themselves?" Keela asked between meaty mouthfuls.

Maya did her best not to cringe at the sight of chewed flesh between her sister's teeth, instead focusing on the small animal's torso she held in her own hand. The remains of a desert scag. Like naked mole-rats but with three tails and a wicked set of canines. Thankfully, the small, furless devils were slow moving and easy prey for the group to hunt as they travelled.

"I'm not sure their intention was to kill Maya," Thelic interjected. He turned his head, regarding the uneaten rodent in Maya's lap with a smile before continuing. "Whatever it was on the dune that strangled you could have finished the job. Like you said, you passed out, you were defenceless. Perhaps the plan was to render you unconscious, then take over your body when you didn't have the presence of mind to fight it off."

"I suppose that would make sense," Keela agreed, discarding the picked-clean bones to the side. "Though, clearly even that didn't work. Could they tear down the veil using her body? Isn't it too soon without the Gouram seals?"

"Maya could tear it down tomorrow, according to Fatari's scrolls," Thelic said. "But it would kill her, and we would still have the gateways to deal with."

Maya sunk her teeth into the crisped skin of the desert

creature and smiled at the surprising succulence of the meat beneath. Looking from the meal to the man at her side, her smile only widened.

We. With Thelic it was never '*she*' where Maya was concerned. Maya could be charged with walking into the fiery depths of hell and his only question would be, 'when do *we* leave?'. Words couldn't express how grateful she felt for that; for his strength and resilience where hers might falter. She didn't deserve it. Hell, she figured she had been a nightmare from the start, coming in and disrupting his relatively peaceful life.

A flurry of wings sounded above, just a moment before Kadhim and Zarina dropped from the sky to land gracefully beside the fire-pit. Taking a seat on the quickly cooling sands, they both reached into the fire to retrieve their share of the cooked creatures.

"All clear ahead?" Thelic asked.

Kadhim nodded as he chewed, then seemed to reconsider as he tilted his head from side to side. "There's a grokusi nest about fifteen dunes away. Shouldn't be an issue though, they only nest when they're mating, so they should have a stockpile of food and won't be hunting."

Maya rolled her eyes at the news. Almost safe, but never quite enough to truly relax. It was a wonder to her that blood-pressure pills had yet to be invented in this realm.

"Thank you both for keeping a lookout," Maya said, looking from one gypsul to the next.

Zarina waved both hands in front of her as she grinned with her mouth full. "Not at all, we're honoured to join you and the others. I've been taking notes in my head, saving bits of information for the scrolls when our duties are over, so stories can be told of our achievements. Humans and gypsul working together for a common cause, it's so wonderful." She leaned forward to point at Maya. "My mama would love to meet you. In fact, she would love to meet all of you. She finds the humans fascinating."

Maya chuckled at the gypsul woman's infectious positivity. "Where does she live? You and Kadhim both come from a Svingoran Tribe, right? Does your mother live with other tribal members?"

Zarina nodded her head enthusiastically, beaming at Maya's interest. "That's right, we both worship Svingora, the friendliest of the Gouram. And yes, Mama lives within the tribal camp with the others."

Friendliest...It was an odd way to describe a god. "What makes the Gouram of air so friendly?" Maya asked.

Familiar with Zarina's mild obsession on the topic and hoping to avoid a longer discussion than intended, Kadhim answered instead. "Svingora is known to make appearances across the tribes. The God of air will appear to those most unfortunate or suffering on hard times to offer them a helping hand." He cocked his head and smiled as Zarina buzzed, her glum reaction to having been robbed of her chance to educate their human companions dissipating as he told his story. "This help might come as the end to a storm, saving those trapped within it. Or perhaps in a wind that carries the rain clouds in a barren desert to those dying of thirst. The God never fails those who worship the element."

"Or it does, and those it fails don't live to talk about it," Keela said with a shrug. Contracted to a Fire Vasiba, she didn't feel any sort of animosity or disagreement with the Gouram. Keela simply couldn't understand the blind faith people had in their gods.

Zarina on the other hand, struggled to fathom such a way of thinking – that the Gouram could be anything but exceptional. She tutted at the Esterbellian and pointed to the sky. "They're always watching." She pressed a finger to her closed lips, a sign for silence that apparently spanned universally across the realms.

Thelic coughed in a poor attempt to hide his laugh as Keela rolled her eyes. They were doing well, all things considered. The battle with the Esterbellians barely a week past had taken it out of them. They had scarcely recovered before starting the second leg of their difficult journey.

Thelic's gaze shifted to Maya. Her long, golden hair was usually tied in a ponytail, but today hung in a loose braid across her shoulder, with errant wisps of hair brushing against her face as she laughed.

Sensing those silver eyes on her, Maya let her hand brush across the sand to lay over his.

Thelic glanced down as her fingers wove their way between his, then looked up to bright green eyes holding him. "Maybe we *should* put the tents up tonight," he said with a suggestive grin.

"No way. I won't have you two getting up to any funny business when you're sleeping next to me. We're blood, Maya…it's beyond weird," Keela stated firmly, pointing an accusing finger at Thelic, then Maya, and then at the couple's interlocked fingers.

Unsure what she meant at first, Kadhim tracked to where Keela indicated, and spotted the clasped hands between Maya and Thelic. He turned his head to the side and clenched his teeth, trying to sober his expression before the others could see.

A hand touched his shoulder and gave it a gentle squeeze. Zarina. She didn't need to be looking directly at Kadhim to sense his feelings. They had known each other too long; were too in tune with what the other felt. That's what happens when you spend your life with someone. Zarina and Kadhim had grown up together in the smallest of the Svingoran Tribes. They were like siblings, related by a friendship so strong, only blood could hope to match it. She had been there when he had first fallen in love as a youngling, only for that love to be ripped from his side; spirited away in the night...to someplace he could not follow...to an entirely different world.

∼

NOBODY HAD SLEPT WELL that night. A sharp wind from the east had kicked up a gale which continued late into the morning. There was no point in waiting. A storm like this could rage for days and they needed to move on. The winds howled like a hungry beast, the sand its claws as it ripped at their clothes and clung to the small folds in an effort to get to the skin beneath.

Maya brushed at the sheer material covering her face, trying to dislodge the silica before any more could make its way down to her neckline. To protect them from the sun, every inch of the travellers' skin was covered. Thin gloves to protect their hands and fingers. A thin piece of material attached to their hoods that could fasten securely against their faces. Without such protection, they would have been stuck, forced to take shelter or suffocate from the blinding swirls of sand choking the air.

Kadhim and Zarina travelled on foot. While they were likely more than capable of flying above the storm, they would risk losing the humans. At times they had no choice but to take to the sky. Walking blind in the storm was risky, to say the least. Every now and again, they would stop and one of the transforming gypsul would take flight and check their position against the mountain regions of the east.

As the storm raged, visibility reduced, and so the group decided to tie a long rope to each of their waists. This way, if one was to wander off, they wouldn't wander far. At the back of the group, Keela stumbled on a protruding rock, the corner of a statue that had long since crumbled with only the four feet of an etiyan remaining. As Keela fell to the side, the rope sprung taut, first pulling Maya and then Thelic.

Thelic turned sharply at the tug on his hips, squinting through the impossibly thick swirls of sand to see what had happened to Maya and Keela behind him. He waited a moment, but Maya didn't emerge. Turning back to face his front, he tugged on the rope – a warning to Zarina ahead of him, then a second tug to indicate he was moving backward. The rope went slack – she had understood his message and was coming back towards him.

Thelic moved quickly, the eastern wind now battering him from the right as he made his way to Maya. The rope remained slack, gliding through his fingers as he made each step. There. A distorted figure was kneeling on the ground, hunched over. Thelic ran the last few steps. Was she hurt? His mind ran wild with the possibilities of what might have caused her to stop. He dropped by her side grabbing her shoulders to twist her body to face him.

Maya planted her face into Thelic's chest, holding her breath as she fumbled with the fastenings on her hood. The material protecting her face had come loose and every breath was thick with the sands of Kavakin, clawing at her tongue and throat.

The howls of the wind made it impossible to speak and be heard, so Thelic hadn't understood. Thinking she might be injured, he pushed her back from his chest to inspect her for any cuts or scrapes. Green eyes blinked rapidly back at him as she waved her hands and pointed to the wayward material flapping to the side of her face.

Finally, he registered the reason for her distress and quickly caught the loosened face guard and secured it to the other side of her hood, tucking the excess material into her collar.

Maya sucked in a whooping breath of dank, dry air, grateful for the noticeable absence of sand. She patted his shoulder in thanks and stood up to look around. Still no sign of Keela. She should have caught up by now.

Behind them, Zarina and Kadhim's figures emerged like a mirage coming into focus. Maya pointed to the rope and then to where Keela should have been at the rear of the group. Both nodded, already noticing the absent member, and followed on behind.

Through the churning grit, something moved and Thelic took two quick paces to shift in front of Maya, holding her rope in his hands as he guided them closer.

Keela stormed backwards and forwards before stopping at the base of the offensive rock that had made her trip and fall. She threw up her hands, pointing to the sky, then to the statue, then swung them to the side in a heated discussion with the Gods. Finally, having exhausted her tantrum, she turned to follow the rope and saw all four of her travelling companions facing her.

Zarina broke from the group, her chuckles lost behind the mask and the wailing gales, and placed a hand on the young Esterbellian's shoulder. She smiled again when her hand was shaken free, the petulant move further indicating the exhaustion of the human. Turning back to Kadhim, she raised both hands and placed her fingers and thumbs together to form a triangle – *should we make camp?*

Kadhim considered this. They had been travelling for hours and his last flight had seen the sun reach its peak in the sky. By his reckoning, they had maybe a quarter day left until darkness. They should push on. A nudge from his left. Maya was nodding her head, understanding Zarina's sign and agreeing with her assessment that it was time for a break.

Without argument, he untied the rope from his waist and took to the sky once again to check their position and find some shelter.

∽

As the others stoked the fire and laid out the blankets, Maya took one of the fabricated torches – made of rough wood and a cloth soaked in scag fat – and explored the mouth of the cave. On his flight, Kadhim had barely spotted a dull shade in the mountain's side and decided to risk taking them off-course on the chance they might find shelter there. This close to the boundary void, they could feel it, the pull of their mind, body and spirit to the chaos.

Maya ran her hands along the dried and dusty walls as she made her way deeper into the cavern's throat. Dust turned to slime as the air cooled further in and she slowed her pace, the floor wet with the mountain's sweat. Stalagmites met stalactites from floor to ceiling, the effect against the torch's glow like chattering teeth dancing across the walls. She shuddered. The break from the storm's winds and deafening howls had come as a truly welcome relief, they just had to hope they hadn't strayed into another creature's home or temporary hiding spot.

"Don't wander off. Knowing you, you'll find something that wants to eat us and lead it back here," Keela grunted to Maya. Every word, every chuckle boomed its way back in an echo, ricocheting like a stray bullet amongst the cave walls.

Maya cringed at the sound, and everyone stopped what they were doing and listened. In the silence between them, a dull and soothing roar echoed throughout the cave. A waterfall, deep in the mountain's belly sustaining the underground's ecosystem. Despite being so far from the molten craters, steam drifted through the cavern's throat, the humidity stifling and uncomfortable. Still, it was a welcome reprieve from the howling sandstorm.

Drip, splash, drip, splash.

That was it. No pounding footsteps of their doom coming to greet them. No distant howl from deep within the cave. It seemed, for now, they were safe.

Unable to hunt from lack of visibility in the storm, there was no desert scag for dinner that night. The children of Etiyan Vale had gathered together some rations of mixed vegetables and dried fashgi for this very reason. Maya tugged at the fish-like meat with her teeth, the salt unwelcome on her parched lips. Nevertheless, she was starving, and chewed the hardened food gratefully, wishing they had more.

"Could you tell how close we are to the southern port from the sky?" Thelic asked Kadhim. He sat crossed legged next to Maya, his face scrunched up as he regarded the fashgi meal with woeful distaste.

"I believe we're just over halfway. The storm has slowed us by about half a day," Kadhim answered as he offered the last of his vegetable ration to Maya.

Maya looked at the outheld hand, Kadhim's claws curled slightly inward over the rounded spud, and shook her head. She was hungry, but so was everyone, and she wasn't going to encourage preferential treatment.

Before Kadhim could take it back, Keela's hand darted out from the side and snatched the offering, then snaffled it into her mouth. At the chorus of shocked expressions around the small fire, she shrugged, tucked the half-chewed vegetable into her cheeks like a chipmunk and said, "What? We all know I'm one of the best fighters we have." She chewed the remainder and swallowed, lifting the leather satchel of water to her lips to wash it down. "I need to keep my strength up if we're going to stay alive."

"Didn't your mother ever teach you any manners?"

Kadhim asked. "We all know Bandaar isn't one to educate on proper etiquette." Belatedly remembering the link between the two sisters, he looked at Maya to offer an apology. But she didn't seem hurt, instead, she appeared worried by his words, hand rising to rub the back of her neck awkwardly.

"What?" he asked, glancing between Maya and Keela.

"My mother didn't live long enough to teach me anything," Keela said quietly. "And you're right, Bandaar wasn't exactly a great role model, though I *am* pretty handy in a fight thanks to him," she added with a cold smirk.

Kadhim, unaware of Keela's history, bowed his head in apology at rekindling what was likely a painful subject. "I'm sorry. Though, I know how hard it can be. The pain dulls, but never truly leaves."

Keela snorted and turned up her nose at the thought of this man, this gypsul pitying her. "I'm no stranger to pain, and I'm not one to look back at the memory of her as something to shy away from. She died. People die. I will see her again, all I need is patience."

It wasn't hard to catch the sadness that briefly flickered behind the hard exterior. Keela was a warrior, a fighter. Growing up in Esterbell under her father's thumb had taught her to hide it, to bury the pain and sadness, because there was no room for weakness by his side.

"You believe in the afterlife?" Maya asked her. It seemed out of place and out of character for someone so logical, so military.

"Of course I do. We live in a world of sprites and spirits for goodness' sake," Keela replied, bewildered by the question. "Though, that belief became true when your soul took a wander to the in-between and met Batshari."

Thelic nodded in agreement with Keela. Maya's little trip to the spirits' domain – though fruitful – had concerned him. For over half a day, he had sat by her side, unable to move or wake her for fear that her own spirit may stay stuck there like so many before her. But now he knew. The Gouram, the Gods, were no fable. The seal across Maya's chest and her power was proof of that.

With exhaustion overcoming them, goodnights were bade and the fire extinguished as each member of the small group of travellers lay on their rolled out mats to sleep. Barely a moment passed before soft snores filled the open space amidst the drips and splashes beyond the curve of the cavern's tunnel.

It was this exhaustion and illusion of safety that meant no watch was left to guard those who slept, relying on the belief that the storm would blanket them from a predator's eyes. But it wasn't what lay outside of their haven that may have concerned them. A blue glow rose from the darkness of the cavern's gullet, iridescent eyes watching their guests with curiosity.

4
A DEVIL IN THE DETAILS

EASTERN OUTLANDS – KAVAKIN DESERT

Maya woke to Thelic stirring beside her, his arm gently slipping from beneath her head as the other brushed across her waist. She opened her eyes and vaguely registered that the cave was no longer cast in darkness. A dim light broke through the shadows on the walls, flickering softly from somewhere deeper inside.

"Quiet," Thelic whispered in warning to Maya. Readjusting, he crouched, resting one knee on the floor as his hand reached for the spear never too far from his side. Slowly, he unwrapped the weapon's head of its cloth barrier.

Beyond the curve of the tunnel, a blue orb bobbed in the distance, jumping in and out between the stalagmites rising from the cavern floor.

"What is it?" Maya asked, reaching for the dagger still secured to her waist.

Thelic shook his head in response. He wasn't sure, and that concerned him. His frown deepened as his eyes followed the strange light.

Maya glanced to the others, their sleeping figures undisturbed. She leaned forward, one hand gently reaching out to nudge Keela. The orb-like glow stopped, its light pulsing from behind a cragged rock. Maya paused, only inches from her sister.

"Don't move," Keela murmured into the crook of her arm. "Whatever it is, it's been watching us for a while now."

Maya pulled back her hand. She should have known Keela would be awake. Little got past the Esterebellian woman, even when she slept. Her knees began to ache the longer they sat, but the little light had yet to move on, seemingly stuck where it had stopped.

Thelic slowly rose to his feet. Still the light remained. He shuffled one step forward and Keela twisted her head, growling when she realised what he was doing. "I said–"

Light exploded across the cavern before vanishing just as quickly, plunging them all into darkness once again. Kadhim and Zarina bolted awake as the searing light broke through their closed eyelids. In less than a second, they were standing by Maya's side, weapons up while one faced the cave's mouth and the other faced its throat.

"It's okay, I think whatever it was is gone now," Maya said placing a hand on Kadhim's outstretched arm. The muscles there strained as he pulled the bow string taut, his eyes darting across the gloom.

"What was it, what did you see?" Zarina asked, lowering the long, thin sword she had acquired at the Etiyan Vale encampment. The weapon suited her, slim and elegant despite its deadliness.

"A blue orb of light. It was a bit like a floating flame…like a will o' the wisp."

At Maya's words, Kadhim sighed in relief and lowered the bow. "It's a spirit, they often linger by Gouram shrines." Slipping the bow over his head to rest across his chest, he strode from the blankets to re-light the fire. With the flame's light to read, he pulled the map from his bag, and everyone gathered around to look over his shoulder.

"Where are we?" Thelic asked, moving to stand beside him.

Kadhim took a moment then pointed to a mountain region. "I believe we're here, it's the closest shrine to the abandoned etiyan encampment we stopped in yesterday." His finger paused over a faint symbol for the element of fire, easily mistaken as part of the mountain region they bordered.

If the weathered scroll was correct, they had travelled much further than Kadhim had expected, well over halfway. Assuming the storm died down, they should reach the ferry port by later the next evening.

"Aren't you worried?' Keela asked. Unlike the others, her weapon was still raised, her eyes never leaving the back of the cave where the light of the fire failed to reach.

"No, it's fine. You said it had a blue light, correct?" Zarina asked, angling from the fire to regard the three humans.

"That's right," Maya said with a nod.

"Good, that means it's a new one, a soul that's passed only recently," Zarina explained. "Over time the spirit's aura will fade, and if it doesn't cross to the in-between…well, then you might have a problem. That's when they can turn malevolent."

Keela seemed unconvinced; her body still rigid as she held her blades close to her chest.

"Zarina, can you head to the front of the cave and check outside? See if the storm has passed and how close we are to sun-up," Kadhim asked. After receiving a nod of understanding from his friend, he returned the map to his bag and stood to face Maya. "We might as well check the shrine whilst we're here."

"I agree. You think it might be one we're looking for?"

Maya asked. It would be an unprecedented stroke of luck, especially considering their previous form up until now.

"No, Fatari insisted the shrines in Kavakin have long remained dormant…but it can't hurt to double-check. I struggle to imagine a better place for the God to rest," Kadhim reasoned. Thelic bobbed his head in agreement, while Keela muttered something about fools seeking peril.

It wasn't long before Zarina returned to inform them that the storm had died and day would break before long. Approaching the fire, she dropped several carcasses on the dusty floor and removed her knife.

"What are you doing?" Thelic asked as he rolled up his mat and attached it to the side of his canvas bag.

Zarina held up the dead desert rodents with a wide grin. "The spirits can wait. Maya's soul isn't going anywhere near the in-between without a little food in her belly."

Maya had forgotten. To reach Batshari she had gone to sleep beside the shine in the Shadow Mountains, only to wake in the in-between with the angry Gouram of water. The experience had been…unpleasant, at best. With that in mind, she was suddenly nervous that they might find Pavinic resting here. She finished rolling her sleeping mat before joining the gypsul by the fire. Zarina was right, the spirits could wait a little longer.

∼

Dust turned to slime as they made their way deeper into the heart of the cave. The further they got, the narrower the passage became as they squeezed, one by one, through the tight contours of the rock. Breathing became more difficult as they shimmied and crawled around the serrated turns, the air dank and musty. With torches abandoned, too dangerous in the small confines of the tunnel, it wasn't hard to pick out the glimmers of light coming from ahead.

Finally, with one last squeeze, they fell one after the other from the tight passage into an open space. The dull light of dawn streamed from large cracks in the rocky ceiling above, the rays highlighting a structure carved into the stone wall that was so grand, Maya had to blink twice to make sure it was really there. A cathedral. So tall and intricately carved, it put the tombs of the Jordanian Petra and great temples of Egypt to shame. Maya sucked in her breath at the sight, so unexpected.

The roar of water echoed around them and together they walked to the ledge. Not far below, an underground river separated the group from the temple, its flow soft and calm. Above that, a waterfall tumbled out of the cathedral's left wing, falling into a rocky pool before joining the waterway.

"Spirits," Keela whispered, equally as awed by the sight as everyone else. As if summoned by her words, two bobbing orbs darted from behind the stone columns supporting the temple's entrance.

"Looks like they're back," Maya said, barely able to take her eyes from the scene ahead to register the will o' the wisps on the other side of the river.

"There," Kadhim said, pointing to a small platform tied to the water's edge. "That's how you'll cross. Zarina and I will fly over."

"Why don't we just swim? I'm dying for a dip. I'm starting to get a little pungent over here," Keela said, giving the hood of her desert attire a cursory sniff and scrunching up her nose at the smell.

Kadhim shook his head. "No. It may look calm, but these desert rivers run deep, and the currents can be deceptive." He turned to Maya. "You can use BB to push the platform across."

Maya cringed at the suggestion. She hadn't seen the irritable water sprite since Etiyan Vale. For all she knew it had abandoned her.

Sensing her trepidation, Thelic smiled. "The great *Blessed One*, cowering before her subservient Finkel."

Maya turned to him with a sarcastic smile of her own. "I'm not sure what you mean. BB and I are best friends, we're like this," she said holding up a hand with her fingers crossed. "We're closer than ever." Turning back to the water, she touched a hand to her chest and summoned BB.

Nothing.

She tried again.

Still no sign of the sprite.

Thelic let out a bark of laughter. "You're being ghosted by a sprite."

"Maybe it's because you haven't offered your blood?" Keela suggested.

"I shouldn't need to," Maya growled, irritated by the petulant sprite. She could feel him in her chest. He was definitely there, and he could hear her just fine. "I don't need to summon a castor circle to move a bloody plank of wood across a river." She closed her eyes, blocking out the others to have a private word with the sprite.

BB. Come on. I know we've had our differences, though I'm not sure what I've done to earn your apparent dislike of me.

A soft, wet nose nuzzled at Maya's neck, Loki coming in to comfort her as his long, white tail brushed across her face in greeting. A growl reverberated through her chest, and it all clicked into place.

Are you jealous? she asked BB.

Was the Finkel of water, jealous of Maya's attention towards the Finkel of air? The growl intensified and Maya chuckled.

I love you, BB. Maya stopped at that, surprised by how

easily those words seemed to leave her. She rarely said them, even Thelic had yet to hear the three little words with so much meaning behind them.

She gasped as BB exploded from her chest and danced around her feet before coming to rest on the opposite shoulder to Loki. The water sprite glared at its elemental brother, nuzzling deeper into the crook of Maya's neck.

"I'm jealous," Thelic said, watching the Finkels' display of affection.

"Don't you bloody start," Maya groaned. "Okay, let's go. BB's back on side to help us now."

"What did you say to him?" Kadhim asked, his eyes dancing with curiosity at the exchange.

Maya blushed. "We just cleared up a little misunderstanding. Nothing too exciting," she said with a quick glance towards Thelic. His eyebrow raised as Maya's cheeks deepened in colour. "Come on, we still need to check the temple and clearly the sun has risen, so we're wasting the day just standing here," she said, turning from the curious party to the small path leading down to the river.

It didn't take much for BB to push the rickety wooden raft to the other side of the waterway. After securing the rope, they made their way up the steep steps and stopped at the temple's entrance. From the base to the tip of the tallest of three spires, it was easily over three hundred feet tall. This wasn't the work of builders meticulously placing stone on top of stone or mere brickwork. This was a stonemason's masterpiece, each divot carefully carved from the cavern wall.

As they passed between tall stone pillars, they felt confident in the likelihood of a Gouram resting in such a place. It was built for a God, no man or gypsul deserving enough to call this place their home. Inside was a single, hollowed out chamber, with smaller crawlspaces to the side for offerings. Lanterns, broken and abandoned, littered the floor; the ropes once securing them to the walls and stone supports long since weathered and fallen to dust.

At the back, standing tall and dominating the room, was the statue of a creature unlike anything they had seen on their travels. Maya had been expecting something close to the fire-bellied etiyan, lizard-like creatures that some of the gypsul were able to transform into. But no, stood on four legs was something closer to that of a devil, with two, angry looking horns and large scales each the size of her hand covering the length of its stone body. A tail, frozen in place boasted power and deadliness, long with a thickly barbed end.

"I don't like the look of that," Maya whispered, a cold fear settling in the pit of her stomach at the very notion of meeting such a creature in the in-between. "Batshari seems damn near cuddly in comparison."

Thelic stood silently beside her as he took in the chosen form of the Gouram of fire. It suited. The thing looked like it had crawled from the depths of hell. Like those on earth, the Avalonians believed in such a place, a place of fire and despair; where those who had wronged others were sent. It seemed unfair. If a hell should exist, then why not a heaven? The humans on earth had a heaven, so why not here? Instead, the stories spoke of a simple, quiet place. A place of rest. He knew that wasn't what awaited him in the afterlife. If the scriptures were true, he was destined, and better suited to the restless throes of this creature's otherworldly dwelling.

A blue light briefly lit the shadows of the temple before ducking behind a stone dais. A second orb darted from one of the columns before coming to rest atop the stone creature's shoulder. Small, translucent feet swung over the side.

"The spirit…it's a child," Maya whispered.

The dull figure of a small boy shook as he silently chuckled. Turning his head, he nodded enthusiastically to the other spirit close by, willing it to join him. The orb transformed and a little girl tentatively poked her head out from behind her hiding place. She looked directly at Maya, then to Thelic and the others, then back to the boy to shake her head in strong disapproval.

The boy seemed to sigh as he crossed his arms, then disappeared. A moment later, he reformed, springing forward to stand directly in front of Maya.

The movement was so quick it surprised her, and she tripped, falling backwards. Thelic, quicker to recover, grabbed her wrist, steadying her and moving himself forward to intercept the boy. He reached out.

"No!" Kadhim shouted, rushing forward to try and stop the human from making contact – too late.

Maya and Thelic fell to their knees, heads dipped as they went slack with sleep. With one of Thelic's hands frozen on Maya's wrist, the other had pushed into the chest of the boy's incorporeal form and hung there, motionless.

"What the–" Keela stepped forward.

"Don't touch them!" Zarina warned, pulling Keela away from their companions. "They'll just have to ride it out and hope it isn't too unpleasant."

The boy looked from Thelic and Maya to the others. He smiled sadly, then leaned his head back and closed his eyes, preparing to guide the couple through his final memory.

※

"Maya? Maya!" Thelic yelled as he shook her sleeping form. He glanced around, raising a hand to protect his eyes from the glare of the desert sun.

Maya groaned as she stirred on the ground. "What happened? Where…"

Taking the curve of her neck in his hand, Thelic helped

her sit up, checking for any winces of pain or discomfort. "We're just outside of the cave, but…I don't think this is real."

Taking his hand, they stood together and assessed their surroundings. He was right, the cave entrance – a unique M-shaped hole in the side of the shallow hill – was only a few feet away. A memory flooded back and she thought of the temple, and the young boy.

"I don't think this is the in-between," Maya said. When her soul had travelled there to meet with Batshari, the world had appeared dull and monochromatic. This was nothing like that. Instead, the colours of the sand and sky were rich in hue, the differing shades unrealistically vivid.

"I've heard the spirits can offer their final memory. They do it at times to offer peace to the family they've left behind. Or, in some cases, offering nightmares to those who wronged them," Thelic explained.

Had they wronged the spirits in some way? Offended them? Maya's mind raced with the possibilities. But she didn't have to ponder for long.

A voice called out by the cave's entrance. The little girl was waving at them. This time she wasn't the same, transparent blue ghost they had seen her as. She was alive, flesh and blood, with long, brown hair down to her waist, and amber eyes that seemed to sparkle in the light.

At the sight of her taloned hand, Maya realised for the first time that the children had been gypsul. She shuddered as something raced through her body from behind. The boy. He was bright like the girl, his clothes a dusted white and hair the same auburn. He stopped just in front of Maya, still facing the cave as he waved back.

"You should come in now, Phanto," the young girl hollered from the entrance. "I'm making scag-mush!"

Thelic couldn't help but smile at the little girl's term for chopped up meat and vegetables mashed together.

The boy, Phanto, put two hands on his hips defiantly. "You're not the master of me, Clajiit. I'll come in when I'm ready."

Maya watched as Clajiit stomped her foot, ready to unleash a tirade of abuse at the boy. Instead, she paused and squinted her eyes, appearing to see something amongst the rocks to their right. Her face, darkly tanned with a light blush of pink, suddenly went pale.

"Phanto, RUN!" she screamed.

Phanto turned to look at wherever she was pointing and gasped.

Maya and Thelic, disturbed by the young gypsuls' reactions, also turned to look behind them. Both had expected a grokus or some sort of dangerous desert creature. But the gypsul didn't fear the desert's natural predators. There was only one thing they truly feared in this world. Humans.

Phanto ran towards the cave as two large men jumped from behind the rocks and sprinted towards him. Maya and Thelic stepped out, blocking the path between man and boy. She held out her palm, ready to summon her Finkels to deter them. The men passed straight through, undeterred. Dread crept into Maya as she turned and ran after them.

The little girl had left the cave, she was sprinting towards them, towards the danger. An arrow burst through her throat, blood dripping down to stain the white of her desert dress.

Phanto shrieked as Clajiit gargled and dropped to the floor. He reached out, desperately racing towards her. He didn't make it. A dagger flew through the air and pierced his back, the blade buried to the hilt between the boy's shoulderblades.

Maya screamed, her feet sinking into the sand with

every step she took. It was a nightmare; one where you had to run, run as fast as you could but it's always impossible. You're never quick enough. She slowed, her feet plodding to a stop beside the men as they stood over the boy's body.

Lying on his belly with his head turned to the side, Phanto's eyes, a rich amber like Cajiit's, were open and blinking at the sand caught in his lashes.

Maya's hand clasped over her mouth at the realisation that he was still alive, despair racking her body at their inability to help. Thelic growled beside her, his fists clenched as he took in the two humans, two murderers beside them.

The hunters laughed, each patting the other on the back in congratulations. "Seems we found a nest. Their hands and runes will fetch a pretty sum," the taller of the men said, flipping a blade over and over in the palm of his hand.

The other man, short and stout, lifted his foot and stepped on the hilt of the dagger. Phanto let out a pained cry, blood bursting from his lips to splatter the sand.

"You're not wrong, I know a few people in Danika and Fortus who will pay good coin for 'em." The man removed his foot, then crouched and pulled the dagger from Phanto's back.

Thelic clenched his teeth as the boy wailed, and stood helpless as the man proceeded to kick the boy in the ribs, forcing him onto his back. But that was nothing. What came next was worse. With the same blade still soaked with gypsul blood, he put the sharp tip to the edge of the stone runes on the boy's face and began to carve them out.

It was a bitter relief when Phanto finally passed. His eyes squeezed shut as blood gargled in his mouth, until finally they relaxed and opened wide as he released his final breath.

As the second man knelt to saw at Phanto's wrists, Maya fell to her knees, no longer able to bear the torturous treatment of the little boy. "Please," she begged. "Please, let us out of here."

∼

Kadhim, Zarina and Keela jumped to their feet as the couple finally began to stir. Without a word, Thelic raised his head and slowly stood. Though clearly awake, Maya remained where she was, her face downcast as her shoulders rose and fell sharply.

"Oh no," Zarina whispered. Ignoring the boy, she stepped forward and took a knee by Maya's side. "Don't, Maya. Don't let it break you."

Maya raised her head to look at the boy. He smiled and she broke, the tears streaming down her face unrelenting as she smiled back at this wonderful, beautiful child whose life had been savagely stolen far too young. "I will find them," she whispered. "I will make them answer for what they did to you and Clajiit."

The boy's smile faded, and he shook his head from side to side. He turned, once again beckoning to the young girl. She had been watching the exchange with fear and interest and decided to trust Phanto. She disappeared, quickly reforming behind his back, poking her head around to look at Maya.

"Nice to meet you, Clajiit. My name is Maya," she said, wiping the tears from her face. The little girl nodded in response to Maya but stayed behind the boy, still fearful of the humans, and for good reason.

"What did you see?" Zarina asked as she helped Maya to her feet.

"Something that will stay with me for the rest of my life," Maya said. "Two men...two humans, murdered them for sport. They butchered these children to sell their runes and body parts in the territories."

Kadhim sucked air through his teeth as he looked again at the boy and girl. For the first time, he registered the darker blue along the collar of the young girl's dress, and the runes missing from her face. He looked down. He hadn't thought to assume they had been gypsul because he had yet to see their hands. He saw them now…well, what was left of them – two cragged stumps at the ends of their wrists.

"Fuck," Keela whispered. She had also seen the missing hands and could only imagine what Thelic and Maya had witnessed.

"When did this happen?" Maya asked the boy. Perhaps if the men were still alive, they could capture them, bring them to the Keepers to pay for their crimes. No. The rulers of the territories wouldn't care, they would just as likely celebrate.

"It wouldn't have been longer than a year ago," Zarina answered in place of the voiceless boy. "Any more than that and we would hardly be able to see them."

Maya smiled coldly at the small victory. If this had happened decades ago, they wouldn't have a chance…but this she could work with.

"I know what you're thinking, Maya. But it's pointless. We'll never find them amongst the five territories," Kadhim said. "This happens, and it's what we're trying to stop. But we don't have time to hunt for their killers."

Maya turned to him. "Don't underestimate me, Kadhim. I used to hunt these bastards for a living back on Earth, and I got pretty damn good at it." She glanced down in shock as the little girl appeared in front of her and touched the stump of her wrist to Maya's hand. A sick dread briefly passed through Maya, fearful that she might be transported back into their memories. But nothing happened.

Clajiit shook her head, then placed her wrist to her heart and smiled. They were at peace. There was no need for more violence and anger. She dashed off towards the dais where she had once hidden from the strangers, and beckoned for them to follow.

With a smile in return at the young gypsul's excitement, Maya followed with the others close behind. In the wall at the back, behind the statue, was another crawlspace. Clajiit pointed inside excitedly before disappearing once again.

"You're not going in there," Keela said sternly. "I don't care if they're kids, you don't know what's–" She stopped and let out a soft curse as Kadhim and Zarina disappeared through the hole. "There's no bloody way we're related," she finished as she watched Maya crawl into the space after them.

Inside the chamber was dark, the air as stale as it had been in the tunnel from lack of proper ventilation. After only a few feet, they were able to stand, and the room lit up in a magnificent blue as Phanto and Clajiit used their light to chase away the shadows. Looking up, Maya realised they were in the tallest of the three spires, the ceiling so high, even the light from the orbs was unable to reach its peak.

"Okay...wow," Keela whispered. Across the back of the wall was a map carved into the stone, each river and mountain intricately engraved.

"This isn't just Avalon. This is the whole realm," Kadhim noted, awestruck.

"Sythintall," Zarina breathed in agreement. Their world. They had forgotten what it looked like, the older maps locked and hidden away to preserve them.

Clajiit bounced up and down excitedly as she approached Maya once again. She pointed to Maya's chest and Batshari's seal glowed in response beneath the jumper. Turning to the mural, she indicated to a place deep in the icy mountains south of Cantor.

Having studied the map the night before their travels, Kadhim knew there was a temple dedicated to Pavinic exactly where the child was pointing. Admittedly, he had assumed it to be a mistake on the Seer's behalf, finding it odd that the Gouram of fire would rest amongst the frigid climes of the southern mountains.

"Pavinic?" Zarina asked the girl.

She nodded enthusiastically, once again jabbing her arm through Maya's chest.

"Seems odd. Why would she know we're looking for the Gouram at all?" Keela asked, stepping closer to inspect the map.

"She can sense Maya's power," Zarina offered in explanation. "We all know the prophecy of the one blessed by the Gouram, the one who can save our realm. With Batshari's seal, the youngling correctly assumes that's Maya."

Keela cocked a dubious brow. "Okay, but how does *she* know where the God rests? She's just a kid."

To Zarina's surprise, Maya already had an answer for Keela's question. "When I was in the spirit realm, I could feel Batshari before I was able to see him. Perhaps the same goes for these children? They feel the Gouram's call." Stepping closer to the mural, Maya knelt down to get a better look at the area. The mountains were dense, white dyes and pale chalking long since faded to denote their wintry environs. If that was to be their next stop after Danika, they would need to prepare for the weather.

Mirroring her thoughts, Thelic stood beside her, smiling at Phanto as he brightened his light for them to better see the finer features of the map. "We can stop in Danika Market to get what we need. I know a guy who travels those mountains hunting bodaari."

"Keero." Maya had forgotten all about Thelic's bodaari. A large and friendly creature with deep purple eyes, akin to a platypus crossed with a bear. "Do you think he made it home?"

Thelic furrowed his brows, not wanting to think about his furry friend. "I can only hope so, but we'll check when we're back in Danika."

With the mural of Sythintall to consider, Kadhim had returned to their belongings by the campfire to retrieve their own map. He checked the location of each temple marked by the Seer, making sure they aligned with the wall's atlas. He nodded his head, satisfied that theirs matched, and returned it to his bag.

Clajiit and Phanto followed along with the travellers until they were back under the unrelenting sun of the desert, skipping together down the rocky lip and onto the sands. Stopping just in front, they turned to the others and bowed their heads, before offering a small wave as they slowly dissolved.

"They've moved on," Kadhim said with a sad smile.

"Why now?" Maya asked.

"Perhaps they were waiting for you. Or perhaps they just wanted someone to say goodbye to. Either way, they're at peace now."

5

TROUBLE AT THE PORT

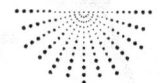

EASTERN OUTLANDS – KAVAKIN DESERT

The temptation was undeniable, the desire to remove every bit of clothing from their bodies and crawl into whatever shade they could find, if only to escape the heat and dank sweat from wandering through the desert. The storm had passed, and with it the wind and sands that had blanketed them from the sun's piercing rays.

They stopped only a few hours into their travels to take on water and rest in the shade of decaying ruins. As had become routine, Zarina took to the sky to check their progress and location. If they continued, they would reach the port by nightfall. But then, that same temptation remained, to stay in the shade and sleep for days, their bones and muscles burning with every dune they climbed.

Still, with every moment they lingered in Kavakin, the more likely they were to become a meal for the desert dwelling creatures. A dull hiss in the distance reminded them of that; a grokus braving the heat in search of food. Picking themselves off the sand and returning their water pouches to the canvas bags, they trekked on.

Zarina guided them to another crater field, the grokusi

cries making her nervous enough to risk the fiery pools beneath their feet. This was the closest they had ever come to the boundary veil. From here they could see the looming, gaseous wall of chaos separating Avalon from the rest of Sythintall.

Maya had been so curious about the barrier void. What did it look like? She already knew how it felt: a constant pull, a beckoning, darkened thoughts willing her towards darker deeds. When she had seen the memory of those children being murdered, she had conjured images of driving her blade through the throats of the men responsible. She had never pictured murder. It wasn't in her nature. Her job had always been to protect people, to *stop* crime.

She stared at the void now. Aptly named, it appeared as a constantly shifting wall of fog, alive with wisps and tendrils reaching out to ensnare any prey that might come too close. They were a mountain away, at least, but you couldn't miss it on a clear day, reaching so high it disappeared into the upper atmosphere.

Zarina dropped from the sky, returning from her second recce of the day. "We may have to stop for the night," she said. "A second grokus is tracking us now."

"I thought you said they couldn't reach us near the molten fields," Maya said, her eyes scanning the dunes on either side of them.

"They can't. But the creatures are intelligent, they're tracking around, probably to meet us on the other side," Zarina explained.

"How long until we reach the port?" Kadhim asked, turning to face Zarina. He had been staring at the chaos, as if worried it might conjure an army of spirits to attack. So many had been lost to the infernal wall, and they were far too close for comfort.

"Only half a day or so," Zarina replied.

"That would make a quarter day travelling at night. It's too risky this close to the chaos, we should move on."

"You and I could lure them away, Kadhim," Zarina suggested. At Maya's worried expression, she smiled. "It's fine, we'll just dash across the sands and take flight when they get too close." She flicked her eyes to Kadhim, waggling her eyebrows excitedly. "Remember that game we used to play?"

Kadhim crossed his arms in response but returned the smile. "It's a bit different with a grokus, but it's not a bad plan."

"What are you two going on about?" Keela asked, dropping her heavy pack on the sand to roll and loosen her shoulders. Her travel bag was at least double the weight of the others, with a special compartment housing replacement blades as well as a large sharpening stone.

"Hook and fly." Zarina chuckled at Keela's blank expression. "It's a game we used to play at Bodhisia's Valley in the north. We would run as fast as we could across the marshes, drawing out the wimble-nooks, then take flight and try to catch them in our alter-forms."

"Wimble-nooks?" Maya asked.

Zarina tilted her head. "Yes. You know, like Loki," she said, drawing out the words slowly. "You *must* remember them, Loki wouldn't have appeared to you in that form otherwise." She smiled, skipping over to Maya, "When you were a little girl–"

"Zarina," Kadhim warned. The gypsul woman winced at the stern tone of Kadhim's voice. "We don't have time for stories. If we're going to do this, we should do it now."

"Wait a second," Maya said, but too late. Kadhim transformed and leapt into the sky.

"I'll explain later," Zarina promised with a wink before taking off after her friend.

"Where the hell are they?" Keela asked, looking to the sky as the last ray of light touched the western horizon. It had been too long since their avian friends had left to draw the sand-predators away. Should they have stayed by the edge of the molten fields? No, the idea had been to get as far from the field and their stalkers as possible.

"According to the map, there should be an old town just up ahead. Maybe we should stop there and wait for them?" Maya suggested. She was worried for their gypsul companions. "We could light a fire as a signal?"

"Good idea, we can have something to eat as well," Thelic said, holding up three desert rodents."

Sooner than anticipated, they reached the ruins and started a fire. When the gypsul had left, they had given their packs to the humans. Now, as the meat cooked, they looked over the map from Kadhim's bag. They were close to the port. This ruined town wasn't as big as the last, but it was still double the size of Etiyan Vale and easily recognisable on the map.

"They're hiding something, those gypsul," Keela muttered as she turned the spit over the fire. "They're always hiding something."

"Where did *that* come from?" Maya asked, returning the scroll to Kadhim's pack.

"You know exactly what I'm talking about. We can't trust them. They know something about your Finkel. I bet they know a lot more than they're telling us."

Thelic eyed Keela warily. Perhaps it was paranoia, but against the firelight her eyes seemed to glow. The light green in her irises overtaken by dancing flames. Reaching for the spear, he tucked it closer into his side.

Keela snapped her head to the ground where his spear lay and smirked. "What the hell do you think you're doing?"

"How do you feel, Keela? Feverish? Any burning in your chest?" Thelic asked, grip tightening on the hilt of his weapon.

"And what would you do if I said yes, Thelic? Kill me?" She barked a laugh, her hand slowly moving behind her. "Why don't you try it?"

"Keela," Maya said, flinching as her sister's eyes snapped towards her. "Let me feel your forehead." Maya reached into her pocket and clasped her hand around the Gouram Stone as she stood. Thelic grabbed her wrist, willing Maya to sit back down.

Keela sighed, then scoffed dramatically. "You two are so paranoid." Putting her hands in front of her, she raised them with her palms facing forward. "Look, no weapons, no fever. I'm just tired and hungry. The sooner we get to the port, the better."

Unconvinced, Thelic kept his hands where they were, one on his weapon, the other moving to Maya's thigh. "Then stay where you are and let me feel your temperature," he said.

"Back off you stupid, blathering, HUMAN!" a voice screamed through Keela.

Everything happened so quickly, Maya barely had time to register anyone had moved when she was pushed roughly to the ground, the Stone rolling from her pocket and onto the sands. Blades clanged, dagger meeting spear as Keela launched herself at Thelic – the immediate threat.

Maya rolled to the side and leapt to her feet. Thelic jumped back as Keela thrust a fist towards his stomach and swung to the side, her dagger intent on slashing his belly.

"Keela, fight it!" Thelic growled, jumping back again and again to avoid the deadly swipes.

Something in Keela roared with frustration at every

missed swing. Flipping one of the daggers in her palm, she hurled it at Thelic.

He moved his spear just in time to smack the blade from its path to his face. There was no doubt she was possessed, and whatever it was had every intent to kill. He was at a disadvantage, forced to use the hilt of the spear to avoid striking her with the sharpened tip. He moved his hands up again to block her, realising too late that it had been a ploy as she ducked to swing her leg out, catching his ankles and toppling him to the side.

Maya darted forward, seeing her chance to grab Keela from behind. She wrapped both arms under Keela's armpits, forcing her sister's hands into the air where the blades couldn't reach her.

"Thelic, grab the Stone!" Maya called.

As Thelic raced back to the campfire, Keela drove her head back into Maya's face, smiling with delight at the crunch of Maya's lip colliding with her own teeth. The grip holding her loosened, and Keela turned, swinging the dagger.

Maya gasped and stumbled back as the blade sliced into the side of her hip. Blood seeped down the leg of her dusty white trousers. No time to assess the damage. Keela was dancing on the spot, readying herself for the next attack, her smile foreign and maniacal.

Thelic searched desperately around the fire. Something glistened, out of place amongst the dull colours of the sand. He grabbed the Stone and turned to see Maya fall to one knee, Keela slowly approaching, her dagger raised with deadly intent. "Keela, no!"

Maya ducked her head, seemingly in defeat. She watched the floor as Keela's shadow loomed closer. Three feet. Two feet. One. Maya launched herself into the air, parrying a deadly jab before driving a fist under her sister's chin. Just as quick, she turned her back, keeping one of Keela's arms locked over her shoulder, then bent over, forcing Keela over her body and onto the ground at Maya's feet.

Thelic was there in an instant and grabbed Keela's arms, his strength far outweighing hers. "Take the Stone from my pocket!" he yelled to Maya.

Crossing to his side, Maya reached into the folds by his leg and pulled out the opal. Keela squirmed on the ground under Thelic's grip, her eyes widening at the realisation of what Maya held.

"No!" the voice possessing Keela screamed. "Stop it! Get that thing away from me!"

Maya paused, holding the Stone to her sister's face. "Why are you afraid of it? This will set you free."

Keela laughed, deep and throaty as she continued to struggle fruitlessly under Thelic. "Set me *free*? Don't jest, stupid woman. That Stone will only serve to trap me. Even the chaos of the void is preferable to that…thing, that place!"

"Maya, just do it," Thelic growled, wincing as Keela curled her fingers, digging her nails into the flesh of his hands.

"Who are you? Why were you trying to kill us?" Maya asked the spirit instead.

Again, Keela laughed, spitting a line of curses and obscenities. "We don't want to *kill* you. I can taste your power, the power of two worlds, the only power that can truly free me."

"I only have the Gourams' blessing," Maya said, kneeling beside Keela on the sand. "You know you can't possess me, so why bother trying?"

"There is more than one way to bend another's will, Mayara Rivers. We have been watching you. Your heart aches for those you care about. You would do anything for them."

Maya recoiled at the sound of her full name spoken aloud. "You wish to use my friends against me?" This time, it was Maya's turn to laugh. "You underestimate them. Better yet, you underestimate me. I'm not one to roll over and take defeat." She thrust the Stone to Keela's chest and did as her grandmother had taught, calling on BB and Loki to focus their energy into the palm of her hand where she could then direct it.

Keela screamed and wriggled, kicking up sand in an effort to get to Maya. She gasped as power shot through her chest, her contract marks glowing under the material of her desert clothes.

Maya shook as power coursed through her, Loki's wind whipping around them in a sandy tornado. She called to Keela's Vasiba sprite, and the ghosts of fiery tendrils seeped from the possessed body in response, expelling the unwelcome spirit.

With one last scream, Keela went limp beneath Thelic. In Maya's hand the Gouram Stone glowed white before slowly fading to return to its opaline hue. Maya fell back into a seated position, panting and wiping the fresh sweat from her brow. As she moved to stand, she winced and dropped back to the floor.

"Your hip," Thelic said, leaving Keela where she lay to kneel beside Maya.

"I'm fine, it's pretty shallow. I think the exorcism just wiped me out."

His jaw clenched as he examined the sliced material and growing patch of mottled red beneath his fingertips. Without another word, he picked her up, ignoring her yelp and demands to be put down. He placed her on the stone by the fire and moved to Zarina's pack where the medicine was kept.

"Yes, don't worry about me. I'm fine," Keela muttered as she struggled to her feet. Stumbling over to the fire, she took one look at the blackened remains of the overcooked meal and resisted the urge to cry. "I hate this place. I hate travelling with you people."

Thelic turned his head slowly to glare at the Esterbellian. It wasn't Keela's fault that Maya had been injured, he knew that, and so tempered his anger and turned his mind back to the task of cleaning Maya's wound.

"Sorry," Keela muttered as she picked the crisped skin off the meat. "I knew what was happening…but I couldn't stop. It was excruciating the harder I tried."

"Like your whole body is being torn in two," Thelic explained on her behalf.

Keela nodded. "It lied though. It *was* trying to kill you, Maya. It didn't want to, but there was so much rage."

"I noticed," Maya said with a chuckle, lightening the mood.

"What it said, about your power being from two worlds, that wasn't a lie. I think it has something to do with our father."

"Bandaar? How so?" Maya asked, wincing as Thelic touched the dampened cloth to her hip.

"Well, we always knew he was contracted to a powerful sprite from Earth before he travelled through the gateway to Avalon…but we assumed his sprite had been stripped like everyone else's. What if that's not true?"

A raucous cry came from above, and a white bird with red tipped wings transformed and dropped to land beside Keela. "Thank the Gods!" Zarina cried, her two, taloned hands grasping Keela's shoulders and pulling her into an embrace. "When we lost one of the grokusi and couldn't find you, we assumed the worst!"

Kadhim followed shortly after to land beside Maya and Thelic. Turning to them both, he stopped, registering the medical pouch opened on the sand and the bright stain on

Maya's hip. Brushing a hand over his face, he sighed and sat on the stone next to her. "What happened?"

"Keela tried to kill us…she claims she was possessed but I'm not so sure," Maya explained shooting a grin at her sister.

"Ha, you're funny," Keela smiled back sarcastically. "Next time I might not fight so hard and let the spirits have their way with you."

After cleaning the rest of the wound, Thelic pulled the material apart to apply the Avalonian version of a plaster – a cloth with a sticky lining made from the mucus of particular vegetation. Being difficult to obtain outside of the territories, they had been used sparingly throughout their journey, but he wasn't willing to risk the filth of the desert causing infection.

"Thanks," Maya said as Thelic packed away the kit. As predicted, the wound was shallow, but she understood his concern, she would have insisted the same if he had been injured. Her chest ached with what she knew that meant. Something she had spent her life avoiding for fear that such a person might leave her, whether through their death, or of their own accord. With the trauma of her mother being taken from her at such a young age, Maya had raised a wall that had hardened over time. *It's better to have loved and lost than to have never loved at all*…that's what people said. But Maya wholeheartedly disagreed. As scary as it was, remaining alone for the rest of your life was *nothing* compared to the feeling of losing someone you loved.

∽

It was close to midnight when they finally reached the southern shore of Kavakin. Small ripples broke across the water as the swell slapped against the supports of a wooden dock housing a single, rickety water-raker's boat. It was woefully short of what they had been expecting, all of them having hoped for a small town and at least a boat large enough to ferry them across comfortably. As it stood, Zarina and Kadhim would have to fly and meet them on the other side.

Only a few feet from the sanded bank of the water stood a small hut. With no lights flickering within, it was safe to assume that the inhabitants had gone to bed for the evening.

Wanting to remain close by and with few other options, the group moved to a sheltered spot near the line of low cliffs to lay out their blankets. With nothing to cook and little need for additional heat, they didn't bother with a fire, instead taking it in turns to venture to the water to bathe.

Leaving the others to chat and snack on what remained of their rations, Thelic and Maya left first. Maya sighed as she undid the last of the buttons on her top, finally freeing her breasts from the scratchy material. Kicking off the slip-on boots, she cursed softly, struggling with the tight fastens along the waistline of her trousers. A chuckle rose from behind and she turned to Thelic. Clearly, he had no trouble removing his own garments as he stood shamelessly naked before her. Without a word, he clasped the material in both hands and ripped the trousers in half before discarding them to the side.

"Thelic!" she hissed.

"If I never see you in those clothes again, it will be too soon. I much prefer you like this," he said, leaning down to kiss the side of her neck. He pulled back, scrunching up his face.

"What?" Maya asked. Disturbed by his reaction, she began to reach for the shirt she had dropped.

"Oh no you don't," he growled. Reaching down, he lifted her into his arms and ran into the soft surf to dive beneath the waves. They broke to the surface and Maya gasped, spitting out the salty water as a giggle burst from her lips.

With his body pulled close and one hand still wrapped around her waist, Thelic used the other to softly wash up her neck, cleaning away the dirt and grime that had accumulated over their travels. The hard-earned callouses from wielding his spear scraped across her shoulders and along her back as he pulled her deeper into his embrace to wash there. Maya said nothing, just closed her eyes and rest her head against his chest to enjoy the sensation.

"How's your hip? The salt in the water must be irritating it," Thelic asked, allowing his fingers to skim the edges of the bandage to make sure it remained.

"That's the last thing on my mind," Maya whispered, lifting her face to convey what it was she wanted.

Thelic chuckled, deep and throaty. His own arousal had become apparent the moment he'd ripped her trousers off. He groaned as Maya wrapped her hand around his tip.

"What do you want me to do?" she asked softly, slightly tightening her grip as she began the slow, careful strokes.

"That," Thelic choked. "Keep doing that." His body shivered, a warning he was already close to the edge. Maya chuckled and ducked her head below the waves. "What are you–" He clenched his fists and bit the bottom corner of his lip, suppressing the moan he knew would reach the others at the camp. He bucked as the tip of her tongue dancing across him, but Maya's hands kept him in place, her fingers leaving periodically to join her tongue. Then she was gone.

Maya sucked in a breath as her head broke the surface of the water, only for Thelic's mouth to crush against hers, stealing the oxygen once again.

"What the fuck was *that*?" he asked, his own breathlessness plain as he pulled away.

"You've never?" Maya gawked at this man, this beast who had pleasured her so expertly.

"I have, but not like that," he said. His fingers slid though the wet strands of her hair as he cupped a hand to her face. The stress, fear and anger of their troubles temporarily replaced with something raw and primal.

Maya was lost in those eyes. "I love you," she whispered.

Thelic's head jerked back and his hand stiffened, shocked by her words. The words he had been waiting for since this woman had broken through the vines caging his heart. No. It was *this* woman and those three little words he had been waiting for his entire life.

"Say something, Thelic," Maya pleaded as her face fell to look upon the water lapping at their waists.

"You know how I feel. How I've always felt." He raised his hand to her jaw, forcing those jade-green eyes to look at him. "What I feel for you transcends love, Maya. A word has yet to be invented. Life is meant to be the most precious thing a man can covet, and yet I would give it up, for you."

The butterflies floating across Maya's stomach turned to fireworks as the corners of her heart squeezed out the last of any doubts or insecurities. She knew he loved her. She had always known. "I...I'll stay. I won't go back to Earth when this is all over. Assuming we live, that is," she said softly.

Moving both hands back to her shoulders, he moved his face so close that Maya could pick out the finer details in the light greyness of his irises.

"We will live. *You* will live, I'll make damn sure of that." He pushed his lips to hers once again, his hips angling forward so his length was pressed against her stomach. "Now. Let me show you just how much I need you in my life." With no other words, his head ducked below the water and Maya clasped a hand to her mouth as his tongue went wandering.

78 | CHAOS DEALS IN DEATH

∼

"Ten coins!?" Keela hollered. "That's beyond extortionate, old lady!"

"My boat, my prices. Pay up, or swim," the port owner huffed, her hands moving to sit on each of her voluminous hips as she regarded the three travellers. "Though, I don't suggest it. Creatures that dwell in the deep tend to mate around the alignment. Makes 'em all hot and bothered," she concluded with a wink to Thelic.

Thelic rolled his eyes and reached into his pocket. He jingled the small, leather pouch and frowned, knowing full well they didn't have ten coins in there.

What would you take in trade?" Maya asked. After spending the majority of their coin reaching the Outlands from the Fortusian port, she figured they had just enough to hire a few karkili when they reached Danika.

As the woman was about to object, assuming the travellers had little to offer, a man opened the door to the humble cottage and stepped out. With a rag in one hand, he meticulously stroked along the edges of a long sword, breaking his concentration to look up and see what all the commotion was about.

"That's my husband, pay him no mind," the woman scowled.

"Ulma, stop being a shiken's arsehole and give them a decent price," the man hollered to the dock where the group stood.

Keela burst out laughing before she could stop herself, and the woman made some noises of protest in her throat, her hands leaving her hips to hang tight by her sides as she spun to face her husband.

"Shut it, you! Get back in bed. We can't afford a funeral if that poison spreads," the woman hollered, then turned back to the others mumbling a curse under her breath.

"What's a shiken?" Maya asked, curious by the amused response.

Thelic coughed to suppress a laugh. "It's a small creature that lives in these parts. They're pretty rare…" He shifted his eyes from Maya to the water-raker. "They're known to die while trying to…relieve themselves." At Maya's confused expression he added, "They're too tight, so sometimes their hearts give out in the process."

Maya turned her gaze back to the woman – who had moved to cross her arms over her chest – and laughed. She couldn't help it, after the stress of travel, the joke about this woman being as tight with money as a small creature's nether-regions was the proverbial straw that broke the camel's back.

"I was beginning to think you lacked a sense of humour," Keela said with a snigger.

The large woman turned a deep shade of red as the joke was enjoyed at her expense, then turned on her heel and stormed back to the desert cottage.

"Wait!" Maya wheezed, trying to contain her giggles. "I'm sorry, please." Spotting the husband just ahead, she realised he was leaning his weight onto one leg and remembered what the woman had said. "We have medicine!"

Ulma stopped at that, and slowly turned. "Stuff to treat a wajeer's bite?"

"Wajeer? They don't live around these part," Thelic said, walking forward. "How did it happen?"

"Well, if it wasn't that four-legged vermin then I don't know what it was. You had better ask my husband. Come on," she said, waving for the others to follow behind her.

. . .

Inside the small cottage was surprisingly roomy, with a second floor like Thelic's acting as a mezzanine for sleeping. The bottom floor, however, was nicely spread out, with cushions lining a seating area and a short table to dine at. Other than that, the colour was sparse, with only browns and creams in the curtains and rugs – any other hue apparently too rich for both their tastes and their pockets.

Maya and the others moved to sit at the table as instructed while Ulma fumbled around the cupboards looking for enough mugs for each of the visitors. As the husband sat down to join them, Maya reached out her hand in greeting, pulling it back at the man's confused expression.

"It's a new way of greeting," Thelic explained to the man. "She's spent a little time at the educators' guilds and forgets that not all have been taught Earth's ways."

The man nodded his head, then offered his hand with a smile. "Is this how you do it?" he asked enthusiastically as he raised it up in the air.

"Like this," Maya said, taking his hand in hers to lift it up and down.

"Very strange. I know we descend from that realm, but its customs still baffle me."

Maya bought her hand back to her side, momentarily saddened at the familiarity of the man's reaction to when she had taught Elkin the 'high-five' on their travels.

"Right, less of this nonsense, can you help my husband or not?" Ulma asked as she set each of the mugs down by the travellers.

"What did the creature look like?" Thelic asked the man. There was no way it was a wajeer. The creatures were fierce to be sure, but they only dwelled near a city's outskirts, scavenging for scraps when the inhabitants went to bed and the streets were empty.

"I swear it looked like one of them beasts. But it wasn't.

I'm not sure if I'm honest. It was elemental though, that much I *am* sure about. Damn thing nearly blew my head off with a fireball before it bit me and ran."

"Sounds like a Fire Finkel," Keela said, standing to retrieve their med-pouch from the bags by the doorway. "Let me have a look, it could just be infected."

The man shifted his weight, pulling his legs out from under the table and across the floor.

Shifting up the material and exposing the man's shin, Keela whistled as she touched the edges of a large, circular wound.

"How does it look?" he asked, closing his eyes and turning his head as Keela continued her assessment.

"Definitely not poison," she surmised. "You're lucky. If it *had* been a wajeer, you'd be in for a world of hurt. They require a specific antidote, and I'll assume you don't have any lying around here."

"Did you say a Fire Finkel?" Ulma asked. Her look of defeat turned into one of mischief as a wicked gleam flashed in her eyes. "You want to trade? Okay then. In return for being ferried to Danika, you lot can take care of that pesky little sprite for us."

6
HUNTER BECOMES THE HUNTED

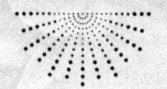

EASTERN OUTLANDS – KAVAKIN DESERT

"What makes you think we can even find it? We don't have time to be messing around, tracking down Finkels," Keela said as she packed away the med-pouch and returned it to the travel bag.

For once, Maya had to agree. They had already lost a day in their exploration of the cave and arriving so late to the ferry port.

"We know where it is," Ulma insisted, interrupting Maya's thoughts. "We just don't know how to get rid of the damned thing."

"It's been terrorising our little slice of home for the past few months now," Ulma's husband explained. "Torching our produce and chewing at the ropes. We've had to use a chain to tie the ferry up now, after the first was lost when the creature bit through it."

It was the reason the couple had charged so much in the first place; a desperate attempt to make up for their losses and live comfortably.

"Why don't you move away from here? Why would anyone choose to live on this gods-forsaken plain?" Keela asked, her sympathy in short supply for those who refused to help themselves.

"This is all we have. I inherited the business from my father and his father before him. Nobody wants to buy it from us, as I'm sure you can understand," the man explained defensively.

"This is getting us nowhere," Maya said, pulling Keela back before she bit the hand they needed to ferry them. "Tell us where the Finkel is, and we'll try and do what we can. But we need to leave for Danika tonight, at the latest."

"Deal! You bring us that pesky creature's head, and I'll ferry you to the other side of Avalon if you ask it," Ulma said.

Maya had no intention of killing the creature, but nodded her agreement, nonetheless.

As they stepped into the sun, Maya spotted the two, red-winged birds on a nearby ash tree. The gypsul, keeping a close eye on their human companions as always.

Kadhim and Zarina watched as Maya and the others nodded their heads to whatever the woman's husband was saying, before leaving their bags and heading towards the sharp incline of the cliff's path. They waited until Maya had passed the tall rocks and disappeared from the couple's view, before swooping overhead and transforming to land just ahead of them on the rocky road.

"What's going on?" Kadhim asked, concerned they were heading in the opposite direction of the water, with no bags and only their weapons.

Keela pointed to Maya, her eyes narrowed in annoyance. "Maya's bleeding heart is causing us problems again."

"That's hardly the reason," Maya said defensively. "Did you *want* to swim?"

"No," Keela mumbled, cursing under her breath. "Fine, it

might not be your need to get involved with every creature in distress, but damn it you're like a beacon for these people!"

"Again, I hardly see how that's my fault," Maya insisted, rolling her eyes dramatically at Keela's temper-tantrum.

"*Again*, where are you going?" Kadhim asked, his tone suggesting he was unhappy with their direction of travel.

"To find a Fire Finkel that's been harassing the water-rakers," Maya offered in explanation. "We didn't have the coin they wanted for the trip, so we were forced to offer our services instead."

Kadhim sighed and tipped his head back. "We don't have time for this."

Zarina giggled and skipped to Maya's side. "Stop huffing, you two. It sounds like we don't have much of a choice," she said, her voice and demeanour a natural relaxant. "Is this Finkel far?"

"Apparently not. The man insisted it lived in a stand of ash trees just up there." Maya pointed to a row of bone-white trees at the top of the low cliff.

"In that case, I think you should take this one, Maya," Zarina suggested.

"What?" Thelic asked. "Why the hell should Maya be the one to kill it?"

"Because it's good practice for her. And I don't think you should *kill* it. I'm sure there's a reason for its misbehaviour. Maya would do well to hone her communication with them."

"Like, talk to them?" Maya asked. "I speak with Loki and BB in my head, telepathically."

Zarina's eyes widened as she clapped her hands. "That's good. But can you sense how they feel? You must practice this so that you may rely on their instincts in battle as much as your own."

Maya considered Zarina's words as they silently trekked up the footpath. As promised, it wasn't long before the group passed the first of the ash trees, their roots poking through the sand in a trip hazard to any who didn't watch their footing. With no leaves and spindly branches, there was nowhere for the creature to hide other than behind one of the large trunks.

Together they moved silently, carefully navigating the uprooted floor as they peered behind each tree they passed. Even Kadhim and Zarina moved on foot, wanting to be on hand should the creature spring out and surprise them.

Something flashed, metal catching the sun.

Zarina screamed, clutching her shoulder as she fell, a small dagger piercing through the skin to protrude above her shoulder blade.

Kadhim rushed to her side, standing over her with his bow drawn and the first arrow nocked. Everyone stopped, their own weapons held ready as they peered into the twisted field of trees.

High-pitched whistles pierced the air before arrows descended on the group. Clutching Maya to his chest, Thelic raised his spear and spun it like a helicopter's rotor blades, summoning his wind to act as a barrier against the rain of arrows striking the trees and floor around them.

Another howl cracked across the silent wood as metal pierced flesh.

Maya turned her head to track Keela. Her sister was safe behind a tree, blocking her face from the splintering bark as the arrows hit. Next she turned to check on Zarina. Kadhim remained stood over her, his bow hanging loosely by his side, an arrow protruding from his stomach. He turned to Maya with a pained expression before crashing to the sandy woodland floor.

Maya tried to push away from Thelic, to reach their two fallen friends, but his grip was like a vice, only tightening the more she struggled. As the whistles died and the arrows stopped, he released her, and they rushed to the gypsuls' sides. Both Kadhim and Zarina were still conscious and breathing, the arrows failing to pierce any vital organs – that was assuming their organs were in the same place as a human's.

A harsh laugh broke from the trees ahead. "And here I thought we were hunting Finkel. You outlanders will fetch a much prettier sum."

Maya and Thelic did a double take as their attacker stepped into view. It was a man, once only a figment of a dream, now standing before them in the flesh.

"You," Maya whispered.

"Have we met, sweetheart?" The tall and stocky man looked down his nose at Maya standing defensively in front of his prize. "I think I'd remember if we had. Unless you're one of the whores from Danika. They all look the same after a while."

A low growl erupted from Thelic, his feet planting firmly into the sand. "You murdered those children."

The man turned his gaze to Thelic, momentarily surprised by the accusation. "I've never harmed another soul in my life."

"Liar!" Maya roared. "I watched you kill the young gypsul by the desert caves and butcher their bodies. You *and* your lackey."

"Ah, the outlander kids," he sneered, realisation dawning. "Well now, those things don't really count, do they? They'd need to have a soul for a man to feel bad about taking it."

Maya moved to take a step forward, enraged by his words and callous disregard for the young lives he'd stolen. Thelic's arm reached out to the side, blocking her. She whipped her head to face him, bewildered by his attempt to stop her from giving this man what he so clearly deserved. But Thelic was no longer driven by rage, he was too busy staring at the man's weapons. A set of knives. Where were the archers?

A cold smile passed over the hunter's face as he raised his hand and snapped his fingers. Whistles rained down on the group once again, the arrows finding more than one mark.

Maya saw the arrow in the split second where time seemed to slow. A large figure moved in front of her, just as the metal pierced flesh. A burst of blood spattered her face but the figure in front didn't move.

"Thelic!" Maya screamed, registering the serrated iron tip protruding through the back of his white shirt, turning it crimson. Thelic said nothing; didn't move, the perpetual human shield eyeing its enemy like a tempered beast waiting for its moment to strike. Where was he hit? It was hard to tell the angle from Maya's position at his back.

"Give us the outlanders, and we'll leave you be," the hunter said, the smirk on his face a clear indicator that he wasn't bothered either way – he *would* be claiming his prize today.

"Fuck you," Keela spat, yanking an arrow from her arm to let it drop to the sand below. She looked at Maya, a thin smile crossing her lips. "Do your worst, Sister."

"No. We can take them without using your power, Maya," Thelic insisted, his gaze still fixed on the knife-wielding man.

The hunter chuckled and shook his head. He raised his hand–

A bolt of fire rocketed through the trees, crashing into Keela's ankles and lifting her off her feet to land in a graceless heap atop one of the larger roots. The fire kept going, darting from tree to tree like a flaming blur as it sought the next target.

"Finkel!" the man screamed, lowering a hand to his knives as he tried and failed to follow the creature's rapid movements.

Two, three, four men raced towards the centre of the barren wood, the archers rallying beside their leader. With Kadhim and Zarina now unconscious, and Keela nursing her two burned ankles, Maya and Thelic would have to protect them. At the emergence of a new and more immediate threat, the hunters had all but forgotten their gypsul prey, their gazes fixed on the surrounding trees.

Pulling Thelic's sleeve, Maya spun him to face her and almost cried with relief. The arrow had pierced through his shoulder. All in all, he would be fine.

As if in tune with her thoughts, he smiled and gripped the wooden shaft before snapping it off. "Stay with Zarina and Kadhim. I'll get Keela," he said, stroking a hand down Maya's face before rushing to the wounded Keela's side.

Maya turned as screams erupted from the group of hunters. Two of them had fallen, their chests and faces singed a gruesome black and pink. The one she needed was still unharmed, the murderer she wanted words with.

Loki. BB. I need you, Maya beckoned silently. Without a moment's hesitation, the two sprites sprang into action, already sensing something was wrong and patiently awaiting their summons.

The red blur stopped for the first time since its appearance, the fiery head of what looked like a small bear turning at the sense of its equal. At the sight of Maya's sprites, the creature's mouth opened in a growl to reveal elongated canines, embers dripping to sizzle against the sand. It sprang forward.

Maya, already clutching the dagger in her hand, sliced her open palm and conjured the castor circle. With the first drop, light sprung from the ground at her feet, the blue ring bright and vibrant denoting her pact with the Gouram of water.

BB shivered as the gifted power soaked between the sapphire-coloured scales of his skin, then darted forward to meet his counter element. Blue and red collided in a crash of snapping teeth, both vanishing only to reappear in another part of the wood. Loki waited patiently at Maya's side, his claws extending to dig into the sand, then retracting back under the fur of his paws in a rare sign of nervousness.

"Communicate with him, Maya," Keela urged weakly as she slumped to the ground beside the gypsul. Thelic had managed to drag her over to the others, but it had cost him. He gripped his shoulder, the rubicund stain now coating the entire right side of his shirt.

Pushing aside her instincts to treat Thelic and the others, Maya focused on BB. He was so fast, every time she thought she got a lock on him, he was suddenly in another part of the wood.

BB, she urged.

A half growl, half purr responded in her mind, the seal across her chest resonating like a shockwave. Maya gasped at the sensation and clasped a hand to her breast.

BB, when I signal, bring the creature to me.

This time just a growl in response. The sprite didn't seem to like Maya's plan very much.

Trust me, she said.

"Did it work?" Keela asked, her eyes flicking from Maya to the two, battling creatures.

"It did. I need you both to stay here. I have a plan," Maya said, turning to regard them both.

"Not a chance," Thelic muttered, gripping his spear in both hands. Before Maya could object, he pointed to the three hunters still standing. "You concentrate on the Finkels, I'll make sure that lot stay where they are. That's non-negotiable."

Maya nodded. She hadn't considered the hunters might use the distraction to attack her. With Keela's assurances that she could still wield her throwing knives, Thelic and Maya ran to a relatively open spot a safe distance from the others. With Zarina and Kadhim lying defenceless, the last thing she wanted was to bring the Finkels anywhere near them.

Okay, BB. Bring it this way. Maya knelt down to stroke Loki. "Do you remember the last time you helped me fight a Fire Finkel, in the woods by Winkler's hamlet? And that time in the glen where we met properly for the first time?"

Loki raised his head, a wide and unnervingly human grin of understanding reaching the corners of his furry face. He knew exactly what Maya intended, and he would convey as much to BB. This time, it wouldn't be a fiery prison that their elemental opponent would be locked in, but a watery one, with the Air Finkel's help.

They were close. Each of BB's manoeuvres bringing the fire sprite closer and closer to the set trap. Maya summoned the second circle, calling on whatever of the Gouram's essence lay deep inside her. A bright, yellow glow responded, joining the blue in a chorus of brilliant hues akin to green.

NOW!

Loki sprang forward at Maya's command just as BB slammed to a stop and twisted, catching the Fire Finkel's throat in his mouth. With the sprite finally immobilised, Loki went to work, zipping around the two sprites in the beginnings of a tornado.

Okay, BB, merge with Loki.

The Water Finkel did as instructed, releasing the gasping sprite and disappearing into the void, the two elements joining as one in a frightening roar of power. The cyclone twisted, moving between the trees as the Fire Finkel slammed into its sides in a desperate bid to escape.

Hold it steady! Maya screamed internally as the elements broke the limbs of a tree close to Keela and the others.

The hunters ran, terrified of the ever-shifting mass ploughing through the trees.

"Thelic, don't let that man escape!" Maya yelled over the storm, her arms shaking with the effort to manipulate the cyclone and keep it in place.

Thelic ran forward, barely dodging the colliding sprites and falling branches. The man screamed and fell to the ground, Keela's dagger stuck deep in his thigh. Clutching his leg, he tried to drag himself to the nearest tree, but Thelic got to him first. He rose his spear, ready to strike the man's heart.

"No, Thelic! I need him alive!" Maya called, dropping to one knee as the Fire Finkel continued to battle against her sprites. It was so strong, stronger than the one they had fought in Danika. *"COME ON!"* she screamed, digging her nails into the wound on her palm in a bid to release more blood, and more power.

The Fire Finkel stopped, a shudder coursing through its body as the flames flickered out. Only its husk remained as it dropped to the floor.

Okay, Loki, that's enough. BB, you keep holding it, Maya commanded. Standing to her feet, she took a wobbly step forward and leaned heavily against a nearby tree. The cyclone died just as quickly as it had started, only a sphere of water left to imprison the fire element. As she approached the floating ball of water, the Fire Finkel opened its eyes.

With the hunter somewhat subdued and under Keela's watch, Thelic returned to Maya's side, holding her steady as she reached the sprites. He winced as one of Maya's hands reached out and clutched his shoulder just above where the arrow still lay embedded in the skin.

"Thelic…I can hear it," Maya whispered. She stared into the Finkel's eyes through the blur of the shifting water and listened as it communicated its feelings. Pain. Torment. Fury. "These hunters, I think they killed the creature's family or friends. It feels lost."

Loki appeared on Maya's shoulder to nuzzle her neck in his usual, comforting way.

"What do you want to do?" Thelic asked. "It might attack us again if you let it go."

Maya shook her head. "No. It won't." At Maya's silent command, BB released the sprite before returning to her side, his teeth bared in warning to the Fire Finkel. Maya took two steps forward to close the distance between her and the wheezing sprite, holding her hands up in a sign that she meant no harm. She knelt down and reached out slowly to place her hand on the rough and wet fur of its hide.

The creature shuddered, closing its eyes and waiting for its captor to strike. When nothing came but a soft stroke of its fur, the Finkel opened its eyes to Maya's smile.

"It's alright. We'll take care of those hunters for you, but please stop hurting the family by the water. Okay?" Maya reasoned. The Finkel blinked twice, then vanished in a wisp of smoke.

"What does that mean?" Thelic asked.

Maya shrugged, as unsure as he was by the Finkel's response. "Where's the man?"

"With Keela and the others. Zarina is awake, but Kadhim is badly hurt...they won't be able to shift with their wounds."

Maya clenched her fists and stood shakily to her feet, both exhaustion from the summons and rage coursing through her. Beside her, Thelic swayed lightly and threw out a hand to steady himself.

"Whoa, are *you* okay?" she asked. With no more than a curt nod of his head to reassure her, they made their way towards the others.

"So, what now? You preach the sin of killing another, and then murder *me*?" the hunter spat as Maya approached. "You're disgusting. How could you side with these creatures when they should all–" The tip of his tongue crunched as

Maya's fist smashed against his teeth. His head snapped back as another came pummelling after, a tooth jarring loose to fly down the back of his throat.

"Maya," Thelic stated calmly from behind her, though he made no real move to intervene.

Maya stepped back, arms shaking with fury. "I will *never* forget what you did to those children, how you *mutilated* them," she roared at the hunter.

"How the fuck do you even know about that? You weren't there!" he gargled, pushing himself up to a sitting position to stop the blood from clogging his throat.

"I saw it all! The whole thing." Maya clutched her fist as the ache began to set in. "Where's your partner, the other man?" When no immediate response came, she lurched forward with her fist raised again in warning.

"Okay! He lives in Danika. He was a client, wanted some gypsul parts to bolster the war effort. You know, for morale, to let people know that the outlanders are easy prey."

Maya rocked back on her heels into Thelic's chest. If that was true, then the Danikans were as eager for war as the other territories. "Was the kill commissioned?" she asked, desperation in her voice.

The hunter stared back with a quizzical expression.

"Did someone *pay* him to come to you, to hire your services for the kill? Or was he acting on his own?" she clarified.

The man shifted under the weight of everyone's stares. "Yes, he was ordered to come here, to the Outlands."

"Who gave the order?" Maya seethed.

"Danika's Keeper, Carnass."

"Shit," Keela hissed. "Are we too late? Has Carnass joined the war effort?" she asked Maya, as if she might be able to see the unseen like her grandmother.

"You're lying," Maya said to the hunter. "I heard you say you were going to *sell* the body parts, not hand them over."

"One kill was for the Keeper…the other for profit," the hunter said with a shrug. With two fingers, he reached into his mouth and wobbled a molar, cursing as he spat out the bloody tooth. "Why do you care so much?"

Turning her back to him, Maya regarded the others. "We should get back to the water-rakers and treat your wounds." Kadhim had yet to wake up. Though his breathing seemed steady, he refused to rise.

The hunter chuckled. "No point. Those arrows were dipped in a toxin. It should be starting to set in about now. Won't kill a human, but it's poisonous to those *things*," he said, jabbing a finger at Kadhim.

"Sikospin," Zarina whispered.

"No wonder I feel like shit," Keela muttered.

Thelic shook his head, still unsteady on his feet. "Sikospin isn't poisonous, it just knocks you out for a bit."

"No. It's deadly to us," Zarina said, her eyes focused on Kadhim's unmoving form. She snapped her head to Maya. "We need to get back to our bags. I have zingan root in there, it should counteract the worst of it."

"Maya, you'll have to go," Keela said with a yawn as she lay her head against the tree trunk. "I think we're going to be out of it for a while."

"I'll go with you," Thelic said. He stepped to the side ready to lead the way, but his legs gave out and he dropped to the floor.

"No, you stay here with the rest of them. Keep an eye on the hunter. I'll be as fast as I can." As Maya turned to run for the path, the hunter jumped to his feet, a hidden blade pulled from his boot as he descended on Maya with her back turned.

"Maya!" Thelic roared as he reached out to grab the man. The last of his energy vanished and all he could do was watch before the darkness swelled along his vision, and he passed out.

Maya turned at the shout and raised her hand to defend against the weapon bearing down on her. She screamed as the knife pierced through her palm, jutting out the back of her hand. Without thinking, she snatched the dagger from her side and plunged it deep into the man's chest, twisting the hilt before releasing it.

The hunter stumbled back before crashing to the floor, both hands clasping the hilt in a mixture of shock and confusion at what had happened.

Maya stepped towards him, nothing but cold contempt plain on her face as she slowly pulled the dagger from her hand. "Sometimes, vengeance can be just as sweet as justice. Enjoy hell," she said. Then she turned and ran for the water-raker's cottage.

7
PROPHECY UNVEILED

DANIKA

"Ouch!" Keela yelped as the heavy-handed Ulma applied the bandage to her arm. "That's too tight, I'll lose my damn fingers if you don't let at least *some* blood get through."

Ulma tutted at the temperamental warrioress, then moved away to tend to Zarina. She paused at the side of the table where Zarina was seated, her eyes hesitant to look directly into those of the gypsul.

"It's okay," Zarina said with a reassuring smile to the human woman. "I can treat this by myself, you can help the others." As she awkwardly stretched one arm over her head, she found her reach wasn't quite enough to dab the cleanser onto the right spot. She tried the other way, leaning to the side to slide her uninjured arm up her back.

"Here, give me that," Ulma said. She gasped at the feel of the gypsul's long fingers brushing against her own as she grabbed the cloth. Swallowing her inherited fear, she pushed Zarina's long braid of silver hair to the side and went to work cleaning the wound.

"I'm sorry you folk got caught up with the hunters,"

Ulma's husband said as he refilled the water jug. "We weren't expecting them back for at least another three days."

"It's fine, thank you for helping me get my friends back here," Maya said, accepting a mug from the man. Beside her, Kadhim groaned as he chewed the last of the zingan root. "Here, have some water," Maya offered, raising the chipped clay cup to his lips. He nodded his thanks, cringing at the aftertaste of the life-saving root.

"It's a good job you thought to bring some of that," Thelic said.

"Fatari gave it to me before we left," Zarina explained, wincing as Ulma moved to clean the entry wound on her chest. "Though, we almost always carry some with us, just in case."

As Kadhim coughed, Maya looked to the husband and wife. "My friend will need to stay here for a few more days to recover. Will you house him?"

"What a ridiculous question," Ulma said with an exasperated sigh. "You people…you not only helped my imbecile of a husband with his leg, but calmed the Finkel and got rid of that horrid man who plagues our doorstep every third moon." She dabbed at the wound with a little more force than intended as the emotion of gratitude overwhelmed her. "It's true we've learned to fear your kind, but whether you're an outlander or a human, we no longer care. Your actions define you, and you've shown us a kindness. For that, you will always be welcome in our home."

"Thank you," the group whispered in unison, each smiling with their own gratitude.

"While I appreciate your kindness, there isn't a chance in all the realms that I'm going to lay here and rest while you all go on without me," Kadhim said, the deep tone of his voice suggesting the others shouldn't push this point further.

Naturally, Zarina ignored it. "Yes, you are, Kadhim Caveneel. You are going to stay in that bed for at least two more days and then we'll *both* meet the others before they move on from Danika." She crossed her arms defiantly, and as Kadhim opened his mouth, Zarina shot him a look of warning. "Don't even try it, Kadhim."

"Caveneel?" Maya asked, surprised to recognise the name. "Why does that sound familiar?"

Zarina and Kadhim glanced at each other before Kadhim answered. "I gave you my full name when we first met, you probably just forgot."

That seemed unlikely to Maya, she was always very good with names; a skill that had been useful as a policewoman. Brushing off the feeling of uncertainty, Maya made a suggestion. "When you're feeling better, you can meet us at Thelic's lodge." They had planned to stop there anyway to see if Thelic's bodaari had made it back from the ice passage in Cantor. "It's south–"

"I know where it is," Kadhim interrupted. "That's where we were first told to look when you came through the gateway. By the time we got there, you had already moved on to Esterbell."

Of course. Thelic had forgotten the gypsul had been following them from the beginning at Fatari's behest. It still unnerved him. Not that it had been *gypsul* following them, but that he had been completely unaware of anyone lurking in his and Maya's wake.

∽

DANIKA'S SHORE was buzzing with activity as boats queued along the inlet, all waiting their turn to dock at the territory's smaller harbour. As Ulma manoeuvred the small boat through the flotilla of bigger, busier rafts, Thelic noted the merchandise. It wasn't unusual for Transumian silks and

Fortusian jewels to be ferried across the channel. Danika boasted a wonderfully exotic market. It was, however, unusual for the type of trade presently visible on the ships lining up to offload their goods. Weapons and Armour. The glint of metals in the mid-afternoon sun was unmistakable, with weapon racks proudly displayed across the platforms.

"Okay, I won't be able to find a space to stay for long, so you'll have to hop off when we get to the dock," Ulma informed them.

Collecting their belongings, Maya and the others readied themselves along the side of the boat, preparing to jump at Ulma's command.

"Now!"

They sprang from boat, each tumbling onto the platform when their ferry-lady slowed. As they found their feet, they turned to see Ulma waving goodbye.

"I'll look after your friends, don't worry!" she called.

Maya smiled and returned the gesture, pleased they had made yet another ally in this complicated world of chaos. A groan from behind caught her attention and she looked down to find Keela still sitting on the rough wooden planks of the dock. Maya reached down, offering a helping hand and noted Keela was clutching her ankles, still swollen from the Finkel's attack. Her own hand wasn't faring too well either, and she suspected the hunter had neglected to clean the weapon he'd attempted to kill her with.

"We'll head to see Brijid, first," Thelic said in his usual gruff tone. "I know we're already behind schedule, but none of us will be much use until our wounds have been properly seen to."

Maya wanted to object. After speaking with the hunter and seeing the imported weapons currently lining the wide docks, she was becoming increasingly worried. It was impossible to know just how much time they had to convince

Carnass against joining the war effort. Still, her hand throbbed and a fever had set in, indicative of infection. He was right, the healer had to come first.

Ulma had dropped the group at Danika's eastern docks, the closest port to the southern tip of Kavakin. Unfortunately, that meant they had over half a day's worth of travel to the Keep which lay forever west of the territory.

As they meandered through the crowds, Maya was surprised when a woman, a guard wearing the signature blue of the Danikan territory and Carnass' sigil, stepped into their path to bar the exit.

"Gloves off and hoods down. Come on, let's see 'em," the guard demanded, the dull and drawled tone of her voice suggesting boredom with the monotony of the same request uttered again and again throughout her shift.

They each did as they were told, removing the gloves they had seen fit to put on with the plummeting temperatures the closer they got to the territory.

Despite the tedious nature of the guard's role, the hand on the hilt of her sword momentarily flexed as she carried out her inspection. No coloured and elongated fingers, no runes. "Fine, move along," she said, only to issue the same demands to the next group of individuals who wished to move past her.

"Seems like things are getting tense in Danika," Keela muttered, pushing her fingers into the stiff gloves once again and pulling up her hood to ward against the biting chill. "I've never seen this port so busy."

"It makes you wonder what the other Keepers have said to sway Carnass," Thelic pondered aloud as he led them forward. "He always swore he would never be baited into war, unless in the defence of his own territory."

Whatever had changed the territory leader's mind, Maya could only hope it wasn't entirely set in stone. What would she say? She had the prophecy, tailored by the Seer specifically for Carnass, but would it be enough?

"Over here," Thelic said, quickening his pace as they came to an area by the side of the only dirt road leading from the docks to the Danikan towns. Carts and karkili lined the grass, some with wares and others with people clambering to find a space in the open-top carriages.

As Maya and Keela stood to one side, Thelic approached one of the few remaining empty carts and its driver. Words were exchanged, to which Thelic shook his head and offered a malevolent smile. After further words, the driver seemed to reassess before chuckling nervously and nodding in agreement.

"Well?" Keela asked. "What's the price?"

"One coin each, we have enough."

A taxi service, Maya realised. An Avalonian Uber. She shook her head and smiled, the small comparison to her home world a brief and heart-warming reprieve from the unfamiliar. As Thelic and Keela stepped up and settled themselves on the open-top cart clearly not designed for human cargo, she regarded the rickety looking wheels dubiously.

Resigned to her fate, Maya stepped up moments before the driver cracked the reigns and the karkili took off as if the devil herself were snapping at their heels. Maya fell back, almost toppling off the back of the cart. Thelic's arm gripped her waist, pulling her down to the seat beside him.

"Bloody hell! What did you say to him?" Maya asked, suddenly aware of the creaks and bumps with each rock the spindly wheels hit.

"Just that we're in a hurry," Thelic said innocently, keeping hold of her waist as the carriage rocked to one side. "I might have suggested his life depended on the speed at which he got us to the Keep. I know what these transporters are like, they require a heavy hand."

Keela barked a laugh and bobbed her head in approval, while Maya sighed and made a mental note to apologise to the poor driver.

∼

Despite the speed of the death-trap that made up their taxi, Maya was surprised to see the high stone walls of the Keep after only a few short hours. With shaky legs and aching spines, they disembarked, pulling their travel bags to reposition them on their backs.

Unsurprisingly, Danika Market was just as Maya remembered; stalls brimming with delectable treats and fine clothes to suit the cooler climes. As they made their way from stall to stall – resisting the urge to barter a kidney for a taste of the sweet, meat filled buns – a cry rang out from the centre of the square.

Maya rose to her tiptoes, trying to see over the heads of the shoppers attempting to squeeze though the crowds. There. Barely twenty feet away, stood Maya's first enemy in this world. The market's butcher.

"Don't even think about it," Thelic warned, seeing the glint in her eyes as she revisited the memory of her previous encounter with the man. "You can't save everyone, Maya."

"Says you," Maya muttered, her stare fixed on the beefy butcher. The squeal had come from the meat vender's customer, a short man who seemed to be asking for his money back. The butcher raised his fist and everything in Maya told her to go, to help. The grip on her wrist kept her steady, preventing her intervention. The butcher's fist stopped short of the customer's face as a boot planted into his chest, rocketing him back into a couple standing nearby.

Maya's breath caught in her throat. The man's rescuer stood between the butcher and his next victim. Red hair tied in a hasty, messy bun. Broad shoulders to rival a heavy weight boxing champion. Maya broke from Thelic's grip and disappeared into the crowd.

"Elkin?!" she called breathlessly, gripping the red-head's shirt and spinning him towards her. An unfamiliar face stared back and smiled, a prominent gap between his two front teeth. It wasn't him. Maya smiled back sheepishly and mumbled an apology as she walked away.

"Maya–"

"Don't, Thelic," she said wearily as she passed. "I just thought…"

"I know," Thelic said. He, too, had been shocked at first. The similarity between the scene before them and when Maya herself had faced the butcher. Elkin had rescued her, and so their journey together had begun. "We need to let go," he said softly.

"I know." If only it were that easy. Elkin's betrayal had left a bite-sized chunk missing from Maya's heart. That hole would slowly fill, but it would take time.

"Hello? Brijid?" Thelic called as they each stepped through the flap of the healer's canvas tent.

"Give me a damn moment," a voice called from behind one of the drawn curtains that offered privacy to her patients.

It wasn't long before the short and flustered healer emerged, rubbing the blood from her hands with a damp cloth. As she took in Thelic and Maya, their weary expressions, and the woman behind with bandages wrapped around her ankles, she sighed. With one hand on her hip, she pushed the stray strands of mouse-brown hair from her face and gestured to three beds lying side by side.

"You two look worse than when I last saw you. How did that djinca sting heal up, Maya?" Brijid asked.

Shortly after arriving in Avalon, Maya had been attacked by a djinca, a creature akin to a lioness...a six-*foot* lioness with hard scales, the ability to fly and a wicked set of teeth. Brijid had attended to Maya's wounds and saved her life that day.

"It healed well. Thank you, Brijid. Maybe one of these days we'll pop in just to say hello instead of needing your skills as a healer," Maya said with an uneasy chuckle.

"You and Thelic are always welcome." Brijid angled her head to peer past as Maya took a seat on the bed. "I see you picked up a stray, too."

"A stray would imply someone unwelcome and in need of constant care. I'll have you know I'm quite the opposite," Keela muttered, gingerly raising both feet from the ground to lie across the thin mattress. "Except for right now, right now I need a little care and attention."

Brijid laughed softly but assessed the same. Considering Keela's small and athletic build, the size of her ankles would have been less surprising on someone twice her hight and four times her body weight. "Let's have a look at those then. Maya, could you help Thelic remove that awful looking bandage on his shoulder?"

Maya nodded and hopped from the bed to help Thelic with his heavy coat. "You should check Keela's arm as well. She was hit with an arrow," Maya suggested.

"My arm is fine, it's these damn burns on my legs that are causing the issue."

"Hmm, yes. I can get rid of the swelling, but you'll have to stay off them for at least a day before the medicine takes effect." Brijid's frown deepened as she peeled away the bandage wrapped tightly around the Esterbellian's arm. "Make that *two* days – this is heavily infected."

Maya frowned. Two days. That was too long. They would have to pay a visit to Carnass without her.

Keela looked up, easily reading the anxiety on her sister's face. She sighed. "You got any wine knocking about, Brijid? If I'm to stay in this tent for two days, you can be damned sure I'm making the most of it."

Brijid laughed and smacked the spot between Keela's shoulder blades in approval. "Of course I do! You can fill me in on all your adventures while I treat you. I'm dying to get back out in the wilds."

The three travellers cast a knowing look at one another. They'd certainly been on some adventures, and for the most part wouldn't wish them on anyone.

∾

BY THE TIME Brijid had deemed Thelic and Maya sufficiently treated to leave her care, dusk had already crept upon them, some of the stall owners tending to the last of their customers before closing early for the night. Thelic rotated his shoulder as he and Maya walked the short distance to the gates of the Keep. With the wound cleaned and rebandaged, the constant sting was replaced by a dull ache. Brijid had treated Maya's hand much the same as she had tended to Keela's arm – with tuts of disapproval and quick-fire magic to burn out the infection and cauterise the wound. It was a crude method of healing, one Brijid wasn't entirely pleased about, but it was the quickest. Maya held it up now, testing and wiggling her fingers with ease.

"How is it?" Thelic asked, pointing to Maya's bandaged hand. "I still think you should have stayed."

"Maybe *you* should have stayed," Maya retorted, registering a small hiss of pain as a gaggle of girls raced past, jolting his shoulder again. The suggestion was half-hearted at best. While Maya was concerned for Thelic, she didn't want to face the Keeper alone, even if it *was* just Carnass. The

Keeper of Danika was rumoured to be a tyrant, a vicious king with nary a care for the lives of those who displeased him. As Maya had come to understand, it was all a facade, the man being more an eccentric teddy bear in comparison to his perceived alter-ego.

"Trying to get rid of me?" Thelic asked as he waved away another group of young men and women offering their sexual services. "It's too late, Maya. You should have thought about that before you said those three little words." He stopped beside a stall selling chunks of multicoloured soaps and pulled Maya to face him. "Where you go, I go. I'm yours as much as you are mine, and nothing will ever change that."

Maya blushed at his words. She should hate it, hate the possessive side of Thelic. But she didn't. It told her everything she needed to know about his feelings for her – not that there was ever any question. He had made it abundantly clear how he felt in the way his eyes touched her very soul. She reached up with a hand and brushed the lengthening stubble that peppered his cheek, then rose onto her toes and kissed him. "I know," she said.

As Maya and Thelic approached the Keep's gate, two guards stepped forward to intercept. "No visitors. The Keeper is not to be disturbed, now move along."

"We're here on business for Carnass," Maya stated to the man. "Tell him Mayara Rivers has his prophecy."

After some debate between the guards, one cursed and sheathed his weapon before turning to walk slowly up the wide stairs of the Keep. It wasn't long before he returned, skidding around the corner and almost tumbling down the steps in his haste.

"Let them through! Spirits, let them pass now!" the guard bellowed, red-faced and sweating profusely in his race to get back to the gate where the visitors waited patiently. His companion stepped to the side, waving a hand to allow entry as the second finally reached them.

"We know the way," Maya insisted as the man bent at the waist to suck in air and catch his breath. He nodded his head and smiled in thanks, telling them the Keeper was waiting in the great hall.

"Seems Carnass is playing the part of the evil king as well as ever," Thelic whispered to Maya as they made their way up the stone steps. "I'd almost forgotten about the prophecy, what did Lifaya tell you?"

"Nothing good, as usual," Maya said gloomily as they passed under the tall arch of the main entryway. Inside the Keep was all splendour in the most boastful way. Tapestries woven with silk and golden threads hung from the lateral beams of the ceiling, each with battle scenes depicting those vanquished to maintain the Keeper's political position. On either side, moroccan-like lanterns encrusted with jewels hung delicately to light their way.

As they turned the corner at the end of the long passageway, they passed through the final door into what was aptly named the grand hall. The same tapestries and lanterns hung in place, light glinting off their gilded frames onto the stretch of blue marbled floor. At the centre of the ceiling, moonlight poured through a brilliant skylight, its glass consisting of multicoloured hues bathing the room in warm colours. Beneath that was the Danikan throne, and Carnass sitting comfortably on his velvet cushions.

"Leave us, and close the doors," the Keeper bellowed to the stationary guards at the hall's entrance.

With little expression, the guards did as commanded, and the wide doors were sealed. Once alone and in private, Carnass transformed into the man they knew him to be.

"Thelic, Maya, you survived the trip," Carnass cooed as he skipped his way across the empty space towards them.

Tossing his long and loose platinum hair to hang down his back, he opened his arms and pulled Maya into his embrace. "I'm so pleased you made it."

"Thank you for seeing us," Maya said, hugging him back and inhaling the rich floral scents of whatever he had dabbed onto his neck that morning.

The Keeper stepped back, holding her at arm's length to make a fuller assessment. She was skinnier than before; eyes seeming wider, set deep in a gaunt and tired face that spoke of suffering. Her dull blonde hair hung in a loose ponytail, the frayed ends splayed across clothes that were both too large and too tattered for a woman of her pedigree.

"You look terrible," Carnass said softly. "Has my Thelic not been looking after you properly?"

Thelic rolled his eyes as the Keeper regarded him with a scowl. "She's alive, isn't she? Believe me I've had my work cut out for me."

Maya offered a scowl of her own to Thelic. "I'd say I more than pulled my weight on our travels, or have you forgotten Yatiken Point? Or Slitter Ridge? Or the hunters and Finkel in Kavakin?"

"Spirits, you have been busy!" Carnass' eyes danced with steady amusement at the thought of Thelic playing the unlikely roll of a damsel in distress. "While you seem to have taken a beating, you're truly a far cry from the woman that graced my hall only moons ago." An approving smile spread from ear to ear as he leaned down and kissed the top of her head. "Well done."

"Maya has your prophecy," Thelic said, keen to change the subject.

"And I have your mother's ring," Carnass replied, tapping the thin, silver chain that hung from his neck. "What did the Seer tell you, Maya? What is my future?"

Maya stepped back from Carnass and resisted the urge to stare at her feet. "You're not going to like it."

The Keeper's gaze held hers steadily. "Nevertheless," he said, unshaken by Maya's warning.

Maya shoved her hands in her pockets and leaned her head back with a weary breath. "On the sixth night of the dark moon's harvest, a man…someone you love, will offer you a choice."

"I see. That's not so bad, though I assume this choice comes with a somewhat dark future?"

Maya nodded slowly. "Fatari told me to warn you not to be clouded by the instincts of a leader, but to follow your heart…" she paused, trying to remember the exact phrase her grandmother had used. "For if greed triumphs or mortal fears take root, your seat on the throne and your place in this world will be forfeit."

Carnass tilted his head to look up at the night through the coloured glass panes of the skylight. "I feel I've been cheated somewhat." Above, the three moons were making their ascent, the central moon no longer full as the closest moved to block its light from the sun. An impending eclipse. A dark moon, barely weeks away.

"I'm sorry, Carnass," Maya said softly. "That's all my grandmother told me. I tried to ask what the decision was or where exactly each of your choices led, but…"

"But the Seer was as fickle as rumoured, only providing that which allows us to make our own choices and follow the path already set." Carnass sighed and cupped a hand to Maya's cheek. "Thank you. At least with this information I know the full weight of the decision I must make."

"Is it about the war? About your place in it, Carnass?" Thelic asked. This had been the first he'd heard of Fatari's prophecy for the Danikan Keeper, and it concerned him. Carnass had given Thelic a role to play in this world, the little lost orphan with no land and little prospects other than to sell his own body like most orphaned children in Avalon. The Keeper had taken him in. Trained him. Given him land. He had likely saved his life.

"That would be my first guess," Carnass said. He frowned as he contemplated the prophecy. "I'm getting pressure from all sides to join the preparations and ready my army. Bandaar is a difficult man to turn down."

"So, *he's* the one convincing you to join," Maya muttered.

Carnass nodded his head and rubbed his eyes, the dark smudge of shadows beneath them more noticeable now with the weight of the territory's future in his hands. "I know Bandaar is your father, Maya."

Unease settled in the pit of her stomach. "Do you know what he intends to do with me?"

The great and supposedly fearsome leader of the Danikan territory looked down at the floor, nudging at something unseen with his foot. "I do." With his head still bowed, he lifted his eyes to search Maya's face. "Would Bandaar's ceremony work? Would it save the realm?"

A low rumble of expletives bled from Thelic. "The only person that ceremony serves is Bandaar and his own agenda." With two quick strides Thelic was in front of Carnass, a finger jabbing at the Keeper's chest. "Surely you can't be foolish or desperate enough to believe him?"

"Careful," Carnass warned, stepping away and resuming the air of a regal once again, back straight and chest puffed out. "I had to ask, Thelic. This is Avalon we're talking about. I'd give my *own* life to see an end to the chaos."

"Then you know the ceremony will probably kill me?" Maya asked. Emotion swelled within her. Carnass had always been an ally, but now she wasn't so sure. "As I'm almost certain my so-called father lied about his true intentions, let me educate you."

Carnass raised an eyebrow, unaccustomed to the tone. "I'm listening."

Maya turned to pace back and forth. "The gypsul want to close the gateways, that much is true. But it *must* be done, Carnass. What the humans fail to understand is that Avalon is sick, the plight being the elemental leak coming from the gateways opened by the Five Majors."

"Ah, but Bandaar's ceremony will seal off that leak. It will allow the sprites from the Earth Realm to live here, with us," Carnass interjected.

"No. The trapped sprites *contribute* to the chaos. By unleashing them, Bandaar hopes to gain a military advantage over the gypsul. And that's exactly what he would get, until Avalon is completely devoured by the colliding essence of two worlds."

"Would you mix wine with sikospin?" Thelic asked the Keeper, simplifying the situation. "Because that's what is happening here. An unnatural concoction with a deadly aftertaste."

Carnass pondered this for a moment. It was too unbelievable. "History passed down from the Five Majors explicitly warned of a chaos born from the third realm…it had nothing to do with the sprites," he insisted.

"Then why would the Majors remove the sprites at all? Think about it, Carnass. There would have been no need to strip the humans of their contracts if there was no issue with the Earth sprites being brought to this world." Maya's heart pounded in her chest. The Keeper was being difficult, desperate to cling to the old texts.

"Why would Maya lie?" Thelic asked, imploring Carnass to understand.

Carnass opened his mouth, but hesitated. Only one reason came to mind for why this woman might lie to him and to the human population of Avalon. "Because she is part outlander, Thelic…like her mother."

Maya closed her eyes and took a deep breath before opening them with a renewed fire in her heart. "Half of my bloodline is gypsul…but why are you so quick to dismiss the part that is also human? I might be the only person in this stupid war that wants an outcome that serves both sides."

"Not the *only* person," Thelic reminded her with a nudge.

Carnass swept his gaze from Thelic to Maya. They had become quite close it seemed. Thelic was trustworthy, a loyal companion and someone he had come to love over their years together.

"We need you to put a pause on your involvement in this war, delay things for as long as you can," Maya said softly. It wasn't an easy ask to say the least. Carnass had already hinted at the pressure he was under from the other Keepers. His reluctance may be misconstrued as a betrayal.

"Spirits, Maya. Do you understand what you're asking of me?" Carnass breathed frustratedly. Something struck him. The decision the Seer had hinted could either dethrone him or claim his life. Was this it? He had assumed that it was something else, something that had been weighing on his mind since his meet with Bandaar. Only time would tell.

"I can stop this chaos, for good," Maya said, placing a warm hand on the Keeper's shoulder. "But I need time to gather the help I need in order to do it."

"You're being impossibly vague," Carnass sulked. He took Maya's hand in his own, turned it over and raised her palm to his lips. "You must give me time to think. Where are you staying?"

"With Brijid Tempin for the time being," Thelic responded automatically.

Carnass nodded in understanding, having seen the bandages from their wounds. "I will send a messenger by the high sun, tomorrow." He closed his eyes and released Maya's hand before turning his back to them. Two things flashed across his face that had gone unseen by the couple – fear and shame. The Keeper's decision had just become significantly harder.

8
MISCHIEF MAKES A MESS

DANIKA

Despite the late hour, Danika's central square remained lively as residents meandered from the taverns to bordellos to spend the day's income. Thelic and Maya walked silently along the streets, their thoughts crowded with questions. Had they done enough? Had they convinced Carnass? Was this all just a fool's errand?

"You're sighing again," Thelic said quietly.

"Something feels…off." Maya continued to stare into the distance, her mind whirring as she replayed their discussion with the Keeper. "I think we need to be prepared for Carnass to betray us. There's no way Bandaar didn't ask him to hand us over if we came knocking."

"How would your father know we'd go to Danika?" Thelic asked. After Elkin's betrayal, Thelic had promised himself he wouldn't blindly put his trust in anyone again. But he'd known Carnass since he was a boy.

"If it were me in Bandaar's shoes, I would cover all my bases. I would approach every single one of the Keepers," she said. Perhaps Maya was being paranoid, but the Danikan

Keeper had clearly spoken with Bandaar. How else would he know she was a halfling? "I'm just saying, we should be cautious."

Thelic nodded, his lips drawn thinly across his face. He would never be anything but cautious where Maya was concerned.

As they opened the door to Brijid's home, two sets of bleary and blood-shot eyes looked up from across the room. Three jugs sat at either side of the two women, both leaning forward with their hands locked in an arm-wrestle on the table.

"That was quick," Keela slurred, yelping as Brigid used the distraction to slam her opponent's arm down in victory. "Shit…that was my weak arm. Again!" Keela bellowed, waving for Thelic and Maya to join them.

Brijid hiccupped and burped as she stood with the jug, her movements wobbly as she attempted to refill it from the large barrel tucked into the corner of the room.

"For spirits' sake," Thelic muttered as he quickly moved to save the jug from Brijid's shaky hands. "Trust you two to get drunk. We were hoping to have a serious discussion upon our return."

"Gods, Thelic," Keela murmured. "Don't be such a shiken's ass."

Brijid howled with laughter, pointing at Thelic and curling her hand into a ball before peering at him through the small hole she'd made with her fist.

Maya shook with the effort to stop herself from laughing at Thelic's irritated expression and the women's state of intoxication.

Mumbling something to himself, Thelic set the jug on the table and scraped a hand through his dark hair. "I'm going back to my cabin tonight. You both need to go to bed. Keela, I'll be back in the morning, be ready to leave by mid-day."

Keela puffed out her chest and mimicked his words in a comical impression before returning her focus to the jug and pouring herself another cup.

"You're going tonight?" Maya asked, surprised by his plan.

"I need to pick up a few things and check on Keero. I want to be ready to head out by mid-day tomorrow, whether Kadhim and Zarina are here or not."

Maya nodded in understanding. He'd taken her cautionary words about Carnass seriously. "I'll go with you," she said. "As tempting as it is to sit and watch these two take another crack at the arm-wrestling championship, I'd also like to see if Keero made it back."

~

Having borrowed Brijid's karkili, the journey to Thelic's cabin wasn't long. Alone at the corner of the wood, the small, two-story cottage appeared eerily silent and abandoned under the shadow of the trees. Dismounting, Thelic reached up and helped Maya from the saddle. He turned to the front door of the house and summoned the wind, muttering words to dispel the trap he'd laid to prevent bandits from robbing the place. A sharp gale whipped around the house before dying instantly.

Moving away from the door, he walked around the side of the property, to where a large pile of straw was messily laid upon the ground. He bent down and ran his hands along the broken stems. No longer sharp and stiff, the hay felt warm to the touch. He sighed with relief.

"Is this where Keero sleeps?" Maya asked, crouching to run her hands over the grain.

A sharp growl came from the trees behind them, followed

by the sound of branches breaking and paws thundering across the earth.

Thelic stepped in front of Maya and smiled with his arms held wide in welcoming. Moments later, a large beast, at least three hippopotami wide with a long and flat leathery tail, came bounding from the trees. Recognition dawned in its large, purple eyes and it growled again, this time in greeting.

Keero, Thelic's mountain bodaari had made it back and had waited patiently for his master's...his friend's, return. The creature's nose collided with Thelic's chest, sending him and Maya back into the straw pile. With his chest bowed to the ground and his backside high in the air, the bodaari's tail whipped up and down, vibrating the ground with the heavy thuds.

Thelic chuckled and stroked down Keero's wide snout. He'd missed his friend, and thanked the Gods the bodaari was alive, happy, and healthy.

After several moments of being welcomed back, Thelic and Maya got to their feet and headed for the front door, leaving Keero to purr contentedly in his pile of straw. The door groaned as Thelic pushed at the handle. Inside, a light blanket of dust coated every surface, the air turning stale in their absence. It felt like years had passed since they were last here.

Maya ambled over to the small, temporary bed beside the empty fireplace and sat down, running her hands over the thin and dusty sheets.

Thelic watched her from the doorway, his own mind replaying the events of their first meeting. He'd been so wary of her then, so unsure about his decision to get involved in her affairs. There was no regret now. He wanted her in every way, troubles and all. As Maya moved to the fireplace and began to load it with wood, he closed the front door and reached into his pocket, his fingers brushing the cold metallic ring that had once belonged to his mother.

"Shall we make some food?" Maya asked, we still have some stock powder for a soup at least. She turned to find Thelic staring at her. Moving the hand from his pocket, he threw a small, silver chain towards her. Maya caught it easily and held it in the palm of her hand.

"Can you keep hold of that for me? The clasp is broken, but you can hang it on the chain with your other necklace." Hooded beneath long, dark lashes, Thelic's eyes shone mischievously with the request.

Maya rubbed the silver band between her fingers. "Thelic–"

"It doesn't have to mean anything. I just want it near me, and I trust you to take care of it," he said softly. Neither was ready for what the ring would promise. But for now, it would act as a reminder, a token of his trust and respect for her.

"Okay," she said, her cheeks warming with her own half promise. "I'll keep hold of it." She reached up and undid the clasp of the necklace Thelic had given her in Fortus, the twisted triangles a symbol of the combined elements. Removing the old chain, she thread the ring to sit alongside it.

Thelic was beside her in an instant, brushing aside Maya's ponytail and taking the two sides of the necklace to help with the clasp. His hands lingered along the curve of her neck, his thumb brushing the line of her hair. He leaned down to replace his fingers with his lips and chuckled as she relaxed against his chest.

"So, what is it you needed to get?" Maya asked numbly, closing her eyes at the sensation of Thelic's hands kneading the knots across her shoulders.

"Hmmm. Chores later…" he turned her to face him and

in one swift movement bent to hoist her over his shoulder. "Pleasure first."

She giggled as he smacked her backside and quickly took the stairs two at a time to the mezzanine level overlooking the lower floor. He threw her on the bed, pushing her shoulders down as his body draped over hers. She clasped his wide shoulders and tugged at the heavy coat preventing her from getting to his shirt. He sat up, his thighs straddling her waist as he removed both garments, pulling her to a seated position so he could quickly do the same for her. A low grumble emanated through him as the softer material of Maya's shirt proved difficult, and he bunched it in his fists, ready to remove the offending item more forcefully.

"Don't you dare," she warned. "This is the only clean shirt I have left." Gripping the underside of his arm, Maya twisted her body to flip their positions and sit atop his stomach, then slipped the shirt over her head along with the elasticated tube top that supported her breasts.

"Fuck," Thelic breathed, reaching up to cup both breasts in his hands.

Maya smiled, then groaned as he kneaded the soft tips of her nipples between his fingers. She moved her hips back and forth across his hardening length, her head falling back to enjoy the soft scrape of his calloused palms on her skin.

Thelic's body vibrated with need, his hands moving to her waist as impatience got the better of him. "Off, get those trousers off, *now*."

They both jumped up, boots kicked to the side and remaining clothes removed in record time before their mouths collided and they tumbled towards the bed in a tangle of limbs.

Maya needed him, needed every glorious inch to take her, but Thelic no longer seemed to feel that same need for haste. He wanted her too, that much was plain enough with his length pressing against her skin. But no, he wanted to savour this rare moment of true privacy.

Capturing both of Maya's small wrists in one hand, Thelic raised them above her head, his other hand trailing down her breasts, to her stomach, to the apex between her thighs. Maya bucked and melted all at once as he slowly thrust one finger inside her, his thumb a tease against that sensitive hub of pleasure.

"Thelic," she breathed.

He chuckled, enjoying her torment as he slipped another finger inside and pumped a painfully delicate rhythm. When he felt the build of her climax and watched her breath quicken, he lifted his thumb and slipped one finger out, denying that release.

"Thelic, please," Maya whimpered.

"Not yet," he growled. He wanted to worship her, wanted to possess and claim every inch as his own. Bowing his head, he took Maya's breast in his mouth, teasing the nipple with errant flicks of his tongue as another of his fingers slipped into her core. She angled her hips, an invite for him to go deeper. He obliged until once again she came close, but again he denied.

With a growl of her own, Maya tugged her wrists from Thelic's grasp and wrapped one leg around his with the intent to flip their positions and take back control.

Thelic chuckled as he easily subverted her attempts. "Patience, Blessed One," he cooed. Then, without warning, he thrust his full length deep inside her core. Overflowing with need and desire, the rhythm was no longer delicate, it was unrelenting as each powerful thrust of his hips cracked against her, the pain lost as they drowned in the moment.

Maya clutched the sheets and cried out as the first wave hit, her moans cut short as his mouth lowered to possess her own in an almost frenzied passion. This time, as the pressure built, he relinquished her mouth and captured her gaze as they rode the storm of an orgasm together.

Sweat dripped from the end of his nose to land on her cheek as their heartbeats slowed. Despite coming to the climax, they stayed like that for a moment longer, just to look at one another, no words needed to convey the unflinching love that lay between them.

∾

Maya raked the remains of the fire and offered another small log to coax it back to life. After their tumble between the sheets, they had come downstairs and barely started the fire before falling into each other's arms again…and again. She clutched the thin bedspread to her chest, not bothering with clothes in the privacy of Thelic's remote cabin.

If her destiny did not already lay elsewhere, Maya could picture herself here. Had someone asked her if she was the sort to settle down into the mundaneness of a quiet life, she might have laughed in their face. But that was before, when the job was all she had. Now it was different. She had finally invested herself in something more than simply existing.

Pots clanked as Thelic prepared a simple meal. As Maya played with the fire, he had gone outside to gather what he could from the overgrown vegetable patch by Keero's bed place. Apparently, Thelic also felt comfortable with their privacy, and Maya admired the dimples on either side of his behind as he worked diligently to prepare their food.

"I feel bad that we have to leave Keero again," Maya said, dragging her gaze from Thelic's nakedness to the window under which the mountain beast slept outside.

"What are you talking about? We're taking him with us. If we're planning to journey through the mountains south of

Cantor, we'll need him to get through the pass. There's no way a karkili would survive the temperatures."

"Oh, I just assumed he couldn't cross the ice. How do you plan to cross the channel?"

"Maelin's Bridge. But we'll need coin first, and lots of it. I have some stashed away in the woods, we'll get it before we head back to Brijid's."

"Maelin…" Maya thought back to Horticus, the Ragashian Elder at Slitter Ridge. He had told the tale of the Five Majors and their leader, a king named Arthur and the king's advisor, Maelin. She shook her head in disbelief at such a tale. A myth born from the crossing of two worlds. "Did you know the tale of King Arthur is almost a myth on Earth? It's pure mystery. Some believe it's true and others believe it's just a story."

"King Arthur is considered a hero in our texts, the one who turned the wheel that saved human castors from those who hunted them on Earth." Thelic scraped the cut pieces of vegetable from the chopping board into a large pot and carried it over to sit on an iron hook above the fire. "It seems bizarre with your world's advancements, that anything so important could be lost to time."

Maya shrugged. "There's perhaps a little truth in all myths. But naturally, evidence is required to determine whether they're fact or fiction, and there's no *real* evidence. Well, at least none that's readily accessible. I can't see historians making the trip to Avalon anytime soon," Maya said with a grin.

Thelic smiled as he gathered bowls and spoons, relieved to hear the lightness in her tone and see her relaxed in the fire's glow. "Is there nothing in your history books of Avalon?" he asked.

"You're asking the wrong woman. I never excelled at history, though I swear that was more to do with the horrid woman who taught it," Maya said with a shudder. "I *had* heard of Avalon though, and I know it has something to do with King Arthur and the legend of Camelot and Vivian, the lady of the lake, I just can't remember."

Thelic scooped the boiling broth from the pot as he listened, handing a bowl to Maya. "They're both in our scrolls, too. Camelot, or Camalet as we call it, is south of Esterbell. And Viveen was Arthur's lover. Though she was known to be crazed. I believe she killed him…or was it Maelin she murdered?" Thelic wondered, trying to remember the old teachings.

It was like an ancient game of Chinese Whispers had been played, with bits of information regarding the not so mythological King being lost in translation and time.

"I'd like to go there when this is all over, to Camalet," Maya said, playing with the ring that hung from her neck. It was more than that. She wanted to make plans, something pleasant to focus on when they faced the darker days ahead.

Thelic lifted the spoon to his mouth and blew on the hot broth. "We'll go," he said, his gaze leaving hers to glance at his mother's necklace. So much pain was attached to the tiny trinket, a reminder of everything he had lost. Now, he could only smile at its new meaning, at the consequent possibilities.

THE NEXT MORNING, Thelic packed some additional items he felt necessary for their journey – namely, snow tackle. Maya admired a set of metal plates with short spikes lining the base, designed to easily attach onto boots for trekking over glaciers. The rest of the gear contained packs of quilted, waterproof clothing. Maya had asked what the lining was made of, but Thelic had warned that ignorance, in this case, might be bliss. She ran her hands along the rough outer layers, mostly coats with large, fur-lined hoods to protect the face and neck.

As dawn crept over the horizon, Maya looked to the sky outside the window, hoping for the familiar squawk of their gypsul companions to ring across the wood. But there was nothing. She knew they couldn't wait, couldn't risk that Carnass might betray them. It was safer to leave the territory while they still could. Kadhim and Zarina would have to catch up.

As Maya sat down to write a note, she realised she wasn't sure if the gypsul could even read. As she pondered the possibility of her friends' illiteracy, she decided to draw a picture in addition to the text.

"What the hell is that supposed to be?" Thelic asked as he glanced over her shoulder.

Maya turned and shoved the paper behind her back. "Hey, I've seen the little drawings on your map, you're hardly one to judge."

"I didn't draw those, one of the kids in the orphanage did…and it's still better than whatever that is," he said, laughing.

Maya resisted the urge to prod him with the sharp end of the stick of lead she had been using. Instead, turning back to the note, she leaned over the kitchen counter and concentrated on the finer details of the shropsin they had seen at the ice passage between Esterbell and Cantor. On one side of the beast, she drew a bridge, and on the other she drew the forest that held the Cantorian portal Jacob had passed through, where Maya had met the Svingoran Elder, Prisia.

With the three objects drawn in line with each other, she circled the bridge, hoping it would better convey their intended destination in relation to the other images. Leaning back, she looked at her work. Thelic was right. A child might have done better, but it would have to do. Hopefully Kadhim and Zarina would either read the coded note, or they would look at the drawing and surmise the same.

"You ready?" Thelic asked from the doorway. They had hoped to leave before dawn.

"Ready," Maya said, taking a small knife from the counter. Following Thelic out, she closed the door and stabbed the knife through the paper so that it sat at the centre of the wooden entrance. "There. hopefully they see and understand it."

Thelic scoffed before putting his hands together and muttering the words that would create his whirlwind security system.

"What if Kadhim and Zarina get caught in your trap?" Maya asked.

"They should know I set traps from the last time they visited here looking for us," he replied with a shrug. "They're tough enough to get out of it, anyway. Don't worry."

Maya regarded the settling leaves around the base of the door dubiously, but decided not to push it further. Walking up Keero's flat, leathery tail, she settled amongst the thick fur of his back as Thelic gently guided the creature onto the path towards Danika's major town.

~

By mid-afternoon, they arrived at the bustling market gates. With Keero and the karkili, they would have no chance of navigating the hustle and bustle of marketeers. So, with that in mind, Thelic guided the creatures around the stone wall that penned in the Keep and the market goers like cattle. Four gates allowed entry into the town, and thankfully Brijid's home was located in the quarter not far from the eastern gate.

As they approached the portcullis, a sense of foreboding

accompanied the weight gathering in Maya's chest. There hadn't been this many guards yesterday. She held her breath as they passed beneath the heavy, iron barrier. But nobody stopped them, in fact the guards barely glanced their way, too distracted with their own affairs.

"Relax," Thelic breathed in Maya's ear.

Maya didn't. Her shoulders remained tense, wary of every soldier as they wound their way to the small paddock in the eastern quarter. Only one other creature was housed in the small, muddy stable area – a bright red karkili. Thelic handed the young stable boy double the normal wage to feed, water and watch over Keero and their belongings. The boy beamed and ran into his hut to stash the coins before returning to tend to the bodaari as instructed.

"That was kind of you. Exactly how much coin did you have stashed in the woods?" Maya asked, smiling as the boy nervously approached Keero to stroke him.

"Enough to keep us going." Thelic watched as the boy fetched water and leftover vegetable scraps from the barn. "Orphans never get paid enough. Not enough to make a difference."

"You think he's an orphan?" Maya knew that Thelic had been forced to stay at the orphanage for a while during his youth, it was how he had come to enter Carnass' service.

Thelic nodded. "It's one of a few jobs set aside for the kids. Most go on to be whores or soldiers though. With no family, there's no one to disappoint by selling their bodies or dying in the Keeper's service." His eyes clouded with the memory of friends lost to such a fate, then he shook his head. "Come on."

Brijid's tent and adjacent home were only around the corner. Maya walked behind Thelic as he pushed and navigated his way through the crowds of people. The busy alleys were strange for this part of town. Here there were no market stalls, only permanent businesses – blacksmiths, tailors, healers, and the like. What came as more of a surprise was the long queue of people outside Brijid's tent. Most seemed to carry the odd cut and bruise, but none seemed injured enough to warrant such a heavy build-up of customers.

Bypassing the tent, Thelic went straight to the front door of Brijid's house. As he raised his hand to knock, he stopped, finding the door was slightly ajar. He pushed it wide and stormed into the room, his spear already detached from his hip. The room was a wreck, and a figure lay unmoving on the floor, her hands and feet dipped in crimson.

Maya dashed past Thelic and rolled the body over. A fist came flying clumsily towards her face, but Maya quickly caught it. "Keela, it's me!" she yelled, pulling her sister into a seated position. Maya checked her hands, looking for the injuries, but found nothing that might explain the bright red hue. "What happened?"

Keela pushed at Maya's hands and rubbed her eyes, blinking away the grogginess of their late-night drinking shenanigans. She regarded the room around her – the table over-turned, three broken jugs…and clothes strewn everywhere. A tight chill passed over her body and she jumped at the sound of Thelic closing the door, keeping his back to the women. She looked down.

"Where the fuck are my clothes?" Keela moaned.

"I'm a little more concerned about where the hell Brigid is. Look at this place. Were you attacked?" Maya asked, standing up to assess the damage.

Keela shook her head. "Attacked? No…I don't think so." Keela brought her knees up and dipped her head between them, fingers massaging her temples. Her head shot up as she spotted the dye on her feet and a memory clawed its way through the post-drunkenness haze. "Oh God."

"What?" Thelic asked from the stairs. He had checked to see if Brigid had managed to make her way up there, but the bed was made and didn't seem to have been slept in.

Keela groaned and buried her head between her knees again. "I think we stole one of Carnass' karkili…yea, we *definitely* stole one of his karkili. Dye…I remember so much bloody nexie dye." She pulled her hands in front of her face, spotted the mottled red and groaned again. "Fuck."

"That still doesn't answer our question," Maya said, resting her knees on the hardwood floor. "Where the hell is Brijid?"

At a knock on the door, Thelic gave Maya enough time to grab a blanket to cover Keela before turning the handle to answer their caller. A Danikan guard.

"I have a message from the Keeper of Danika," the woman announced as she held up a scroll of paper to read from. "The healer, Brijid Tempin, has been arrested for the following: theft of the Keeper's personal property, damage of the Keeper's personal property, public indecency–"

"Oh please, you can hardly give that as a charge when half of the bordello women strut around town half dressed!" Keela insisted angrily.

The guard gave a short cough, then continued. "And finally, theft of resources from the tailor, Borokin Lisker."

"What do we do, Thelic? What's the procedure here?" Maya asked. Back on Earth it would be simple – bail Brijid out and get her a lawyer. For some reason she doubted the proceeding would be quite as smooth in Avalon.

The guard answered Maya's question instead. "The Keeper of Danika has requested the audience of Mayara Rivers to plead in defence of the accused. Which of you is Miss Rivers?"

Maya stepped forward.

"Do you accept?"

"Do I have a bloody choice?" Maya murmured. This was a dirty play by Carnass, and Maya had the sinking feeling that, if she went into that Keep, she might not make it back out without shackles firmly attached to her wrists.

"I'm going with her," Thelic said, stepping forward to stand by Maya's side. "You know he'll want to see me, too."

"I was instructed that only Miss Rivers was to attend," the guard insisted. "I know you are Thelic Anthon, and I was specifically instructed that you are *not* to attend."

"Shocker," Maya grumbled. There was only one reason Carnass didn't want Thelic there – it would be much easier to detain a lone woman. Luckily for Maya, Carnass had no idea that she was never alone, never without BB and Loki. "I'll be fine," Maya said turning to face him.

"You're *not* going alone," Thelic insisted, flicking his gaze from Maya to the guard.

Maya held up the pendant of the elements. "I've got *them*." She nudged her head to the side, to where her backpack was lying next to Keela. "The Stone is in there." The Gouram Stone. No way was she willing to risk it falling into a Keeper's hands.

Thelic glared at the guard who began to shift uncomfortably from one foot to the other. This felt wrong. None of this was in Carnass' nature, his *real* nature, the one he hid from the masses. That begged the question – where was the puppeteer? There was no question Maya's father was behind this, but was he here? In Danika?

"I must speak with the Keeper," Keela announced, standing up on two wobbly legs. "I am equally as responsible for this mess."

"Only Miss Rivers–"

"I am *also* Bandaar's daughter. You know, Keeper of Esterbell? You sure you want to turn me down?"

Again, the guard shifted uncomfortably at the decision

she felt was a mighty leap from the meagre pay grade she was offered. "Fine. You may come with us to the Keep, but I cannot promise you an audience."

Keela rolled her eyes and headed for the stairs, asking for a moment so she could change. *Never again*, she promised herself. *I will never drink again.*

9
DECEPTION AND DEALS

DANIKA

Keela smiled as she handed over the blades on her belt to the guards manning the gate. As her and Maya were guided towards the steps of the Keep, she was comforted by the cold touch of hard steel against her ankles – two more blades hidden from view, tucked into the lining of the leather. She hoped she wouldn't have to use them. Her head was pounding in retribution for her drunken mischief, and all she craved was the comfort of a bed

As they passed under the final arch, Maya spotted Brijid. The healer seemed fine, all things considered. Her hair, usually pulled back into a neat bun, was determined to defy gravity, odd strands sticking out at various angles. Her clothes were just as bad, covered in red dye and torn at the sleeves…though, at least she was still wearing clothes, unlike how her drinking partner had been found.

"Have fun?" Maya joked as she stopped beside the small healer, her eyes searching for signs of mistreatment.

Brijid groaned and looked at her feet. "Sorry about this, Maya." She looked up at Keela, at the grim expression and the woman's bright red hands. "Sorry to you, too." Brijid remembered it had been her idea to steal the karkili. Keela, too intoxicated to think reasonably, had gladly accompanied the mission for a bit of ill-advised fun. Keela merely offered a grin in response and shrugged.

The room became hushed as Carnass entered the hall with a line of servants and guards in his wake. Barely acknowledging the others in the room as he swept past, his silken coat trailing behind as he approached the throne.

"Well, here I am, Carnass," Maya said as she stepped forward. "How does this work? I assume you want something in return for their release?" She flinched at the Keeper's glare. With so many in the room, it was expected he might hide his true colours. But Maya felt the pierce of that gaze, perfected over many years of ruling a territory to instil fear in his subjects and challengers.

"For such an insult to the Keeper of a territory, she should be put to death," Carnass said menacingly through his teeth. He flicked his gaze to Keela, then to her reddened hands. "Both of them, in fact."

"Death?" Maya cried. "Surely you're joking?" She laughed nervously, looking from the Keeper to Brijid. The healer had expected as much, and hung her head in shame.

"Indeed. People have been executed for less, Miss Rivers."

Miss Rivers. Carnass *was* serious. "What do you want, Your Lordship?" Maya bit out. "Maybe we could talk this over in private?" She pleaded with her eyes, willing Carnass to send the others away so he could return to the fun and friendly Keeper she so desperately wanted at that moment.

"That's not necessary. In return for the release of these miscreants, I am willing to take *you* into custody instead." Carnass leaned back in the deep seat of his jewel-encrusted throne, no smile or note of pleasure in the thin line of his lips.

"I knew it. I knew you couldn't be trusted," Maya cursed.

"Then you should have trusted those instincts and left when you had the chance."

"Thelic will damn you for this. You know that." Butterflies fluttered across Maya's stomach, and she relished the small moment of pleasure as the Keeper flinched. Thelic was important to Carnass, a friend of sorts. "You know the prophecy. What if *this* is your decision?" she said.

"Do you accept my proposal, or not? Will you come willingly in exchange for the release of your friends?" Carnass waited patiently as Maya turned to the other women. She was trying to calm them down, but both were insistent that this was all wrong, that Maya couldn't possibly consider his offer. Carnass crossed his arms as he listened. His stomach felt as if it were lined with lead, like something deep inside him had died. His humanity? His dignity? He raised his chin as Maya turned to give her response.

"Fine. Release them both and drop all charges. I'll remain here with you, willingly." A thousand thoughts crossed Maya's mind in that moment. She had the Finkels. She could escape the soldiers – maybe whilst they were on the road? That was assuming their plan was to transport her to Esterbell. But Brijid's execution might have been instantaneous. Maya had to take the risk.

"No. I wholeheartedly disagree with this decision," Keela said, striding towards the throne. A guard stepped in her path, and Keela ducked, removing the blade from her boot as she spun to kick the feet from under the man attempting to grab her. Two more guards stood in her path, each lunging to restrain her arms, knocking the blade from her grasp.

"Are you mad?" Carnass roared from his throne.

"You're working with my father, aren't you?" Keela snarled.

Recognition flashed in Carnass' eyes for a brief moment,

before a smile tugged at the corner of his mouth. "Your father has been looking for you, Keela Rivers. Two prizes for the price of one."

"That wasn't the deal, Carnass. Release them *both* or you can be damned sure I will fight you every second of my captivity," Maya snapped, the words as much a threat as they were a promise. She had been hesitant to show Carnass the extent of her power, but desperate times called for a little lack of restraint.

After a long moment of deliberation, the mask Carnass had perfected broke for just a moment, and he smiled sadly. "I'm sorry, Maya." Raising his hand, he clicked his fingers and the guards manning the doors descended upon them.

Maya called on the Finkels as she dove to the floor to grab the knife Keela had dropped. She rolled and jumped to her feet in one fluid motion and dragged the knife across her palm. The Finkels manifested to stand beside her, four times the size of their usual, fox-like form.

Carnass leaned forward on his throne, holding a hand up to stop the guards barely ten feet from Maya and the others. A blue and yellow glow burst to life across the marble floor with the first drop of blood. A castor circle. The rumours were true, Maya had contracted with a Gouram.

"You had your chance to resolve this peacefully, Carnass," Maya said menacingly as she stroked the top of BB's head. The Water Finkel growled at the Keeper, drool dripping from sharp teeth as he snapped them in warning.

The room stilled; the Keeper's guards frozen just beyond the glowing circle. Some seemed confused and crept closer to inspect the sudden light at their feet. But most knew what it meant, most Avalonians had heard the stories of such power, and it frightened them.

Carnass stood and took one step towards Maya. He

stopped, his hands rising in defence as both Finkels snarled and focused their gaze on the approaching threat.

"This...this is why your father wants you? For *this* power?" Carnass whispered. The sight was a wonder, truly splendid in the way it reflected off the metallic surfaces to bounce around the room.

"I can stop the chaos, Carnass. I can stop all of it. We just need the time, and we need everyone to leave us alone to get it done," Maya said. "Bandaar...my father, he can't be trusted."

"It's true, Carnass," Keela said, shaking herself free of the guards with ease now that they had more pressing things to concern themselves with. "I've seen what Maya can do. I've seen her contract with the Gouram. She is Avalon's only hope now. My father's lack of sense will destroy this world...if you let it."

Carnass let out a long breath and bit his lower lip. These could be lies, a story cleverly concocted to save themselves. But perhaps not, perhaps they were telling the truth. "How much time do you need?" the Keeper asked.

Maya's eyes widened, and she stuttered to hastily respond. "I...we're not sure. A year, preferably? There are things we need to do. We need to enlist help if Fatari's ceremony to banish the chaos is going to work."

Carnass stepped back and sat on the edge of his throne. That was too long. Bandaar was breathing down his neck as it was. With a steely look, he demanded all but his commanders leave the hall. Once the doors were closed and only his most trusted of soldiers remained, he looked apologetically to Maya, "I can't give you a year."

"When does Bandaar intend to spark this war?" Keela asked. She had never been privy to the finer details of her father's plans, but a timeline would certainly be useful at this point.

Carnass threw his hands into the air and released an irritated laugh. "How should I know?! That man is unpredictable, and until I commit my forces to this war, he's as tight-lipped as they come." Resting one arm on the side of his chair, he rubbed his temple. "It will take Bandaar no longer than a month to finish his preparations, but he wishes for Transum's Keeper to join the fight. With her being a recluse, that particular task is proving more difficult than your father had expected." Carnass chuckled at the memory of a discussion he'd had with Bandaar about their Transumian equal.

"Have a guess, at least give us *something* to work with," Keela urged.

Sitting up straight, Carnass crossed his hands in his lap. "I would say you have about four months, maybe five. Bandaar will not move without at least one other territory by his side. As it stands, that will be Jaxum, the Keeper of Fortus. His preparations were nearing completion, but I have been told their little set-back will take several months to solve – something to do with an explosion in the weapon district."

"Not even half the time we need," Maya muttered. "Even if we manage to gather what's required, we'd have to wait for the next alignment to carry out the ceremony. Damn!" She banged a fist on the supporting column beside her, the castor circle flickering with the emotion coursing through its conjuror.

"I'll buy you whatever time I can, Maya," Carnass promised solemnly, holding a hand over his heart to further demonstrate his intent.

The skylight above shattered, glass raining down on the Keeper and his former captives. Carnass leapt from his throne, his commanders hurrying to surround him as three figures landed beside Maya, Keela and Brijid. A bow, a spear and a sword were raised the minute the intruders' feet hit the floor, each holding a stance within the light of the castor circle at Maya's defence.

"What took you so long, Thelic?" Carnass crooned as he pushed his protectors to the side. "I expected at least one of my guards to die in the attempt to remove young Maya from your care."

"What the fuck is going on, Carnass," Thelic spat. He turned to Maya, his eyes grazing her body from head to toe. He lingered on her palm, where the blood still dripped from her fingertips. The grip on his spear tightened as he took one step closer to the Danikan Keeper.

"Hang on a moment, Thellie," Carnass laughed nervously, holding up his hands in surrender. "I'll admit, there was a minor misstep on my part, but our little Maya wasn't being entirely honest about...well, everything," he said waving a hand at the Finkels and the castor circle. "However, now I'm sure she can do as she claims. I mean, if not her, the first of many generations to have such a power, then who?"

Thelic only glared at the Keeper in response, before reaching into his pocket and handing Maya a small pad of lint-like cloth. "Use this for your hand. We're leaving." He glanced at Kadhim and Zarina, their weapons still high and ready should the Keeper decide to act against them. "Let's go."

The gypsul nodded and Zarina ran across the marble to the grand hall's entrance to check for more guards.

"No one will stop you or your...friends," Carnass shouted to Thelic's back. The sight of the gypsul made the Keeper curious but all the more wary. Would they sway Maya to join their side against the humans? "I have decided to trust you, Maya, and I will steady my forces until Bandaar and Fortus look to start the war. Then I will have no choice but to join in their alliance."

Thelic stopped at the door, one hand still gripping Maya's arm. Without looking at the Keeper, he gave a solitary nod of understanding. He was furious that Brijid had been captured in such a manipulative manner, and did not trust himself to speak. Carnass was in a difficult position. The Danikans wouldn't think twice about overthrowing a Keeper too cowardly to fight a war, and the other Keepers would be glad to assist in such a coup if that were the case.

Maya tugged her arm from Thelic's grip and turned to face Carnass. "One more thing. If I find out you've hired more hunters to track down and murder young gypsul after today, I won't hesitate to return and show you just how big of a mistake that would be. This is your one and *only* warning, Carnass. Do whatever it takes to ensure it doesn't happen again."

Carnass stared at the woman across from him, so different to the tired and frightened girl he had met all those moons ago. A girl who had been new to their world and now thrived despite the burden she carried. "You have my word," he said.

∽

"What do you suppose the choice is – the one Carnass has to make?" Maya asked as she strolled through the market with Keela and Thelic. For obvious reasons, they had decided to leave the territory that evening. Brijid had hurried home to put together several medical packs, and to send a runner to Winkler's Hamlet for a ferry to be prepared for their arrival. With that sorted, all they needed was some winter gear and fire pots for their trek into the southern mountains.

"What do you mean?" Thelic asked as he closely inspected a pair of heavy boots with a furry inner lining. "He already made his choice, he let you go."

"No. The choice was prophesied to happen on the sixth night of the dark moon's harvest. The eclipse hasn't happened yet," Maya said. The prophecy may have had nothing to do with their quest to find the seals, but not knowing bothered her.

"Well, just one more reason for us to leave before nightfall," Keela said as she inspected a smaller pair of boots. "We can't trust anyone, not anymore. Carnass alluded to the fact that gossip is spreading about your abilities. And with the war oncoming, people will want to use you. Human and gypsul alike."

She was right. After the string of betrayals, Maya would be hesitant to put her faith in anyone until the chaos was calmed and the war stopped. For now, the people she trusted were those around her, the friends she had gathered and been with through the dark times. They all knew the importance of the path they were following, they all had faith in one and other to see it through till the end.

After what felt like hours of bouncing from stall to stall, each of them carried a bundle of clothes, shoes and coats that would see them through the unforgiving temperatures and terrain of the south. Their final stop was a merchant selling small pots of paste that Thelic insisted they would need to cook and keep warm in the mountains.

With everything they needed, they all but tumbled through the door into Brijid's home. Before long, the bags were packed and loaded onto Keero and the sun made its descent. Brijid had insisted the travellers stay for at least another night. Though, with the way she stood in Thelic's shadow, it was clear the gypsul made her uneasy. They all declined, each member of the group keen to make a move for the port and get out of the territory before Carnass could change his mind.

~

Quiet yips and howls of night-time creatures rang from every corner of the wood as the moons settled overhead. Beneath the heavy footfalls of the bodaari, critters crawled through the deadened leaves, the crunch of broken twigs making it impossible to sleep. The last time they had trekked through this wood to Winkler's Hamlet it had taken a full day, so Maya relaxed into the blankets to further contemplate their timeline.

Four months before the war would start. God only knew how long it would take them to gather the seals. Even then, what would they do while they waited for the alignment? Could they do the ceremony without it? Maybe. Perhaps the seals alone would be enough. Maya cursed under her breath at the seemingly impossible task before them. The young ghosts in Kavakin had claimed the Gouram of fire slept in the cold mountains in the south. Fatari claimed the Gouram of earth lay by the Deadland Lakes in the far west. And the scrolls were in Bodhisia's Valley in the northwest. But what about the Gouram of air?

Loki swirled as Maya's thoughts spoke of his element, rushing along the fur of Keero's back to land weightlessly on Maya's chest. She chuckled, her musings immediately eased by the creature's sweet persona. Almost as soon as she had reached up to stroke him, BB emerged from the seal on her chest, a snarl on his face as he snapped at Loki. With dominance asserted, he spun three times and settled between her breasts, a soft snore following as the tiny breaths caressed her neck.

"You know, I think I fancy myself a Finkel sprite," Keela said, indicating the creatures with a knife she had been using to slice pieces of an unfamiliar fruit. "The fear they caused those guards at the Keep, I liked it. I liked it a lot," she finished as she popped a slice into her mouth.

"I thought you hated Finkels?" Maya said, chuckling again as the two creatures looked up to glare at the Esterbellian warrior.

"Well, that was before. I've only known Keepers to be capable of mastering the little devil sprites. That and the only Finkels I've ever actually met, other than yours, are always feral and out for blood."

"I'm beginning to learn that isn't their natural temperament," Maya said softly as she stroked the hard, glistening scales of BB's back. "The Fire Finkel back in Kavakin was in pain. Humans had hunted the creature's friends or family, it was hard to tell what the relation was. But it was hurting."

"That reminds me," Keela said. She paused, wondering if she should bring it up at all, but thought best to get it out in the open, should Maya need to talk. "That hunter…that was the first time you had taken a life, wasn't it?" Keela watched carefully as Maya's shock at the chosen topic suddenly morphed into discomfort. "You don't have to talk about it, but it helps," she said.

Thelic angled his head to glance at Maya from where he sat by Keero's neck. He had also wanted to visit the matter, but wasn't sure how. His gaze turned to Keela, noticing the small lines of worry on her forehead. The warrioress had changed. When they first met, the fiery woman had wanted nothing to do with them. Now she was prepared to comfort and support Maya, not just in battle, but in affairs of the heart and mind too. He smiled.

"It was my life or his," Maya said as she concentrated on the scales of BB's back. "The decision was easy. It was barely a decision at all with how fast it all happened." Maya hesitated momentarily, wary of voicing what had truly gone through her mind at the time. "I was prepared to kill him anyway, for what he had done, for what he would continue to do." She sat up as her stomach churned with the admission, dislodging BB from his spot. He growled his annoyance before disappearing into the seal. She had intended to kill, to murder another human being. What the hell was happening to her?

"Maya?" Thelic asked when her silence seemed to drag.

"This world is fucked up," Maya muttered.

Keela relaxed against the packs tightly strapped to the top of the saddlebags. "You're not wrong. I took my first life when I was fifteen."

"Twelve," Thelic called from his spot. "You're not alone, Maya. We've all done and thought things we're not proud of. Your actions that day not only saved your life and undoubtedly ours, but it also saved those gypsul that came next."

The deaths were justified. At least in this world they were. Though she knew Thelic and Keela meant well, their admissions only further proved the point Maya had made. This world had problems, and not just in the chaos that threatened to suffocate it.

As they continued in silence, Maya drifted in and out of sleep, waking every now and again to the larger crack of Keero's plods through the brittle wood. She woke with a jolt as a sharp squawk came from overhead, the gypsuls' warning to be on the lookout. She sat up and gripped her small dagger as Keero came to a halt.

Keela jumped in fright and cursed as Zarina landed softly on the ground beside the bodaari. Bringing a finger to her lips, the gypsul gently took the reins of Keero's harness and guided the beast to a nearby bush large enough to hide his form.

Once settled, the others dismounted to stand by her side and Zarina pointed to a tree several feet away, to the figure hidden within the canopy. Kadhim had taken a position that overlooked the worn and beaten path. Camouflaged in black amongst the leaves, he waited patiently with an arrow ready to fly should their group be spotted.

"What's going on?" Maya whispered.

"Soldiers," Zarina replied quietly, peeking around the bush just as the first figure came into view. "I think they're from Esterbell. That territory wears black, correct?"

Keela nodded her response and edged forward to get a closer look. At least twenty armed soldiers walked in single file, with a carriage pulled by two karkili at the centre of the parade. The Esterbellian crest stood proud on the side of the transporter.

"Bandaar," Thelic whispered, gripping his spear tightly.

"No," Keela said. "He isn't here. That's a captive box. See the seals on it? They block elemental summons, there's no way he would travel in that." She looked to Maya.

"That's for me, isn't it?" Maya asked, and Keela's face dropped in a grim look of confirmation. "That bastard. Carnass must have sent a message to Bandaar of our capture as soon as he knew we were in the territory." She turned her nose up at the sealed box with its singular, iron door as the soldiers passed. "So, dear old Dad sent a transportable prison…charming." She wasn't sure what annoyed her more – that Carnass had temporarily sided with her father; that Bandaar hadn't even come to collect her himself; or the sheer amount each Keeper seemed to underestimate her.

None of the soldiers were particularly quiet as they ambled along the path. Maya's grip tightened on the dagger's hilt, then eased as she closed her eyes and took a breath. She reminded herself that these were just ordinary men and women following orders, with no personal grudge about their intended captive. They didn't deserve her anger. Crouching lower amongst the brush, she peered through a crack in the fauna. *18, 19, 20…that's all of them. Maybe I'm not being entirely underestimated*, Maya thought as she counted each soldier that passed.

When the coast was clear and the Esterbellians were far enough away, Kadhim jumped down from his perch in the canopy to stand with the others. The soldiers had been an unexpected threat so early in the journey, and didn't bode well for their chances at remaining hidden after their crossing.

Zarina seemed to echo Kadhim's thoughts, making suggestions that might allow them to skip the port at Winkler's Hamlet and stay off the main roads. But none were viable. The only other port was in the west, but that would take them at least a day longer, and closer to Bandar's Keep.

"It might be fine," Maya said as she stroked the long fur of Keero's hide. "The soldiers are expecting us to be with Carnass, why would they bother setting up a checkpoint at Winkler's?"

"That's what I would do, just in case I arrived only to find my quarry had escaped," Thelic said, pacing back and forth and attempting to concoct a better plan.

"Also, I don't like the idea of leaving you again when we get to the port," Kadhim added somewhat gloomily. "Every time we do, it's like a bad omen. Something terrible is almost certain to happen as it so often does when we go." The gypsul would be unwelcome in the human town and would have to remain in their animal form to avoid spooking the residents.

With no other option coming to mind, they continued along the non-existent road to the Hamlet, quieter than before, none daring to speak and all listening for the warning cry of their gypsul lookouts. But nothing came.

. . .

Chimneys coughed with lazy smoke as the villagers of Winkler's Hamlet lit their fires for the evening. The group had arrived earlier to the shoreside settlement than expected, the water-rakers having been informed by Brijid ahead of time that the travellers would arrive that evening at moons' peak. That would be a little while yet, the sun barely having dipped below the horizon.

"We can't afford to wait around," Thelic said. He had stopped the group just before the edge of the forest and searched the slowly emptying streets for any sign of the Esterbellian emblem. "Those soldiers won't be far behind us, and I want to be out of here before they show up."

A flap of wings passed overhead and the gypsul dropped to land behind them.

"I'll go to the port and see if they're ready," Keela offered, about to take a step in that very direction.

Thelic grabbed her arm, pulling her back into cover. "You're the last person that should go," he rumbled in annoyance.

"What? Why? They're not looking for me."

"Face it, Keela. You chose a side. Bandaar knows you're with Maya, so who are the guards going to look out for? A woman's face they have never seen? Or her accomplice, a princess whose face is all too familiar?" Thelic asked, lifting one eyebrow to emphasise his reasoning.

After a moment, Keela's shoulders sagged. Thelic was right. "I hadn't thought of that," she said softly. She hadn't thought that her own father might be hunting her just as much as he was hunting Maya.

"I'll go," Thelic said. "Follow the line of the trees until you hit the water's edge. I'll meet you there."

Kadhim seemed ready to object but held his tongue. He himself couldn't offer to go. Even with the long coat and gloves provided by Brijid for both him and Zarina, the clothes would only draw attention. These days the humans were actively searching, hunting those who wished to hide their features. Instead, Kadhim nodded his head in a silent promise when Thelic's eyes met his. He would watch over Maya.

10

FRIEND OR FOE?

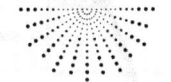

DANIKA ~ ESTERBELL

"I've been meaning to ask...what the hell happens to your clothes when you...you know?" Keela flapped her arms as she asked the question, unsure how else to put across the gypsuls' transformation.

Zarina chuckled as she led the bodaari to the water's edge. "That's a good question. Nobody is *really* sure, though many rumour that when we shift into our other form, our body shifts onto the spirit plane to be replaced with the creature that we turn into."

"What is it? The bird I mean," Maya asked, equally as interested in the gypsuls' special abilities.

"It's called a winshik, a beautiful creature only found in the northern mountains of what you humans call the Outlands." Zarina's gaze dropped to her hands as she released Keero to feed on the nearby fauna. "Those birds are a rare sight these days. Most were hunted in the early years for their eggs."

"I'm sorry," Maya said, unsure what else to say. "What's so special about their eggs?"

"They contain a property that, when consumed in the

right dosage, allows your spirit to leave your body for a short amount of time. Human and gypsul priests used them in the early days in their attempts to commune with the Gods. Now the eggs are hunted for the pleasurable effect they provide in much smaller quantities."

Maya thought back to her time with the Gouram of water. "Did you give me one at Batshari's temple? Is that how I managed to travel to the in-between?"

Zarina quickly shook her head. "No! Using the eggs is highly dangerous. Most never return to their bodies. Being Svingoran, we have a closer connection to the spirit realm. We can enter and exit as we please and take other souls along for the ride. It's risky and we rarely do it. Mostly the Svingorans use their abilities to help families who have lost a loved one. We are able to provide a connection that allows those very important goodbyes to be said."

"I see." Maya sat down amongst the cracked twigs. She swore as one lodged itself where no twig should go and readjusted her position. The lull in the conversation became uneasy, everyone tense as they awaited Thelic's return.

"Have your clothes *ever* failed to return with your body when you transform?" Maya asked, trying to lighten the mood once again.

Kadhim chuckled then remembered the note he had stashed in his pocket. "I forgot to ask," he said, retrieving the thin paper to hold in Maya's face. "What in the name of the Gods is *this*?"

Maya blinked twice then cringed as she registered the note she had left for the gypsul at Thelic's cabin. "I thought it was pretty good, actually," she muttered.

"Why the drawing? Did you think we couldn't read? And what exactly *is* the drawing?" Kadhim asked, more amused than irked.

Keela snatched the note from Kadhim's hand and

squinted, turning the paper clockwise then anti-clockwise. "Ah, I see. It's a picorin bird…riding a grokus? Or is that something naughty?" Keela asked with a wink in Maya's direction.

Maya snatched the paper back and scrunched it into a ball before shoving it into her pocket. "It's a bloody shropsin, like the one we saw on the ice passage between Esterbell and Cantor. I was trying to indicate where we should meet, in code."

"Spirits…that's awful. Good job you're a powerful castor or you might have little else going for you," Keela said with a smile as she leaned back against the tree trunk. She ducked her head as Maya launched a twig in her direction. The projectile fell just short of its mark and prompted another snort of laughter from the group.

"Wait a second," Maya said, lowering the second stick she had chosen. "If you had this, how did you know we were at the Keep?"

"Thelic arrived just as we were about to leave his cabin." Kadhim purposefully failed to mention that, if Thelic hadn't ridden home to find them, he and Zarina would probably still been stuck in the booby trap Thelic had left at his front door. "We flew him back to the Keep."

"I thought you couldn't fly with others," Keela said, perking up at this new development.

"If we had flown over water, we wouldn't have had a chance," Zarina explained with a chuckle. "We had to stop and take it in turns, he's quite heavy."

"All muscle," Thelic insisted loudly as he wove his way through the trees to where the others sat.

Maya breathed a sigh of relief at the sound of Thelic's voice and rose to stand along with the others. "How did it go?"

After checking Keero, Thelic explained that the water-rakers would need the agreed amount of time before leaving port. "Turns out we're not the only ones seeking passage over the channel."

"Soldiers?" Maya asked.

Thelic smiled and shook his head, the disbelief still evident in the crease of his brow. "He *was* a soldier, but he left Bandaar's service years ago. I thought he was dead."

"Okay," Keela said, drawing out the word with her mounting impatience. "Friend or foe?"

"Oh, he's definitely a friend." Thelic dipped his head to look pointedly at Maya. "I think we should bring him along."

"What?" Kadhim snapped, stepping forward to stand at Maya's back and square up to Thelic. "You've got to be joking? The last man you trusted almost got us all killed."

The words were like a slap that rippled across the group, a harsh reminder of Elkin's betrayal. Zarina put her hand on Kadhim's shoulder, both in warning and to remind him of the hurt that still remained.

"If memory serves correct, Kadhim, we *all* trusted Elkin," Maya seethed, turning on the gypsul. "*You* included."

"I had no choice but to trust Elkin. He was there whether I liked it or not. But now you have a choice, Maya. No one else should be brought in on something this important. Why risk it?" Kadhim directed the last question to Thelic. He had expected better, expected the warrior to be more cautious, at least with regard to Maya's safety.

"There *is* no risk because the man I have in mind has spent the last three years trying to *kill* Bandaar," Thelic said, his temper quietly growing with Kadhim's tone. "Do you honestly think I would risk it otherwise? That's how he was rumoured to have died, struck down by Bandaar himself during an assassination attempt."

"What's his name?" Keela asked. Bandaar had a long history of attempts on his life, much like all the Keepers, but only three had come close enough to be remembered – Maya being one of them.

"Merthus Kraquin," Thelic answered with a wide grin.

Keela laughed, the sound a shock amongst the quiet of the wood. "Oh yes. I remember him. In fact, he should still have a scar from the last time we saw each other." She chuckled again at the memory of her duel with the somewhat legendary man. "I thoroughly approve. The man is a beast, both in nature and in the sheer size of him."

Maya searched Thelic's face but found no sign of doubt in the confident glint in his eyes or grinning set of his mouth. Still, she didn't like it. Not at all. Her trust had been shattered. It wasn't a jigsaw puzzle she could simply piece back together. But she trusted Thelic entirely, and they could use all the help they could get.

"I'd like to meet him before we make a decision," Maya said.

Kadhim cursed and threw his hands up dramatically. "Unbelievable. Fucking unbelievable." He turned on Thelic, pushing past Maya to face him properly. Despite his tall frame, the gypsul came up a little shorter than the human, somewhat lessening the intensity of his stare. "I swear to the Gods, Thelic, if this decision costs us–"

"It won't," Thelic promised through gritted teeth.

"Cut it out," Maya said, stepping between the two. "The more people we have on our side to help us, the better," she insisted as she placed a hand on each of the warriors' chests to placate them.

※

"You're looking a little more rotund than I remember," Keela said, striding up to the large, cloaked figure by the hamlet's port and prodding his belly. Her finger hit solid rock, or at least that's what it felt like.

Two golden teeth shone in a wry smile of recognition. "Not likely, sweetheart," Merthus replied, moving his hand up to the hilt of a large sword strapped to his back.

"Easy, Merth," Thelic said, raising both hands to calm the beast.

"What the fuck is *she* doing here, Thelic?" Merthus bellowed, jabbing a finger in Keela's face as the other hand swung the sword from its strap.

Maya stopped in her tracks. She could see what they meant now. At over six foot six, and built like a bear, Merthus was impressive. His scarred, dark-skinned face stretched in a malevolent grin as he hoisted the sword into a fighting stance. With no hair to speak of, a clean bead of sweat was allowed to trace its way down his forehead and across a crooked nose that had seen a great many fist fights.

"She's with *us* now," Thelic explained, stepping between the bear and the all too calm Keela.

"Bollocks," Merthus spat. "It's a trick. She was so far up her father's arse it's a wonder she didn't suffocate."

A quick burst of laughter broke from Maya as Keela's expression leapt from boredom to annoyance. Maya raised a hand to her mouth as the two warring parties looked her way, momentarily distracted. With a grin, she stepped forward and offered her hand to the new member of their team. "I'm Maya, nice to meet you."

Merthus looked at Maya, then to her outstretched hand and tilted his head ever so slightly in confusion. "What are you doing?"

"Oh right, sorry." Again, Maya had offered the Earthly form of greeting. She really needed to stop doing that. Trying to salvage the awkward moment, she raised her hand in a half-hearted wave.

"She's from the other side," Thelic explained, pushing down on Merthus' sword until it touched the ground. "I told you, we're helping her."

"You told me fuck all, and I told you I can't help. I'm off to Esterbell to kill *her* bastard of a father once and for all," Merthus said, trying and failing to raise his sword under the pressure of Thelic's hand holding it down.

"I changed my mind," Kadhim said, stepping up to stand at Maya's side with Zarina. "I like him."

"Oh, Gods in a swamp," the bear cursed. "You're running with *outlanders* as well?" he hissed, moving the weapon to face Maya and the gypsul.

Kadhim and Zarina tilted their bodies to block Maya, each reaching for their own weapons should the man decide to attack all the same.

"Merthus," Thelic warned. "Don't even try it."

Maya sighed, getting increasingly irritated. "Bloody hell. Listen, we're no threat to you, Merthus. Thelic thought you might be able to help us but I'm assuming he forgot to mention with what?"

Merthus nodded his head.

"Okay then. We're trying to gather the Gouram seals, find the scrolls that will help us enact a ceremony that can tear down the boundary veil, and hopefully stop Avalon dying, all while trying to stop the war between gypsul and humans." Maya took a deep breath and waited for his reaction.

Merthus remained quiet for a moment as he processed her words. "What the hell are you trying to drag me into, Thelic?" he finally said, glaring at his old friend.

"We don't have time to fully explain now, we have to leave before the Esterbellian soldiers show up," Kadhim said, pointing to the moons above. It was nearing the time they had promised the rakers they would be ready to leave.

That only seemed to further agitate the dark, bald-headed

man. Or perhaps it excited him. It was difficult to tell what Merthus was feeling when all he offered was a half-smile, half-grimace. Nevertheless, Kadhim was right. If it wasn't for the heavy prison they lugged behind them, the soldiers would have caught up already, so they likely weren't far from the town.

Merthus stumbled back, almost dropping his sword as Kadhim and Zarina transformed quickly into their alter-forms and took flight. He muttered an oath, waiting for the others to pass as they headed for the dock before reluctantly trailing along behind them.

As promised, the rakers were positioned and ready to leave the moment their cargo was loaded. The long boat dipped as Keero stepped onboard and plodded into the lower cargo hold. As each of the rakers took their positions, the passengers moved to the front of the ferry, where their words might be kept private, masked by the lapping of small waves against the boat's hull.

"There's no need to explain," Merthus insisted, removing the straps that kept the sword's sheath firmly attached to his back. He sat down, leaning his head back against the rough wood as he rested the sword across his lap. "I have my own shit to get on with. I love you like a son, Thel, and it's great to see you again, but I can't help you."

Thelic took a seat on the opposite side of the ferry's bow, resting his spear as Merthus had done. "I understand. All I'm saying is, your goals line up with ours…somewhat."

Merthus snorted and nodded his head to Keela. "You expect me to believe she'll have any part in bringing down her father?"

"Gods, you're as short-sighted as ever," Keela muttered. After a day of travelling on the bodaari's back, she opted to stand, taking the moment to stretch cramped limbs. "We don't plan to kill him. At least, I don't think we do," she said, glancing at Maya and Thelic.

The couple shared a look and shrugged unhelpfully.

Keela rolled her eyes. "What's your problem with Bandaar anyway? Why are you so desperate to kill him?"

"He murdered my wife. That a good enough reason for you?" Merthus asked, glaring darkly up at her.

Keela had been ready with a sarcastic retort, but it caught in her throat as his words took hold and she registered the flicker of sadness hidden behind his deeper-seated anger. "When was this?" she asked quietly instead.

"During the executions. She wasn't even involved, she had nothing to do with the outlanders."

Keela had figured as much. Her father had gone through a phase five years ago, one that had cost many Esterbellians their lives. Accusations of helping the outlanders or refusing to assist in the coming war against them. The other Keepers had turned on Bandaar for his cruelty, and her father had learnt a valuable lesson. It had stalled the war, until now.

"Bandaar doesn't fear death," Keela said quietly. "His biggest fear is losing his place and power as Keeper, and humans falling to the gypsul."

"Gypsul?" Merthus asked, the term unfamiliar to him.

"The outlanders," Maya explained. She had stopped pacing as Merthus spoke of his wife's death, but continued now, back and forth across the bow. "Bandaar craves more power. And he thinks he can get it from me, which I suppose is true, in a way."

"In a way that sucks the life from you," Keela muttered.

Keela's sour tone took Methus by surprise, but he put it aside and looked to Maya. "Why you? I understand he wants war with the outlanders, but what use does he have for a young woman like yourself?" To him, Maya looked perfectly average. But he knew he had yet to see beneath the sleeves of her coat for any tell-tale marks of a contract with the elemental sprites.

Maya looked to Thelic who nodded his head encouragingly, knowing her intentions. She pulled at the tabs of her coat so they flapped loosely, and pushed the collar of her shirt to the side, revealing the seal on her chest.

At Merthus' confusion, she explained. "I'm contracted with a Gouram, and I have two Finkel sprites."

His eyes bulged as recognition dawned, a memory resurfacing of old scrolls he had been forced to learn like all human children of the realm.

"You fool," he whispered. "Power like that can't be managed. You must have…what, three casts before your body gives out and your essence depleted? One Finkel is bad enough, but two Finkels and a Gouram…"

"We don't know the cost of her contract," Thelic said. It was the reason he had tried to prevent Maya from using her abilities against the hunters in Kavakin. There was too much they simply didn't know. "She doesn't have the usual marks that signify the remains of her life. She doesn't have *any* marks, in fact, other than the Gouram's seal."

Merthus scratched the top of his head before dropping his hand to rub his cleanly shaven face. "So, you want my help getting the other contracts. You are a damned fool if ever I've met one, and I've met my fair share." He lifted his gaze and grinned pointedly at Thelic before once again sobering his expression. "What's in it for me? If I help you, and I'm not saying I will, what do I get out of it? I have no cause to involve myself in this bloody war, and I'm less inclined to help you tear down the only thing that's stopping the rest of this world's outlanders from killing us."

It was a fair point. Saving Avalon from choking to death would save them all, but the humans would be faced with a new threat if the gypsul banded together and decided to go to war or expel the humans. Why should he help? Maya wasn't sure she could answer that question. To her surprise, Keela answered instead.

"You want Bandaar to pay. Believe me, when this is all over, he will have lost everything he holds dear."

Merthus considered this for a moment, then flashed his gold teeth in a wide grin. "Okay then, I'm in."

∽

Dawn broke as the boat docked. Each member of the group kept their weapons ready as they watched the gathering crowds at the port. All around them, merchants hustled to replenish their stock from the port stalls before rushing to market to set up shop. A queue gathered along the worn, wooden planks across the water, people eager to claim their spot on the ferry for the trip back across the channel to Danika. The planks creaked and groaned as Keero was offloaded, and everyone moved to the side as the beast passed, trying not to fall into the water below.

Thelic stopped at the head of the group, prompting the bodaari to halt just as suddenly and cause everyone in his wake to bump into one and other like a stack of dominoes. The reason became clear quite quickly. A line of soldiers dressed in the signature Esterbellian black were checking those who passed and any large cargo crates they wished to load onto the ferry.

"Shit," Thelic grumbled.

Passing the others, Merthus moved up to the front beside his friend. He spotted the soldiers instantaneously and muttered his own string of profanities. They would recognise him, thanks to the three long scars that stretched from his chin to his cheekbones – a parting gift from Keela years ago, when the two had fought on opposite sides.

"We'll have to kill them," Merthus said quietly, moving forward as the people either side of them began to complain about Keero.

"Whoa, that's a bit drastic," Maya whispered from behind.

"He might be right. If they recognise us, there's no way they'll let us pass without a fight," Thelic interjected.

"Maybe create a *distraction* then?" Maya suggested in a patronising tone, withholding the 'duh' she was so sorely tempted to add at the end. The soldiers would recognise Keela, and Merthus was a difficult man to forget. But the Esterbellians would only have been given a brief description of Maya and Thelic, and neither had any obvious visual aspects that might set them apart from the average traveller.

A plan formed in Maya's mind as they drew closer to the dock's end, and she quickly explained it to the others before nudging Thelic to one side and taking charge of Keero's reins.

"DON'T talk to me," Maya roared behind her as she stormed down the dock with Keero close at her side. "I NEVER want to see you again!"

Thelic suppressed a grin at the absurdity and simple nature of Maya's *plan*. 'Everyone loves a bit of drama', she had said.

He chased after her and grabbed the back of her coat, spinning her to face him just as she reached the guards. "I didn't mean to…" a brief hesitation for dramatic effect, "I didn't mean to sleep with her!" Thelic finished, shouting in Maya's face.

With her back now turned to the guards, Maya smiled and whispered, "Ready?" Not waiting for a response, she took out her blade and slashed at his gut.

The action was intentionally predictable, and Thelic jumped back, already prepared to counteract the move.

Some of the guards chuckled, whispering amongst themselves while others moved forward to break up what appeared to be a marital spat going horribly awry.

"Break it up, you two," one of the soldiers shouted, motioning for another to move around the back of the pair.

One of the men grabbed Maya and hoisted her back, knocking the blade from her hand to drop onto the floor. She yelped in pain as her wrist was twisted in the process and the man's arm wrapped around her stomach.

Thelic momentarily forgot about their distraction. Reacting purely on instinct at Maya's pained expression, his anger surfaced and he jabbed a fist into the approaching guard's stomach. Stepping forward, he wrenched Maya free and held her close as the others piled in.

Reacting quickly, Maya spun in Thelic's arms to face him. Grabbing the sides of his face, she brought it down and crushed her lips to his. She moaned theatrically and threw her arms around his neck, resisting the urge to wrap one leg around his waist to further sell the act.

Thelic's eyes went from wild disbelief to understanding as he carefully watched the soldiers from the corner of his eye. The older of the men and women sighed, each pointing to the very public display of affection in annoyance while some of the younger of the Esterbellians blushed.

Maya broke the kiss. Remaining as she was, wrapped in Thelic's arms, she twisted her head and smiled at the soldiers. "Sorry about that, this is all a bit new."

"That's right," Thelic added. "Finally managed to tie this one down, if you catch my meaning?" he said with a wink to some of the older men. He squeezed her backside for added effect and only smiled wider as Maya dug her nails into the back of his neck.

Maya lowered her hands and finally turned, readjusting her ponytail as she stepped forward. "Are we free to go? Oh, of course, you need to check our belongings," she said with a bright smile.

One of the soldiers, a commander by the looks of things, sighed and shook his head before waving them on. "No, you're fine, just get out of here."

Maya and Thelic continued past the guards, pulling Keero behind them. Thelic risked a glance to where the soldiers continued with their checks. No sign of the others. Astoundingly, the distraction had worked.

"I LIKE YOU," Merthus said with a nod of approval as Maya and Thelic approached. "That was a ballsy risk and you pulled it off. Though, I must admit I'm a little disappointed. Been a while since I smashed some heads together, at least a week or two." He jumped back as the two gypsul landed with little warning in their winshik forms beside him.

Maya chuckled at their new companion's disgruntled look, and decided she liked him, too. While she would avoid a fight where she could, the man would be a handy addition when the need arose.

The hike from Esterbell's eastern port to Maelin's Bridge would take at least two days, assuming they didn't come across any more hiccups on their journey, and the path would be easily navigable if they stuck to the eastern line of the Bloodywood. Nevertheless, Thelic checked his map as they set off, eager to find a route that would avoid settlements of any nature on the journey, and thus reduce their chances of coming across any more soldiers.

Despite the territory's reputation, the weather held steady, offering sunshine instead of the usual snow and sleet. Maya abandoned her coat as the mid-afternoon sun glared down overhead. It wasn't hot, not even slightly, and goosebumps puckered the skin of her forearms. Still, she took a moment to stretch her upper body without the added weight of the heavy material. Standing up, she tucked the coat under her arm and stepped over the bags to Keero's shoulders where Thelic was sitting. Settling next to him, she tucked the coat around them both and leaned into his side.

"Two acts of affection in barely half a day." Thelic lifted his hand to feel her forehead. "You feeling alright?" he asked teasingly.

Maya nudged his shoulder with her own before snuggling into the luggage at their backs and pulling the coat up to her chin. "The first didn't count, I was pretending. Got to keep you on your toes, Mr Anthon," she jibed in return.

Thelic's chest rumbled with a chuckle as he wrapped his arm around her shoulders. "You've got me all riled up after that little act. I hope you plan to finish what you started." For a moment, the others faded away, leaving only himself and Maya. For a *moment*, they weren't on a mission to save a world. But that moment wouldn't last forever, it couldn't. He had offered to spirit her away. Somewhere he could keep her safe. Somewhere nobody would think to look for them. But Maya had refused. Now he had to make sure that choice didn't get her killed.

11

A SECRET BETWEEN FRIENDS

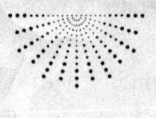

ESTERBELL

Early in the day, the roads had been packed with travellers, merchants and even some holiday-goers, all heading north for work or a break from the dreariness of everyday living. However, the further south Maya and the others travelled, the emptier the paths and fields became. Maya had forgotten how cold the Esterbellian territory was, its southern temperature seeming to drop with every step towards the mountain region.

Keela held her hands in front of her face, a crisp cloud appearing with every breath. She placed her fingers in her mouth and blew with all her strength through the leather gloves, but to no effect. She lifted the material from her wrist and tried to blow into the glove instead, desperate to feel her fingertips once again. No luck. Now the fur-lined inside was wet with condensation. She tutted, flumping back amongst the blankets on the bodaari's back and tried to distract herself from the biting wind by counting off the reasons she had decided to come on this nonsensical mission.

One…I like to breath, so the chaos void needs to go. Two…fuck.

Nothing came to mind. Of course, Keela had grown closer to Maya – despite her original intentions – and wanted to help her sister…Who was she kidding? Keela lived for this. Lived for the adrenaline rush that came with every bend in the road. During her early years training with Bandaar, Keela hadn't been allowed to leave the territory, and certainly wasn't allowed anywhere near the Outlands. But that had changed the older she became. Slowly, more responsibility had fallen on her shoulders. Emissary. Representative. Messenger. Commander. The list went on. But still, she could never please Bandaar, not truly. Right here and now, she was doing something for herself. She was helping those she had begrudgingly come to care about. Not to please her father, quite the opposite. With that thought in mind, Keela finally smiled and closed her eyes as she burrowed further into the blankets.

As Keero's pace gently slowed, they decided to stop early to set up camp. The bodaari had done well, nearly a whole day of travel without a need to stop and rest. But despite his impressive strength and stamina, even he needed a little down-time. They had come across a series of large boulders jutting up from the ground. Considering the relative flatness of their current surroundings, it was a strange sight and seemed somewhat out of place.

"We shouldn't stop here," Merthus said. His voice, naturally loud and deep, shocked the quiet of the group. He slid down from Keero and the bodaari seemed to sigh in relief as it stretched its long legs.

"Don't be so superstitious," Keela said with a smirk. Sliding down from Keero's back, she followed Merthus to the edge of a crater just a few feet from the group.

"I'm surprised you're not *more* superstitious…especially after what happened in Kavakin," Thelic muttered. He had certainly learnt his lesson. Ghosts and spirits were a lot more active, a lot more *deadly* than he would have thought possible.

"Oh please, we're days away from the boundary void," Keela threw back at Thelic behind her.

"What is this place," Maya asked. "Why shouldn't we stop here?"

Merthus made his way to the top of a large, stone slab clearly displaced from its natural resting place. Peering down, he noted the flowers that bloomed along the craters and broken rock of the former battlefield before him. Without looking back, he answered Maya's question. "This was a place of death. Still is, in fact." He finally turned and skidded down the loose scree of the steep slope. "It was one of the battlegrounds from the first war. A lot of people died here, both human and…gypsul, alike."

Kadhim and Zarina had landed once they saw the others stop and dismount. Now they listened to Merthus. They had also heard the tales and been shown the sites of the major battlegrounds from the first war. Many had died, too many. While the gypsul had continued to dwindle in number, the human population had only grown as more and more came through the portals. It was a miracle there were any natives left.

"And you think it's haunted?" Maya wanted to chuckle at the absurdity but held her tongue. She knew better than to laugh at something they had come face to face with only days before.

"Not so much haunted, as cursed," Merthus replied, his eyes widening dramatically to emphasise his point. "I've known soldiers who have ventured to this spot – most to pay their respects, some to be bloody idiots and prove the rumours wrong."

"And? I assume something happened to them?" Maya

asked, a shiver running up her spine despite her own disbelief.

"They all died."

"They didn't *all* die, Merthus," Thelic interrupted with a roll of his eyes. He stopped, his expression darkening as he lowered his tone to an almost whisper. "No, it was worse than that. Some were left to live after losing everything. Others went mad, killing entire families before disappearing altogether. Worst of all, some were forced to travel across Avalon on impossible missions with a reckless, impulsive blonde." Thelic stood back and watched with delight as Maya's face went from dark intrigue to the deadpan expression of being utterly unimpressed with his attempt at humour.

"You're real funny," Maya retorted sarcastically. "Let's see that smile linger when you sleep in your own bloody tent."

"I'm not the one who'll be shivering, princess. I thrive in the cold."

She had to admit, Thelic had her there. Maya was self-proclaimed as being solar-powered, simply not built for the colder climes. Refusing to rise to the bait, Maya brushed past him and clambered up the steep rock to where Merthus had stood. She had seen battlegrounds before, been to museums and plots of land dedicated to remembering those who had fallen in the World Wars. This was nothing like the places she had seen, those flat grasslands filled with flowers. Here, what lay before her was much different. Boulders removed from the earth and the odd tree growing at a slant, peppered with prickly flowers. A war fought with the elements instead of bombs and missiles. A war that was slowly coming for them now.

∾

A SMALL FIRE crackled at the centre of their makeshift camp just within the treeline of the Bloodywood. While the forest presented a greater risk from predators, it was deemed preferable to a troop of soldiers or braving the night's howling winds on the open plain.

As it turned out, Merthus had more to offer than simply his intimidating stature. He was an excellent hunter. This had been surprising, considering the sheer size and weight of the man, but yet he effortlessly swept through the trees, ducking and weaving under the branches and avoiding the crack of twigs underfoot in the hunt for their evening meal.

Three rasicus were attached to a spit and turned over the flames until the skin was crisp. They would eat well tonight thanks to their new companion. While they had made sure to pack food for their journey to and from the southern mountains, it was only just enough. Now they had an addition to their party, that food store would likely dwindle much quicker than anticipated.

With bellies full, Kadhim, Zarina, Keela and Merthus each bade their goodnights and retired to their tents, all eager to sleep while they could before taking a turn keeping watch.

Maya settled amongst the blankets, once again tucked into Thelic's side. He stroked her leg with one hand, no longer bothering with the gloves as he soaked up the fire's warmth. Relaxing, they both allowed a moment of companionable silence as their body heat intermingled and the cold that had crept into their bones slowly dissipated.

Thelic's thoughts echoed Maya's. The battleground had been a stark reminder of the importance of their task. It was so easy to listen to stories of war and hardships, both in this world and on Earth, and not apply them to reality. A mere fable left in the wake of what was once a terrible chaos provoked by ruling parties. But it wasn't just a story. War was real and utterly devastating.

"You okay?" Thelic asked, concerned by Maya's deepening frown.

"I am. I'll admit, I was tempted to take you up on your offer to run away from all of this." She chuckled sardonically under her breath. "How selfish can a person be to even consider such a thing?"

Thelic shifted slightly to look at her, then placed two fingers under her chin, lifting it to face him. "You're only human, Maya. Well, half human at least," he said with an easy smile. "In our world, anyone who claims they feel only pleasure and honour in committing to something that may take their life, is a liar…or a fool."

She smiled up at him and raised her hand to brush the side of his jaw, the muscle taut with frustration and worry. "I have so much more to lose now than I ever have before. So much more I want to protect. That alone could be my reasoning. Not honour and certainly not pleasure," she said, her scars and never-ending aches proof of that.

Thelic smiled and placed a gentle kiss on her forehead. "It's my job to protect *you*. Just concentrate on keeping yourself alive long enough to finish this quest you feel determined to see through."

Maya smiled at the soft touch. "That's not how love works, Thelic. It's certainly not how I work. We protect each other." She rested her head on his shoulder and asked for a story, something about his past, anything to better know and understand him.

He stayed quiet for a while, wondering what to tell her that he hadn't already. She knew about his father, his mother, his job as a shifter for both Carnass and Fortus. What else was there to tell? "Want to hear how Brijid got conscripted for running a drug den?" he asked.

Maya shifted to the side and looked up at him bemusedly.

"Drug den? Brijid? Wait, I thought drugs were allowed here in Avalon?"

"Certain ones are, yes. But she was a tyrant, believe it or not. Escaped from the orphanage at about twelve years of age and joined the seedy underbelly of Danika. Well, she more or less ran it, actually."

"Twelve?!" Maya squeaked, quickly covering her mouth and hoping she hadn't woken the others. "Are we talking about the same Brijid? The healer? Small? Brunette?"

"The very same." There was pride in his voice and in the way he looked distantly into the fire. "She had managed to do what the other children had only dreamed of doing, running off to create her own life of meaning. A terrible meaning, but at that age we were none-the-wiser."

Maya listened, intrigued by the healer's tale. According to Thelic, Brijid had run into a gang of somewhat unfriendly small-time dealers on the outskirts of the Keep. In return for their protection, she had offered to double their income. Brijid had spent the majority of her years at the orphanage studying medical scrolls, wishing for some way to grow up faster so she could go to the market stalls and shop with the wealthier ladies and gentlemen she so often saw parading past the orphanage gates. Instead, she discovered a means of amplifying a popular drug that not only healed whoever used it, but offered increased strength and stamina that lasted days.

"Waker?" Maya asked. Brijid had offered her the same drug when they had first met, after treating Maya for a djinca sting.

Thelic nodded his head. "Though, the concoction is much safer now and diluted for medical purposes. Her first batch was prone to causing chest pain. But she perfected it soon after, and as promised, the gang made a lot of money from their customers. She ended up ruling the whole lot of them," he finished, chuckling again.

"So, what happened?"

"Carnass. He had her arrested, but instead employed her as his personal herbologist and healer. While she wasn't doing anything technically against his ruling, she was conscripted for using the Danikan people as test subjects for an un-perfected drug. He wasn't wrong, I suppose. Brijid doesn't like to dwell on those days, though she is quite wealthy because of them."

Maya shook her head at the absurdity. Brijid was so… proper. Maya loved the story, loved that she now had another snippet into the lives of her friends.

"And you?" Thelic asked. "Tell me something I don't already know."

Maya considered, then smiled. "I punched a purple dinosaur in the face once." At Thelic's equally bemused expression, she explained. It was something much harder than she had anticipated, as he had never heard of a cinema or the children's tv sensation known as 'Barney'.

"My partner and I hadn't expected to be called in on a job to a children's open-aired cinema," she said, after explaining the mechanics of projecting a moving picture onto a large screen. "But there he was, a man in a purple dinosaur suit, terrorising the parents and children who had simply wanted a nice day out with their families."

Those days had been so simple. Now the monsters were real and out for blood. She had loved being a police-officer. Her purpose had been set, helping those in need. But here, it wasn't so much the people as it was the world that needed saving.

Thelic chuckled at her story and asked more questions. Earth history. Technology. Favourite meal. Favourite place. He wanted it all. As he listened intently to Maya's description of something called a 'toastie-maker', a rustle came from the canopy above. He glanced up and squinted as the moons' glow peaked through the trees. Midnight had come far quicker than expected. He could have stayed there all night and listened to Maya's stories, but they needed to rest, and it was time to switch shifts.

∞

KEELA AND ZARINA took their spots at opposite sides of the fire, each loading a rough cut of wood onto the flames to reignite their only source of heat. Keela rubbed her hands together, willing away the southern chill before pulling another blanket over her shoulders.

Zarina, comparatively unaffected by the cool temperature, left the blanket to one side and leaned back against a fallen log to stare at the Esterbellian warrioress.

"Would you like mine?" Zarina asked as she held out the rough, cotton material, careful to avoid the fire.

Keela declined and resisted the urge to remove one of her own in childish competition. She leaned as close to the fire as she dared and slowly felt the shivers subside. With her chin resting on her knees and her arms wrapped around her legs, she took a moment to admire the gypsul woman. While the humans had dressed for the occasion in long, thick coats and fur-lined boots, the gypsul had kept to their thin and skin-tight attire. She glanced at Zarina's cloak, discarded on the ground next to the fire, used only when they ventured near towns to hide their features.

"You'll make me blush if you keep staring like that," Zarina said softly as she played with her silver braid of hair. "What's on your mind?"

"How the hell are you not cold?" Keela muttered after a moment.

Zarina laughed quietly. "It's going to get much colder where we're going. This is nothing." The humans' healer friend, Brijid, had packed the gypsul some warmer clothes for when the temperatures truly plummeted and even they would be forced to cover up a little more than had up until now. It was a marvel, really. Brijid had clearly been frightened of them, and yet when Maya and Thelic had spoken to her, referring to Zarina and Kadhim as friends and not merely temporary allies, the healer had gone to the trouble of finding clothes that might fit the gypsul.

"Doesn't it strike you as odd that the Gouram of fire would go to rest somewhere so cold?" Keela asked, dispelling Zarina's train of thought. "It makes no sense. In fact, the whole thing feels like a wild goose chase at the whimsical fancy of two ghost children."

Zarina shrugged as she leaned over to place another log into the fire. "You wouldn't find it strange to light a fire in a desert any more than you would to light one on a snowy mountain. Fire is everywhere, and with it, the great Gouram."

Keela scoffed at Zarina's explanation, a tad too preachy for her tastes. Though, what she said made sense, in a way. If a human could be found in the colder climes, why not a God?

"What's the deal with you and Kadhim?" Keela asked next. "Are you family? Friends? Lovers?" She said the last with a wink and waited patiently for the gypsul's response.

"We're friends, but more like family, though we're not related by blood. I've known him my entire life."

"I see, and no sneaky romance bloomed over the years?"

Zarina smiled at Keela's eager look, the look of someone who craved a little drama. "Not even slightly. He fell in love a long time ago." The moment the words had left her, she regretted them.

"Oh? And who is this man or woman that stole his heart?" Keela asked, shifting slightly forward.

Zarina hesitated, unsure how to keep Kadhim's secret without further eliciting the woman's curiosity. But the bait had been taken, and Keela wasn't prepared to let this juicy little tale escape.

"Someone who was taken away. It was a long time ago, but he never forgot her," Zarina said softly.

Keela leaned back, allowing her arms to hang over her knees as she regarded the cautious woman. "Why are you holding back? It's not like I'd know them or run around telling everyone Kadhim's got it bad for an old flame."

Zarina gave a tight smile in response. She hated gossiping, but she hated lying more. And perhaps if Keela knew, she could help ease or at least understand some of the underlying tension coming from Kadhim. "You *do* know her."

Keela jerked forward, scanning her memory banks for any gossip or rumour about a human with a gypsul. None came to mind, and she didn't know any other gypsul. "Who?"

"Come on, think. Who do you know that has a history with gypsul, only to be spirited away at a young age to live in the human realm?"

Keela's jaw dropped as it clicked into place. "Kadhim is in love with *Maya*?!" She lowered her voice as Zarina flapped her arms and told her to shush. "How did *that* happen?"

"Maya's mother was of the Svingoran Tribe. Despite having her runes removed and her hands changed to that of a human, she was always welcomed back on her visits home. Jaseen would often leave the Keep in secret to visit the tribe and her mother, Fatari, when times were hard. My own mother was best friends with Jaseen, and so she and Maya would stay with us when Fatari was away."

"So, young Kadhim fell in love." Keela whistled. "That's a long time to hold on to a crush, and they were only kids."

"It was intense. He used to follow her everywhere, and then cried every time Maya's mother took her home to Esterbell." Zarina chuckled, fondly remembering the young and innocent boy. "One year they simply stopped showing up, and Fatari told us that Maya and Jaseen had gone through the portal to escape from Maya's father. Kadhim was devastated."

"Wow. You know, I thought I sensed something there. He's incredibly protective over her. Maybe not as much as Thelic, but still. There was an intensity I hadn't really understood. I wonder if Maya remembers him at all."

"She doesn't. I'm almost sure of it. She didn't even remember this world, never mind the people in it," Zarina said with a hint of sadness. She glanced sharply at the Esterbellian. "You mustn't tell Maya, or anyone. It's Kadhim's secret to tell."

Keela rolled her eyes and promised she wouldn't breathe a word, invoking the Gods to strike her down should she break her vow. Zarina nodded, content with Keela's risky deal by involving the Gouram.

For the remainder of their shift, they sat in silence until dawn broke and the others were woken, each taking a seat by the fire to enjoy a warm drink and some cold meat before continuing their journey.

As she drained the contents of her mug, Keela glanced surreptitiously between Maya and Kadhim, and noticed for the first time that his gaze never seemed to wander far from Maya; never broke for too long before resuming to watch over her. Between them, sat Thelic. Keela sighed as she sipped at the hot soup. This was a recipe for disaster.

12
MAELIN'S BRIDGE

SOUTHERN OUTLANDS

Lush green grass turned to blades of ice the closer they came to the channel separating them from the Southern Outlands. Before long, they pulled away from the trail skirting the Bloodywood and continued farther east to follow the shoreline. A great expanse of ice lay before them, much like the passage between Esterbell and Cantor where they had once happened across a shropsin. But this part of the frozen channel was broken up, icebergs cracking like gunshots against one and other as they moved with an underlying thermal current. There was no way they could cross on foot or via ferry – the cracks between the bergs too small for a ferry and too wide to jump.

With the slow pace of the bodaari, Maya had opted to walk and stretch her legs the moment they had reached the southern tip, easily keeping up with the beast and its other passengers as they trekked parallel to the shore. Snow had begun to fall in thick flurries and lightly obscured the path ahead, but across the plain directly in front of them, stood what appeared to be a towering monolith. The closer they came, features began to stand out – the details of a staff or perhaps a sword in a figure's hand.

Within what equated to an hour or so, they finally reached what turned out to be two, intimidating guardians to the bridge. Maya stopped and stared up, each statue looming at well over fifty feet tall. The first statue was of a man, the lines of his cloak intricately carved, and a beard almost equal in length. He held a long staff in one hand, with the other held out as if to stop any who wished to cross the bridge behind him.

Maya shifted her gaze to the other. This statue was also a man, this one wearing a crown and clad in brilliant armour emblazoned with three more crowns across his breastplate. In one hand, he held a long sword, its tip piercing the ground at his feet, while the other was held out in a mirror image of the statue next to him.

"Let me guess," Maya said, pointing up to the guardians. "Maelin and Arthur?"

"Indeed, they are," Thelic said. "Camalet is just over the bridge and further east than we are now. We won't pass it as we need to head west, but I promise I'll bring you there one day."

Keela snorted, "Why do you want to go there? It's completely barren, mostly rubble left after the first war."

Maya touched the pendent at her neck, and Thelic's mother's ring beside it. "I'm just interested, that's all."

Keela spotted the small, cylindrical item on Maya's necklace and realised what it was. Had Thelic offered a proposition of marriage to Maya? That wouldn't go down well. She bit her bottom lip and searched Kadhim's face, for once wishing that she wasn't in on the secret.

As they passed beyond the guardians, Maya was surprised to find that neither the statues nor the bridge had been made of stone, but of a dull, grey marble instead. With closer inspection, she noted the lines of gold veins as she ran her fingers along the balustrade, likely erected to stop travellers from toppling onto the ice below. In length, the bridge spanned the entire channel, at least two miles as far she could tell.

"That's odd," Thelic said. He had removed a pouch of coins, expecting to be stopped by the bridge's toll-man responsible for the upkeep and maintenance of the passage.

"Very odd," Merthus agreed, walking up to a small door set into the side of the King Arthur statue. With a heavy, steel-toed boot, Merthus kicked the wooden entrance in a series of knocks.

No response.

"Reskin never leaves his post," Thelic said as he regarded the empty landscape around them.

"Never? Doesn't he ever take a break?" Maya asked, feeling a little naive when the others responded with a simple raised brow.

"Never. He wouldn't risk missing a chance to line his pockets with more coin," Merthus said with obvious disdain for the toll-man. He lifted his boot to bang on the wood again. A sharp crack followed, and the door creaked open. "Oops, weaker than I thought," he said as he backed away, now more concerned that Reskin might barge through and charge an extortionate price to fix it.

Nobody came.

Removing his spear and unwrapping the head, Thelic moved cautiously over the threshold, and peered into the dull and dark interior of the marble house. The layout was small and simple in nature – a bed tucked into the statue's left foot, with a cooker built into the right and a cut in the stone above for its vent. Scrolls and books had been stacked neatly on one side, and a winding stone staircase led to the tip of Arthur's crown, where Reskin often sat as lookout for any incoming customers.

With Merthus and the others on guard downstairs, Maya and Thelic took the twisting steps two at a time and pushed open the hatch, before stepping out onto Arthur's full head of marble hair. A rickety wooden chair sat to one side, a layer of snow slowly building on it like a padded cushion. Below that, under the protection of the seat, was a pipe. Maya lifted it and removed one glove before using her pinkie finger to dig out the tobacco-like substance. The base of the shredded plant was still soft, not yet dried out from days of sitting in the open air. Wherever the toll-man had gone, he likely hadn't ventured far, and he hadn't been gone long.

Joining the others downstairs, Maya presented the pipe and her findings to the others. Keela had been impressed with the deduction, lifting the pipe from Maya to see for herself.

"We found something too," Kadhim shouted from the side of the bridge. The others moved to join him, and he pointed to where an iceberg lay below. Blood spattered the snow, along with the crumpled form of an old man with an arrow protruding from his back. Reskin.

"Damn," Thelic muttered upon seeing the body sprawled on the berg. Merthus grunted the same and began debating the risk of continuing on this path.

"What are you all so riled up about? Now we don't have to pay to cross the bridge. That's a win in my book," Keela protested.

"That arrow, the one currently lodged in Reskin's back, it's bandits, I'm sure of it," Merthus said. "Plus, you said it yourself, Maya – Reskin hadn't long left his post."

Maya held up her hands defensively. "I couldn't be sure without checking the body…" She leaned over the bridge's marble rail and regarded Reskin once again. Only a thin layer of snow lay across the dead man's back. The blood around him leaked into the frost to be watered down, never turning dry or brittle.

"What do you see?" Keela asked, the taps of her impatient foot lost in the deepening powder.

"Well, considering the temperature and level of snowfall, I doubt it will have been long since he died. His body was still warm until recent, so only a little of the snow is starting to stick. That's a guesstimate though, I wasn't trained to carry out autopsies or estimate times of death."

Despite being unfamiliar with Maya's terminology, they caught her meaning, the main message being that whoever had killed the toll-man likely wasn't too far away. It was impossible to determine the direction the killers had travelled, any recent tracks to and from the bridge now lost to the weather.

"They're just bandits," Keela muttered, swinging an arm to indicate the number of skilled members of their group. "We've been up against far scarier things than a bunch of men and women with crude weapons. Anyway, we haven't got any other choice. It would take at least another three days if we went via the Cantorian Ice Passage."

Keela made a good point. And as they had already learned, that particular route came with its own dangers. Despite the heavy feeling of unease shared amongst the group, they mounted Keero and made their way across the flat, marble surface of the bridge, each on the lookout for any movement.

⁓

As they passed two small columns on either balustrade, Thelic explained to Maya that they had reached the half-way point. Only a mile to go before they hit the Southern

Outlands. Darkness had fallen, for once a welcome relief as it cast them in shadow. Even the moons seemed to be on the travellers' side, their light hidden by nimbus clouds further allowing for stealth. None talked, only the intermittent huffs of breath from the bodaari breaking the silence.

Thelic had warned the group of a bandit's signal – a sharp series of whistles, often mistaken for that of a fulsin, a small bird found throughout the territories. They each listened for it now. Would the bandits hide under the bridge? Would an ambush be waiting at the other side, leaving nowhere to run but back the way the group had come?

Unease gnawed at Thelic's stomach. Bandits were ruthless, vile, and utterly determined to wreak havoc whenever they could. At one time, he had thought the gypsul shaders and the bandits were kin of sorts, each brutal in their methods. At least the shaders had a purpose. Bandits on the other hand were unpredictable and deadly.

The wind, only a whisper moments before, began to pick up until a strong gale whistled across the bridge. They covered their eyes against the sleet as it bit into their faces. Visibility was poor, to say the least, the snow falling heavier than it had only a mile back. In a way they supposed it was yet another blessing, but at the same time, if the bandits were ahead, they wouldn't know until it was too late. As the wind whipped and screamed against them, gaining its momentum, all other sounds were lost as they clung to Keero and battled their way forward.

Thelic's spear was out the moment their sight had been lost, the bodaari's reins abandoned as he gripped the shaft with both hands. It might have been helpful if the gypsul were able to fly, to provide any sort of prior warning to an impending attack, but taking flight was out of the question. The winds were too strong to keep a steady bearing above the group. For now, they would stay together, weapons held tightly to their chests in preparation.

Something loomed in the distance, stretching from the blizzard's veil to grow taller with every step towards the end of the bridge. Two more statues, different this time; one a crownless knight, a sword held mid-swing and ready to cut down any who dared pass; the other a woman, her long hair touching the marble sash around her midsection.

With the end of the bridge barely in sight, the group dismounted to walk by Keero's side. Maya quickened her pace, weaving between the others to stand at the front of the group by Thelic's side. Even through the storm, she could tell he was unhappy by the way he leaned in. He wanted to object, to send her to the back of the group where it was safest, but he knew her better than that now. She allowed a small smile as she watched him straighten and quicken his pace ever so slightly to keep ahead.

They had made it to the foot of the statues, their imposing height only serving to fray the group's nerves that much more. Just beyond and barely visible in the storm lay a rocky landscape, their path stretching between two mountains laden with boulders the size of small buildings, the beginnings of the cold mountain region forever south of the territories.

The moment they stepped off the bridge, Maya pulled Thelic to a stop, the others coming to a halt behind her. She closed her eyes and summoned Loki to clear the wind, feeling sure she wouldn't need the added power of a castor circle. Instead, she had a quiet word with the sprite, requesting that he form a large bubble around them, blocking the storm. She had considered doing it earlier but didn't want to prematurely drain her energy reserves should she need them for a fight down the line.

Loki somersaulted in the air before springing into action.

A tornado picked up, forming just ahead of them before bursting apart to surround the travellers twenty feet on either side like a large snow globe. The sleet that had moments before been ripping at their faces, stopped suddenly, and hung in suspended animation, ironically frozen in place.

Merthus let out a breath and lowered his hands from his face. Beyond Loki's barrier the wind continued to rage, but from where they stood, the sound whispered like an echo in a cave; soft, barely touching them. "Spirits," he said quietly, poking the floating pieces of hailstone to watch them drift away. "Is this a Gouram's power?"

"Nope," Keela said as she brushed the frozen fur lining her collar. "That's just Loki. He's a mischief maker at the best of times, but he has his uses."

A low growl seemed to surround them, and the sides of the dome began to rapidly close in, the space becoming smaller and smaller. Keela squealed at the back of the group as the barrier moved closer, before thrusting her into the storm once again. She fumbled with the gloves she had only just removed to tidy her hair from her face, and tried to force her way back into the calm void.

"Loki," Maya warned with a laugh. "Please let Keela back in, I think she's learnt her lesson."

The sprite howled a complaint, but did as Maya commanded, expanding the dome's walls to encompass a very windswept Keela once again.

"Little bugger, he did that on purpose!" Keela gasped as she quickly jabbed her hands into her gloves and tucked her hair back under her coat.

"You don't say," Maya replied, smiling wryly at her sister's expense.

"Pay attention," Thelic barked, his posture rigid as everyone turned to see a blurred figure making its way towards them. A second figure appeared from the shifting gloom. And another. Another.

Maya swore as smaller blurs ducked amongst the rocks at their front. She instructed Loki to be ready, to strengthen the barrier in case things got ugly. The closest figure stopped just as they hit Loki's ever-shifting wall. With a look to the others, Maya commanded the sprite to allow the stranger entry.

Wind and snow blew in from the gap created in the shield, and the hooded figure passed through to stand before them. Another, smaller person broke into a sprint in their attempt to make it past the barrier with their companion. A *whump* came before a yelp as the individual was thrown clear across the open space to land in a heap amongst the boulders at the base of a snow drift.

"Please," the figure before them said. "We don't mean any harm."

As it turned out, the stranger was in fact a very tall, very muscular woman. Lowering her hood and scarf, she revealed a face so badly scarred, Maya almost looked away. She wasn't disgusted, she pitied the woman. Scars like that must have come with a lot of pain, and plenty of healing.

"Thelic," Merthus said, stepping up beside him. "The arrows."

Thelic fixed his gaze over the woman's shoulder, where a quiver had been strapped to her back and a large hunting bow hung from one hand. The colouration of the feathers matched. Either she, or one of her people had killed the toll-man.

"We need to pass. Tell your people to stand aside," Thelic demanded, the deep rumble in his voice as clear a warning as the hard clang of his spear's hilt meeting a rock beneath the snow. Thelic's finalising gavel.

"Of course," the woman said as she smiled sweetly. Or at

least she tried to smile. One side of her face remained impassive, frozen by thick scar tissue that had the look of badly welded steel. Maya caught the minuscule change in the grip the woman had on her bow, the way her fingers twitched, wanting to retrieve an arrow. She was no friend, that much was clear. The dome flickered around them, the floating hailstones dropping to sink into the snow.

Thelic risked a glance to his left, where Maya had begun to shiver. Her energy was waning, and much quicker than usual. The cold didn't help, even without the wind, each breath felt as if they were inhaling thin shards of ice.

"Everything ok?" the woman asked, lifting her head to regard the shimmering dome. "You have some impressive skills." She narrowed her eyes, her focus catching signs of movement at the back of the group. Despite their wishes to shield Maya, Kadhim and Zarina had remained where they were, partially hidden behind the sheer size of the bodaari. Kadhim, however, had knocked an arrow and kept it trained on the woman. It was that movement that had caught her eye.

"Everything is just fine," Merthus bellowed, smacking the space between Maya's shoulder blades. "Now, if you don't mind, we'll be on our way." He took a step forward, now placing himself between the rest of the group and their waylayer. "Unless you have a problem with that?"

The woman's gaze remained fixed on Kadhim for some time, but she finally relented, composing her features until they once more appeared as friendly as possible. "Not at all. We were just passing through ourselves. I must say though, you're an interesting party. It's not often you see outlanders in the company of humans…well, not *live* ones, anyway. We could take them off your hands if you like? Pay you a pretty penny, too?"

Maya glared across the space between them. "Not on your life."

The woman laughed, the sound ugly and rasping as she shook her head. "Okay, okay. No need to snap. I'll tell my people to clear a path, if you'd be so kind as to drop your shield so they don't all go flying."

It's definitely a trap, they all thought in unison. Maya didn't have a choice, she was moments away from having to break the cast anyway. Only a second, that's all she needed to regather her strength. Without waiting for the others to agree, Maya dropped the barrier, calling Loki back to her side. The dome dissolved, and the wind rushed hungrily into the void. Maya swayed as it hit her, but Thelic's arm was already there to keep her steady.

The woman turned to her people and signalled with her arms, holding them up, then down, before swinging them both in a wide circle. While whatever the woman conveyed to the bandits was undecipherable to Maya and the others, her people seemed to understand just fine. Even through the snow and hail, it wasn't difficult to catch the sideways glances and looks of confusion as weapons were sheathed and the bandits effectively seemed to withdraw.

Thelic and the others stepped away from the bridge and passed slowly, one member of the group always with their eye on the rear as they faded into the storm.

"Everyone onto Keero, now," Thelic commanded, easily hopping onto the creature's back before reaching down and helping Maya up after him. When everyone was carefully seated, he held Maya tightly to his chest, his arms caging her on either side as he snapped the reins and Keero took off at a galloping pace through the snow towards a mountain pass.

13
SHADOWS AMONGST THE HERD

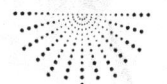

SOUTHERN OUTLANDS

The world was pure white. Underfoot the snow crunched and the ice cracked with each pad of the bodaari's paws, the sound an ominous boom over the ripping winds that served to keep the group on edge.

They were blind in the storm, with no stars to navigate and every mound and crevice a twin of the next. Their only guide would be a distant mountain, but it was invisible to them now through the hailstorm. That boom, the frozen water beneath their feet, was the only indicator they were on the right path. They would have to follow its course, all the way to the stagnant waterfall, then southwest into the mountains.

From experience, Thelic knew the storm wouldn't endure. They should have stopped much earlier to find shelter in one of the many caves and crevices they had passed. But he didn't trust that the bandits wouldn't follow. Not only had the heathen rogues seen a trophy in their gypsul companions, but Thelic had recognised the way the bandit leader had looked at Maya; seen that all too familiar hunger in her eyes from desperate days of surviving on very little. Word had already begun to spread of a powerful castor. Soon, like wildfire, that rumour would grow arms and legs and become unstoppable. For now, only one Keeper hunted Maya; two had already tried to capture her, but how long until the others joined the chase?

Despite day breaking, there was no end in sight to the blizzard. Kadhim, Zarina, Keela and Merthus huddled together at the centre of Keero's back, blankets pulled over their heads to capture their combined warmth. At Keero's shoulders, Maya remained encaged in Thelic's embrace. Her strength had returned quickly from her cast the previous evening, but now her shakes, shivers and chattering teeth threatened to lull her into an exhausted sleep. Thelic rubbed her arm with one hand, while maintaining Keero's bearing with the other.

Maya pulled the blanket from her face and leaned up to shout in Thelic's ear over the storm. "We should stop, just for a bit!" She had heard of adventurers trekking through Antarctica on insane missions to be the first to accomplish something in the barren and ruthless terrain. She had never envied or wished to join such a mission. She hated the cold. But this wasn't just *cold*. Her very bones ached with every cautious breath, her jaw weary with incessant chattering. Even her eyelashes felt heavy, the frost brushing her cheeks in rapid blinks to keep the hail from blinding her.

"We can't stop!" Thelic shouted in return. "Not until we get to the end of the flats. Once we're in the mountains we'll find somewhere." He burrowed his face in her hair, the mound no longer soft, but brittle and frozen. Keero's pace was forced to a slower trot, the wind too biting to go any faster. It was an impossible conundrum. Too fast and the freezing gale was too much to bear, but too slow and they risked frostbite or possibly cold induced comas.

The sun had dipped behind the mountains before they

reached the frozen waterfall, and the terrain finally began its incline as they made their way northeast. They all felt the shift in Keero's weight as he began the climb up the quickly steepening slope. Poking their heads from beneath the blanketed cover, they each kept watch for any deep shadows in the mountain's side, any caves which might be large enough to afford them shelter.

"There!" Keela yelled. When Thelic failed to respond, she shouted again much louder this time, and pointed to a small break in the rock.

Keero wouldn't fit through the crack, not that it mattered. This was the beast's natural habitat; he was far happier than any creature should be in such a desolate place. With that in mind, Thelic halted Keero and slid down. His decision was immediately met with regret as the bottom half of his legs disappeared into the snow. Still, he pushed through until he made it to the crevice Keela has spotted, a natural fault in the rock just large enough for them to fit through.

The others watched as he squeezed through, temporarily disappearing from sight. Maya was about to jump down, worried he had wandered into a predator's den, but he soon reappeared, waving Maya to bring Keero closer so they wouldn't have to trek so far.

Inside, the cave was larger than they had anticipated. The roof hung at least two feet above the staggeringly tall Merthus, while the depths seemed to plunge deep into the mountain's belly. Once the gear had been unloaded from Keero, Thelic gave his fur a calming stroke before retreating through the small opening, and the creature proceeded to lay where he had been left against the entrance. His bulk blocked the majority of the crack, and the roar of the storm was replaced with quiet, only the scuffle of feet on rock and the odd drip of water coming from deeper within.

Keela, being the only fire-master, left the others to navigate the darkness to set up blankets as she set about making a fire. In a land with very few trees and little to no shrubbery to use for firewood, Thelic had been prepared and brought with him small pots of paste made from animal fat and petroleum distillate. Being expensive and difficult to make using natural tar deposits found only in the deserts of Kavakin, they would have to be used sparingly. With shaking fingers, Keela called upon her Vasiba sprite and lit the paste. The cavern flickered with light and everyone sighed, both happy and relieved by the radiating warmth.

"While I'm h-hesitant to boost your ego more than it already is, you are a g-goddess" Maya noted teasingly as she raced forward to crowd the fire with the others. It wasn't long before the feeling seeped back into their fingers and toes, a burning tingle that skirted the line between pleasure and discomfort.

"When did you make the contract with your sprite?" Merthus asked Keela as he removed his boots and discarded them to the side. "You always said you wouldn't bother."

"I didn't have much of a choice," Keela said. From a young age, Bandaar had insisted Keela join with a high-level sprite. Instead, throughout her teens she had worked tirelessly to perfect her skills using a multitude of bladed weapons. There came a time, however, when that simply wasn't enough. It was never enough. "I'm guessing you never contracted?" she asked Merthus.

He shook his head. Merthus had always taken pride in his skill with a sword and thought fools of anyone who contracted with a spiritual being for power. "No way, I'm all natural," he said with a wide smile. "And I suppose you've yet to remove those cuffs from your wrists," he asked, pointing to the leather bands that hid the lifeline of Thelic's marks.

"I'd rather not dwell on it," Thelic said with a noncommittal shrug. "What's the point? When it's my time, it's my time."

Maya stared at the leather bands. *She* wanted to know. In the short time they had been together, Thelic had been forced to use his power – sometimes to protect Maya or even save her life. What had she cost him in terms of years? How much *more* would she cost him?

Sensing Maya's thoughts, Thelic wrapped an arm around her shoulders and whispered private reassurances that quickly turned to kinky ways she could reward him. She blushed, simultaneously cursing and commending his affinity for finding humour in even the most dreadful of topics. Something Merthus said caught Maya's attention, and with a hush to Thelic, she leaned in and listened intently to the others.

"You don't have the bands? You're not contracted?" Merthus asked the gypsul.

Kadhim regarded Merthus cautiously. He was still unsure if inviting the large stranger had been a good idea. Against what he assumed was his better judgement, he answered. "We're typically joined with a sprite at birth. Our runes are our lifeline." He pointed to the cobalt stones that stretched across each cheek. "When our time is nearing its end, they fade to white."

Maya was pleased to note that theirs were still the rich shade of blue she had come to love. "Does it take away from your life essence every time you shift into your other form?" she asked.

Kadhim shook his head. "That's born from a different power. Warriors who make a pact with sprites from the in-between are granting the beings a measure of freedom, allowing them to stretch their wings or loosen their claws in this realm. Those sprites prolong our life, in the hope of more time and the opportunity for that freedom."

"I see." Maya smiled and bobbed her head. She was about to lean back when another question struck her. "Wait, how old are you then? If the sprites prolong your life, then I assume you're much older than you appear?"

"No, I was born only a few years before you." Kadhim momentarily froze at the careless admission, then quickly tried to rectify his answer to avert any suspicion. "I assume, anyway."

"That sounded like more than mere assumption," Maya said, not easily fooled by his quick tact. "Back in Kavakin you began to tell me about a game you used to play, about Loki and the wimble-nooks his form imitates." She paused and shook her head. She had forgotten until now, the stress of the journey pushing it to the corners of her mind. "You knew me when I was a little girl, didn't you? That's what you were going to say." She held Kadhim's stare, daring him to object.

Keela flicked her eyes between Kadhim and her sister. This was it. It was all about to come out. She suddenly wished she had some form of snack so she could properly enjoy what came next.

"That's right. Zarina and I both knew you back then," Kadhim said softly.

"Why would you hide that from me, Kadhim?" Maya asked, confused by his hesitation.

Zarina wanted to say something, to come to her friend's defence, but the moment she opened her mouth, Kadhim cut his eyes to her in warning not to interfere.

"We knew you as a child. There isn't much else to tell," Kadhim said with a casual shrug.

"That's bollocks," Maya snapped. "Why are you being so secretive? Did you know my mother? I know bits and pieces, like how she used to visit Fatari from time to time. But, what else?" Maya's gaze turned from accusatory to pleading as another morsel of her past was presented in front of her.

Kadhim curled his clawed fingers into his palms and blew out a breath. He hated dwelling on that part of his life. Maya could never understand. She was in love with Thelic now, and the half gypsul in her would never let him go. Like mated fulsins, once that bond was made there was little that could break it. He would go the rest of his life loving her, with no hope of his feelings ever being returned. Thelic had beaten him to it, and Kadhim would always resent him for that.

"Please, Kadhim," Maya's whisper echoed alongside the crack and pop of the fire.

Kadhim sighed and shimmied his arms from the cloak before placing the heavy material over his knees to allow it to dry. There was only so long he could avoid telling her, but he didn't have to tell her *everything*. "You're right. Jaseen would bring you to our tribe from time to time to visit her mother and get away from the humans. You, me, and Zarina became very close. We did everything together."

And then you fell in love with her, Keela thought as she hugged her knees, listening intently. *Go on, say it.*

"You may not know this, but your mother was born to a Svingoran Tribe," Kadhim continued.

Keela sighed.

Maya jerked back at Kadhim's admission. "Does that mean I'm a Svingoran by birth?"

"No, you may choose your own tribe, assuming you wish to join one at all," he said, a shrug suggesting he wasn't bothered either way. "Jaseen was always welcome amongst our people, despite falling in love with a human. Some despised it and shunned your mother, but for the most part she was admired for her desire to unite the two sides."

"I don't remember any of that," Maya whispered, somewhat perturbed that she could forget something so different from her everyday life back on Earth.

"I'm not surprised." A dark look passed over Kadhim's face and he began sharpening his arrow tips. "Whenever you and your mother visited, you were never entirely present." He paused to look at her hands. "You always had bandages over your palms, and you held a troubled look that no child should wear."

Maya felt Thelic tense beside her and didn't have to turn to know what he was thinking. On her first meeting with Elkin, he had educated Maya on the rumours of her past. According to Elkin, Bandaar had bled Maya in his effort to strengthen her ability to summon the castor circles. She had only been a child at the time.

Merthus, either oblivious to the sudden tension or all too aware of it, jumped up from his spot. "Right. I'm starving. Shall we put on a pot of stew?"

The others exchanged smiles, Maya especially grateful for the change in topic, and each nodded their heads.

∼

Nudging the heavy bodaari from his spot against their exit, one by one they squeezed through the hole and were thrilled to note the cloudless blue sky overhead. At some point through the night the storm had died, leaving a crystal landscape of sharp mountains, peaks ablaze with the creeping dawn. It was perilously beautiful, offering a quiet sanctuary and willing travellers to adventure and explore the frozen paradise, but at the risk of almost certain death with one wrong turn into one of the many hidden crevasses.

After hauling the last of their packs onto Keero's back, the straps were tightened and everyone checked the fastenings on their boots and clothes. Though the weather had improved, the air was colder than before, and even the gypsul had opted for an additional layer of clothing to fight off the bitter chill.

Once Thelic and Merthus had checked their bearing against the map, they mounted Keero and were about to take off when Maya spotted something in the distance. At her guidance, Thelic directed Keero to where a deep channel had been tamped down in the snow.

"Do you typically find many people or creatures in the mountains?" Maya asked.

Thelic shook his head, as surprised as she was to see the flattened snow. "Not typically. Perhaps the odd hunter or bandits." From the size of the track, either several bodaari or a great many humans or gypsul had trekked this way through the night.

"Would Keero have gone for a wander while we slept?" Maya asked.

"No. And we would have known the moment he moved from the exit." Thelic slid down Keero and stepped onto the flattened path. It was heading in the same direction they planned to travel. "It could be another bodaari…"

"But?" Maya prompted.

"But it's doubtful. Bodaari are territorial and travel in large packs, and I'm almost certain Keero would have sensed one nearby and made a noise. Humans travelling in a storm, however, would have easily slipped by him. And they might have mistaken him for another mound of snow." Thelic raked a hand through his hair and cursed again before climbing back onto Keero.

Following the channel of cleared snow, Zarina and Kadhim elected to fly to check the path ahead. Meanwhile, the humans kept a wary eye, each on the lookout for any sort of movement amongst the cliffs that bordered their path.

Hemmed in, this stretch of their journey was dangerous for one reason, it was the perfect ambush point.

Three days of silent travel passed by like a blur. Shifting from one canyon to another, scrambling up icy and cragged mountain sides and holding onto Keero's straps for dear life. Other than Thelic, nobody had been prepared for this. Thelic was accustomed to the mountains, often called to venture this way at the Keeper's behest hunting bandits and villains who might have fled the territory. Though, even he was suffering from the long and arduous days of trekking the unforgiving landscape.

It was nearing nightfall when Keero approached what looked to be the remains of a rockslide. Each boulder was sharp and stood well over the bodaari's head, yet he expertly clambered over the rubble as if it were child's-play. Had Maya and the others travelled on foot, it might have taken an entire day just to navigate the rocky graveyard.

In no time at all, they cleared the slope and Keero stepped into yet another level of the deep canyon, then stopped at the bend of a sharp incline. Assuming the bodaari needed a moment to catch his breath, Thelic stroked the side of Keero's head and loosed the reins slightly.

Whump. Whump. Whump.

Everyone looked to Thelic at the sound of Keero's tail slapping against the snow, its rhythm slowly gaining momentum.

"What's going on?" Merthus asked from his more central position on the creature's back.

Thelic rubbed the spot between Keero's ears and leaned over to check something. "Well, he isn't growling, he's… panting." The muscles of Keero's back tensed, shifting as the creature lowered into a bow. "Shit, HANG ON!" Thelic wrapped one arm around Maya's waist a second before the creature sprang into a run towards the bend.

Snow spat from Keero's underbelly to wash the riders' faces as he galloped, his speed undeterred despite its depth. The bend was tight and Thelic pulled on the reins to slow the creature down. Keero pulled his face further forward, straining against the leather straps as he skidded around the bend and into a large, open plain.

Twenty, maybe thirty bodaari were dotted across the open snowfield, some lazing about, others with their faces buried in the snow to hunt the dead ground beneath. One by one the creatures raised their heads as the new arrivals came hurtling towards them. At first, they appeared bored, continuing to chew on whatever grub they had found. But as Keero continued forward at a speed even Thelic was surprised by, the creatures' hackles rose, and they bent their chests to the ground in warning.

Thelic pulled on the reins and roared for Keero to stop. As if reminded of his passengers, Keero's two front feet went rigid and he slid to a complete stop. Keela and Merthus, less prepared for the whiplash, went hurtling forward to land in a heap in deep snow. Maya and Thelic had barely managed to stay astride, though Maya's ribs had suffered for it with Thelic's corded forearms bunched around her chest like a corset.

Bursts of laughter streamed from the couple as two heads popped up from the snow – one a very unimpressed Keela, the other a somewhat bewildered Merthus. The laughs died quickly as the wild bodaari began their approach. Thelic placed his hands on the side of Keero's chest, expecting the rumble of warning when presented with danger. His fingers vibrated with the bodaari's quivers; its breathing hitched in excitement.

"Maya, slide down Keero and stand to the side. Merthus, Keela, move out of the way," Thelic instructed in a soft voice.

He lifted his head to the sky and spotted the gypsul just above. Raising a hand, he hoped they understood his meaning to stay put and not transform at the risk of frightening the wild beasts more than they already were.

Maya did as Thelic asked without a word, realising the threat was far from over as the bodaari continued their approach. Thelic slid down after her, and they all reconvened at a safe distance to the side to watch.

Keero, more wary than before, took hesitant steps forward. When face to face with the wild bodaari, he lowered himself ever so slightly, his bearded chin touching the snow in a sign of respect to the herd and a natural instinct to prove he was no threat.

The largest of the bodaari nudged its way through the others to stand at the front. It seemed to assess, perhaps listening to a sixth sense as those large, amber eyes searched Keero's purple ones. After a painfully long time, the wild bodaari leaned forward and pressed its forehead to Keero's in a sign of acceptance.

The bodaari alpha turned its massive head to regard the humans. Keero padded the snow with his paws in a nervous gesture and rumbled his chest, not so much in warning to the wild beasts, but in explanation. *These are my friends. These ones are safe.*

The alpha moved forward and growled when Keero attempted to follow behind. Merthus raised a hand to his sword's hilt while Keela and Maya slowly reached for their daggers. Thelic's own growl of warning caused them to stop and lower their hands.

The beast stopped at Thelic first. It sniffed the ruffled, frozen hair and prodded Thelic's stomach with its nose. With an approving snort, the bodaari moved on to Maya next and did the same, almost causing her to topple over. The same was carried out with Merthus and Keela until the alpha turned and galloped back to its herd, then lifted its head and roared. They had all passed the leader's judgement and could roam freely amongst the pack.

Keero appeared ecstatic by this and bounded to each of the bodaari, rubbing his face against theirs before digging his head into the snow to snack on the hidden ice weevils as the others had been doing.

"We should rest here tonight," Thelic suggested. "This herd will protect us now and alert us to any trouble passing by, so there shouldn't be any need for a watcher."

"Here? In the open?" Keela complained. "What about those mountain cliffs over there? We're heading that way anyway."

"Staying at the centre of the herd is safer. Keero can feed here, too."

"Okay, and how do you suppose we set up tents on snow that's up to our knees, Thelic?" In Keela's defence, they had spent only one of the last three nights under proper shelter. She was cold, wet, tired, and very irritable.

A wide grin spread across Thelic's face as he whistled for Keero. The creature bounded over with a new spring in his step and Thelic climbed onto his back to retrieve three scoops. "We'll use these."

Keela's expression wasn't the only one to sink in obvious despair at the prospect of an hour of hard labour shifting the tightly compacted snow. While impressed with Thelic's preparedness, Maya was equally as dismayed but took one of the scoops from his hand.

"I could melt it?" Keela offered instead, stepping back and regarding the scoops like they had personally offended her.

"No. Save your essence, little one," Merthus said with an exaggerated, patronising tone. He was never one to shy away from a chance to show off his strength, and after days of sitting he was eager for the workout. He snatched one of the scoops from Thelic and went to work shovelling.

Keela's fingers glowed with the beginnings of a summon. "Little one? I'll show you *essence*, you pompous prick–"

Thelic caught her wrist before she had a chance to finish the cast. "Don't. You could spook the herd, Keela. It's not worth it."

Just behind them, the gypsul landed on Keero's back, remaining in their winshik, bird-like forms. Zarina, all white with the ends of her feathers dipped in ruby-red, squawked and opened her wings to span across Keero's back. While Keela and Thelic bickered between themselves and Merthus fervently shovelled snow like treasure might lay beneath, Maya realised what the gypsul was trying to convey.

Taking Keero's reins, Maya clambered onto his back and prompted him forward ten paces. Stopping, she turned him back towards the group then went forward another ten paces. By this point the others had stopped to watch, stepping to one side, onto the flattened snow where the bodaari had passed.

"Well, I hate to admit it," Keela said, mimicking Maya's previous words, "but it seems I'm not the only goddess in our midst." She smiled gratefully at Maya, who insisted the credit go where it was due and pointed to Zarina.

Merthus, robbed of the chance to show off his prowess in strength, begrudgingly thanked Maya and the gypsul, before helping the others unload the gear to make camp.

∾

HOWLS and the pounding of paws dragged the travellers from their intermittent dreams. Thelic's bare chest slammed into Maya's face as the tent was ripped to the side, the entrance flying open to reveal the blur of bodaari stampeding around the snowfield.

"Get up!" Thelic yelled to Maya. He grunted as something slammed into the tent a second time, ripping the side wide open. He grabbed his clothes and dragged Maya to her feet before pushing her out of the tent. Something unseen had spooked the creatures, but the more immediate danger was the bodaari themselves. Thelic pulled Maya to the side just as another of the beasts barrelled through their tent, crushing it into the snow. Quickly throwing on his shirt and heavy coat, he glanced around for his spear. There. He raced forward, only to be tackled my Merthus as another creature thundered past them.

Maya screamed as the bodaari slammed into her shoulder, knocking her to the ground. She hadn't had a chance to grab her outer layers and felt the snow melt through the shirt to dampen her skin.

"Maya!" Grabbing his spear, Thelic hunted but failed to find her coat in the heap of trampled snow. He cursed, preparing to shake off his own to give it to her. Something distracted him, a line of silver glinting in the moonlight. Weapons, their wielders fast approaching. "Bandits!" he called in warning to the others. He turned to run to Maya, but she wasn't there. He spun, desperate to locate her amidst the blurs of stampeding creatures.

Having stayed in a tent by herself, Keela hadn't been afforded the offer of another human's body heat, so her clothes were still on and her weapons strapped to her side. Scrambling from the tent, she twisted at the sound of pounding paws heading towards her, and jumped from the path of a bodaari. Just as she regained her footing, a wild battle cry rang out from her left and she raised her blades as a dagger plunged towards her heart.

Kadhim and Zarina watched as Keela parried the attack

and sliced the bandit's throat. Putting their backs together, the gypsul raised their weapons.

"We should fly," Zarina yelled over the howls and yips of the creatures. "We need to find Maya!"

Kadhim was about to agree when he spotted Maya several feet away, grappling with a man attempting to rearrange her face with a blade. "Over there!" he shouted back, lowering his bow and pulling Zarina after him.

Maya gripped her attacker's wrist and roared as she slammed her head forward. Bone met cartilage and a wet, sickening crunch forced the bandit to drop his blade and clutch his broken nose. Maya caught the dagger as it fell, then twisted her body and jerked forward until steel met flesh. The man fell back, holding his side as gouts of blood sprung from the deep wound. But Maya had no time to stop as she quickly spotted two more bandits running towards her.

Holding up her fists, Maya was about to swing a punch when the man was thrown off his feet, one of Kadhim's arrows plunging into his chest. The second bandit, unfazed by the death of her partner, leapt forward. Having lost the dagger still buried in her first opponent, Maya fell back and cried out as a sharp rock dug into her ribs. Momentarily distracted by the blinding pain, she gasped as the woman's knee landed on her chest.

Thelic, embroiled in his own battle with two bandits, swung his spear in a wide arc, slicing the bellies of his attackers. He spun at Maya's scream and watched as a woman dug her knee into Maya's chest and raised a small dagger. He scrambled forward, then fell back as another bodaari swept into his path. Clambering to his feet, he let out a relieved breath as Maya's attacker fell back, Maya's fist pummelling her in the face. But the danger wasn't over, and two more bandits were on her at once.

As Maya swung again, her fist was caught and she was pulled to her feet, the hilt of a small sword slamming into the side of her head. Dazed, she barely had time to react before a second blow landed in the same spot. Her head rolled back, the raging sounds around her becoming a dull roar as black spots crowded her vision. She vaguely noted the world had turned upside down, the thumping pulse of blood rushing to her head as she was hoisted over the bandit's shoulder.

Again, Kadhim halted on his path to Maya, a raging bodaari barrelling past him. He raised his bow, trying to find a spot to aim without hurting Maya, but every time he thought he had a clear line of sight on her captors, another of the creatures would intercept his path or force him to shift position.

Thelic watched helplessly, blocked by the rioting bodaari as Maya's body swayed limply over the bandit's shoulder. Three more men had joined her captor, someone he recognised now as the scarred woman from Maelin's bridge. Together the kidnappers raced towards the canyon with Thelic in close pursuit, dodging and weaving past the bodaari, and cutting down bandits as he passed.

Zarina had sprinted forward. She was close to Maya now, her sword raised and ready to plunge into the first bandit she came across. She didn't make it. A bodaari slammed headfirst into her side, casting her into the air before she dropped, her head landing with a sickening crunch on the sharp edge of a rock protruding from the snow. After a dizzy moment, she lifted a hand lazily to the spot at the back of her head, then pulled it away to see it slick with blood. A scream rang out from somewhere behind her, but she continued to lay there, admiring the trail of red streaming down her fingers, unable to move from the path of the second creature heading straight for her.

Zarina closed her eyes, waiting for the blow she felt sure

would kill her. A sharp tug on the collar of her coat and she gasped in pain as her body was yanked from the creature's path. Merthus released the gypsul's collar and looked down at her, then turned his head as Kadhim caught up. Seeing Zarina was safe, both men barely afforded her a second glance before retraining their sight on Maya.

The path of Maya's captors was blocked, part of the herd banding together to run in tight circles and ward off any attackers. The bandits skirted around, giving the bodaari a wide berth, then stopped as a thundering crack reverberated across the plain.

Thelic had heard the ominous boom of ice cracking, and some small part of him screamed in warning to run towards the cliffs and away from danger. But that voice was strongly overridden with every step closer to Maya. He was barely ten feet away now, close enough to watch in grief-stricken horror as Keela launched herself at the group of bandits holding Maya, only for the ground to give way, plunging the women and the bandits into the dark crevasse below.

14

A DEVIL'S DEN

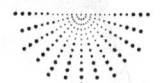

SOUTHERN OUTLANDS

Thelic skidded to a halt, his face ashen as he replayed the sight of Maya disappearing into the chasm. As the shock passed, he carefully scrambled to the edge of the hole, dropping to lie on his stomach and better distribute his weight. Below was an abyss, with nothing to light the way and no means of telling how far Maya, Keela and the bandits had fallen.

He twisted onto his back and raised his spear at the sound of boots crunching through the snow behind him. Merthus was carrying a very pale Zarina in his arms while Kadhim fired off arrow after arrow at approaching bandits, cutting them down without a single miss.

The bodaari had begun to disperse, Keero swept along with the crowd as they headed for the outer rim of the plain, a natural instinct to run from the continued rending of the ice beneath their paws. Only five bandits were left standing, and with no bodaari blocking their way, they descended on Thelic and the others.

Kadhim reached for an arrow and shot down the first of the approaching men. He realised a moment too late that he had shot the wrong one, as an archer appeared from behind the downed man and let loose his own arrow. Kadhim fell back as the iron tip pierced his side, the wound not fatal, but enough to keep him down.

Merthus roared and ran headlong into the remaining four, raising his sword like it weighed no more than a feather and cutting down three at once with a single swing. The last raised his dagger and thrust it at his significantly larger opponent, but the blade never found its mark, as an arrow ripped through his throat, undoubtedly saving Merthus' life. The warrior turned his head and nodded his thanks to Kadhim, who quickly dropped his bow to attend the searing pain in his side. Merthus swept his gaze once again to survey the surrounding area for any further challengers. Finding none, he turned and hurried back to join the others.

Thelic rolled back onto his front, confident his companions would take care of any further trouble. He shouted Maya's name but received only an echo in return. What was at the bottom? Rocks? Water? Snow? He prayed it was one of the latter. But then, if the fall was far enough, even that might not have saved them. He shook his head to dispel the thoughts. Maya was alive. She *had* to be alive.

∼

MAYA'S EYES fluttered open as something dripped onto her face. She blinked, trying to adjust her eyes to the gloom. From somewhere beyond the darkness, a faint glow illuminated a passage to her right. Another drip. She glanced up and found the wide eyes of a man staring back at her, blood streaming from the spiked rock jutting through his chest. Unable to look away, she watched as a small rivulet of blood ran down from his mouth to catch in the roughly cut stubble along his chin. The droplet fell and Maya flinched, lifting a hand to wipe it from her cheek. As the second bead formed, she tried to roll away and a sharp pain ripped through her side.

The glow from the passage steadily brightened, before a soft voice called out, "Maya?"

Maya let out a ragged breath of relief. "Keela!" A moment later, Keela's sharp features appeared over Maya's face, bearing a smile that quickly morphed into concern.

"Is that your blood?" Keela asked, moving her flaming palm closer to Maya's body. She wasn't pointing to Maya's face, now painted red with bandit's blood, but to the floor where a small spattering had forming beneath Maya's back.

"I don't know, but I'm not sure I can move," Maya admitted. She tried again and gasped as her side protested with a sharp pain. "I think I've broken a rib."

"Then you're lucky you're still breathing okay…You *can* breathe?"

Maya tested by filling her lungs. The pain was extraordinary, but she could do it, and nodded her head to Keela. "How come you fared so well?" she asked. Somewhat impressively, the Esterbellian seemed almost perfectly unharmed, considering the height from which they had fallen.

"I had a cushion," Keela said with a grin, pointing to a bloody, flattened bandit laying several feet away. "Here, let me help. You can't keep lying on the snow, you'll freeze to death. Where's your bloody coat?"

"Lost it in the chaos," Maya groaned, accepting Keela's hand and swallowing a scream as she was hauled to her feet. She almost toppled over, but caught herself and lifted one foot. "My damn ankle is buggered as well," she realised. Not broken though, she had suffered a broken ankle from a climbing accident a few years ago and knew the difference between a bad sprain and a break.

Just in front of them, the wall of the chasm was a sharp drop before sloping off in the shape of a frozen wave. They were lucky. If it hadn't been for the slope, even Keela with her cushion would have perished from the height.

Leaving Maya leaning against a boulder, Keela approached the slope and attempted to clamber up it. She slipped and skidded back down, unable to get a look at the top of the hole.

"We'll have to find another way out, there's no way we're getting back out that way–" Keela paused at the sound of a deep moan, then turned, registering a dark shape moving by the far wall.

∽

"Did you see that?" Thelic asked Kadhim and Merthus who lay on their stomachs beside him. "I swear I saw something glowing." He shouted into the hole again and waited, but no response came. "Fuck!" He scrambled to his feet and paced along the edge.

"Do we have any ropes?" Merthus asked. He searched the distance for Keero amongst the bodaari still trotting nervously along the sides of the cliffs. One stood out from the others with a harness and several packs still miraculously strapped to its back. "Over there, look!"

Thelic stopped his pacing and shifted his gaze to where Merthus had pointed to Keero. He let out an irritated sigh. "No, I took the ropes from the packs to let them dry in our tent. The same tent which is currently buried somewhere out there under mounds of snow!" He kicked at the offensive substance beneath his feet then spun to face Kadhim. "You! You can fly down there and check on her."

Kadhim shook his head in annoyance. "I already tried to

shift." He lifted the hand from his side now drenched with blood. "I couldn't do it."

With a growl of irritation, Thelic spun to face Zarina who lay unmoving where she had been left. He strode over to her, all sense of compassion removed in his fear for Maya's life, and took Zarina's shoulders in his hands to shake her awake. He stopped as he held her, alarm building in his gut. "She's not breathing!"

∽

Keela gripped both blades and approached the groaning figure. It was the woman, the bandit leader from Maelin's Bridge. Anger surged through Keela and she lunged forward with her blades raised.

"Wait!" The bandit held both hands up to ward off Keela's attack. "Please, I can help you!"

Keela paused. Spotting a blade lying idly beside the woman, she jumped forward and kicked it away before holding the knife to the bandit's throat. "And why the hell should we believe you?"

"Because these mountains are my home. Listen, I never wanted to hurt your friend, we wanted to sell her. There's a bounty on the head of a gifted female caster." The woman leaned to the side to cast a glance at Maya. "Blonde, powerful, skinny as a scag, and travelling with a big fella wielding a spear. She fits the description!"

"You're not doing a very good job at convincing me you should live," Keela grumbled, gripping the bandit's coat and pushing the blade deeper into the curve of her neck.

"I know this place!" the woman gasped. "Please, I know where we are. There's a safer route back to the surface, I'll show you!"

"I'm quite certain we can find the exit ourselves," Maya

muttered. Holding her ribs, she slid to the ground to sit, her right leg tiring from holding all her weight.

"I wouldn't be so sure. These caves stretch all across the mountainside. You're more likely to get lost, or worse, you might find yourselves at the Devil's Gate."

"The what?" Maya asked sardonically. "As daunting as you make that sound, you underestimate our ability to survive. We've become quite good at it."

The woman shook her head desperately and gasped as Keela's blade nicked her skin. "No, I don't mean you'll die and go to the spirit realm, I mean an *actual* devil, living here, in these parts."

That caught Maya's attention, and the smile fled from her lips to be replaced with interest. "Do you mean the Gouram of fire? The temple is here? Can you show us?"

"Wait, you want to go towards the God's den?" The bandit glanced from Keela to Maya and found no sign of a joke. "Fuck it. Just kill me now. I'm not going anywhere near that place." She closed her eyes and held her breath, waiting for the cut that would end her life.

"Wait, Keela," Maya instructed. "Turns out we *do* need her."

Keela muttered an oath. From the woman's reaction, she wasn't sure she wanted to go near this temple either. "What's so scary about it? It's not like the God actually lives in this world, it can't hurt you."

"Ha!" The woman cackled nervously. "That's what *you* think. I've lost many men and women to that blasted thing! It crawls from the depths of its pit and lures people in with promises of warmth and riches. No men or women who venture there ever return."

"Then how do you know the stories are true? If nobody returns, who's to say it's not just made up?" Maya asked. She was dubious at best of the woman's tale and refused to be so easily swayed from their mission.

"There's only one reason someone wouldn't return to their homes and families," the woman stated darkly. "That *thing* killed them. And I've heard the rumblings myself, heard the whispers when I've gotten too close to the temple. Believe me, miss. Whatever your reasons, they're not worth the risk. Best to just leave this place and go back to your happy little life with your fella."

Maya snorted a laugh then hissed at the reverberating pain. Still unfazed, she struggled to her feet and hobbled forward. "You're going to take us to this temple, or we won't just kill you, we'll split you apart from nose to navel until you're begging for us to end your life."

Keela's eyes bulged at Maya's threat and at the unmistakable look of someone willing to go through with it. After some consideration, the woman finally nodded in agreement and Keela helped her to her feet. It appeared the bandit had fared just as bad as Maya during the fall. Her arm hung loosely from one socket and a bright red stain spread across her heavy winter coat showed signs of what was probably a serious abdominal wound.

"Lead the way," Maya said, with little sympathy for her former captor.

As the woman hobbled forward, Keela bent to gently sling Maya's arm over her shoulder. "Where the hell did *that* come from," she murmured quietly, questioning Maya's previous threat.

"Read it in a book somewhere," Maya replied with a cheeky smile. "Always wanted to use it, but back on Earth you'd get arrested for such a threat. And as a police officer it's more than a little frowned upon."

Keela chuckled, finding a new respect for her half-beaten sister. Perhaps they had more in common than she thought.

~

"Merthus, go and fetch Keero. The med pouch should be in the central pack. Hurry!" Thelic continued to pound on Zarina's chest. It hadn't been long before they realised her heart had stopped along with her breathing. Kadhim paced beside him, helpless as he watched Thelic's attempt to save his friend's life.

Zarina had begun to breathe for a short moment when they had initially started, her heartbeat pounding beneath his palms. But she soon passed out, her chest once again falling still.

~

"What's your name?" Maya asked the bandit to distract herself from the pain. She leaned heavily against the tunnel wall as they stopped again for a short break.

"The name's Clippin. I'd say it's nice to meet you, but I wish you'd never crossed our bloody path."

"You're the one that attacked us," Maya countered. "If it weren't for you and your merry band of bellends–"

"If it weren't for *me*, you probably wouldn't have found this place. Come on, I haven't got all day." Clippin pushed herself away from the tunnel wall, keeping one hand on her wound and her neck inclined to avoid bumping her head on the low and curved ceiling of the cave.

Keela reignited her flame to light the way as she helped Maya down the passage behind the bandit. Crossing several forks in the road where additional tunnels spread out into the darkness, Maya had the odd sense of wandering through a continually descending ant hill. Clippin had been right. As they turned left, then right, then right again at another fork, Maya was so turned around she wasn't sure she would be able to find her way back to where they had fallen through the ice, never mind find a temple in this place.

"You feel that?" Clippin asked.

They did. The air had warmed considerably the deeper they travelled, to the point where their breath no longer fanned out in front of them. Without her coat, Maya still shivered violently against Keela's side, but was glad of the increasing temperature.

"It's not far now," Clippin assured them. "And there are steps to the surface just around this bend." Leading them down the winding passage, Clippin stopped and held a hand out in front of her. "See, told you."

Maya and Keela both gasped at the staggeringly high arch etched into the rock. As Clippin had promised, to the right was a winding, roughly hand-carved stairway, from where a fresh but bitterly cold breeze emerged from its peak.

"Now, if you'll excuse me, I'll be on my way. You two can take it from here," the bandit said, inching her way towards the stone staircase.

"Not so fast," Keela said sternly, grabbing the back of Clippin's coat and hauling her backwards. "You're coming with us." At the bandit's stream of verbal abuse, Keela pushed her blade to the woman's throat. "You really think we're going to let you go now, so you can gather your little friends and come back on the hunt? Not likely."

Maya moved towards the temple's arched entrance. She could hear it now, the whispers Clippin had spoken of. But these were different to the spirits she had heard before, they seemed further away, only a quiet echo in comparison. Above, mounted on a keystone at the arch's apex, was the stone head of the same devil-like creature they had seen at the temple in Kavakin desert. She shivered under its heavy gaze, frightened to know she would eventually come face to face with the creature in person. The Gouram of fire.

"Hang on, Maya" Keela shouted as she dragged Clippin to stand alongside her. "We should gather the others first and tie this one up."

"No," Maya said, her eyes glazing over as she tried to pick out the voices. "This is it. This is where we need to go."

Keela released a frustrated breath, failing to realise that Maya had stopped shivering and was suddenly walking just fine on her own. "Okay, just wait a moment then." Pushing Clippin to the floor, Keela removed the laces from her boots. With the first lace, she tied the woman's hands together, then tied her feet with the second.

"He's here," Maya mumbled, continuing forward.

"Who's here?" Keela asked, looked to the stairs for any sign of the others.

"The one we're looking for. He's been waiting for me."

A harsh laugh caused Keela to glance up and find her captive looking past her to the temple entrance, where Maya continued to walk into the darkness. "Damn it, Maya. Stop!"

Maya couldn't hear Keela. She heard nothing but the voices now. They were singing, beckoning her further into the void. Her senses snapped back as her feet slid out from underneath her, and she plummeted down a slope to where a dull light waited at the slide's end.

"Maya!" Keela sprinted to the spot where Maya had fallen and watched as she disappeared with a scream into the glowing bottom before rolling out the other side. Keela was about to head down after her, then thought better of it. She needed the others.

Racing back to where Clippin lay awkwardly against the wall, Keela raised the hilt of her dagger and brought it down swiftly onto the back of the woman's neck. Clippin went limp the moment she was struck, and Keela wasted no time as she raced up the slippery stone steps.

∼

MAYA GROANED and spat the dust and blood from her mouth. She appeared to be in a cavern of red, every wall colourfully painted in the dull amber light. She tried to sit up but clutched her ribs and whimpered quietly. At least she was herself again. She remembered hearing Keela's voice, like a soft song playing in the background of a bustling cafe. She hadn't really registered it, the only thing at the forefront of her mind to go deeper, to see more, to meet whoever so desperately seemed to be calling to her.

Gritting her teeth, Maya struggled to her feet as she took in the room. It was magnificent. Whoever built these places for the Gods were truly masters of stonemasonry. Four curved pillars stretched up to the domed ceiling, each one roughly carved out from the living rock wall. In fact, the entire room seemed to have been carved directly from the cave wall itself.

At the centre of the long chamber featured some sort of slightly raised platform, a dais. Maya took a step towards it and cursed, having momentarily forgotten her injured ankle. She limped to the first pillar and leaned against it, glancing towards the next. Something caught her eye, small mounds lining the walls. She squinted into the furthest shadows of the temple where the light almost failed to reach, and just about managed to pick out the familiar forms of hands, feet, and a head.

Bodies, she realised, and lots of them. Leaning lazily against the walls, they were the bones of those who had ventured into the deep as she had done, only to be stuck here with no hope of rescue. Maya swallowed the lump in her throat and shuffled forward, moving from pillar to pillar before reaching the circular stone slab. Beautifully designed, it featured the frightening and familiar face of the Gouram of fire etched in fine stonework. Just beyond that, a fountain bubbled at the far end of the room. The glow was coming from there, and it wasn't water that tumbled from the fountain's spout, but lava.

"No wonder it's so bloody warm in here. We're over one of those fire pits." Maya turned automatically to share the news with the others, forgetting she was alone. With a sigh, she hobbled back towards the entrance.

She froze as something swept around her at considerable speed, then disappeared just as quickly. She steadied her breath and summoned the sprites, determined to keep her mind and body to herself this time. The sprites never came. She tried again, then a third time, but still they refused to appear. The entity swept past her again, this time more forcefully, and Maya tripped, falling onto the edge of the slab. She shouted at the pain rippling through her ankle and ribs and clawed her way to the centre of the stone circle, away from the shifting and shimmering thing that slowly approached.

A bright red light burst throughout the room and the very chamber shook with frightening force. Maya covered her head as slivers of rock broke free from the ceiling and crashed to the floor around her. She tried to stand, but her body seemed to seize, something inside her insisting she lay down and close her eyes. Powerless to resist, she did as it willed, and soon succumbed to the darkness.

The moment her eyes closed, she was falling – no… floating down, down to somewhere warm and inviting. This couldn't be the depths of hell. Hell was not inviting, or so Maya had read. Maya opened her eyes to…nothing. No more glow from the lava fountain, no more cavern, just empty darkness. She blinked, unsure if her eyes were open or closed, until a figure glided towards her. It was a woman, utterly beautiful with shining silver hair and hands so red they seemed dipped in blood. The woman stopped in front of Maya and offered a familiar and reassuring smile.

"Zarina?"

∼

THELIC WAS HUNTING through the snow for their tents and rope when a bright light lit up the pre-dawn sky. He twisted towards the far mountainside just as a bolt of fire reached its peak and exploded. From halfway up the cliff, a person was trying to wave them down, her hands ablaze with amber flames, further emphasising her wave.

Keela.

But where was Maya? Only one figure stood at the cliff's edge. Thelic turned and shouted to the others, but they had seen the signal and had begun to move in that direction. Not bothering to wait for them, Thelic hurried in Keela's direction, his pace painfully slowed by the thick snow underfoot.

He had almost reached her when the earth shook beneath his feet causing him to fall. He remained still whilst the crack of ice and rock rumbled around him, waiting for the floor to fall, to take him to his death. After a moment, the shakes receded along with the threatening sound. He carefully regained his footing and hurried to the base of the cliff.

"Thelic!" Keela shouted with relief as she helped him over the last rocky lip. She had spotted a longer and flatter path up the cliffs and tried to indicate as much to Thelic, but he had seen the quicker route and managed himself well on the climb. She gasped as he grabbed her shoulders, an almost delirious panic in the hard set of his eyes.

"Keela, where's Maya? Why isn't she with you?" he asked, voice rough with concern.

Keela shook herself from Thelic's stone grip and indicated the passage behind her. "She's down there, we found the temple."

He had already started running for the passage entryway but stopped at Keela's words and turned on his heel, dread lacing his tone. "Tell me she didn't go into the temple on her own." It was a demand more than a question.

"I'm not sure she had a choice, Thelic. She wasn't herself," Keela explained at Maya's defence.

He all but roared in frustration as he threw himself at the passageway and took the icy stairs two at a time. At its base, he saw a crumpled form and for a fraction of a second thought it was Maya. He soon realised it was in fact the chief bandit who had attacked them; the woman responsible for this entire mess; responsible for the death and carnage; the reason Maya was currently alone. A dark thought crossed his mind, one that envisioned him driving his blade through the bandit's gut. A slow death. One fitting for such a person.

"Maya's down there," Keela said from halfway down the staircase. Her eyes danced over Thelic's white-knuckled grip on the hilt of his spear and recognised the dark look he harboured, but made no move to stop him.

"Go and flag down the others, I'll get Maya," he ordered without looking at her. He tore his gaze from the bandit leader and headed for the passage, jumping onto the slope without a second thought, his spear ready for whatever lay at the bottom.

∼

"Zarina?" Maya asked again. "How...What..."

Zarina's glowing body shook with a silent giggle. Without answering any of Maya's half-formed questions, she held out her hand.

Maya couldn't help but wonder if this might be a trick. A cruel and clever trick if Zarina's form had been the chosen vessel for such a falsehood. The gypsul was so easy to trust, so wonderfully calming even in the face of utter chaos. Without realising it, Maya had reached out and touched her hand to Zarina's.

The gypsul smiled kindly and closed her eyes. Colour exploded and Maya screamed as her body was seemingly ripped apart. She looked down, half expecting to find nothing but shreds of flesh, but she was whole and unharmed. When she raised her head, the pain was gone and she was no longer in darkness, but a place of greyness, entirely monochromatic. A marble bridge similar to the one they had crossed only days earlier stretched out before her, the only thing separating Maya and a sea of bubbling lava.

The In-between. The world of the spirits.

∼

AT THE BOTTOM of the slope, Thelic rolled and jumped to his feet, spear raised and ready. A scream echoed along the cavern walls. Maya's scream. In the soft glow, he picked out a human form thrashing about on a raised slab of rock. He raced forward only for a blurring shape to wisp into his path. His feet left the ground as the entity blasted into his stomach. He struck the far wall causing the rock to splinter at his back with the force of it, then dropped to the floor, the breath ripped from his lungs.

By the circular dais, another swirl of dark matter joined the first, then another, all joining as one to surround the unconscious Maya.

Thelic heaved in a laboured breath and retrieved the weapon knocked from his grasp. The spirits, or whatever they were, continued to swirl in a wide circle. He approached them again, slower this time, until he was beside the barrier. Beyond, Maya lay still. He couldn't tell if she was breathing or not, the blur of the shield too thick to see her clearly.

He raised his hands and slammed them against the shimmering dome. The entities shuddered, and Thelic got the sense they were mocking him, laughing at his powerlessness. He slammed his fists again, and again. When that didn't work, he raised his spear and sliced at the barrier. It went through, then was sucked from his grasp to skid across the stone and land by Maya's side. He roared in frustration and fell to his knees, continuing to pound on the barrier.

15

A PHOENIX RISES

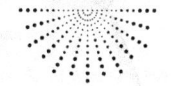

SOUTHERN OUTLANDS

"Is this where the Gouram of fire lives?" Maya asked Zarina. For once, Zarina wasn't her usual, chatty self. The gypsul would have been the first to offer a long-winded explanation of anything that might have interested Maya. But now she was painfully silent, offering only a small smile of reassurance.

"This is not my true resting place," a voice rumbled from somewhere ahead.

Boom…Boom…Boom…

Maya instinctively reached for her weapon despite knowing it wasn't there. The footsteps continued forward; their echoes intensified the closer the invisible entity came. A figure glistened several feet ahead, a mirage that became crystal clear in seconds.

"I've been waiting a long time to meet you, halfling," Pavinic, the Gouram of fire chuckled.

Maya blinked at what appeared to be…a cat. An orange tabby cat, to be precise. The beginnings of a wild giggle bubbled up her throat at an alarming rate and she clamped her jaw shut, lifting a hand to her mouth.

The cat frowned, its small whiskers twitching in annoyance. "I see you're distracted by my appearance. That was never my intention. I simply did not wish to frighten you." With a malevolent grin unbefitting of a small feline, a crack sounded as its bones broke, the bright orange fur along its spine ripped down the middle as a devil-like figure rose from the body to a terrifying height.

Maya shrank back as the Gouram transformed into the creature she had expected. The devil statue she had seen in the caves of Kavakin had not done this creature justice. While it sported the two blazing horns and a spiked tail, it was double the size. The Gouram's horns were a burst of fire, embers dripping down its back like a mane of flaming fur. Hard scales rippled at the power that thrummed beneath as the creature's tail whipped back and forth excitedly, smashing into the marble rail until chips of the hard stone burst apart.

"Is this better?" Pavinic bellowed, drinking in Maya's distress and further rising in height to stand on his two back paws.

"Not even slightly," Maya uttered with a tremble. Feeling Zarina's soft hand touch her shoulder, Maya clenched her fists and straightened her spine. "You said you've been waiting for me, well we've been looking for you as well. We need your help."

A chilling chuckle broke through the silence of the bubbling world. "Do you not yet know the cost of joining with a Gouram?"

Maya opened her mouth to respond, only to realise she didn't know, and couldn't even offer an educated guess. "I can only assume it's nothing good?"

"That depends on your sense of what is good and what is bad," the God said with a sly smile. "The cost is something many crave, both in this world and those beyond. Though *they* are naive fools."

"I don't suppose you feel inclined to tell me what it is I've given up?" Maya asked, sensing the Gouram's predilection for teasing.

The God scowled. "Where's the fun in that?"

"You want something from me. And I want something from you. I've been told you are the most feared, but also the most gracious of the Gods. If that's true, then please, tell me. What is my cost?" Maya had never heard such a thing about Pavinic, but hoped his ego would bend to her request. His smile suggested her gamble might have paid off.

"Very well, I am reticent to disappoint my worshippers," he said, flicking his tail with a sense of glee. "Your cost, halfling, is immortality."

∽

"Thelic?"

Thelic raised his head and turned at the sound of Keela's voice. After what felt like hours of pounding hopelessly on the barrier, his knuckles were bloody and his arms exhausted from his efforts to reach Maya. He rose to his feet and staggered towards the end of the slope.

Keela's face appeared at the top. "Thank the Gods," she muttered. "Is Maya there? Is she ok?"

Thelic bit down on the surge of despair. "She's here, but I can't get to her."

A grumble of annoyance came from above along with muttered arguments before the large, bald head of Merthus appeared in Keela's place. "I found the ropes! Keela and Kadhim are coming down, I'll stay here and haul you all up when you're ready," Merthus bellowed.

Thelic sighed in relief. Perhaps with all three of their strength, they could break the barrier and reach Maya.

A yelp echoed through the passage before Keela came barrelling into view. Thelic caught and set her on her feet, before doing the same for Kadhim. A grunt of pain caught Thelic's attention, and he glanced down to Kadhim's torso, where blood had seeped through his clothes to speckle his coat with red.

"It's fine, the bleeding has stopped," Kadhim said, reading Thelic's expression.

Thelic took one look at the gypsul's ashen and tear-streaked face and didn't push the matter any further. "Maya is over here, but there's a barrier blocking the way to her," he said instead.

At first, Keela saw nothing but Maya's body lying on the stone dais. As she moved forward, Thelic caught the corner of her coat, stopping her just before she reached her sister.

"What are you doing? She's right there!" Keela cried.

"Look closely," Thelic insisted. "They almost knocked me out the first time I tried to interfere. They'll do the same to you."

Keela saw the swirling mass, barely visible in the glow of the fountain's light. "What are they doing to her?"

Kadhim stepped up beside them, so that they were all forming a line against the shifting wall. "They're protecting her, ensuring nobody interferes. Maya is with the Gouram now," he said.

"What? But I thought she needed a guide for the in-between?" Keela shouted. "I thought she needed you or she would be lost?" Keela hadn't meant for it to sound so harsh, but worry gnawed at her insides as she turned from Kadhim to look at her sister. Maya's body was so still, she could be dead for all they knew.

"She has her guide," Kadhim said, his voice heavy as a

fresh tear sprung to the corner of his eye, its trail down his cheek halted as he swiped angrily at his face. "All we can do now is wait."

"Fuck that," Thelic spat. "You have no way of knowing Zarina is with her." A thought occurred to him. "Can I go? Could I be her guide?"

Kadhim looked scathingly at Thelic, his sadness momentarily forgotten. "Of course you can't go." He clenched both fists and reined in his temper at Thelic's respondent look of agony. "I'm sorry, we just have to trust that the Gouram wants Maya alive as much as we do."

~

"IMMORTALITY?" Maya asked. That didn't sound so bad. And the Gouram was right, humans throughout history had longed to find the holy grail, or whatever they could to live just a little longer than fate intended.

"Don't be fooled, little halfling. Immortality in this sense means your body *and* soul are bound to this world, to this plane of existence." Pavinic gave her a moment to see if the weight of such a cost would come to her. When it didn't, he continued. "You may never rest in the spirit realm. You may never spend your next life with those you have lost in this one. When your beloved dies, he will move on, and you will remain here."

Maya felt the blood drain from her face. Her mother. She would never be able to join Jaseen in the afterlife. Thelic. Maya raised a hand to her lips where the ghost of his kiss remained. How would she tell him?

The Gouram continued, his words a sharp blade carving deeper and deeper. "Your body will cease to age, and you will spend the rest of your days in that form. Do not be fooled, you are still weak to mortal weapons, and overuse of the

Gourams' powers will see your body fail. You *can* be killed, but your spirit may never move on."

"Yes, I get it!" Maya snapped. She dropped to her knees and covered her face with her hands. No tears fell. Instead, she wanted to scream at the unfairness of it all. She was saving their world; how could they ask such a price?

It is just as much your world as it is ours, Mayara, Pavinic's voice echoed in her mind.

Maya dropped her hands and looked up, her temper barely contained. "He should have told me. Batshari allowed me to accept his seal without a hint of warning at the cost. He's lucky I won't be able to pass fully into his realm, because I'd like to wrap my hands around his big, scaled throat before I rip his heart out."

Pavinic roared in a mighty laugh that seem to shake the world. Bubbles of lava popped, sending globules of searing molten rock onto the marble bridge at their feet. "I like your fire, girl! I will be sure to inform my brother of your misgivings about him."

Maya muttered an oath, not bothering to object to Pavinic's plan of dobbing her in to the God of water. She rose to her feet. "Well, I guess I'm all in now. Shall we do this, or what?"

Pavinic experienced something he hadn't felt in a long time. Pride. The small halfling had finally accepted her charge and showed little fear in the knowledge of its cost. "I believe you have been through something similar before, with Batshari?"

Dread crept up Maya's spine and she shivered as a morsel of that boundless courage escaped her. With Batshari she had allowed the element of water to fully encompass her, had relinquished her body and her soul to it. In that moment she had felt as though she were dying.

"I'm ready," Maya said with a single nod.

Pavinic grinned. "Then step into the fire."

⁓

Thelic picked up a small pebble and thew it half-heartedly at the forcefield, watching it bounce back as the previous ones had. He reached down to retrieve another just as the room filled with light. He dropped the stone, holding his arms up to cover his eyes.

Beyond the barrier, a scorching fire roared from the centre of the dais, with Maya at its source. Thelic jumped to his feet and braced his hands against the shifting wall, his roar lost as the sound of the flames and Maya's harrowing scream filled the room.

Keela and Kadhim leapt up, but stood back, watching as a sister and a friend was burned alive before their very eyes. Maya's body convulsed, her skin turning black, her hair and clothes singed until there was nothing left but her writhing body floating at the centre of the inferno.

Keela cried hysterically and joined Thelic to pound at the impenetrable wall while Kadhim simply stood frozen, beginning to fear they had failed. Whatever this torture was, whatever Pavinic was doing, surely Maya would not survive it.

Thelic and Keela fell forward as the barrier vanished, no longer required now that the God's meeting had met its conclusion. As they rose to their feet, the flames simmered down until only Maya's charred body remained.

"Wait!" Kadhim shouted as the others stepped onto the platform. "Just hang on a moment."

Despite shaking with the need to go to her, Thelic stayed where he was and waited. Slowly, golden strands broke through the seared scalp of Maya's head and cracks appeared across the blackened remains of her skin, revealing a pale pink beneath. Flakes of the ashy flesh peeled away, the burnt pieces falling to the floor like dust to lay beneath her. This continued, more of her skin glowing in the soft light of the fountain, until finally Maya was whole again, unharmed, her cuts and bruises completely healed like she had never fallen through a hole in the ice…never been burned alive.

She was a legendary phoenix, risen from the ashes.

When the healing process appeared complete, Thelic took a tentative step towards Maya, dropping to his knees by her side. An emblem blazed beneath the skin of her abdomen, slowly fading to a soft glow. A Gouram's seal. She was breathing, her pulse steady beneath the tips of his fingers across her naked breast.

"Well?" Keela asked, not daring a step forward for fear of somehow disrupting what she could only describe as a rebirth.

"She's alive," Thelic whispered, barely believing it himself. He lifted Maya into his arms and cradled her. "Open your eyes, Maya. Come back to me." Her head moved beneath his chin and he looked down as she opened her eyes. Those green eyes he had grown so accustomed to, had grown to love, were no longer just the pale jade. Brilliant amber glowed at the edge of each iris, a fiery circle slowly fading as she blinked away the fogginess.

"Thank the fucking Gods," Keela breathed, dropping to her knees as the adrenaline seeped from her body. "If you hadn't just been burned to death, and I had any strength left in me, I'd strangle you for the fright you gave us. You little twerp," she added with a broken smile. Keela had been so sure Maya was lost to them, that all of this, all of the pain and suffering they had gone through had been for nothing. More than that, she thought she had lost her sister. Tears sprang angrily to Keela's eyes as she muttered curses and rose to her feet, turning from the others in embarrassment.

"Christ, Keela. Anyone would think you actually *cared* for me," Maya said weakly.

Keela spun on her heel, astonished and hurt by the accusation, then softened at the sight of the small and teasing smile on Maya lips. Her shoulders dropped in defeat as she smiled back, allowing the tears to fall.

"Thelic," Maya whispered, peering up into the raging silver of his eyes, his face heavy with a storm of emotions. She raised her hand to cup his cheek. "Any chance you brought an extra set of clothes with you? Mine got a little...incinerated."

He wanted to scowl and laugh and shake her all at once. It's not every day you see the woman you love burn to death. He needed a damn moment to pull himself together. As she stroked the scruff of several days' growth along his jaw, he closed his eyes and quietened his temper. She was alive.

∼

"BLOODY HELL, woman. What happened to your hair?" Merthus asked in awe as he helped Thelic over the lip of the slope. Maya, still weak from whatever had transpired in the in-between, had been clutched to Thelic's chest as their beastly companion hauled them up. It was an impressive feat, Thelic alone weighed at least twice that of Maya.

"Oh, and your clothes, too?" Merthus asked shyly with a grin.

Maya touched her hair gingerly, worried the new locks might fall from her scalp. With the rebirth, her hair had grown several inches longer and now sat just below her waist. She hastily pulled Thelic's coat closed, the heavy material far too big as it swept across the floor.

"Merthus, did you manage to find our bags where you found the ropes?" Thelic asked.

Tearing his gaze from Maya's newly covered nakedness, Merthus met Thelic's overtly threatening stare and coughed to clear his throat. "Sure did. I didn't think you'd need anything other than the ropes so that's all I brought. I'll help get the others out and then go and fetch the bags."

With everyone reunited at the top of the temple's slope, Merthus and Keela left to retrieve Maya's clothes and to track down Keero.

Maya sat by Zarina's side, stroking the pretty silver hair now stiff with dried blood. Her face, once rosy across the cheeks and slightly tanned, was now pale and lifeless.

"She guided me to Pavinic," Maya whispered to nobody in particular.

Kadhim leaned heavily against the passage wall, barely able to stomach looking at the body of his oldest friend. His family. A pain burned in his heart at the thought of informing Zarina's mother of the news. She would be utterly crushed. He would have cried, if he had anything left to spare. But his reserves were depleted. He had no more to offer...except vengeance.

By the stone stairs Clippin began to stir, her panic mounting with the realisation she was still in the company of her captors. Lifting her hands, she bit at the crude bootlaces tied around her wrists, then yelped in fear as clawed hands latched into the folds of her coat and dragged her up.

"Kadhim," Maya croaked, her throat as barren as the sands of Kavakin. "Don't do it." But Maya was too late.

Kadhim thrust a dagger deep into the bandit's gut, then twisted, his rage and pain clouding all sense of right and wrong. He held her there and stared into the woman's eyes until her head dropped forward and a final, laboured breath passed her lips. Her body dropped to the floor, blood pooling around her.

Maya tried to gasp, tried to feel anything other than a

grim sense of justice. It was because of bandits that Zarina was dead. But the brutality of it…she had been tied, defenceless, with no means of fighting back. It was dark, too dark. A step so far over the moral line, Kadhim may never come back from it. And yet…Maya felt somewhat content.

Kadhim spoke softly, shifting his gaze from the woman at his feet, to Zarina's body. "A leader must take responsibility for those who serve her. Her actions, her decisions led to Zarina's death. So, she paid with her life."

With little compassion, Thelic continued with his task of regathering the rope from the temple's entrance. If Kadhim hadn't killed her, Thelic might have. The gypsul had saved him from making that choice.

ONCE MAYA HAD DRESSED and Keela had assisted with braiding her hair to keep it manageable, they lifted Zarina and carefully carried her body to the surface. On the cliff overlooking the bodaaris' plain, they set Zarina's body alight in accordance with gypsul tradition. Slowly, over time, her skin would turn to ash and drift away with the wind, carried by the God she loved with all her heart.

They each took a moment to say a few words. Some wishing her well, others promising to find her again in the next life. Maya thanked her for all she had done, but said little else. Unlike the others, Maya would never see the gypsul again, her soul now forbidden from the spirit realm with the pacts she had made with the Gouram.

With the ceremony concluded, they trundled through the snow on the hunt for the remainder of their gear. So much had been lost; four tents, nearly all their rations, and at least half of their fire paste. After hours of searching, they decided to cut their losses and began the long trek down the mountain passages, back the way they came.

16
PLANS AND DREAMS

SOUTHERN OUTLANDS ~ ESTERBELL

"I hope we never come to the mountains again. It's beyond cold. I think I might have lost a toe," Keela complained.

"You should get yourself a Maya," Thelic said, turning his head to regard the shivering Esterbellian behind him. "She's like a small furnace now." At first, he had thought Maya was running a fever. But after several days of trekking through the mountain pass, her strength had slowly returned, and yet the fever remained.

"Maya, come and have a cuddle," Merthus called from beside Keela.

Thelic's grip tightened across Maya's waist, forbidding it.

"You're warm enough as it is, Thelic. Let me go and warm the others," Maya said, trying to wriggle free from his hold.

"Not in this life *or* the next am I letting you snuggle next to that man. I know where his hands have been." While it had been intended as a joke, Thelic felt Maya's body go rigid against his chest. "What is it? What's wrong?" He loosened his grip, worried he might have squeezed her too tightly.

In this life…or the next. The words churned over and over in

Maya's mind. Thelic didn't know. How could she tell him that she wouldn't be able to join him in death, something that came increasingly close with every stretch of their journey together?

"Maya?" The soft edge in Thelic's tone pulled her back to the present. He knew she was hiding something, and she knew it would only hurt him more to think she wasn't able to confide in him.

"Pavinic…the Gouram, he told me something." She leaned her head back against Thelic's chest and closed her eyes. "You were wondering what the cost was for using my powers, for contracting with the Gouram. Well, he told me."

Thelic shifted his weight slightly back to see her face. "You have no life band – well, none that I can find," he said with a sly smile. "I'm assuming it doesn't take your essence?"

Maya turned her head to the side, away from him. "No, it doesn't. Though, both Pavinic and my grandmother warned there was a price, that too much use of the Gourams' power could cause my body to fail."

"Then you won't use it. Not unless your life is already in danger," Thelic said. To him, it was that simple.

"That's not the only thing," Maya said, her breath hitching slightly. "My all-access pass to the spirit realm has been revoked. When I die, which could be tomorrow or… thousands of years from now, I won't be able to move on. I'm immortal, Thelic. We won't be together in the next life." Tears sprung to Maya's eyes. It was absurd. She had never been religious or believed in any sort of afterlife, and yet now it meant the world to her. She had seen ghosts and met with Gods, there was no doubt in her mind that such a place existed. And she had been barred from it.

Thelic was frozen at her back, with no words of comfort or barks of outrage. He stayed that way for so long, Maya's tears had dried, and she turned her head to look up at him. His jaw was solid, and his eyes held a determination that warmed her.

"I'll find a way, Maya. Whether my soul has to remain here with yours or we ask the Gods to remove your seals, we'll find a way." Thelic brushed a gloved finger along her jaw and lifted, leaning over to seal his promise with a kiss. "Let me worry about it, you have enough in your cup."

Maya chuckled. "I think you mean plate, not cup." At Thelic's confused expression, she explained. "The saying is – you have enough on your plate." She felt the tension ease from them both and relaxed against him. They *would* find a way; she was sure of it.

THREE DAYS HAD PASSED before the sounds of Keero's soft plods through the snow turned to the cracks and booms that told them they had made it back to the frozen river. Maya had spent her time moving from person to person, acting as the group's portable heater. All except Kadhim. He had refused her offer of warmth, instead sitting at the back of Keero's tail away from the group as he tended to his wound. He barely spoke – not entirely out of character for the gypsul, but more concerning was the look in his eyes. A fire had burned there, a fight that Maya had admired. But that blaze was gone, it had died and been replaced with a dull glaze as he answered their questions with mumbled responses or a simple shake of his head. He was mourning, enduring a new fight that would either serve to make him stronger, or break him. Only time would tell.

The chill was one thing, but there was little Maya could do to stave off the aching hunger. With the majority of their gear lost in the bodaari stampede, their rations had depleted two days ago. Keero had managed to forage beneath the snow for bugs, ice weevils and hardy shrubbery, and at first, all but Thelic and Merthus had declined the rare, skittering feast of creepy crawlies. However, after a day of no food and at least two more days to follow, the others had eventually given in. While the hard-shelled beetles, writhing weevils and thorny stems of bitter plants had kept them going, tempers had mounted after day two and everyone was relieved to see the statues of Maelin's Bridge in the distance.

"I'm going to order a whole lipen," Keela muttered with a shiver as they passed the space between the stone statues of Lady Viveen and the crownless knight.

Maya had heard of a lipen before but had yet to see one. From what she could tell it was an Avalonian farm animal, and at the thought of bacon or ham with a tavern's concoction of honey glaze, her mouth watered.

"Just one? I'm ordering three," Merthus grumbled longingly. With it being his turn to borrow Maya's heat, he caught her waist between his thighs and tickled her ribs like an excitable school-boy.

"Knock that off, Merthus, or you'll lose your privileges... and a hand," Thelic warned from the front of Keero.

Merthus smiled slyly and locked his legs tighter, then tickled Maya again until she was wheezing and wriggling to escape. "What about you then?" he asked Maya. "Lipen? Or perhaps rasicus? You could do with *both* if I'm honest. You're far too skinny for my liking."

"Oh? And how exactly do you like your women, Merthus?" Maya asked, finally escaping his hold and crawling with her blanket to sit beside Keela.

"Big and boisterous. The more meat on their bones, the better!" he bellowed, wrapping his arms around himself as if such a woman were right there in front of him. His mood sobered and he dropped his arms to his sides, a soft smile replacing his grin. "My wife was an incredible lady, almost as tall as me and quite the looker."

"I liked your wife," Thelic said, glancing back to smile at Merthus. "She was a hell of a woman, especially with the way she kept you in check."

"How did you and Thelic meet?" Maya asked. Merthus had been an Esterbellian soldier, while Thelic had been in the service of both the Danikan and Fortusian Keepers. They were unlikely friends to say the least.

"Don't answer that," Thelic threw back in warning.

Merthus grinned, all traces of sadness gone and glad for the distraction from the loss of his wife. "I met Thelic when he was only a young lad, in a bordello of all places."

"I swear to the Gods, Merthus. Don't," Thelic seethed.

"Maya would have found out eventually, Thel. You should be proud of your past." Ignoring Thelic's threats, Merthus shuffled closer to Maya to relay the tale. "Thelic was under orders by Carnass to spy on Bandaar's daughter for a while."

Keela perked up at that. "*Me*? Why?"

Merthus waved a hand and shushed her, stating it was unimportant, before continuing. "Thelic knew that Keela would frequent a bordello to meet with a friend. And at the time, when I still worked in the Esterbellian Keeper's service, I was charged with protecting Keela from the shadows."

Keela's jaw dropped and her eyes almost popped from her head. She hadn't known that Bandaar had afforded her a protector during her younger years.

"Mm-hmm, that's right," Merthus said, catching Keela under the chin with a light touch of his fist. "Anyway, one day Keela was sitting at one of the tables with her friend, and a young dancer came onto the stage, dressed in a sheer and very pretty ensemble. It was unusual that the dancer was dressed at all, but the skills were...memorable, and I could barely take my eyes of her. Because of that, and my lack of intoxication from being on duty, I realised that the girl was in fact a young boy."

Maya dragged her gaze to Thelic. He had turned and was looking directly at Merthus with a mixture of disbelief, betrayal, and revenge. He scrambled across the packs on Keero's back with his arms outstretched to silence Merthus, but the former soldier had been prepared. With barely a halted breath, Merthus grabbed Thelic's arms and twisted, flipping him onto his front.

With a quick move, Merthus sat astride Thelic's back, keeping the younger warrior's hands locked in his grip whilst he proceeded to tell his story. "As I was saying, the boy possessed great skills – his little belly on show for the entire tavern's perusal, would dip and wave in the most mesmerising of ways."

Maya and Keela had been listening intently, then shared a look and burst into fits of giggles. Even Kadhim couldn't help but crack a hollow smile at the infectious laughter.

"You…you posed as a belly-dancer?" Maya asked, tears falling down her face as she gripped her aching stomach. The title seemed to reinvigorate Keela's own hysterical fits and they both fell on their backs at the mental images of a young Thelic thrusting his hips in an enticing and erotic dance for the bordello's patrons.

"That was you!?" Keela crowed as she remembered the dancer and his unusual performances every evening she had visited. "You were good!"

"See, Thelic? There's nothing to be ashamed of," Merthus teased with a squeeze of his thighs on Thelic's waist.

"So, now we know how you met, but how did you become *friends*?" Maya asked.

"Well, if Thelic behaves enough for me to let him up, I'm sure he will be happy to tell you." He leaned over Thelic's back and to the side to look him in the eye. "No maiming, okay?"

Thelic growled a reluctant promise and coughed as the bulking weight of Merthus was removed from his back. Coming up to his knees, he turned and gave his old friend a hard swat to the back of his bald head, then sat back and crossed his legs.

"Merthus wasn't the only one to discover I was acting under Carnass' orders," Thelic began, resigning himself to telling the short story. "Another Esterbellian soldier discovered I was a spy and tried to have me killed. I was beaten half to death and left to die at the back of the bordello, where Merthus found me. He took me back to his home, and his wife took to healing me." Thelic's eyes crinkled in a smile at the memory. "Mathild was entirely too good for you, Merthus. How you managed to convince her to wed you is still a mystery to me."

Merthus grinned then stroked from the shining top of his head to the end of his heavily scarred face. "It's all this charm and rugged handsomeness. How could she *not* fall for me?"

Maya had figured their newest companion was at least thirty years of age, but according to this tale – already wed and working as a soldier by the time he had met with Thelic – Merthus was probably closer to fifty. Maya leaned back against the tightly packed gear and smiled at her new knowledge. Who knew Thelic had lived such a colourful life?

∼

NIGHT HAD FALLEN by the time they reached the recognisable shapes of Arthur and Maelin. Taking a north-western path, they headed towards the Bloodywood in search of food and shelter from the gathering storm.

As Thelic, Maya and Kadhim set up what remained of

their tents, Keela and Merthus left on the hunt for food. With only two tents remaining, Keela and Maya would take one, while Merthus and Thelic shared the other, much to Thelic's annoyance.

Kadhim had been insistent that he would rather rest in his winshik form than sleep betwixt the snores and bad smells that would abound in the men's tent. Maya couldn't blame him. Even from the opposite side of the campfire, she had often woken to Merthus' bellowing snores.

It wasn't long before the hunters returned with rasicus and woodland scag. With the last of their fire pots, the food was skinned and cooked, the flames kept safe from errant drops of rain using a combination of shredded tarp and thick forest leaves.

As Maya picked at her food, she regarded the others. Mealtimes had become quiet in recent days. While exhaustion was evidently a factor, the death of their friend weighed heavily on them all.

"I miss her," Keela said, holding her half of a rasicus limply in both hands. "She was so bloody talkative, and sometimes I thought she would never give it a rest…but now I miss it."

Maya chuckled softly. Keela had once seemed determined to invest as little of herself as possible in the lives of those around her. But slowly they had broken her down and made a small space for themselves in her heart.

Kadhim stiffened as he always did when the sadness threatened to overwhelm him. "She was very fond of you all. And she talked so much because she was proud of her heritage."

"She was a good fighter, too," Thelic offered. There was more; like how much he had trusted her, not just with his own life but with Maya's.

"I would still like to go to your tribe. I think we all should, to meet with her mother," Maya finally said.

Kadhim nodded appreciatively, first to Maya and then to all who had spoken kindly of his friend. "When we have the final Gouram seal, we will need to travel to the Northern Outlands to Bodhisia's Valley. My tribe lives in that region, and it would only take us a day off-course to reach them. Her mother would appreciate it."

Maya and the others looked to each other and then, in a chorus of agreement, nodded their heads. They had almost forgotten about Merthus until he spoke up.

"You want to go to a gypsul tribe?" Merthus asked incredulously. "I mean, I know *you* are trustworthy, Kadhim. You saved my neck back in that snowfield. But can we really trust that *all* your people will be so welcoming?" Merthus held out his hands and shrugged. The question was innocent enough, and he didn't want to offend Kadhim or the memory of Zarina. Still, he had only recently decided to join this quest to save a world, and already it was proving to be more dangerous than he could have imagined. He had to be sure.

Kadhim's emotions were barely held in check, and if Merthus had asked the same question only days before, he probably would have lunged for him. Now he sighed, it *was* a good question. "Some will probably reject bringing humans onto tribal territory, that's true. But those who stand behind you will far outweigh those who don't. I can avow to that much," Kadhim said quietly.

Merthus seemed to assess the gypsul, watching him closely for a moment before shrugging again and resuming his meal. "Had to ask. So, where do we start? You have the water seal and the fire one, where's the next?"

Thelic pulled the map from the bag at his side. He traced his finger from their position in the south of Esterbell, all the way up to a temple marked in the north of the territory, seemingly smack bang in the centre of the Keep. "I guess we'll probably skip this one, shall we?"

Maya shuffled closer and saw where his finger lay over her father's heavily guarded home. Nudging his finger aside, she noticed the triangle was simple, the right way up and with no lines in the middle. "That's the symbol for fire, and we already have it as I'm sure you remember. We need to head west, so what about Cantor?" She traced her finger over the channel to the next territory. Three symbols were spread evenly along the landmass of Cantor, one in the north, one in the south and one in the middle. "Two of them are smudged so it's hard to tell."

"Let me see," Keela said, leaning over Maya's lap to take the map from Thelic. "Hmm, the southern one is definitely water, see the way it's upside down?" The triangle was smudged and barely recognisable, but Maya nodded. "The central one is clearly earth, and the last one...not a clue," Keela finished.

"Well, that's two possible contenders for the earth seal then," Kadhim said, glad to have a line of bearing on their next target to distract him.

"Is it worth the risk though?" Maya asked. "My grandmother seemed sure the Gouram of earth was resting in the Deadland Lakes, right here." She pointed on the map to a mountainous region in the Western Outlands, across the channel from Cantor. "I think we should avoid staying in the territories whenever we can and head straight there."

"Fatari has been wrong in the past. If we're in the area it makes sense to check out the other temples before moving on," Kadhim insisted.

"I'm inclined to agree with him," Keela said thoughtfully. Her particular experience with the Seer's miss-telling of a prophecy had painted Keela as the one to betray their group, when in fact it had been Elkin all along. "Sika supports our goals for now, so we're in no danger of him or the Cantorian soldiers. I think we should check it out."

A tight clench in Maya's gut suggested otherwise, her instincts compelling her to object, to insist they continue past the Cantorian territory and head for the Lakes. But they had a point, and it would waste a great deal of time if they got to the western mountains only to find that her grandmother had been wrong about the Gouram's location.

"Sika? The Cantorian Keeper?" Merthus asked Keela as he ripped at the meat with his teeth. "How'd you manage to get *his* blessing?"

"He's...an old friend," Keela said, her smile serpentine as she added, "And Maya's future husband if all goes well." Sika's note to Maya after assisting their escape from his territory had suggested as much.

Thelic chucked the scag bones to the side, imagining Sika's body lying next to the discarded carcass. "I'd like to see him try," he muttered. Eager to move on from the topic, he returned to their previous argument. "We'll need to head to the ice passage tomorrow then. It means leaving Keero behind again, so we'll be travelling on foot until we can purchase some karkili, unless you're so sure about Sika's loyalty that you would risk getting a ferry into the main port?" he asked pointedly to Keela.

"Those aren't the only ways," Merthus pointed out. "I know a fella who could take us over the channel. It'll cost a fair amount of coin though, and I don't have enough for all of us."

"Coin isn't an issue. Who do you have in mind?" Thelic asked.

Merthus looked anywhere but directly at Thelic and muttered a name under his breath. When Thelic and the others continued to stare at him, he sighed and repeated himself. "Falkin."

"Falkin Regold? As in the same man that's being hunted for running huffer across the territories?" Keela asked, the food in her mouth barely chewed as she swallowed the hard lump. "Are you mad? How do you even know him?"

Merthus scratched the top of his head, wondering how best to describe his acquaintance with the most notorious drug runner in Avalon. "He's saved my backside a few times, and I used to work with him after leaving Bandaar's service."

Keela spluttered an unintelligible response, but Maya interrupted. "What's huffer? And how can this man help us?"

While Keela and Merthus tried to find their words, Thelic filled Maya in on the substance known throughout the realm as huffer. "You remember I was telling you about Brijid's days as a drug runner? How she invented the old variant of waker? Well, she also helped Falkin create huffer. It's nasty stuff if I'm honest, and one of Brijid's greatest regrets. She had intended the drug to act as something to be used in conjunction with a healant. It numbs the body and mind so surgical manoeuvres can be carried out with little pain to the client. It's also highly addictive."

"I've known soldiers to lose their minds over the stuff after a single dose, it's *more* than addictive. And you're *friends* with this guy?" Keela asked, surprised by Merthus' choice of social circles.

"Friend is a bit of a strong word, but I know he'll help us for a decent price, and his vessel is big enough that Keero can come with us."

Thelic considered that. He loved his shaggy comrade and knew he would be useful in a number of ways, not least of which being they could travel with all the heavy gear required for the wilds. If they could bring Keero along, he would be glad of it. "That sounds like the best plan so far."

"It sounds like the *only* plan," Maya agreed. She didn't want to leave Keero behind again any more than Thelic.

Quietness descended as they each tried to come to up with something different. None prevailed, and the rest of their meal was enjoyed in companionable silence, before the first watch began their shift.

MAYA SLEPT FITFULLY THAT NIGHT. Haunting nightmares of villagers with pitchforks, all chanting for death. In the dream she walked along a path, her hands covered in blood. She didn't know or understand where she was or how she had come to be there, but she had a sense of regret, reflected in the way she ambled forward in a desperate bid not to glance behind her. At first, she thought she was alone, but as she looked around, Merthus stood to one side, his face and clothes stained with the blood of his friends and his enemies. On the other side stood Loki and BB. But there was one more that stood alongside the Finkels. A third creature. A tabby cat.

17

FROSTED FIRE

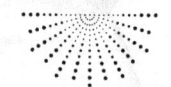

THE BLOODYWOOD – ESTERBELL

Merthus' plan to use the drug runners' port would require travelling through the centre of the Bloodywood. They had considered trekking around it, taking a semi-circular route heading first south and then following the wood's edge back up north along the shore. However, that ran the risk of meeting more bandits known to frequent the ice passage.

Maya had forgotten what the depths of the Bloodywood was like; how the wood itself seemed alert to those who passed. Something always seemed to be lurking, stalking… hunting. Some might have found the place to be tranquil in its soft sounds, but the odd hoot and snapping branch kept the group on high alert with the knowledge that this place had earned its ominous name.

At the first stream, Keero was allowed to stop and rest while the others refilled their water pouches and foraged for roots, berries and herbs along the embankment. Initially, Maya had been unsure about drinking from the river, the water running slightly reddish and honouring the forest's name. Thelic had put those fears to bed, teaching her the colour was due to harmless mineral deposits further upstream. That wasn't all she learned. Over time, Maya was being taught to correctly identify the edible varieties of plants and their deadly toxic cousins.

Maya yelped as her hand was smacked barely inches from a mushroom with black spots speckling its stem. Once Keela was finished chastising and accusing Maya of trying to poison the lot of them, she helpfully pointed to an almost identical mushroom with very dark *brown* spots. It became a conditioned response, to the point where Maya would indicate to a root or shroom before even attempting to pick it.

They carried on in this way as they trekked through the forest, stopping every now and then to hunt and replenish their supplies with rasicus meat and small fashgi from the streams. After a while, they began to relax as Keero plodded along their bearing, each chatting about the meals they planned to order from the first tavern they came across, or how long they intended to soak in a nice hot bath.

Maya suggested they spend an extra day at the Cantorian tavern that Merthus believed they would encounter half a day after crossing the channel. She had barely gotten the words out when Thelic hushed them, holding a finger to his lips with a look of warning.

As their voices died down, the sounds of the forest became more pronounced, and a low growl echoed amongst them. A warning from Keero, the beast's sensitive ears picking up on something their eyes and ears could not.

An arrow whizzed past Maya's face, the fletched feathers grazing her cheek on its flight. The shock of it caused her to cry out, and she rolled backwards off the bodaari just as a storm of arrows followed after. Thelic sprang to the centre of Keero's back and lifted his spear, spinning it at such a speed, sparks flew as the arrows clanked against the whirring shield of the metal haft.

A grunt of pain sounded nearby, and Maya turned from behind Keero to check on the others. Everyone had taken shelter behind Thelic's shield of metal and air, all okay with no signs of injury. All except Kadhim.

"Where the hell is Kadhim?" Maya shouted. The arrows had stopped, and further grunts erupted from the forest directly in front of them. A shock of red in the depths of the darkened trees caught Maya's attention amidst quickly moving figures. Kadhim's hands were wielding a thin sword, Zarina's weapon, something he had kept close since her death.

"He's over there!" Keela called, breaking from cover.

With instructions for Keero to stay put, they sprinted towards the sound of clanging blades and stopped short as two gypsul sprang from the underbrush to ambush them. Thelic stepped in front of Maya, bringing his spear up just in time to stop the stone dagger from penetrating his heart. Merthus lifted his blade, cutting the gypsul's blue hands at the wrist in one swing.

Keela stepped back as the second gypsul swung his dagger at her throat. With her own blades gripped in both hands, she ducked and lunged forward, only for a fiery creature to cut her off as it crashed into her chest. She flew backwards, hitting an adjacent tree-trunk with so much force, leaves from the canopy drifted onto the battlefield like snow.

With Thelic and Merthus occupied by another gypsul coming to the aid of the first, Maya sprang forward to intercept Keela's attacker. With her blade raised, she parried her opponent's jab then thrust a fist into the man's throat before delivering a powerful, round-house kick to the side of his head, knocking him out.

A hiss accompanied the sound of tittering feet along dead leaves. The fire sprite slithered amongst the trees, a blaze of fire in its wake as it watched its master fall. Hundreds of tiny, flaming legs moved lightening quick to pull its snake like body along the ground. Sweeping into a wide curve, it doubled back to intercept Maya as she summoned her own sprites.

The Finkels launched into action without waiting for a command, cutting their opponent off before it could reach Maya. Water, air, and fire collided in a snarling mass as BB tried to drench the creature, only for its size to grow and expand too quickly to be quelled by the water. Loki morphed into a tornado, desperately trying to imprison the fire sprite, but it broke free.

A grunt of pain sounded behind Maya, and she risked a glance back. Another sprite had joined the fray, attacking Thelic and Merthus alongside its gypsul master. The mud and clay gollum-like creature broke apart with every one of the humans' strikes, only to rebuild itself from the ground around it. An impossible enemy.

A chilling, chattering hiss sounded at Maya's front and she returned her attention to her own opponent. The flaming centipede was impossibly quick, its tendrils licking the spots along its body to relight wherever BB had quenched.

Maya slid the blade across her palm and concentrated on forming a plan to relay to her sprites. Perhaps sensing Maya's power, the creature's body twisted to where she stood, just as the first of the castor circles emerged and a fierce light illuminated every shadow, every corner of their surroundings.

With the gypsul momentarily distracted by the glow of Maya's power, Kadhim stepped forward and brained his opponent with the hilt of his sword. He turned to where another gypsul stood a few feet away, watching the scene before him with interest as he idly picked leaves from his long, blonde hair. He flicked his eyes to Kadhim who had begun his careful approach. Utterly unperturbed, the stranger smiled and pointed a long, taloned finger to indicate something behind him. Kadhim turned, just as the fire sprite leapt at Maya.

Maya grunted as the top half of the flaming creature slammed into her chest and knocked her to the ground. She had tried to regroup her Finkels, but the fire sprite had appeared within half a second and knocked the breath from her lungs. She found her voice again and gasped as its sharp legs dipped into her skin, hundreds of thick needles burying themselves along her chest and abdomen, where the glow of the Gouram's seal intensified.

All of a sudden, the creature's weight shifted as BB and Loki slammed into the sprite and cast it into the trees. Maya swore as small spots of blood marred her coat. She rolled to the side and blinked, her pain momentarily forgotten at the sight of a bright orange tabby cat grooming itself beside a tree not too far from her.

"Pavinic?" Maya whispered, unsure if she was hallucinating the house pet she had seen in the in-between, so oddly out of place in Avalon.

The cat lowered its paw and rolled its dark amber eyes in a disturbing display of comprehending her words. Rising from a casual seated position, it sauntered over to Maya, pausing temporarily as Loki, BB and the fire sprite whipped past in a swirling mass of chaos. Once the path was clear, it continued forward then stopped to sit by Maya's side.

"You're not doing terribly well at controlling our power. Are you, halfling?" the cat purred with a hint of irritation.

Maya baulked at the familiar voice of the Gouram, taken aback by the unexpected words from a very unexpected source. Behind her, Thelic called her name, trying to determine if she was alright before ducking to avoid another strike from his gypsul opponent. She raised a hand and waved, still awestruck by the talking cat and wanting him to see it too.

"Pay attention, Mayara. You are better than this," the cat growled.

"You *are* Pavinic! How are you here, outside of the spirit realm?"

"Silly child," he muttered, flicking his ringed, ginger tail in annoyance. "The creature I currently inhabit is merely an extension of my essence, just as the others are. Use your contracted sprites wisely, or you will be quick to suffer the cost of immortality before you have had a chance to fulfil your duty."

"You suit being a cat," Maya grumbled as she rose to her feet.

"Quiet. Close your eyes and harness the power we have given you. Project it to your guardians, and command."

Maya did as the cat instructed and closed her eyes. Beneath her feet, the three circles shone with a blinding brightness and the battle paused as each opponent cast a hand over their face to block out the light.

Combine.

Only the single word was uttered in Maya's mind. Loki, BB and the cat shuddered as power rippled through them. Slowly their forms dissolved into a smoky mass, before reforming as a single entity. A fox-like hybrid emerged, three times the size of a single Finkel, with three tails formed of fire whipping from left to right. Its body was as hard as rock. No fur and no sapphire scales. Instead, it bristled with dagger-like icicles as it pawed the earth menacingly. Maya's hybrid leapt forward, twisted, and battered the fiery centipede with its tails, sending the creature sprawling onto the forest floor. Without hesitating, the fox-like sprite bowed to the ground, its entire body vibrating with an unseen force, just before the razor-sharp ice along its back launched at the quickly recovering opponent.

The fiery centipede roared in pain as the sharp projectiles

broke through its hard-shelled skin. Maya thought it wouldn't be enough, that the ice would surely melt upon impact. Instead, thick frost bloomed from the impact sites to spread across the creature like a fast-forming disease.

The hybrid dashed to the writhing centipede's side, then transformed back into a smoke-like mass to flood down the fiery throat. Flames burst and crackled along the creature's gut, until its many legs began to slow and freeze completely. It stilled, a statue of ice, then exploded into crystalline fragments that melted and faded until nothing remained.

Maya's body shook as she finally lowered her arms. Growls and grunts rang out from behind her, a reminder that the threat was far from over. Instructing her sprites to return to their original forms, she turned and almost toppled to the floor.

Kadhim and Keela rushed to steady her the moment Maya's hands had dropped, signalling the end of her cast.

"Stand back," Maya ordered them, shaking her hands free as she faced the next opponent. It was hard to get a clear line of sight as Thelic and Merthus ducked and lunged, narrowly avoiding the vicious swipes of a creature Maya had never seen before. The earth sprite had taken the form of the rabbit-like rasicus, only twice the size and double the deadliness with impressive stone claws.

Maya raised her hands again and prepared to send one of her guardians to join the fight. Pulling the power from the castor circle, she pushed it out towards the first of her sprites and gasped at the strain on her chest. She coughed, almost faltering as blood splattered the sleeves of her outstretched arms.

"Maya, stop!" Kadhim called. He reached out for her, only to meet an invisible force that instantly repelled him. Loki. Maya had instructed the Air Finkel to act as her defence, should the earth sprite decide to cut off her power at its source.

With BB remaining by her side, Maya sent the cat to assist Thelic and Merthus. The sight was almost laughable – a small tabby racing to join them in battle. Just before it reached the scene, fire burst from its fur and it morphed to the size of a flaming lion. It leapt onto the earth sprite, sending them both careening into the trees behind in a clash of fire and claw.

Maya dropped to her knees and gathered what little energy remained to steady her command of the cat. From the corner of her eye, she saw Thelic turn and shout something. He was coming, he would try to stop her. She could just about make out the cuts and bruises along his jaw and the line of blood from a slash across his chest. She had to stop the earth sprite now, before she passed out. Marshalling the last of her power, she willed the cat to destroy the clay monstrosity.

Thelic slammed into Loki's wall and cursed. He dropped to his knees directly in front of Maya. "Let me in," he growled.

"Move, Thelic," she warned. She could barely see, his face a blurry twist of shapes and colours. Red stood out the most. Blood. *His* blood. She had to stop the sprite.

"Maya, remember what the Gouram said. Stop, now!" he roared, slamming his fists into Loki's shield.

A whistle rang out over the forest and the earth sprite ceased its attack, then disappeared. Thelic twisted his body to search the surrounding trees and spotted a man, a gypsul, standing over the body of one of his comrades. Thelic clenched his teeth and raised his spear. He hadn't realised any of the gypsul were still standing.

With its opponent pulled from battle, the cat returned to Maya's side, walking straight past Thelic and through Loki's barrier before jumping onto her shoulder and licking her face. The feel of the cat's tongue left a wake of warmth across her cheek and Maya dropped her hands, calling her sprites to return and rest within her.

The moment Loki's wall disappeared, Thelic rushed forward, brushing a hand over Maya's cheek and restraining the urge to voice his complaints for using so much of her contracted power.

"This is an odd sight," the gypsul stranger said, abandoning his semi-conscious friend to approach them. "Humans and gypsul working together." He peered down at Maya as he brushed leaves from his golden hair and mud from his dark jacket. "Strange to see such power, and from a *human* of all creatures. This seems like a story worth knowing."

"Why did you attack us?" Kadhim growled, stepping forward and raising Zarina's sword till the tip met with the stranger's chest.

The gypsul glanced down, unperturbed by the threat, and crossed his arms. "From what I could tell, *you* were either a very placid captive, or a traitor to your kind. Why *wouldn't* I attack you?"

"We were no threat to you, why not just let us pass?" Maya asked, accepting Thelic's outstretched palm as she struggled to her feet.

"Haven't you heard?" the stranger asked with a tilt of his head. "The war is soon to be upon us. A few dead humans now would mean less dead gypsul when the fighting finally breaks out." He paused and dropped his gaze to the exposed seal on Maya's chest. "Something inside me whispered, instructed me to capture you, woman. Now I see why. You are human, and yet you harness the favour of a god."

A faint outline of the circles continued to glow at Maya and Thelic's feet. Maya tried to stand tall, to look formidable and deserving of the power. "You're right. And I'm not just human, I'm half gypsul as well." She wobbled, nausea accompanying her clouded vision. Spotting a fallen log, she pushed past the gypsul to take a seat, and pretended to fix an errant lace of her boot. All three of the sprites appeared by her side, Pavinic's cat nudging under her arm to gain access to the wound on her palm.

As Thelic and the others joined her, the gypsul turned to regard them all once again. Seeing Maya's Finkels, he was quick to make his assumption. "And not just *one* god, I see. You've certainly been busy. What foolish person, gypsul or otherwise, would ask for such a power?"

"Enough," Thelic said with a deadly calm. "She doesn't have to answer any of your questions. Don't be fooled, she isn't the only one with power among us. Move along, or I'll cut you down."

"No," Maya said, the sound more like a wheeze and prompting her to cough up the acidic bile at the back of her throat. "You and these people, you're shaders, aren't you? You've gone rogue, left your tribes to attack the human settlements."

The stranger looked down his nose at Maya and smirked. "We don't answer to that. Our hearts aren't shaded, they finally see the truth. The humans would see us destroyed. We simply want to save our people."

The gypsul that Kadhim had knocked out several feet away began to stir. Sitting up, he turned his head and locked on to Maya. "That one, we need that one. Trivan, get her!" he bellowed to the man standing before the group. When Trivan refused to move, the gypsul sprang to his feet and darted forward, raising his dagger with a guttural scream.

Merthus jumped up to intercept, but Trivan was upon his raging comrade first. He lashed out an arm, catching him by the throat before moving his hands to hold the man's face. He muttered an apologetic prayer, then twisted, snapping the gypsul's neck. The stranger, Trivan, released his friend and let him slump to the floor.

"How many of you have gone mad since you all decided to leave your tribes?" Maya asked, her gaze shifting from the dead gypsul to Trivan.

Turning to face the puzzling woman, Trivan's head tilted to one side, surprised by what he saw. Sympathy had softened the corners of Maya's eyes, a small, apologetic grimace across her closed lips. "You pity me?" he asked, mystified by her reaction.

"No," Maya said. "But I know what's happening to you and your people. That man, I'm betting he was possessed by a spirit previously trapped in the chaos of the void. I assume he became enraged not long after you ventured close to the boundary?"

Trivan considered this, thinking back to when his friend had first displayed the symptoms of mania. "We came from the southwest...and yes, we did come close to the boundary void. But he has been fine for days, no more than mildly irritable."

"I believe that's how it starts. The spirit begins to fester in the human or gypsul host, slowly driving them mad. How quickly that happens depends on the strength of the spirit and that of the person it inhabits." Maya thought back to her discussion with her grandmother and relayed to him the source of her information.

"You are the Seer's kin?" Trivan asked.

"Yes, and if you're willing, I can help you and the others here." Maya looked past him to the several dead bodies littering the forest floor. Only two had been left alive and had already begun to stir nearby, groaning from their injuries.

"Maya," Thelic warned. She turned to face him, and he reached to wipe the blood from her mouth, his shoulders rigid. "You don't owe them anything, and you've used too much power as it is."

Maya smiled and placed a hand on his thigh to give it a reassuring squeeze. "Trust me, Thelic. We need them." Shifting forward on the fallen log, she made a move to stand and a second wave of nausea threatened to finish her completely. Placing both hands on her thighs, she allowed a moment for the world to stop dipping and swaying.

"Perhaps you should rest first?" Trivan asked, though the clipped edge of his tone implied he wasn't in any mood to wait for a human to sleep off her power hangover.

"I'll be fine. Do you want my help or not?" Maya asked with an exasperated sigh.

"I'll listen to your proposal. But I can't promise my men will agree."

"Fine, but if I do assist you, I want something in return."

Trivan's brows shot up and an amused smile replaced his irritation. "Oh? And what might a halfling want from the likes of us?"

"Have you heard of Slitter Ridge?" Maya asked. "Do you know Horticus, the Elder there?"

Thelic realised what Maya intended and something inside him was pulled in two directions. She was trying to bolster the gypsuls' fighting force. But Thelic himself was human, and while he had come to know and respect a number of tribesmen, he couldn't help but feel concerned that he had already been forced to choose a side in the coming war.

Trivan nodded his head, amusement fading as suspicion bloomed. "Yes, I know of the Ragashian Elder. What about him?"

"When I have removed the spirits from your bodies, I would like you to gather as many of your people that are willing and go to the Ragashian Tribe. Their forces are already building, and he can help you understand what it is I'm trying to accomplish.

"And what, exactly, are you trying to accomplish, halfling?"

Maya ground her teeth and tried to ignore Trivan's patronising tone. "My friends and I will take down the boundary void and close the gateways. But in return, we want the humans who reside here now to have the freedom to live out the rest of their lives in peace in this realm."

All emotion left Trivan's face, until he tipped his head back and laughed. "You!? You think you can take down the chaos? Not even the Gods have managed such a feat!"

"I can do it. The Seer has seen it happen, and as you can tell, the Gouram are on hand to assist." Maya held her hands wide, indicating the last of the circles glowing beneath her.

For the first time, Trivan noticed the flowers newly blossomed beneath their feet as they had been talking, brown and black, camouflaged but utterly beautiful next to the patches of deadened forest floor. "What in the Gods…"

"It's the Gourams' essence, it renews life," Maya explained. "When I help you, go to Horticus. He will explain everything you need to know. Do you accept?"

Trivan wasn't sure. This power, it was too much for a human. Half gypsul or not, it would consume her before she had a chance to do any good with it. A voice in the back of his mind told him no; told him to ignore her; or better yet to kill the others and take her for himself. He could use her power to kill all the humans plaguing their realm. Trivan shook his head to rid the instinct for chaos, and watched as the young halfling appeared crestfallen, misreading the shake of his head for a refusal to her request.

Maya sighed. "You must understand–"

"If you help us, I will rally the remainder of my forces and go with them to Slitter Ridge" Trivan said.

Pleased with the result, Maya jumped up more quickly than she had intended. Her legs locked then turned to jelly and she mumbled a curse as the ground came up to meet her. Before she knew it, Thelic caught and gently lowered her to lie amongst the flowers around them, his body leaning over hers.

"You asked me to trust you," Thelic muttered softly. "Normally I would, but when it comes to you looking out for your own well-being, I'm afraid that's asking a little much." He looked up at the others to relay the only plan he was prepared to stand for. "We'll set up camp and treat everyone's wounds first. Maya can help once she's had the chance to rest."

Trivan nodded reluctantly and turned to gather the remainder of his men. Maya closed her eyes and smiled, finally allowing the darkness to take her.

18

SHADED EXORCISM

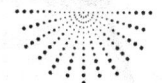

THE BLOODYWOOD – ESTERBELL

Whispers. Someone is whispering…

Maya tried to open her eyes. A sliver of amber light radiated through, and she promptly shut them again. Too soon. Too tired. The whispers continued and Maya recognised the slightly irate tone of Keela's voice coming from somewhere nearby. She forced the lead weights of her eyelids open again to see a flicker of light dancing along the inside of what she assumed was her tent. Gathering her strength, she turned her head to see Thelic was sitting to her left, one arm wrapped loosely around his spear as his forehead leaned against the shaft. A soft snore rose with every long breath and Maya realised he was sleeping. She tried to sit up as quietly as she could, but automatically groaned in pain at the stiffness across her body.

Thelic awoke with a start and pointed his weapon at the tent's opening. Seeing nobody there and confused at what had woken him, he turned and saw Maya in a half-seated position, trying to right herself.

"You shouldn't push it," he said, lowering his spear.

"How long was I asleep? I'm starving." Maya blushed as her stomach agreed with an audible rumble.

"Two days."

"What!? Are the gypsul still here?" She noted the dark circles under Thelic's eyes and the lengthened stubble he had grown during her rest.

"They're still here, unfortunately. I'm surprised you slept through the debates, they got quite...heated," he said with the ghost of an amused smile. "How do you feel?"

"Exhausted. Sore. Tired. You know, the usual," Maya said with a soft chuckle. A cold nose bumped the side of her arm, followed by another and the soft flick of a tail.

"They've stayed by your side the entire time," Thelic said, indicating the Finkels and Pavinic's cat. "Anyone that tried to approach the tent soon changed their mind with this lot growling at them." He smiled and stroked the soft fur down Loki's back. It was because of the sprites that he had managed to get any sleep at all.

"I'm sorry I worried you," Maya said softly.

Thelic's jaw tightened. "You said you were going to use your powers wisely. You said you would only use them to protect yourself."

"No, I didn't. *You* said I should do that. At the end of the day, Thelic, I need you. I need all of you if I have any hope of doing what needs to be done. So, when I see the man I love and our friends in danger, I won't just stand by and watch. This isn't me being reckless, this is me being pragmatic."

Thelic softened at her words, at three words in particular. "You know, you shouldn't be so quick to throw that sort of declaration around. There are consequences."

"What declaration?"

Abandoning his spear to the side, Thelic sprung forward to straddle Maya's body, careful to hold his own weight as he pushed her shoulders lightly down, forcing her to lay back amongst the blankets. His hands moved to either side of her face, his arms a defensive wall as he leaned down to kiss her.

"A declaration of love, Maya. I spent so long waiting for those three little words, now they drive me mad anytime I hear them. While you may not be in any fit state to suffer the consequences now, I'll be happy to take it from you later."

She chuckled. "Promises, promises, Thelic Anthon. I think I'm well enough to pay my dues right *now*." She raised her hands and was about to pull him down to her, then stopped at the sound of someone retching just outside the tent.

"Don't you dare!" Keela barked from where she sat by the campfire. "There isn't enough moss in this forest to drown out the sounds of you two fulfilling promises."

When Maya and Thelic finally emerged – promises unfulfilled – Maya was embarrassed to see not only Keela by the fire, but Kadhim and Merthus too, alongside Trivan and another of the gypsul. She dipped her head, hiding the blush that accompanied her mortified realisation they had heard hers and Thelic's private conversation.

"Breakfast?" Merthus asked, holding the gypsuls' gifted frying pan towards her with strips of scag and roots cooking in the centre. "Or have you had your fill of *meat*?" He smiled at the symphony of responses offered in return for his comment:

Kadhim coughed, accidentally inhaling a little piece of meat.

Thelic gave a wink in appreciation for the smutty joke.

Maya scowled and rolled her eyes.

Keela looked vaguely ill.

The tribesmen, however, looked mildly confused by the odd reaction to Merthus' question, much to the giant swordsman's surprise. Who knew the outlanders could be so innocent? Merthus chuckled at the odd mixture of people and refilled the pan after handing the cooked strips over to Maya.

Chewing hungrily on the slightly overdone meat, she regarded the gypsul. "I'm surprised you stayed. You didn't seem entirely convinced by my ability to help you."

"I'm curious to see how you intend to do it," Trivan said. "If you *are* right, and my people have been infected by the chaos, then history dictates the Gouram Stone is needed to draw the entities out."

Maya smiled at Trivan. "Well, it's a good job I have the Gouram Stone then, isn't it?" She reached into the sewn lining of her pocket and pulled the threads apart to release the Stone before holding it up to show them.

Trivan grinned, surprising Maya with the sincerity of it. "Aren't you full of surprises." He nudged the man to his left, whose withdrawn expression seemed to indicate he wasn't quite so convinced.

"Where's the other one?" Thelic asked as he accepted the food from Merthus. "There were three of you last I checked." He eyed the surrounding forest suspiciously, as if the other might be lying in wait to attack them.

"He isn't faring well, so we tied him up. He's over there if you don't believe me," Trivan replied, indicating a curled up, shivering mass a few feet away.

"Bloody hell," Maya muttered, shoving the rest of the meat into her mouth before rushing over to the hobbled and hog-tied gypsul. Half-buried in fallen leaves, his teeth chattered wildly as his whole body seized in violent shivers. "We shouldn't wait any longer, I don't know how long he might last if he stays like this."

"Why do you care?" Trivan asked, clearly unconcerned with the state of his friend. "It makes no difference to you if he lives or dies."

Maya clenched her teeth and faced Trivan. "On second

thought, maybe *you* should go first. Clearly whatever spirit has overtaken you is an asshole. Best we get rid of it before it leaves too much of an imprint."

Trivan flashed a grin, this time in challenge as he held his arms wide. "I'm all yours."

∼

TRIVAN LAY PLACIDLY on the ground and closed his eyes as Maya readied herself with the Gouram Stone. It took a moment as she calmed her breathing and thought of her power; of the steps she needed to take to carry out her task. With one hand clutching the Stone and the other lying across her chest, she summoned her power and channelled it through the opal. The Stone's colourful veins glowed and pulsed with renewed energy.

Something in Trivan moved and his eyes flew open. His hand shot forward against his will and latched onto Maya's wrist, talons digging into the soft flesh there. She winced but didn't pull her hand away, only looked to Thelic with a light nod of her head. With the silent command, Thelic came forward and secured Trivan's hands.

"I need you to fight it, Trivan," Maya said sternly. "It knows what we're up to, and it will try and kill every last one of us to maintain control of the host, of you."

Trivan struggled against Thelic's grip and kicked his legs into the air, trying to hit Maya. Thelic barked for one of the others to hold him down, and Keela stepped forward to assist. The other shader tried to barge his way past Merthus and Kadhim to help his panicked leader, but the duo easily subdued him.

Maya muttered the words, imploring the Gods to help her, and pleading with Trivan's original sprite to assist with pushing the uninvited entity from the gypsul's body. Trivan screamed as Maya thrust the Stone to his chest, using its power combined with her own to exorcise the chaos. She stubbled back and fell to the floor as the spirit was sucked into the opal, Trivan's body violently convulsing before falling still. He breathed raggedly, then sat up.

"Well? How do you feel?" Maya asked tentatively as she got to her feet.

"It's…quiet. I had gotten so used to the voices in my head, telling me…well, nothing good." He lifted his head to gaze at Maya, and just from the look in his eyes, Maya felt she was looking at a new man, a softer gypsul, one not so accustomed to the violence the spirit had seemed to crave.

"Excellent," Maya said, content with their success. "Bring the next one over."

Merthus and Kadhim dragged the struggling gypsul to where Maya was sitting and held him down as she steeled herself to go through the entire process again.

BY THE TIME the last of the shaders had been relieved of their chaotic spirits, dawn was breaking. Maya had spent the last two days tucked up in bed and recovering from overexerting herself, and yet she was ready to curl back under the blankets and block out the world once again to sleep for a week. As the others joined her by the remains of the fire, she remembered the taxing nature of the exorcism didn't just affect her, but them too.

"How does everyone feel?" Merthus asked. "We have enough meat and roots to feed a small village, so I can cook off some more if you want?" Everyone, including the shaders, nodded their heads enthusiastically at the offer.

After reassuring himself that his kin were well, Trivan took a seat by Maya's side. "I can't thank you enough for what you have done. I know there is a toll to be paid for using your power like that, and I'm struggling to understand why you would do it for folk that very recently tried to kill you and your friends."

Maya patted the gypsul's leg and accepted the cooked meat from Merthus before responding. "I told you, there *is* a price, both for you and for me. You must go to Slitter Ridge and meet with Horticus, but I also want you to give him a message."

"Yes, yes, I remember, and I will of course hold up my end of the bargain and gather those we left behind to go with me. What do you wish for me to tell him?"

Thelic and the others went quiet as Maya relayed her message for Horticus. "We found another of the seals, and we're close to the third. I want Horticus and his tribe to go to Bodhisia's Valley, where they will create and hold a united front against the humans until we get there."

"What!?" Keela squawked. "Are you forgetting that you're half human as well, Maya?"

"I don't want them to *attack* the humans, I want to afford the gypsul a chance to defend themselves, something that would only be possible in great numbers," Maya assured Keela and Merthus, who had stopped his cooking and stepped around the fire to confront her.

"Whose side are you on, Maya?" Merthus asked quietly.

"I'm not on anyone's side, but the gypsul are heavily outnumbered by the humans from what I can tell. At least this will give them a chance, and they might sway others who join them and advocate peace."

Keela and Merthus looked to one and other before he went back to cooking and she went back to picking at her meat. "I hope you know what you're doing, Maya," Keela said.

Maya's thoughts echoed the same, but her mind strayed to the faces of the children from Etiyan Vale and Traccia, the djinca from Slitter Ridge. They had all become friends, loved ones. Equally, Brijid's face crossed her mind, and she wondered for a moment.

"Maybe we should try and convince some humans to join the gypsul at Bodhisia's Valley? A *truly* united front. It might stop some of the Keepers' soldiers from an outright attack."

Keela and Merthus laughed coldly at Maya and shook their heads before Merthus responded. "They won't hesitate, Maya. That's how they're trained. If Bandaar or any of the Keepers command their forces to rain fire on a settlement, the soldiers will do just that, whether those who live there are gypsul, or human."

~

AFTER TAKING the rest of the day to restock their supply of meat and to rest, Trivan and the gypsul left Maya and the others in the night, with nothing but thanks and promises to relay Maya's message and bring his people to the eastern edge of Bodhisia's Valley.

Maya settled amongst the blankets of hers and Keela's tent and slowly drifted off to sleep, all the while wishing for Thelic's companionship in the hopes he might help stave off the dreams she now expected every time she closed her eyes.

SCREAMS ERUPTED around Maya as the villagers lifted their pitchforks and readied their bows. She stepped forward, as she always did when the dream took hold, and summoned the sprites. Pavinic's cat smiled ruefully up at her, enjoying the chance to exert its power and suppress the humans that descended upon them. Fire rushed from Maya's fingertips, spreading out of control to burn whatever stood in its path. She turned her head and felt her heart break at the sight of a little boy, dead, clasped in the jaws of Loki. Such a gentle sprite. Another gargling scream caught her attention and she turned to where a score of villagers were being trampled and smothered by the waves of water karkili summoned by BB.

A man knelt before her, begging, crying, cursing Maya for what she had done. Maya glanced down at her hands. Blood. So much blood. A dead woman was at her feet. Her pretty, auburn hair fallen across her face, her throat. A pool of blood pumped freely from somewhere beneath that beautiful hair.

"You killed her, you killed her, you killed her, you killed her…"

MAYA WOKE thrashing beneath the force of whatever had her pinned against the floor. A grunt of pain broke her panic, the sound of Keela cursing in the darkness.

"Dammit, wake up!" Keela shouted, pulling at the blankets Maya had tangled herself in. "Hey! Kick me again and I'll kick you back."

Maya stopped moving, her heart beating furiously with the words the man had chanted in her dream. It was a dream. Just a dream. She allowed Keela to help disentangle her from the blankets, then sighed in relief as her limbs pulled free. "Thanks, and sorry," she muttered, watching Keela nurse a sore spot on her jaw.

"Were you dreaming you were in a sparring match?" Keela grumbled.

Thelic and Kadhim broke through the canvas flap simultaneously, summoned by Maya's screams. She smiled at them sheepishly, but before she could offer her reassurances, a pillow smacked into their faces with Keela's warning to get out before something sharper followed.

"I'm fine, just a nightmare," Maya called as the two men sighed and retreated from the tent

"You're having those a lot these days. Every day, in fact, since your meeting with the Gouram of fire," Keela said, her tone mildly accusatory. Since that day, neither had managed to get an unbroken or decent night's sleep.

"I know. It's always more or less the same dream, too," Maya admitted with a shake of her head. She had once heard that the faces in dreams were always of someone you knew, someone you had met at least once in passing. But she was so sure she had never met anyone from these nightmares.

"Do you think..." Keela trailed off and shook her head. "Never mind. Get some sleep, it's nearly my shift."

Maya lay down and closed her eyes. *Burning. Death. Chaos.* Her eyes flew open and she bolted upright. "On second thought I think I'm rested enough. I'll take your shift."

Keela figured she probably should have insisted her sister rest, but with Maya on watch, she knew she would get a decent amount of sleep. "Okay, you do that," she said instead, rolling over with a wave goodbye.

Outside, Merthus was adding more twigs to a wonderfully intimate fire, with a small pot of broth bubbling at its centre. Upon hearing the ties of the tent loosen, he turned and was surprised to see Maya coming out to relieve him instead of the prickly huntress he had been expecting.

"That smells amazing," Maya whispered delightedly. She leaned over the pot and smelled something that brought back the memory of her mother's stew. "What is it?"

"Shrooms and fashgi, with the odd vegetable in there for good measure." Merthus grabbed the second bowl he had put to the side and filled it to the brim before handing it to Maya. "What are you doing up and about? I heard you tossing like a wajeer in heat. Bad dreams?"

Maya nodded and inhaled the steam rising from the bowl, washing away the worst of the nightmare's remnants. "I dreamt I was in a village and people were trying to kill us. I'm not sure why. Perhaps it's because everywhere we go someone tries to make our lives difficult." She chuckled and dipped her head to blow on the hot contents of her bowl.

"Well, from what the others have told me, you've all been through a fair whack of bad luck," Merthus said with a sigh. He stilled, staring across the fire at the woman before him. "But yet you carry on, you fight for a world that has done nothing but deal you ill-fated cards. I can't decide if I admire you, or pity you."

"Admiration is always preferable," Maya said, lifting the spoon to her mouth to taste it. Sweet, spicy, and instantly warming, the stew didn't disappoint. She tipped her head back and closed her eyes, focusing on the lingering aftertaste. "This is delicious, thank you."

Merthus chuckled and offered a curt bow for the comment. "My wife taught me. It's the best thing I can cook, and I do her justice with it." His face turned serious, fatherly almost in the way he raised a brow for the beginning of what would be his first lecture to the young woman. "Thelic told me the cost of your contracts with the Gouram. Did you know what you would be giving up?"

As the stew rapidly cooled, Maya drank hungrily from the bowl, draining half its contents before lowering it to her lap. "No. By the time Pavinic told me, it was too late as I had already made a contract with Batshari. I'm not sure it would have made a difference though. If I had tried to do the ceremony with just the small amount of the Gourams' essence I'd been granted at birth, it probably would have killed me."

Merthus stirred the pot, poking at bits of meat floating on the surface as he carefully considered his next words "I see. I'm sorry for the position you've been put in. You should try to keep in mind your overall purpose. Start putting yourself first. Otherwise, what is the point of your sacrifice?"

She knew he was talking about her summons against the shaders. "I can't just stand by and watch my friends in trouble, Merthus. You all seem inclined to believe that I'm ready to throw my life on the line for any old reason, but that's not true."

"Then educate me. Why would you risk yourself, knowing that you are the only one capable of saving this realm?"

"Because I can't do it alone. I need all of you just as much as you need me. And when it comes to Thelic, he's…" Maya couldn't find the words to emphasise just how much Thelic meant to her.

"He *is* your realm, your world. Meaning Avalon is nothing without him in it," Merthus offered with a sad and knowing smile.

"Does that make me selfish?" Maya stared into the empty bowl. She couldn't cook. She was a terrible hunter and even worse at foraging for roots and shrooms. She relied on their knowledge of this world's cultures and landscapes, each so different with every territory they entered. But she could fight, she could bleed, she could summon…She could do that much at least.

"No, it doesn't make you selfish, Maya."

Her shoulders slumped and she looked up, then released the breath she hadn't realised she was holding. Kadhim, Keela, even Thelic, none of them seemed to understand. But perhaps Merthus would.

"I almost died trying to save my wife, I would have given my life in her place if that offer had been on the table. I understand, Maya, truly I do. All I'm saying is, be careful. Be thoughtful before jumping into a fight, and give us a little credit, we're tough. We can take on a handful of soldiers, or shaders, or even the villagers from your nightmares.

Maya shivered at the memory of exactly that, of Merthus fighting and falling to such an enemy in her dreams. "I know. Thank you for coming, for helping us."

Merthus raised his hand and scuffled the already tangled

mess of Maya's hair to dispel the air of uneasiness. "Well, if you insist on staying up, then I will leave Keela's shift to you. I'll see you at dawn."

Maya said goodnight and stoked the fire, pulling the blanket around her shoulders more for comfort than for warmth.

"The human is right, in a way."

Maya jumped at the unexpected purr of the cat's voice and turned at the waist to see it cleaning its paws beside her. "You know, it's rude to sneak up on people," she mumbled, holding a hand to the thumping beat in her chest.

Narrowing its eyes, the cat lowered its paw to look tiredly at Maya. "You have a long way to go to realise the full extent of your power, Mayara."

"Teach me then. *Show* me what I'm supposed to do."

"I cannot show you, nor can I teach it. Just remember, you do not simply command our gift, you *are* the power, child. By taking water and fire into your spirit, you became those elements."

Maya stared blankly back at the God of fire. "That's not particularly helpful. Do you mean I can turn into a puddle of water?"

The cat rolled his eyes. "I will be watching. Remember my words," he warned, then vanished in wisps of smoke, leaving Maya alone once again.

Muttering an oath to the cryptic God, she pondered his words as she lay back amongst the blankets. Somehow, she had to learn to become the elements themselves. But for now something more pressing gnawed at her gut. By the following evening they would meet with the drug runners. What could possibly go wrong?

19
SMOKEY DECEIT

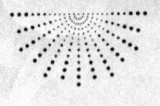

ESTERBELL

Maya was pleased to see that while her rest had meant they were several days behind on their journey, the others had made good use of the time and their location in the wood. With Merthus and Keela's hunting skills and roots littering the forest floor, they had gathered enough food for everyone to eat heartily for a week. Additionally, with the time they had been afforded, the meats were thinly sliced and dry-cured using a handy combination of Keela's heat and Thelic's air, making them suitable for storage in their packs.

By the time dawn erupted through cracks in the canopy, Keero was loaded up, and they began their trek with the plan to stop at Brushkin's Break first, where they hoped to gather more travelling essentials. Somewhat understandably, this particular idea had come from Thelic. After sleeping beside a man whose snores rivalled a bodaari, he was eager to return to Maya's bed, for the peace and everything else that came with sleeping beside a beautiful woman.

"You're still having nightmares," Thelic whispered in Maya's ear. "Anything I should be worried about?" He pulled the reins slightly left, navigating Keero around a prickly bush, then returned his attention to her as he kept their bearing.

Maya cringed at the reminder. Once again, her active dreams the previous night had woken the entire camp. "I'm fine. I think after everything we've been through my mind is entitled to go a little stir-crazy."

"Do you want to talk about them?"

"There really isn't much to talk about, Thelic. They're just not very nice. I'm sure they'll go away soon enough. I used to have them as a kid all the time. We call them night-terrors on Earth."

Thelic nodded, barely content with her answer. While he was doing all he could to protect her body, there was little he could do to guard her mind.

Less than half a day had passed before they reached Brushkin, and they barely stayed long enough to make an impression on the small town's people. With two new tents and medicine to replenish their pouches, they took to the path once again to head north on Merthus' bearing to the drug runners' hidden port.

"What exactly should we expect from these people?" Kadhim asked. It was the first time in a while he had indulged in idle chit chat without being prompted.

"They'll probably try and kill us at first," Merthus replied casually. "That's why I'll go alone to meet with them. Then, when I know they're not going to try anything, I'll return for you."

Maya opened her mouth to object to his solo plan, but relented as Merthus gave her a pointed look, reminding her of their previous conversation not to underestimate her comrades and better look out for her own well-being.

"I'll be going with you," Keela said matter-of-factly, "just in case things go awry." Though, she failed to mention that her trust was still a little lacking where the former Esterbellian guard was concerned.

Merthus rolled his eyes, suspecting as much, but gave no notion of rejecting Keela's intent to join him. Kadhim in turn nodded his head. He, too, planned to shift into his winshik form and keep an eye on them from the sky. While he had grown to trust Keela, he still wasn't entirely sure of their newest companion.

Following the shoreline, the group eventually left the Bloodywood behind and entered an open plain, with rocky outcroppings and deep hollows that hid beneath the waves of green hills. As they travelled adjacent to the water's edge, they passed a surprising number of people, some resting in the smaller caves, while others seemed to strike camp amongst the larger of the stony dunes.

The farther north they trekked, and the harder the rocks became to navigate, the less people they seemed to pass. Soon the landscape became eerily quiet, with only a gentle breeze rustling through the long grass. In contrast to the Bloodywood, the undulating plains appeared lifeless, with no creatures or skittering bugs. It seemed unlikely that in a place this open, albeit difficult to traverse, that drug runners would set up shop where any who passed could see what they were up to.

Smoke rose in the distance and Merthus instructed Thelic to stop Keero and pull into a rocky inlet where the others could rest while he and Keela continued forward. Maya slid down from her position astride the bodaari and clambered up one of the rock faces, ignoring the pain from her scabbed skin as she peered over the top.

In the near distance, a small stone cottage sat just off the shore overlooking a tiny island in the centre of the channel dividing Cantor and Esterbell. Despite being alone and far out of reach from any major town, the home was picturesque and lively, with two young children chasing each other on the back lawn.

"Are you sure we're in the right place?" Maya called down to Merthus, who was readjusting the straps of his sword's harness. "It doesn't seem like somewhere a drug operation might run from." She had been involved in several drug busts while serving in the Police in London, and no matter what front they used to hide their business, it almost always gave off a sense of seediness.

"Do you have the term, 'don't fornicate where you eat', in your realm?"

Maya suppressed a giggle. "Ours goes something like that," she said.

"Well, Falkin threw that out the window the moment he started the business. Seems to be working for him considering he has yet to be caught."

Maya scrambled down the rock to join the others, helping Keela with one of her blades that refused to go back into its sheath. "Is there any way you can signal us if things go nasty?" She hated the idea of sitting to the side while the others risked themselves, but understood the necessity. She wasn't sure why, perhaps something about the brutal honesty of their new friend, but she felt she could trust Merthus…to a degree.

"Keela signalled us with a bolt of fire when we were in the mountains, that's how we found you," Thelic explained to Maya. He turned to Keela. "If you get any sense of danger from the runners, do the same. We'll be watching from here."

∽

"Stay at my back, and let me do the talking," Merthus warned Keela as they approached the cottage from the shoreline. "I don't know how they'll react to me, but they never react kindly to someone they've never met before."

Keela nodded, sticking to his side and keeping one hand on each of her blades. As they wound their way up the pebble-dashed path, the stone cottage came into view. The place was oddly picturesque, with a roof, rich with thick moss and a stone chimney. Small, grimy windows occasionally broke the monotony of the grey walls, inside appearing dark with only the odd flicker of light from somewhere within.

Sitting on the porch steps, two children watched the strangers' approach. One girl and one boy, both dressed in innocent white with dark locks of hair tied in loose buns. The little girl stood and without a word rushed through the creaky front door. The little boy, no older than twelve, narrowed his eyes as he got to his feet and walked down the short path to meet them.

"You're a bigger fool than I thought, baldy," the boy said. "Falk's still looking to tear you apart after the last time. Best turn around before Sis tells him you're here." He proceeded to shoo them away, wafting his hands back and forth and taking a step towards them.

"Cheeky little shit," Keela muttered, appalled that a mere boy had been used as a gang's early warning system. "Go and fetch your father, leave the business to the adults," she said, offering the same offensive wave and taking her own step towards the boy. She yelped as an arrow burst against the rock at her feet, and gladly allowed it when Merthus pulled her back to stand behind him.

"Falkin, you old git. Come out here and greet an old friend properly." Merthus' request was met with a harsh laugh from within the house, moments before a very rotund and red-faced man opened the door and stepped outside.

"You've got the gall of a horny shropsin, Merthus. What could have possibly possessed you to come knocking at my door after so many years?" Falkin asked, his large body rumbling in a dark chuckle. "You're lucky I don't have my boy gut you from tit to toe."

"Now, now, let's not scar the poor lad, nobody wants to see my toes," Merthus replied with his own uneasy laugh. "We need your help."

"We?" Falkin's eyebrows rose in surprise as Keela stepped out from behind Merthus to offer a half-hearted wave. "I see. And exactly what do you want from me?" he asked.

"We need you to transport us to Northern Cantor–" Merthus paused at Keela's rushed whisper, that they in fact wanted to avoid the north and subsequently the Cantorian Keep. "Apologies, it's *central* Cantor we need to travel to. Myself, Keela here, and two others along with a bodaari will all need transport."

Falkin narrowed his eyes at the two, one chubby hand rubbing his belly thoughtfully. He turned and snapped his fingers to someone inside the house, telling them to bring him a chair. An archer appeared shortly after and placed a stout wooden stool just outside the door for the drug-lord to sit on. Using a thin, golden pick, Falkin picked at something in his teeth as he carefully considered the request. "So, it's true then?"

Merthus glanced down at Keela who had stiffened beside him. "Is what true?" he asked.

"There's a bounty on that young woman's head, and on the heads of those traveling with her," Falkin said, his wide and greedy smile stretching from ear to ear. "Bandaar himself issued the warrant I believe. He's offering a lot of coin for your return, princess."

"Damn," Keela muttered quietly. They should have used aliases. "We can offer you a lot more than what my father offers," she said.

Falkin's eyes widened considerably at the bold offer, a tad disbelieving. "I'm listening."

"Well, we can save this realm for a start. We know how to bring down the wall and end the chaos encroaching on Avalon. We can stop it all." Keela knew it was a long shot that Falkin would even believe her, but the rip-roaring laugh that bellowed from the man was not what she expected.

"Ha! I'm less inclined to help you then. The Gods know how many outlanders I've killed, and that scum will surely descend on me like a plague when their reinforcements arrive from beyond the chaos wall."

"It's going to happen, Falkin, whether you help us or not," Keela stated defiantly. "But if you *do* help us, we can promise you protection from the outlanders. And I can personally assure you that we will terminate the only real threat that stands between you and your trade, providing the freedom to carry out your business with no hassle when all of this is over."

Falkin regarded the woman before him in a new light, recognising the prospect of a very useful business partner in the future to come. "So, the little bird seeks her father's place on the highest branch. It's an interesting proposition," he murmured, lifting a hand to one of many chins. "And what of *your* debt to me, Merthus?"

Merthus sighed ruefully, having had high hopes the old man had forgotten what he owed. "It's yours. You will find it at my old home," Merthus assured him.

"Excellent! Well then, with a written promissory note from the lovely Keela, my associates and I will escort you across the channel and then to your home, Merthus, before going our separate ways," Falkin said, a new and excited sparkle in his eyes.

∽

"Can you see them? I don't like this, and Kadhim has flown off to God knows where as well," Maya muttered nervously as she paced back and forth by Keero's side.

As if summoned by her words, Kadhim dropped from the sky to land directly in front of her. "The others are coming now. I'll say it once, Maya, I don't like this man. He's driven by his own greed." He gripped her hard by the shoulders, his claws accidentally piercing the thick hide of her coat.

"Firstly, Kadhim, calm down," Maya said, taking his hands and holding them in hers. "Secondly, I'm not sure we have much of a choice." She pulled herself from Kadhim's almost pleading gaze as Keela and Merthus came rushing around the corner.

"Falkin will take us, though I'm not sure I trust him," Keela said as she bent at the waist to catch her breath. "He wants something in return for passage, and it's not coin."

"We *definitely* shouldn't trust him, that much is obvious," Merthus chimed in with a shake of his head. "He wants me to repay my debt, and…Keela, would you like to tell them what *you* promised?"

Keela groaned and rubbed the nape of her neck before holding her fingers up to count off the promises she had made. "That we would protect him and his runners from the outlanders; that he would be allowed to continue his business in peace; and…that I would carry out a coup on Bandaar, therefore rendering the first two promises possible," she finished with a tight grin.

"Oh, is that all?" Maya spluttered. "And what's your debt, Merthus?"

An almost imperceptible sadness flickered in his eyes before the casual look of ease slipped back into place. "Just a painting that I stole when I last saw him. My wife painted it. I wanted it, I stole it, then I ran away. Not much else to tell, really. It's hanging on the wall of my home. Falkin will accompany us there and then leave us to our business once it's in his possession."

Maya quietly regarded the man's clenched fists but said nothing of it. He had made his decision. "Well, like I said, it doesn't look like we have much other choice. Kadhim are you okay to fly?" she asked.

Kadhim gave a tight nod as his only response and turned to look at Thelic.

Thelic had remained quiet as he listened to the toll that would need to be paid, and found it odd that the notorious huffer runner hadn't asked for more. He would have expected them to pay at least a little coin on top of what had already been promised. Feeling Kadhim's stare, he turned to face the gypsul's anger, as if Kadhim blamed him for not saying anything. Thelic merely shrugged. Maya was right, what else could they do?

INTRODUCTIONS WERE MADE and Maya grimaced at the extended time Falkin lingered with her hand raised to his lips. He smiled as he finally released her, his face blotched and his eyes pink from alcohol raking over her body like she were a midnight snack.

It came as no surprise that the drug runner would want to wait until dark before crossing the channel. He made claims of port taxes and mooring fees being too extortionate to even consider landing at one of the official docks, and the ease at which he was able to conduct his business in the darker hours of night. As it turned out, Falkin had been preparing to ship some of his 'merchandise' that evening, hence in his boundless benevolence, he required no coin for their passage and only an understanding of their contract.

As Keero and the others were carefully loaded onto the small ship bereft of sails, Maya walked up the wooden ramp behind them and looked nervously to the water-rakers and the guards who stood motionlessly along the rails. Each wore masks to hide their features, with a bow and a quiver of arrows slung over their shoulders. The last of the guards to board also harboured curved swords. It wasn't entirely unexpected for the runners to be armed, but with Maya and the others at the centre of their quarry, it was unnerving when they were so clearly outnumbered.

"All settled? Good," Falkin said. After lumbering up the ramp behind them, he ambled around the deck, lighting what appeared to be small, clay incense pots before blowing each out and then finally taking his seat on something close to a throne at the stern of the long boat. He seemed to melt into the chair, his folds dipping over the sides as he lounged back and smirked at Maya. "Would you like a drink?" he asked her.

Merthus respectfully declined on behalf of himself and the others with such diplomacy that Falkin's feathers remained unruffled.

Doubling as water-rakers, the guards used their contracted sprites to push the boat from its mooring and into the open channel. The water below splashed and churned as the heavy cargo pressed through the waves at an impressive speed, rocking the passengers above.

Falkin's eyes, hard as steel in a mellow face, never left his guests. His teeth flashed in a broad smile as he took yet another hearty glug from the curved decanter of heavy liquid. Slamming the bottle on to the arm rest of the chair, he regarded Maya greedily, and beckoned her forward.

"You are Mayara, yes?" Falkin asked smoothly. "I know some powerful people searching for you and your friends. Come and sit with me."

Maya felt Thelic grip her wrist in warning. She would rather have chucked herself into the churning water of the channel than step any closer to the foul-smelling man. Yet, she couldn't risk insulting their host. With a graceful smile, she tugged her hand from Thelic's and stood up to walk clumsily across the boat's swaying deck.

"Please, have a small taste. It's some of my better stuff," Falkin said proudly.

Maya had seen Falkin drink from the bottle, and therefore doubted it was laced with anything too serious. Still, she trusted the man about as far as she could throw him – and with his size, she doubted she could even pick him up. "I'm really not thirsty, thank you," she said.

"I insist. It's a lengthy trip to Cantor, and it's not enough to intoxicate, otherwise how would I carry out my business?" His smile was playful and his tone suggestive, but his eyes held a hard edge, a warning not to deny him something so small.

Maya glanced at the two guards on her left, whose hands had almost imperceptibly risen to the hilts of their swords. It wasn't the first time she had been faced with a pushy man, but it was the first time the threat of death had been implied if she refused. Gritting her teeth, she took the decanter and raised it to her lips. With her tongue held against the bottle's opening to block the contents, she bobbed her throat, simulating the liquid moving down in gulps.

"Well?" Falkin asked, stoking a finger down the length of her arm.

Maya lowered the bottle and took in a deep breath, then grinned. "You're right, that *is* good!"

The drug lord smiled and licked his lips before taking

Maya's wrist and tugging it sharply until she was sitting on his lap. Beside his quarry, Thelic half rose, but Maya cut him a warning look and gave a slight shake of her head.

Falkin was no fool. He had already seen the possessive, protective look on the younger man's face; the way he always stood with his body slightly angled, ready to act defensively and offensively to whatever came their way. Enjoying the moment tormenting his guests, Falkin slipped a hand under Maya's coat and stroked down her back to the base of her spine.

Maya shivered at the rough hand moving across the thin shirt, but kept her eyes on Thelic. His breathing was quick and shallow, and at some point, the head of his spear had been unwrapped. He was close to snapping.

When the bottle was raised to Maya's face again, she imitated the same motion, pretending to drink before handing it back happily and insisting she was already light-headed. As she reached out, the bottle neck slipped from her fingers, only to be caught at the last second by Falkin. Maya closed and opened her fist experimentally. She couldn't feel her fingers. She raised a shaky hand to her lips but wasn't sure when exactly she had touched them as the numb feeling continued to spread.

"Are you feeling ok?" Falkin asked with mock concern, increasing the pace of his strokes along her back. "Perhaps you should lie down? I have private quarters just below."

It wasn't possible. Only the smallest amount of the liquid had touched her tongue, certainly not enough to cause such an adverse effect.

"Maya?" Thelic's anger faded, and he looked at her with concern.

She glanced up at him and tried to move her mouth to say something, anything. But her voice seized in her throat, unable to make it past the lips she no longer seemed to possess.

"Maya, what's wrong?" Thelic knew she hadn't drunk the liquid; she was more intelligent than that. Something else was wrong, something he couldn't see. A light breeze swept over them, moving the incense along the deck like a fog cloud. Thelic moved to his knees then swayed and leaned forward on his hands.

"It's the burners," Keela said, managing to sway to a standing position. "They've drugged us."

Maya shot to her feet then swayed and felt Falkin's meaty palm land on her backside, then shift to her waist as he gently pulled her back down onto his thighs.

"Falkin, what the fuck are you playing at?" Merthus rumbled from the bow. Being so large, the intoxicating incense had only marginally affected him, and he got to his feet. He glanced to the water-rakers who stopped their raking motions to ready their bows. The masks they wore, the ones concealing all but their eyes, not only hid the guards' identities, but acted as filters making them impervious to the smoke's effects.

"Like I said, Bandaar has made quite the tantalising offer for the capture of this young woman and her friends," Falkin replied, squeezing Maya tightly to his side.

"How...how are you not affected?" Keela gasped, clutching her stomach to stop from vomiting with the ship's sways.

"Years of micro-dosing," Merthus answered through his teeth. "I should have known you'd pull something like this, Falkin. I just hoped your greed would overcome your nature of being an absolute bastard."

Falkin clicked his fingers and motioned for the guards to subdue their new quarry, holding Maya tightly as she drifted to the side. The rim of the bottle was heavily laced, and she would almost certainly lose consciousness soon. No need to shackle her pretty wrists.

Merthus went to remove his sword but stopped at Keero's snore as the creature rolled heavily to one side. The boat swayed with the movement, and a plan formed instantaneously. Reaching for Keela, Merthus snapped one of her blades free, then muttered an apology before jabbing its hilt into the creature's side. He rocked back as Keero let out a roar of annoyance and clambered to his feet.

The approaching guards teetered to one side. Merthus prodded Keero again and the bodaari jumped back, knocking two of the guards over the side and into the murky depths of the channel below.

"Stop it, Merthus, you'll make us tip!" Falkin shrieked in panic as he abandoned Maya and stumbled from his seat.

Maya dropped to the floor, no longer able to feel any part of her body.

"That's the whole point!" Merthus snarled, poking Keero again. The bodaari roared and darted to the other side of the boat, flicking his tail to smack Merthus who barely dodged the heavy blow. The boat rocked, one side climbing into the air. With the guards busy trying to cling to the ship's side, Merthus scrambled into a run towards Maya. Skidding to a halt in front of Falkin, he jabbed a punch into the drug lord's throat then lifted Maya and tucked her under one arm.

Thelic was standing now but couldn't seem to unclip his spear from its sheath. The breath was knocked from him as a guard saw what he was doing and delivered a brutal punch into Thelic's stomach.

Thelic doubled over, then fell to the floor. Barely able to lift his head, he spotted Merthus racing towards him with Maya in one arm. Keela dropped to the floor at his side, unconscious, a bruise beginning to bloom on the left side of her face. The boat rocked again, and barrels rolled towards him, smacking him in the face and knocking him out.

Merthus cursed as he spotted Thelic and Keela on the floor. He couldn't carry all of them, the tell-tale signs of the drug's effects had already numbed his lips, and his eyes were beginning to blur. Barrelling through the guards, he slammed into Keero and the beast raced to the other side and pounded its two front paws. The boat lifted and Keero toppled over the side, taking Merthus and Maya with him into the choppy waves of the channel below.

20

DIVIDED

CANTOR

Maya woke to a pounding on her chest and the breathless huffs of someone leaning over her. Her eyes shot open, and she turned to the side to hurl the salty liquid from her throat. Clawed hands stroked the centre of her back, giving a light tap to help dislodge what remained of the channel's contents.

"Thank the Gods," Kadhim muttered, resting back on his haunches. "I was flying above when I saw Keero and you two go into the water. Are you ok?"

Maya rolled onto her back. Her throat burned with the salty residue, but she nodded her head, not yet able to speak past the heaving coughs. Something he said had her bolting upright. "Two? You only saw two of us?" she wheezed.

She spotted Merthus immediately, tending to Keero with a grim look of regret written all over his face. Keero whimpered at the soft bruises on his sides, then licked Merthus, as if forgiving his actions.

They had landed on a beach, with no trees, grass or any sign of life other than themselves. No Thelic. No Keela…no boat.

"Where are they? Where are the others?" Dread crept over Maya at the look Kadhim returned.

"I'm sorry, Maya. I couldn't grab all three of you," Merthus explained, offering an apologetic look. "The boat didn't capsize completely, so they'll still be alive."

"How do you know? How do you know Falkin didn't just kill them out of anger or spite!?" She knew her tone was unfair. She was blaming him, and it wasn't his fault. "It's my fault," Maya realised. "I should have listened to you, Kadhim."

"Don't do that. We all decided to take the risk with the drug runners. This is *not* your fault," Kadhim insisted as he continued to stroke her back.

She looked up at him gratefully then accepted his help to stand. Two of the three moons shone above. While one had darkened in the looming eclipse, the remaining moons' light reflected off the water and glassy sands that surrounded them. Maya turned and then turned again. Across the water on one side, the twinkling lights of Falkin's home on Esterbell were barely visible. To the west, the dark shadows of Cantor's shoreline. They had made it to the small, island spit between the two territories.

"Shit. How the hell are we going to get back to Esterbell?" Maya didn't want to think of the creatures lurking in the depths of the water surrounding them.

"Esterbell?" Kadhim asked. It dawned on him what she meant. "You want to go and rescue them?"

Maya turned back to Kadhim, perplexed by the bite in his tone. "Of course I do. Bandaar will kill Thelic, and I wouldn't put it past him to do the same to Keela."

"He'll kill *you* if you get too close!" Kadhim reached forward and stopped as she stepped back. "Don't you understand your own importance?"

"How can I forget? That's all I'm ever bloody told! You

have no idea what I've already given up to fulfil my role. I won't lose Thelic and Keela as well," Maya seethed, backing away from Kadhim. Ignoring his rising protest, she summoned the Water Finkel.

"I like Maya's idea," Merthus said perking up considerably. "Let's go to Esterbell's Keep and rain fire on those bastards." He rose his eyebrows in challenge at Kadhim's glare before sighing. "Bandaar does have a pretty impressive Finkel sprite, though. And his guards will be on high alert."

"What would Thelic want you to do, Maya?" Kadhim urged.

Thelic would want to kill her himself for recklessly charging into the Keep. Deep down she knew Bandaar wouldn't kill them. He was too smart. And they were too useful as leverage if Bandaar ever managed to get hold of her. Maya would do nearly anything to stop the people she loved from getting hurt, and her father knew that.

"You would be putting them at greater risk if you went," Kadhim continued softly, reading her thoughts. "He'll hurt them just to get you to do his bidding. At least for now you know they'll be left unharmed."

Maya wanted to scream, to do something, anything other than what she was about to do. But Kadhim was right. With only two of the seals and little control over the Gouram's power, she wouldn't stand a chance against Bandaar's army. She needed more seals. Tight-lipped and shaking from a mixture of the anger and despair, she called BB to her side.

∼

MAYA DRAGGED her body from the surf and onto the beach of Cantor's shore. With the Water Finkel's help, the journey had been fast, waves conjured to lift Keero and propel him over the channel until Maya could no longer keep up the cast. She slumped to her belly on the sand, allowing the water to lap over her feet a moment longer. She turned her head to the side and spotted Merthus a few feet away. He was diligently collecting the packs that had come loose from Keero, rushing back into the wash to snatch up the waterlogged satchels before securing them onto the bodaari's back.

"You okay?" Merthus called to Maya as he ratcheted one of the packs into place.

"Fine, just catching my breath," Maya called back. Managing to get to her feet, she shrugged out of the heavy coat and almost shivered at the breeze. For once, she was grateful for the Gouram's seal and the benefits she reaped. Without it, she would be less human and more icicle after a long dip in the freezing channel separating the coldest territories. She glanced at Merthus. His lips had turned a pale shade of blue. They would need to start a fire right away if he wanted any sort of chance at keeping all fingers and toes. Even Maya wouldn't last long in the colder climes with wet clothes.

It had been a while since Kadhim had gone ahead to find shelter, and Maya was beginning to worry. She looked down as something soft bumped against her ankle. Bending down, she scooped up the last of the wayward satchels and hoisted it over her shoulder, a fresh set of shivers pouring through her as the water drained down her already drenched body.

"Good, that should be the last one," Merthus said. Taking the pack from Maya's shoulder, he rung it out as best he could then flopped it over Keero's back. "If Kadhim isn't back soon, we'll have to make camp just up the beach."

A faint swoosh came from above and Kadhim landed behind Keero. "There's nowhere that offers cover close by. There are some remote houses along the shore, but I'm not sure it's worth the risk asking the residents for shelter." The territory was called the 'Flat Lands' for a reason. Cantor was a farming community, with only small pockets of trees and small towns scattered throughout.

"We can set up a shelter there," Maya said, pointing to what looked like the remains of a home that had burned down a long time ago. Upon closer inspection, not much was left, only the bare bones of a house, with no roof and only crumbling walls to offer protection from the elements.

As Maya cleared some of the debris, she organised the rubble to create several pits for fires. Understanding her intent, Kadhim and Merthus unloaded their packs, laying it all out to dry. With the fires lit, they set about preparing a meal.

"At least we can eat well tonight," Merthus said with a small and hopeful smile. "These rations won't last another day now they've been soaked through. We'll have to start collecting more." He lifted one of the bags and demonstrated his point by tipping it to the side and watching the water drain from a small hole.

Maya summoned Pavinic's cat to help dry the remainder of the bundles of kindling. With each dried bit, she would command the next to be warmed as she wandered to one of the fires and loaded it, stoking the embers until they crackled satisfactorily once again.

"You should sit down, Maya. You need rest, and the food is almost done," Kadhim said. Being the only one to avoid being drugged and soaked through, he had more energy to spare and had thus taken it upon himself to act as their cook and watchkeeper that night.

With instructions to the fire sprite to continue with its task, Maya returned to the fire to sit by the others. "Once the kindling is finished, the cat and I will warm the rest of the gear up until it's dry. Until then, you should both get some sleep. I want us out of here and on the road by dawn."

Kadhim and Merthus shared a look, and Merthus sighed,

taking Maya's hand and rubbing the top of it lightly. "Maya, I know you're worried about Thelic and Keela, but you can't forgo sleep for speed. We'll find the other seals, but it will take time."

"I'm going to get the seal from the Gouram of earth, and then I'm going back to Esterbell," Maya said sternly. She had been thinking about it from the moment the decision had been made to go to Cantor.

"Damn it all, Maya. What do you think will happen when you go to your father?" Kadhim asked, dropping the cooking pot's spoon to run both hands through his hair and pace a storm through the sand. "He will take your power. And then he will use it against you, against all of us."

Maya looked up at him through her lashes, her hands clenched tightly against her thighs. "You're wrong. I've beaten him once already, and that was before I had any of the seals."

"Yes, and your mother was sacrificed to secure your victory," Kadhim snapped. He squeezed his lips together, shocked the words had come from them, and slumped back to sit amongst the rubble. "Maya–"

"You're right," Maya said quietly, momentarily rocked by a wave of grief at the reminder of her mother's death. "Have you ever been in love, Kadhim?"

His mouth dropped open and he froze at the blunt question, more so at who had asked it. "No," he lied. "What does that have to do with this?"

"It has *everything* to do with this," Maya said with an exasperated breath. "When I was with Pavinic in the in-between, he told me to step into the fire, into a sea of bubbling lava beneath my feet. He was asking me to burn myself alive."

Merthus tensed beside her and gave a low whistle. "How did you do it? How does anyone willingly do that?"

Maya looked at him with a sad smile. "Would you step

into the fire if you knew your wife would be safe and well on the other side?" Perhaps it was unfair to ask such a thing. Maybe it was callous to bring up Merthus' dead wife, but she needed them to understand what they were asking her to do.

Merthus bowed his head, hiding the pain that gripped him at the thought of his wife, his soul's mate happy, and alive. "Yes. I would do it without a second's thought," he whispered.

Maya smiled as Merthus raised his head to fix her with a stare that held all of the understanding she needed. "I stepped into the fire. I felt the air blacken in my lungs and my skin bubble in a torture that seemed to last a lifetime." Maya looked back to Kadhim. "And I would do it again, for him."

Something deep inside Kadhim broke. He had lost her, completely. Until that moment, a small part of him hoped, dreamed that he could win her back. A darker side of him, one he refused to acknowledge was twisting his thoughts, hoped that Thelic was never rescued. He knew it was no spirit that poked and prodded and warped those feelings. It was the darker side of love that possessed him.

"I have two more seals to get. The Gouram of earth, and the Gouram of air," Maya continued. "The first two damn near killed me, so who knows how the next will go. But something has always brought me back from the edge of that abyss. *His* voice. Don't you see, Kadhim? He's as important to this mission as I am. How can you expect me to go through this with half of myself missing?"

The blows kept coming, every word from Maya like a dagger to Kadhim's heart. But he needed to hear it, because with every confirmation of her love for another man, the darker side of him died. He would always love her, but that love could be expressed in supporting what she needed. Putting her first, for once.

Maya sighed as Kadhim slowly nodded his head. She

wasn't trying to be reckless or foolhardy, and she could only hope they understood that. She was strong, and she could get Thelic and Keela back. But not without the Gouram of earth if she hoped to match her father's army and powerful sprite.

"Okay then," she said. "Which one is the closest temple?"

21

THE VOICES WILL TELL YOU

ESTERBELL

"You know, I never thought I would see the day where I found myself here," Keela muttered, giving an experimental tug on the wrought iron bars of their holding cell. "Where do you think they're keeping the others?"

Thelic growled something unintelligible, the only response he had given since they'd woken up in the dungeon of Esterbell's Keep. He paced back and forth along the far wall, like an animal awaiting the moment its master became careless. He stopped at the sound of a door closing somewhere beyond their cell, and placed his back to the far wall as footsteps approached.

Keela stepped back from the bars of the wooden door's small tile as an unfamiliar face appeared. With a quick glance into the room, the guard muttered something, and a second voice issued an order to be ready. Keela took several paces back until she was side by side with Thelic. With one glance between them, they silently issued the same warning to one and other. *Get ready.*

The door opened and the two prisoners raced forward as

the first guard stepped into the confines of the cell. They stopped, gasping as the shackles around their wrists burned, singing the skin beneath. Thelic ignored the pain and raced past Keela, slamming his shoulder into the fire master controlling the shackles.

Two more guards raced into the room and wrestled Thelic to the floor. He thrashed about under their weight, desperately trying to summon his sprites to assist, but with no luck. A quick glance at the iron manacles told him why, the glowing symbols inscribed to block a user's elemental links.

It took three additional guards to subdue the two prisoners, with short chains applied to their ankles which they attached to the far wall to prevent any future attempts. The guard commander entered soon after to ensure the prisoners had indeed been locked up sufficiently, before ordering one of the lower ranks to fetch the Keeper.

Keela couldn't help but hold her breath as the imposing figure of her father filled the cell's entrance. So, this is how it felt, being face to face with Bandaar as his enemy instead of his ally. She repressed the shudder that warned her not to speak or move, unless she wished to find out the extent of his cruelty. He smiled at her now, the sight not entirely unpleasant, and she relaxed.

"You," Bandaar said, the disdain in his voice betraying the calm and pleased look he wore. "You have disappointed me, Keela."

Disappointment might have seemed mild to many, but it shook Keela to the core with the way he said it. Damn him. Damn everything he had done to get here. She wouldn't cower from her father any longer. She couldn't. "Where are the others? Where's Maya?" she asked.

Thelic's anger at the man evaporated the moment Maya's name was spoken, a new, burning need to see her taking over. "Where have you taken her?"

Bandaar sneered at his captives, a darkness inside him enjoying the pain and desperation he saw. "Your friends aren't here. But Maya will be joining us before too long, I've seen to that."

Thelic sagged with relief. The last he had seen was Merthus carrying her away from Falkin. They must have made it off the boat. "You won't get her," he said with a small smile. "And even if you do, she's too powerful for you now." Thelic's victorious smirk faded as the Keeper regarded him with a look of amusement.

"You're wrong about that. She has one more seal to get and then she will be right where I need her. I'm proud of what my daughter has accomplished. I never imagined the Gouram would answer her call."

"You *wanted* her to get the seals?" Thelic asked.

"That's right. But I never thought it possible. With the seals, my ceremony will almost certainly work, and now she may not have to die in the transition." Bandaar narrowed his gaze and stepped forward to stand toe to toe with Thelic. "I don't want to hurt you, and I've never wanted to hurt my daughter. I only ever wanted to protect her."

"Protect her?" Keela laughed. "You've done everything in your power to capture and kill her up until now! What's changed, Father?"

"Everything!" Bandaar snapped, his face contorted as he fought to control himself. Stepping back, he rubbed a hand over his face and the cool calm returned. "Neither of you understand, the old woman has scored herself so deeply into your minds that you fail to see the truth. But I can help you, just like I helped Elkin."

"You're talking about Fatari," Thelic realised. "You think she's lying to us, trying to mislead us somehow?" Thelic searched the cobbled floor as if it might hold the answer to his next question. "Why? What does she have to gain?"

Bandaar smiled. "That Seer has everything to gain from her deceit. The voices will tell you, you'll see as I have, as Elkin has. You will finally understand what needs to be done."

Keela stared at the man she had once looked up to, all love and respect disintegrating with every spoken word. He was deranged, of that she had no doubt. Something in his voice, in the way he spoke and held himself no longer painted the picture she had once admired. He was no longer her father.

She turned her head away as he glared at her, only realising he had left the room when the cell door clanged shut behind him.

"I have a bad feeling," Thelic muttered, perching on the edge of a weathered straw mattress. He looked up at the sound of early birds out on the hunt with the break of sunrise. He looked up, hope blooming at the sight of wings flapping from the small hole higher up the prison wall. But those wings were brown, with no sign of Kadhim's red-tipped feathers. He told himself that was a good thing, that Maya shouldn't come anywhere near here.

"*Just* a bad feeling? That's it? Wherever Maya is, my father knows about it, and there's not a damn thing we can do to stop him. I have a *catastrophic* feeling," Keela grumbled, taking a seat next to him. "What was he raving on about Fatari? That she's somehow betraying us? That's almost funny, considering *he's* the twisted one."

Thelic shook his head. He wasn't sure himself. Perhaps just the murmurings of a man slowly losing his mind. "I'm more concerned about his plan for *us*, if I'm honest."

"What do you mean?" Keela asked. Thelic rarely thought of his own safety, especially when he knew Maya was in trouble.

"Bandaar seems to think he can change our minds, that

'the voices will tell us'. Correct me if I'm wrong, but the only thing that springs to mind is–"

"Oh Gods…" Keela whispered. "But that's not possible. He would have to house them somehow."

"I wouldn't put it past him to find a way," Thelic muttered grimly. If Bandaar was able to corrupt him and Keela and use them against Maya…Thelic would never forgive himself.

They both stood to attention as the wooden door to their prison swung open and a guard stepped forward. "It's time. The Keeper is ready for you now."

22
WALKING NIGHTMARE

CANTOR

According to the map, they were close. Kadhim leapt into the sky and searched the surrounding plains in the north, but saw no signs of a temple or any caves in which one might be hidden. He swooped down to where the others were waiting and shook his feathered head to convey he'd had no luck.

"Maybe it was destroyed?" Merthus suggested, peering over Maya's shoulder. It wasn't unlikely. Some of the humans regarded the temples as an insult to the Five Majors, and the more suspicious Avalonians suspected the temples somehow amplified the gypsuls' powers.

"Would a God visit a desecrated temple?" Maya asked Kadhim. Even in his winshik form, his doubt was evident in the squawk and flap of his wings. It was unlikely that a god would stay where an insult has been made.

Nevertheless, with little choice, they headed south to continue hunting the area. The Gouram of earth *had* to be here. By Kadhim's calculations, travelling to the Deadland Lakes in the Western Outlands would take a little over five days, assuming nothing interrupted their journey. Leaving

Thelic and Keela with her father for that long didn't sit well with any of them.

As they trekked along the weather-beaten path, they happened upon two villages further inland. Still conscious of the bounty on Maya's head, she would stay with Keero and Kadhim while Merthus ventured into each, enquiring about the temples and stocking up on food for their journey.

Maya sat up with renewed hope as Merthus approached from the second village with a steady grin. The first had yielded no results, most refusing to speak with someone brazen enough to ask about the Gourams in the first place.

"You know where the temple is?" Maya asked.

"I do, and I've been assured this one is intact. Better yet, it's definitely a temple dedicated to Ragashi." With one finger raised, Merthus dragged it through the air, writing the triangular symbol for the element of earth. "I'm feeling pretty good about this one, Maya."

"Didn't the villagers question why you wanted to know where the temple was?" Kadhim asked, peering warily down the path that Merthus had approached from. "This territory doesn't look kindly on those who show interest in the gypsuls' Gods."

"Of course they questioned it," Merthus said with a laugh. "Initially I told them I was an educator, doing research for the guild in Esterbell. When that didn't win me any favours, I said I then wanted to destroy the damned thing. After that, I got all the information I could ask for. Oh, and this!" He held up a bag of dried fashgi and waved it about like a victory trophy.

Maya laughed and offered a high five, to which Merthus took her hand and shook it awkwardly, already forgetting what she had taught him about this otherworldly custom.

"How far is it?" she asked.

His grin beamed from ear to ear. "Not even half a day's ride."

With morale finally on the rise, they each chatted amongst themselves as they guided Keero to the next temple. Maya told them bits about her world's technology, and once again found herself struggling to explain something she never thought she would need to – a tractor.

"That seems a bit lazy to me. The people here till their lands with the sprites, working together to harvest. With all these machines, how is there enough work for everyone in your world? How do they make any coin to support themselves and their families?"

Merthus made a good point, and Maya tried to explain how homelessness and poverty were both major issues in the Earth Realm.

"When you take over the territory, please don't make your technogogoly here. I think Avalon is better without it," Merthus said.

Maya chuckled inwardly at his incorrect pronunciation of the word, but saw no need to correct him there. She did, however, find his second assumption surprising. "You think *I'm* going to take over the territory in Bandaar's place?"

"Of course. Well, you or Keela," Merthus stated automatically, matter-of-factly. Though, he supposed he had never really thought about it up until then.

"I have no intention of running Esterbell. For all we know, the territories might be disbanded altogether when the barrier falls." At Merthus' shocked expression, Maya modified her response. "I don't mean the humans will be forced out, that's the last thing I want. But it may be the case that gypsul and humans rule together, or nobody rules at all."

"There must be a ruler, just as there must be an elder for every tribe. Right, Kadhim?" Merthus asked.

Kadhim nodded his head. Merthus *was* right. Whether it

be human or gypsul, where a settlement stayed a leader must be elected. Someone to settle disputes, or ensure that the village, town or city administrations ran smoothly.

"Well then, I don't know. That can be somebody else's problem. For now, I'm more concerned with finding this bloody temple. Are you sure it's around here?" Maya asked, standing on Keero's back to search the surrounding area.

Merthus regarded the map across his thighs and pointed to a drawing of a small cluster of houses. He looked up and spotted a village in the near distance. "We're close. The temple is just southeast of Thackerpin village. Look directly ahead. Can you see any rock features?"

Maya squinted against the sun's glare and spotted two stone structures, both jutting from the ground at odd angles but easy to spot amongst the gently rolling hills of Cantor. "I see them! They aren't far. Is that where the temple is?"

"Yes, according to the woman in the village. Fatari's marking was quite a bit off, maybe that's why we couldn't find the other one," Merthus wondered aloud, rolling up the map and securing it back in their only waterproofed sack.

Deadened grass turned to pebbles as Keero plodded into a stone field. Pulling the bodaari to a stop, Maya slid down and poured the water from three of their packs into the creature's mouth, giving him a warm stroke along his side and praising his hard work. She turned to the stone pillars, and admired the careful, decorative carvings that would once have looked impressive. However, after years of rain, wind, and cold temperatures, the finer of the geometrical designs had faded and dulled.

She stepped up to the monoliths and placed her hand on one of the swirls. A part of her had expected something to happen, to immediately be transported to the in-between to face Ragashi's judgement. Maya's hope faded slightly, and she looked to Kadhim. He appeared just as disappointed, but quickly softened his expression and motioned for Maya to follow him.

Walking behind Kadhim, they skirted around the front face of the rocks, and spotted a circular stone dais, similar to what they had seen in Pavinic's temple. This one was cracked in two, with brittle vines covering the motifs beneath.

"Maya, lay on the slab," Kadhim instructed, brushing away the dirt and stones so she could lay more comfortably. "Merthus, can you grab the medical pouch from Keero, there should be some bottles in there. We need the one to induce sleep."

As Merthus left to do as he'd been asked, Kadhim explained his plan to Maya. "I'm going to try and guide you like I did at Batshari's temple. You won't see me, but I swear I will be there."

Maya sat down on the edge of the platform and stroked the stone beneath her. She felt nothing from this place. At Batshari's and Pavinic's temples she had felt their power – like calling to like, their essence inside her had answered that call. She dropped her head into her hands, feeling the last of her hope diminish. "Ragashi isn't here, Kadhim."

"But perhaps we can call him here. He has a vested interest in helping you. You're saving the realm he governs. He *has* to answer your call." Kadhim swallowed the lump in his throat and the doubt along with it, refusing to acknowledge the possibility that the God of earth could be so callous as to ignore them.

Merthus returned shortly with a small bottle of faintly pink liquid. Dabbing it onto a cloth, he handed it first to Maya and then to Kadhim who lay down on the stones beside Maya and the dais.

Merthus watched as Maya's eyes fluttered closed, and bit his lower lip to calm the storm of concern flooding through him. Turning to one of the monoliths, he shrugged off the heavy sword and began his climb. Once at the top, he found he had a view of the village to the west and the surrounding farmlands. Maya and Kadhim were helpless, wordlessly depending on him to protect their bodies as their souls sojourned in the in-between. He wasn't sure if they would succeed, but he would do what he could to assist, and carry out his role as the watchful guardian.

~

Merthus turned his head and peered down at the sleeping figures. The temperature had dropped considerably the moment the sun kissed and fled the horizon, and his concern grew for the empty vessels below.

He climbed down from the rock and retrieved blankets to drape over Maya and Kadhim to keep them warm. Neither moved, not even a twitch as the heavy cotton was gently placed over them. He waited a moment, watching the fog of their breath to ensure a steady rhythm. He felt as he supposed a new father might, which was odd considering he had no children of his own. But after seeing Maya's constant struggle and the burden placed on her small frame, he had come to care deeply for her.

With little else to do, he made the climb back up the stone structure and settled at the top. He squinted, spotting a glow bobbing in the distance.

Torchlight.

Merthus muttered a curse and slipped silently to the ground. His sword lay propped against the larger structure, and he picked it up, resting the blade over his shoulder as he made his way to the path. The glow of the torches was closer now, and he counted them. Twelve, all moving in a group barely visible under the waxy light of the dark moon.

Merthus was a skilled fighter, but safeguarding the others whilst taking on a mob wouldn't be easy.

He heard the chatter of villagers egging each other on, bellowing reasons like, 'we must protect the village', or 'we must protect Avalon'. Merthus braced himself and waved to the approaching mob. Twenty in total.

"We have no issue with you, let us pass." It was an older man with greyed hair that had stepped from the crowd to address Merthus. Too skinny, with eyes sunk deep into their sockets, he looked half starved.

"And who, exactly, do you have an issue with? I'm the only one here," Merthus insisted, placing a hand to his chest innocently. Behind him, Maya and Kadhim were hidden by the towering stone, and couldn't have been seen by the villagers.

"Liar!" a woman squawked, equally as gaunt as the man, but much younger. The crowd muttered angrily in agreement as they each rose their farming tools menacingly.

Merthus narrowed his eyes and moved the sword fluidly from his shoulder to pierce the ground between his feet, before resting his forearms over the hilt. "I'm insulted. You don't even know me. Why do you assume I'm a threat to you and your kin?"

Merthus' intent had been to perturb the simple farm-folk with his calm assurance, and it was working. The front row of people shifted back a step, all looking at the mighty sword and its wielder.

"The village you came through, one of them followed and saw who you were travelling with," the old man hissed, a greedy, almost desperate look intermingled with his rising anger. "It's bad enough that you travel with one of *them*, an outlander, but the *woman*...how could you help her? She wants to destroy our world!" he spat.

Merthus flinched at the old man's vehemence, but it was

the confidence in his accusation regarding Maya that peaked Merthus' interest. "Destroy it? She wants to save it, you fools."

"Ha! So, she *is* here!" a different man shouted from further back in the crowd. The villagers shuffled forward at his words, their surety renewed by the accidental confession.

"I do have a woman here, she's sleeping, and I'd rather not wake her. But you're wrong, she's my daughter, and *not* the woman you're hunting for. That much I can promise you." Merthus wasn't really lying, Maya *was* like a daughter to him, and these people were searching for a world destroyer.

"Only one way to be sure," the old man said. "Let us by so we can check. The woman with the bounty has a mark on her chest. I'd like to look for myself."

The way he licked his lips told Merthus the man wanted to do much more than just look for a mark. Anger erupted inside him and he straightened his back, removing the sword from the ground to hold it ready in a fighting stance. Gold teeth flashed as he said, "The first fool forward is the first fool to die. So, who is it to be?"

The crowd parted and three women stepped to the front. Merthus grimaced, appalled by their tactics. He didn't want to kill any of the villagers, but the innate need to protect the fairer sex had his blade dip ever so slightly.

The women raised their hands and simultaneously muttered one word.

Open.

Merthus looked down as the stones at his feet vibrated, some jumping a foot into the air as the ground rumbled beneath them. A crack appeared between his feet, and he had just enough time to jump to the side before the ground was able to gobble him up. Earth castors, he realised. Rocks flew from every direction, pummelling his back as he blocked the ones hurtling towards his face. He roared both in anger and in agony as the storm of stones slammed into both arms.

"More! Give him more!" someone from the crowd shouted, and the others erupted into jeers and taunts at the stoning before them.

Gripping his sword, Merthus darted forward. He was fast despite his size, and the women barely had time to react before each fell, clutching at the guts spilling from their bellies. Not daring to reflect on what he had just done, Merthus leapt over the fallen bodies and swung his sword at the next closest target, the old man.

Someone pulled the man back just in time and Merthus' blade cut through air. He grunted at the added weight of a body clambering up his back, and swiftly flipped the sword so the blade was pointing at himself, then jabbed it through the space between his ribs and his right arm. The weight, a woman, gripped his neck and screamed as the sharp tip cut into her armpit then toppled to the side, bringing Merthus down with her.

Bodies descended on Merthus all at once, people scrambling to pile on top of the human pyramid while others tried to wrench the sword from his grasp. Over the muffled shouts and screams he heard someone say they had found the woman and the outlander. Adrenaline roared through his body, and he abandoned the sword to slowly roll under the weight above him until he was on his stomach. Both knees scraped along the ground as he brought them up, his back straining as he pulled his hands to sit under his shoulders. One knee rose slowly up until his foot was on the ground. Here came the tricky part. With every ounce of strength, he threw his weight back, and a young man yelped as he was thrown clear from the pile of humans now struggling to maintain their grip.

With a roar, Merthus was free. Jumping over the bodies,

he fell to the other side and rolled, picking up his sword before rising to his feet. His teeth slammed together as something cracked against the side of his head with mind numbing force. He looked down at the rock, one side of it covered in blood, then lifted a hand to his head. Warm liquid trickled down his face, and the ground rushed up to meet him as the darkness crowded in.

~

Maya woke to a shout. She tried to sit up, but the haze of the drugs still remained. Orbs hovered around her, torchlight she realised, just before an angry face leaned over to regard her with a sneer.

"I've found the woman and the outlander. They're over here!" the angry man shouted.

Fear swept through her as she regarded the glint of a farm tool in his right hand. She squeezed her eyes shut, willing herself to wake from the nightmare that had plagued her dreams since meeting with Pavinic. "Wake up, Maya," she whispered.

"Come and help me! You two, grab the outlander," the man called.

Maya's eyes bolted open as rough hands pulled at her coat, forcing her to sit up. Her body was numb, still asleep and paralysed despite her mind's wakefulness. Her eyes locked with Merthus just as a rock slammed into the side of his head. She opened her mouth to utter a scream, but nothing came out. Her head flopped to the side as a stranger lifted her into his arms. Kadhim was there too, woken from his sleep by a swift kick to the ribs. Another boot smashed into his face and his eyes closed again as he slipped into unconsciousness.

"Enough of that, bring him to the village. Everyone deserves a chance at him," Maya's captor ordered.

Maya's head lolled back to rest over the man's forearm, and the chaotic world turned upside down.

A rope was tied to Kadhim's feet, and he was dragged behind the gathering crowd, while Merthus was pulled along by the strength of two men, one man under each of the large warrior's arms.

Tears rolled down Maya's face as she watched, unable to look away as her friends were hauled along behind her, Kadhim's head striking every rock they passed.

Just before reaching the village, Maya wiggled her fingers and curled her toes experimentally. In the short amount of time it had taken them to reach the town's gates, she had slowly tested each finger, not wanting her captor to realise that the woman in his arms was ready to fight. It took all her strength not to turn her head and check on Kadhim. He had been silent despite the thrashing his body was taking being dragged down the rocky path.

"Put them over there," an old man shouted. "Someone go and get the others, wake them up if you have to. Tell them we have the woman, we have Mayara!"

Shock preceded the sickening dread at the sound of her name muttered amongst the people. The bandits and drug runners had already spoken of a substantial bounty offered for Maya's capture and that of her friends. But how far had word travelled? Was it Bandaar who had issued this particular order? Or were other Keepers just as keen to get their hands on her now?

Maya was jolted from her thoughts as the man dropped her onto a pile of straw. She kept still, keeping her eyes closed as whoever it was seemed to linger. At the sound of footsteps padding away, she carefully opened one eye.

A metal cage door clanged shut and Maya turned her head

slowly, noting the back of the prison's wall was all stone, with hay strewn across the floor. At first, she thought it might have been for the comfort of their prisoners, but the karkili grazing in the far corner suggested otherwise; the prison simultaneously used as a pen for animals.

She rolled her head to the other side to assess what lay beyond the wall of iron bars. The town was formed like a stadium, wooden houses built one on top of the other in a wide circle carved out of a hill. From the animal pen, Maya surveyed the arena. One exit. Too many villagers. They all seemed excited, some pointing to a figure laying on the ground at the centre of the crowd. Kadhim.

Beside Maya, someone groaned, and she almost jumped at the unexpected sound.

Merthus rolled onto his side and clutched his head. "Damn it all. That fucking hurt." He sat up and spotted Maya looking over at him. "You alright, love?"

Maya nodded, still not daring to speak in the hopes that she might dupe the guards. She froze at the sound of someone shouting close by.

"Hey, this one's awake!" the woman guarding the prison yelled excitedly.

Had she seen Maya, or just Merthus?

"Give him some sleeper or knock him out again. We're not ready for him yet," someone in the gathering crowd shouted.

The gate groaned and footsteps pounded quickly across the floor. Merthus grunted as the woman's fist cracked against his jaw and Maya sprang into action. With the guard's back turned, she failed to see the threat coming from behind.

Maya snatched the dagger from the woman's waist, then grabbed one of her arms, twisting it painfully up into the centre of her back.

Shouts rang out from the village square in warning to the

woman, but it was too late. Maya brought the blade up and held it to her captive's throat, then turned them both to face the approaching crowd.

"Stop right there or I'll slit her throat!" Maya bellowed, sliding the dagger to lightly nick the skin.

"No! That's my daughter, please don't hurt her." An older man broke through the looming mass to stand in front of Maya, holding his hands up in a plea.

"Well, that's my *friend* you've got beaten and bloody at your feet. You didn't think twice about hurting *him*, did you?" Maya snapped in return, feeling no sympathy for both the man and his daughter at the sight of Kadhim's broken body on the ground.

The young woman thrashed in Maya's grip, only to whimper as the blade dug deeper and the dislocating pull across her shoulder tightened painfully.

"We should have killed you," the woman hissed.

"You have no idea," Maya murmured in her ear before raising the arm just a fraction higher. A sharp pop vibrated under her hand as the clavicle parted from the shoulder, and the woman screamed in pain and fury, but dared not move with the knife still tucked under her jaw.

"Maya, let me through and I'll get Kadhim," Merthus said from behind her. As Maya shuffled forward, he was just about to pass when the woman in Maya's grasp laughed maniacally and slid her neck to the side.

Blood spurted forward, spraying Maya's hands and the man kneeling at her feet, before the guard went limp in her grasp and dropped to the floor. She looked in a daze at the gore streaming down her arm, painted differing shades of red and almost black under the torchlight.

Her nightmare.

Her prophesy.

This is what Maya's dreams had foretold. A dead woman

at her feet and angry villagers coming to collect for their loss. The mob descended and knocked Maya to the ground before she could command the Finkels sleeping within her.

Merthus fell back as Maya was shoved into him, a sea of angry villagers piling through the doorway of the small prison. "Summon the sprites!" he yelled.

Maya bit down on the hand covering her mouth and screamed for the Finkels to attack. Pavinic's cat rose like a ghost from the seal on her stomach and angry flames spread across the cell's ceiling.

Some of the men and women scrambled back, instinct outweighing their fury. Others remained, trying to silence her once again. But Maya didn't need to speak.

Loki and BB sprang from their seals, and a wave of water and air blasted the remaining villagers from the confined space. Maya coughed as the hand that had been choking her was ripped away and jumped up to help Merthus to his feet. Gathering herself, she dragged the dagger across her palm and focused on the villagers. Some had darted left, while others raced to find cover in the houses on the right. As the castor circles came to life, Maya called for fire and sent it roaring forward to spread across the arena.

"You killed her, you killed her, you killed her..." The man, the father continued to kneel by his dead daughter's side, his voice lost to Maya as she watched the village burn.

Tinder-dry barns and houses hungrily absorbed the flames, allowing them to spread to the next, and the next. Maya walked forward, standing protectively in front of Kadhim as the inferno roared around her. She was a woman possessed, angry at the greed and violence of the villagers. Angry that the Gouram of earth had failed to answer her call. Angry that Thelic and Keela were trapped with no immediate hope of rescue.

"Maya!" Merthus called, his voice a whisper amidst the

roaring flames. He reached out and twisted her to face him. Blazing emerald eyes stared back. He shook her by the shoulders, shouting for her to stop. That she had beaten them, that everything was well.

His voice broke through, and Maya blinked past her crimson rage to see the carnage before her. *This* was her nightmare. Death and destruction at the hands of her and her sprites, she looked to the right. Loki had transformed into a creature the size of a bodaari and was lunging towards a boy, Maya's infectious rage urging him to kill.

"Stop!" Maya screamed, and Loki skidded to a halt. The flames froze, still licking at the wood around it, and the wave that had trapped a dozen shivering men and women sank into the earth. Maya dropped to her knees where three charred bodies lay beside Kadhim. She stroked the gypsul's bloodied hair and almost cried with relief when he stirred beneath her hand.

Merthus remained where he was, still dazed by the level of destruction Maya's power had caused. His head snapped up at the sound of a whistle, just as an arrow ripped through Maya's shoulder. She screamed at the searing pain and staggered to her feet. Merthus moved to grab her, to try and protect her, but dropped to his knees as something heavy landed on the base of his neck.

∞

"Look at what she did! My girl is dead, and for what? A few coin?"

"It's more than that! With the bounty we can easily rebuild our village. Better yet, we can strengthen our defences for when the war breaks out."

Maya bolted to her feet at the sound of the voices, then cried out as pain rippled through her shoulder. The arrow. It must have been dipped in something. It had been seconds after she was hit when the familiar haze had descended. She moved her hand to touch the wound, only to realise metallic cuffs had been attached to each of her wrists. She almost laughed. They had seen her power, what made them think handcuffs would stop her? She summoned the sprites with the plan to use the cat's fire to melt through the metal. Nothing happened. She tried again, but still the sprites refused to rise from their seals.

"It's no use," a woman said from outside Maya's cell. "Those shackles block your power." She regarded Maya with a mixture of hate and regret. "Even after all you've done to our homes, I'm sorry for what you're about to see. You said he was your friend?"

Maya looked down, realising that her prison was much smaller than the last, and raised from the ground. She glanced behind her and noticed two karkili harnessed to the front of the cage. She was in a transporter. Turning back to the woman, Maya spotted Merthus just behind, back in the animal pen. He gave her a grim look, then dropped his head as he pointed to something at the far end of village square.

Kadhim was there, on a wooden stage held together by twisted rope. Maya's hand rose to her mouth as she finally understood the device beside him. A short guillotine.

"No. Stop this! He's trying to save you! He's trying to save your entire realm, don't do this!" Maya screamed at the woman, at anyone who would listen to her.

Kadhim raised his swollen face at the sound of Maya's voice, and she watched him, grief-stricken as he tried to form the words he wished to tell her. Three words repeated over and over until she could finally read what she couldn't hear.

I love you.

At the crack of a whip, Maya fell forward against the bars as the karkili shifted their weight to pull her carriage. She screamed, threatened, begged for the villagers to listen, but could only watch as Kadhim's hand was placed on the chopping block. She passed under the gate's arch and rounded the corner out of view before the rope was released. The sound, however, was clear enough to paint what her eyes could not see. The singing sound of a sharp blade hitting stone rang out over the small village, followed by Kadhim's scream.

23
DEATH SUMMONS A GOD

ESTERBELL

After days of rough travel, Maya was tired and sore but resisted the urge to snap at the children running beside the carriage, some throwing rocks into the pen to further entice the human cargo locked within. Instead, she stared ahead at the looming Keep with its midnight-coloured roof. Esterbell Keep. She had done everything in her power to stay out of her father's hands, and yet here she was, being delivered like a prized goat tied neatly with a power-blocking bow. She hugged her knees to her chest, avoiding the curious gazes of the market goers.

"Maya?"

Maya's head snapped up at the familiar voice, spotting Brijid drop her bags to run alongside the carriage. "Brijid! What the hell are you doing here?"

"I was enlisted to join Carnass as his healer. We arrived a few days ago," Brijid said breathlessly as she tried to keep up with the karkilis' pace.

"Have you been inside the Keep? Have you seen Thelic or Keela?"

"Yes! But, Maya, they're not the same. Something is

different–" Brijid yelped as her foot caught on the edge of someone's foot and she toppled to the floor.

"Brijid, go to Cantor!" Maya yelled as the carriage pulled away. "Go to a town called Thackerpin and find a man called Merthus!" she begged.

Brijid shouted a reply, but under the thundering of the karkilis' hooves, whatever she said was lost as the carriage entered the Keep's gates.

Kadhim would likely be dead by now, but perhaps Brijid could barter for the release of Merthus. If there was one thing the villagers would respond to, it was money, and Brijid had plenty to offer if Thelic's story about her past had any truth to it.

Maya shuffled along the straw to the back of the cage as two Esterbellian guards unlocked and opened the iron door. One of them grabbed her feet, dragging her forwards so the other guard could pull her from the transporter. Together, they roughly manoeuvred Maya towards a stone arch, half dragging, half carrying her through the corridors until she was finally pushed into a tall and beautifully decorated room.

The doors at Maya's back slammed closed, and despite knowing they had locked her in, she still turned to tug at the handles just in case. She vaguely noticed that one door was a dark and heavy oak, while the other was slightly lighter, like it had been replaced recently. She turned to face the room and immediately recognised the king-sized bed, the silk tapestries and gilded furniture. The carpets were different from when she was last here, likely changed after failing to remove the blood stains.

Maya dropped to the floor in the same spot where she had held her dying mother in her arms. She dragged her hands across the carpet, as if waiting to feel some lingering essence of Jaseen. Of course, there was nothing, only the memories remained, a wound reopened as she faced the room in which Jaseen had been imprisoned for all those years.

A lock clicked and the doors to the room swung open. A burning hatred crept into every corner of Maya's being at the sound of her father's voice.

"Welcome home, Mayara."

Maya furiously fought to prevent the tears that streamed down her cheeks and the quaking anger that surged through her. She rose to her feet and turned to face Bandaar, hoping he might see her revulsion towards both him and this place where he had murdered her mother, the place he called *home*. Apparently, Bandaar failed to register her emotions, or he simply chose to ignore them as he stepped forward and wrapped her in an embrace.

"Mayara, I'm so glad to have you back," he said softly.

Maya felt sick, felt the acidic tang of bile rise in her throat as she struggled from his grasp. She wanted to say something, ask a question, hurl abuse, but the words failed to form.

"Come, you must be hungry. All of your friends are waiting for you in the dining hall." Bandaar tugged at Maya's shackled wrists, pulling her along behind as he moved through the corridors, past several courtyards and into a high-ceilinged hall. Maya jerked herself free as she stepped from behind him and regarded the chamber with distaste. The same tapestries and varied taxidermy adorned the walls as they did throughout the rest of Keep. At the centre of the hall, however, stretched an immense stone table heavily laden with food and with three people seated and ready to eat.

"Thelic…Keela," Maya whispered. They were okay. *Better* than okay, she realised, as both laughed at a joke another was telling. The third and final diner was a tall and heavily muscled redhead. Maya sucked in a sharp breath at the sight of Elkin passing a bowl of vegetables to Thelic, at the sight of that heart-breaking, easy smile she had longed to see again.

Thelic looked up and spotted the newcomers. "Bandaar! The food is getting cold, old man, and Elkin is likely to eat the lot before you've had a chance to get your fill." He stopped, his gaze falling on Maya. "She's here," he said softly.

Maya blanched at the scene before her. Thelic offering his hand to their enemy, and Keela barely bothering to register her sister's arrival before continuing her conversation with Elkin. "You're all...okay," Maya said, as she slowly walked towards the table.

"Of course we're okay, Maya," Elkin said with a smile. "I told you, Bandaar is on our side. The others will tell you now that they've seen the truth."

Thelic rose from his chair and walked around the table to meet Maya. Resting one hand on her shoulder, he grinned down before gently steering her into the chair adjacent from his. He loaded her plate with an assortment of meats and vegetables, enough to fill her twice over despite having consumed little to nothing on the journey from Cantor.

"And how do you expect me to eat?" Maya asked, raising her cuffed hands.

"I would be happy to feed you," Thelic replied teasingly, scooping some of the food onto a spoon and offering it to her mouth like he would a lover.

Maya turned her head and lifted her hands, smacking the spoon from his grip. "What are you doing? Why are you acting like this?" She looked to him, then to Keela and Elkin whose happy expressions had turned to growing irritation. "What have you done to them, Bandaar?"

The Keeper took his seat at the head of the table just as the doors to the hall burst open.

"Fashionably late but I'm here nonetheless, and that

smells absolutely divine." Carnass froze as Maya turned in her seat to stare at him. "Ah, so *this* is why you summoned me. A warning might have been nice," Carnass muttered sulkily before taking his seat at the other head of the table opposite Bandaar.

"I see you have yet to make your decision," Maya said, her tone dripping with cold sarcasm as she regarded Carnass. She had been counting the days of the eclipse. This was the fifth night of the dark moon. Tomorrow, he would be faced with the prophecy Fatari had foretold.

Carnass dipped his head and released a deep sigh. "Please, Maya. No business over–"

"I think I can hazard a guess as to which way you're leaning," Maya continued, cutting him off. The decision *had* to be about whether or not he would join Bandaar in the war, or why else would he be here?

"I'm sorry, Maya. But I must put the Danikan people first," Carnass said softly, his eyes pleading for her to understand.

Maya leaned back in her chair and shook her head at the scene around her. Nearly everyone she had come to love was seated around this table, breaking bread with the man who wished to use her and release the creatures that would destroy their world. And yet, she knew it wasn't them, not truly. Brijid had warned that Thelic and Keela were different somehow. And she was right.

Maya leaned forward, pushing the plate away to allow her hands to rest on the table in front of her. Thelic had resumed eating and looked up with his mouth half full of food. "What's wrong with you?" she asked. Thelic stopped chewing and grinned again, crumbs dropping into his lap.

"What do you mean, Maya? I thought you loved this man," Bandaar said, laughing along with Thelic and the others.

Maya glowered at her father, fists clenched as she resisted the urge to lunge for him. "That is *not* the man I love, and that is *not* my sister."

In a snap movement, Keela dropped her spoon and slammed her hands onto the table. "What would you know, filthy halfling?" she snarled.

Maya shifted slightly back in her chair, shocked by the viciousness in her sister's tone. No, this wasn't Keela at all. "You're all spirits from the chaos void," she whispered.

Carnass whipped his head from Maya to the others, then rested his questioning gaze on Bandaar.

The Esterbellian Keeper's jovial mood had lessened considerably with Maya's revelation, and he gave a bored sigh before lowering his goblet to the table.

"How did you do it, Bandaar? How the hell did you manage to trap them?" Maya asked.

His jade eyes pierced hers as father and daughter battled silently with their stares. Not bothering to answer her question, Bandaar barked an order to the guards, requesting his 'guest' be removed from the table and returned to her room.

~

MAYA WOKE from her dreams in a cold sweat as she rolled from the bed to land on the hard oaken floor. Gathering herself, she took three deep breaths to calm her pounding heart, and noticed some food by the door. After padding across the room to retrieve the tray, Maya moved to sit within the slatted light by the window to eat. She was starving, and yet her nightmare had stolen her appetite. She couldn't help but wonder, was it prophetic? Would all her dreams be some sort of warning of what was to come? Couldn't she envisage a picnic by the shore instead of death and destruction?

Maya remained by the window until well past dawn, staring out at the bustling city below. The door to her room opened without a knock, tearing her from her thoughts of Camalet as she idly twirled the ring on her necklace. Two handmaids were ushered into the room and hesitated as the door was shut behind them. They had been sent by Bandaar to help Maya bathe and dress.

Being twins, the mirrored prettiness in their wary faces softened Maya somewhat. Seeing no sense in fighting such a simple thing, she waved a hand for them to continue, and they each scurried past her into the adjoining bathing room.

Maya looked down at her clothes, wrinkled and stinking from so many days without a proper bath. The smell of flowers drifted from the other room, and Maya left her seat by the window to join the handmaids. One squeaked at Maya's quiet appearance, then stepped forward and held out her hands.

"What?" Maya asked, eyeing the outstretched palms distrustfully.

"Your clothes, miss. If you will?" the more timid of the twins insisted. Looking down at Maya's handcuffs, she furrowed her brows and then snapped her fingers before retrieving a small knife, as if this were a problem she had faced before. "It'll be easier to cut the coat and shirt from you, the Keeper is having new clothes brought up anyway."

Maya bit down on the series of expletives bubbling to the surface at the mention of her father, not wanting to frighten the women any more than they already were.

"Okay, now your breeches, and then we'll help you bathe," the braver twin announced.

"Ah, no. I'm quite capable of doing the rest myself. Thank you though," Maya insisted.

The two maids looked at one and other somewhat fearfully, and explained that if they didn't help, they would be accused of failing to fulfil their roles and be expelled from the Keep.

Maya sighed upon seeing their distress and told them they could wait in the main bedroom until she was done. They both seemed to relax a little at her suggestion and hurried from the room.

Finally alone, Maya peeled the trousers from her body and placed them in a second, smaller bucket beside her. Stepping into the wide, copper tub, she groaned as her body submerged in the hot water, scented bubbles washing away the grime of travel.

"Miss, are you sure you don't need any help? We could wash your back?" the braver twin asked as she scurried back into the room to collect Maya's clothes.

"Really, I'm fine. Though, would you mind answering some questions?"

"Of course not! What would you like to know?" With a smile that touched her eyes, the maid beamed with honest delight at the potential to be useful.

"What is it like working here?" Maya enquired. The maid tilted her head, seeming somewhat confused by the question, and so Maya asked again. "I mean, do you get paid and treated well? I'm a prisoner here, so feel free to be honest, I promise I won't tell."

"A prisoner, miss? We have dungeons in the basement for that sort. You're a *guest*, and those shackles are for everyone's safety, nothing more. But to answer your question, yes. We're all paid and treated very well here. The Keeper isn't as bad as some make out, it's those infernal guards that rile *me* up the most!"

A small hiss came from the main bedroom and the timid maid popped her head around the corner with a scowl to her sister. "Shush it, or we'll be back on the streets again before long!"

The braver of the two shook her head with an amused smile. "You see, we're all grateful for our positions in the household." After wringing out Maya's clothes, she moved into the bedroom and placed them by the fire to dry. "We'll leave you for now, unless you need us for anything else?" she called back to Maya.

Maya insisted she was fine and thanked them before sinking deeper into the tub. She tried to slip her hands from the cuffs and grunted when they refused to slide over her knuckles. In the movies, the heroes and heroines would dislocate their thumbs to slip free from their restraints. But this wasn't a movie, and she had no idea how to do that.

Long after the water had turned cold, Maya wearily rose from the tub and stepped from the water, grimacing at the pain and stiffness in her shoulder. Bandaar's healer had done his tricks and treated the wound so that only an angry line of stitches remained. She banished the thoughts of Kadhim and Merthus, still trapped in that village, and did her best to dry herself – something surprisingly difficult when your hands are manacled together.

Pausing at the arched doorway, Maya spotted a bundle of white material on the bed and strode across the room. With a muttered oath, she released the towel from her chest and picked up the sheer, chiffon dress, its heavy folds decorated with golden threads sewn into blooming flowers. It was beautiful, and entirely bewildering. She was a prisoner. She had expected a shirt to go with her trousers, or something plain, something that wouldn't be a loss if Bandaar's ceremony got messy.

Dropping the dress back onto the bed, Maya sat on the mattress beside it and lay back. The guards could come in at any moment, and she would be utterly naked. But she didn't care. As she lay there, it was questions more than idle worries that occupied Maya's mind. Bandaar had somehow managed to trap spirits from the chaos void and placed them into Keela and Thelic, and possibly Elkin. She needed to free them first.

At that thought, Maya leapt from the bed and shot across the room to where her trousers lay by the fireplace. "Please, please, please," she muttered, frantically searching for the sewn pocket.

It was gone.

The maids, they must have found and taken the Gouram Stone when they were washing her clothes. And they would take it straight to Bandaar.

In a fit of rage, Maya threw the trousers into the fireplace, then immediately regretted it. Now she would have to wear the dress. But that was fine. It was always in good taste when someone dressed up for a funeral. And the Keeper of Esterbell deserved the best funeral he could get.

∽

That evening, the maids returned with an air of excitement to help Maya with her dress. As she stepped into the puddle of material, one of the twins held it up to Maya's breasts while the other secured the buttons at the back. Her hair was next, cut to a manageable length and brushed to sit neatly down her back. Once the maids were placated and approved of her appearance, Maya was ushered from the room, to where the guards awaited to escort them all through the Keep.

"Bandaar is going to kill me," Maya whispered to who she hoped was the bolder twin. "This ceremony requires my blood to succeed."

The young woman averted her eyes and shook her head rapidly, insisting that wasn't the case.

"You're going to be fine. You're the Keeper's daughter,

and even *we've* heard of your power," the other twin insisted quietly, linking her arm with Maya in a surprisingly relaxed gesture. She leaned in close, casting a quick glance at the guards behind. "But just in case you're worried, I've sewn a place for your good-luck charm just below the waist of your dress."

"My what?" Maya asked.

The maid lifted a finger to her lips and gave Maya a wink before patting the waist of her own dress. Maya mirrored the action, lifting her hands to feel the pleats by her midriff. Her fingers paused on a hard lump.

The Gouram Stone.

Maya almost cried with relief and whispered her thanks to the young woman, who with one small act of kindness had unknowingly increased Maya's odds of surviving.

They soon arrived before an enormous set of double doors, and the guards stepped forward to push them open, revealing an antechamber beyond. Large, flaming lanterns lined the atrium's walls, their light broken by columns spanning the length of the room. At the centre was a stone dais, similar to those seen at the Gourams' temples, although this one was much larger.

Thelic and Elkin approached at the sound of the door opening, dismissing the guards and maids as they each took one of Maya's arms and led her down what she felt was the last stretch to the gallows.

"Thelic, I know you're in there. I know you can hear me. You have to fight this, please!" Maya begged. His face and expression were stony, leaving her to wonder if she had waited too long, if Thelic was even in there anymore. Back at Etiyan Vale, he had fought with everything he had. But he seemed at ease now, with no sign of an internal battle raging beneath the skin.

"Little fulsin, Thelic is at peace with what must happen,"

Elkin said softly, turning to face her as they walked. "You know that neither of us would ever wish you harm. Bandaar assures us he will do all he can to safeguard your life during the ceremony. He swears it."

"He's a liar!" Maya roared, struggling in their grip. "Thelic, look at me."

Thelic sighed and stopped them several feet from the others. He looked down at Maya, then raised an expectant brow. "Speak. It may be the last chance you get."

Maya winced at the cold words. He had never spoken to her that way, even when they had first met. She felt the weight of the necklace, the promise that hung there. She moved her hand to the small ring and rubbed the cool metal between her fingers. "Remember, Thelic."

His eyes tracked her movement like a hawk would its prey. He blinked, then shuddered, something stirring within. A memory. A promise. The ghost of Maya's touch and her love locked away deep inside him.

Maya gasped as her feet left the ground, both men holding under her arms to carry her on towards the waiting spectators.

Carnass and Bandaar stood from their wide, throne-like chairs. While Maya's father seemed pleased to see his daughter clean, well dressed and prepared for whatever came next, Carnass was the opposite.

The Danikan Keeper was deathly pale, eyes ringed with dark smudges attesting to his sleepless night. He opened his mouth to say something, then slammed it shut as Bandaar stepped forward to embrace Maya.

"I know what I've said in the past frightens you, Mayara" he said softly, stepping back to brush a strand of hair from her cheek. "But now that you are contracted to the Gouram, I am almost sure we can transfer your power without risk to your life."

"And if you're wrong, *Father*? You won't just have killed your wife, but your daughter, too, all for more power," Maya snapped. "The chaos deals in nothing but *death*, yet you're still intent on releasing it."

Bandaar shook his head, anger surfacing with her words. "You wish to destroy the boundary, to bring it down and let those vermin reclaim these territories. What you don't realise, my dearest daughter, is that by destroying the barrier you would be destroying your brother, and all the spirits trapped within."

"My brother? The one who was taken as a child? He's dead," Maya spat, the words a cruel blow in the heat of her temper and fear.

"Yes, but his spirit is still very much alive, and he wouldn't have the chance to move on to where I could see him in the next life." Bandaar narrowed his eyes and gripped Maya's chin in his hand. "You have lived a good life. If you die here and now, you can move into the spirit realm and rest peacefully with Jaseen. Does Qaylan not deserve the same?"

To Maya's left, Thelic twitched. Without realising, he had reached up to grasp Bandaar's wrist and wrenched it from Maya's face. With a soft curse, Thelic stepped back and clenched his fists before apologising to the Keeper with a mild look of annoyance.

Thelic is still in there. He's fighting it, Maya thought hopefully. She looked to Keela and noticed her body was ramrod straight, a stark difference to the lazy posture she had held at the table the night before. They were *both* fighting, struggling against whatever spirits had taken control of their bodies.

Confused by Maya's smile, Bandaar grabbed her by the back of the neck and marched her to the centre of the dais. With his eyes focused forward, he failed to notice Maya reaching into the hidden pocket of her dress, and the small object she pulled out to hold, concealed in her closed fist.

Carnass stepped into Bandaar's path, the once proud and powerful man now a cowering and frail mess in front of his Esterbellian equal. "Bandaar, are you sure no harm will come to Maya?"

"I never said no harm would come of this ceremony, now get out of my way," Bandaar hissed as he brushed Carnass aside and led Maya into position. With a snap of the Keeper's fingers, Thelic walked forward, before coming to a rigid stop at the edge of the stone circle. Taking the spear from his side, he unwrapped the head and held it to his own throat.

"No, wait!" Maya shouted, reaching towards him.

"Stay where you are or he will take his own life," Bandaar said menacingly, pulling Maya back into the centre of the circle. "Now, I'm going to remove your cuffs, and you will do only as I say, or I *will* order Thelic to cut his throat."

Maya's face fell in horror as a thin line of blood rose beneath the blade on Thelic's neck. "Okay, I'll do what you want." She held her hands out, careful to keep her fists closed as Bandaar removed the cuffs.

Beside the Keepers' chairs were two small tables, one with goblets of wine, the other with a roll of parchment. Bandaar skirted the edge of the dais and retrieved the scroll, then turned to face Maya.

Thelic's fingers trembled, and a sheen of sweat coated his brow. While Maya was relieved to see the man she loved was fighting, the shake of his hands had caused several more cuts to appear across his throat.

"Hang on, Thelic," she whispered.

A dagger skidded across the stone slab to stop at the base of Maya's dress. She bent down and picked it up, then turned to face her father. His eyes were flicking along the worn words written on the scroll, and he muttered the steps to himself despite having memorised them long ago.

"Cut your palms, Mayara. Your blood must flow freely," he said, not bothering to look up at her.

With a desperate look to Thclic, Maya made the first cut in the palm that held the Stone, then slowly did the same with the other. Loki, BB and Pavinic's cat sprang from the seals at the sense of Maya's power unleashed. Wind whipped through the air and BB growled, Maya's distress bleeding into the sprites. For a moment, the room was cast into complete darkness as Loki's wind extinguished the lanterns' flames.

As the first drop of blood fell to the stone, light flooded the room as the castor circles came to life. Yellow, blue, and red rings, thick and unbroken and spreading wider than they ever had before to fill the large stone circle. Maya groaned as the power flooded through her, and she embraced it, let it course through her veins, up, up, and into the Gouram Stone.

"Good, Maya!" Bandaar called over Loki's wind. The sprites growled at the Keeper, the cat raising its hackles. Bandaar laughed, vibrating with his excitement at the prospect of being able to control such creatures. He returned his attention to the scroll and began the chant.

I offer my body, I offer my soul to the power before me, given willingly by its master to another…

Bandaar relinquished the parchment to retrieve a second dagger and made a small cut in the centre of both his palms. Stepping up to the stone, he knelt before Maya and leaned forward to place his hands on the floor at her feet. "Maya, kneel. Place your hands on the stone," he commanded, before continuing to mutter the chant under his breath.

The glowing circles flickered, and Maya shuddered as the

breath fled from her lungs. She gripped her chest as her body was forced down to the stone by an invisible force, sucking the very life from her.

This was her only chance, she had to free the others from their spirits all at once before the ceremony could properly begin. Gripping the Stone, Maya closed her eyes and called on the Gouram.

Bandaar flew back from the circle, skidding along the marble tiles as the stolen power was drawn from his body, back into the dais and into Maya. She called upon everything she had, drawing it from the seals and from deep within herself. The sprites lay on the ground, their essence suffering under the call for more power to be sent into the Gouram Stone. Maya rose into the air, water and fire curling as one beneath her feet as she continued her own prayer to the Gods.

"Stop her!" Bandaar roared, struggling to his feet. "Do it, Thelic, do it now!"

The being inside Thelic sensed the threat, it knew what Maya was trying to accomplish. It would not kill this host and risk being sucked into the Stone.

With no way to overpower the being, Thelic removed the blade from his throat, and watched helplessly as his finger pressed the trigger to extend the shaft. He raised his arm... and launched the spear.

Maya's eyes flew open, her prayers cut short as blood filled her mouth. She bowed her head to look down and saw the hilt of Thelic's spear poking through Batshari's seal on her chest. With the last of her reserves, she closed her eyes and opened her arms, unleashing her power across the room to ensnare the angry spirits.

Thelic, Keela and Elkin fell to the floor simultaneously, trapped in violent convulsions. Guards raced through the door at the sound of their Keeper's anguished roar, and

Carnass stepped back as Bandaar fell to his knees, gripping his head as the spirit inside him battled for control.

Maya's eyes were open now as she strained to pull the power back into her body, and the spirits into the Stone. She watched, shocked as Bandaar writhed in pain on the floor. He had been possessed the whole time, his anger and violence on behalf of another being. She had yet to meet the real man, the father that had long been overtaken by a cruel and angry force from the void.

She slowly floated down until her feet touched the ground and she called the last of the spirits into the Stone. A smoke-like essence wisped through the air, souls vibrating as they struggled against the pull, before disappearing into the powerful opal.

Maya's hands dropped to her sides and the Gouram Stone fell to skip across the dais, the sound echoing across the now silent chamber. She turned her head weakly to the side to stare at Bandaar, an unconscious heap on the floor. *I'll never get a chance to get to know the real him*, Maya realised, as her eyes flickered closed, and her legs buckled.

Emerging from their shock, both Esterbellian and Danikan guards raced across the hall to surround their respective Keepers, blades held high in warning despite being unsure as to who the real enemy was.

Carnass had moved back, confused by what had happened, and looked to Thelic.

Barely able to raise his head, Thelic barked for Carnass to make a stand. To take Bandaar while he was weak. To make a *choice*.

In a snap judgement, Carnass ordered his guards to seize the Esterbellian Keeper, fear outweighing his better judgement. His guards leapt forward and chaos ensued.

Thelic finally managed to rise to his feet and beamed at Carnass, pleased he had chosen Maya's side.

Maya.

Thelic whipped around and froze as all colour seemed to leave the room, only the bright red of Maya's blood standing out against the grey and black. He stumbled forward, tripping on the edge of the stone circle to land on his knees in the crimson pool. His hands shook as he lifted Maya into his arms, careful not to touch the spear jutting from an angry, fatal wound on her chest. His spear. The spear he had sworn to protect her with. He clutched her tighter. She had been so warm after gaining Pavinic's seal, her body a small furnace in his arms. Now she was cold and deathly pale.

"Is she breathing?" Keela asked. Behind them blades clanged and elements roared as the Esterbellians and Danikans fought for their Keepers. Bandaar had yet to wake, and one guard stood over him protectively, ready for the first to break through their defences.

"No, Keela," Thelic murmured in a grief-stricken daze. "She's not breathing because she's dead. I killed–" his voice broke, and he squeezed Maya's broken body to his chest.

Elkin dropped to his knees by Thelic's side, his eyes wide as the memories of Maya flooded across his mind. A voice had told him this would happen, that it was necessary. His own invading spirit was kinder than the rest, allowing Elkin to feel and move as he pleased, all the while influencing those thoughts and actions. He should have known that he was possessed, but it was so subtle, so easy to dismiss.

Placing Maya's body gently on the stone, Thelic shook with barely contained rage as he rose to his feet and searched the battleground for Bandaar. There. Hidden at the side of the room, one of the guards was trying to wake him.

Snatching Keela's blade from her side, Thelic sprinted into the mass and unleashed his fury on the soldiers, no matter which side they fought. He cut them down, one by one on his mission to reach the man that had caused all of this. Driven by grief, his swings were clumsy, but deadly, nonetheless.

Fire relit the lanterns as more guards piled into the room and entered the fray. Some broke off, racing for Maya, while the others jumped in to protect their Keeper. Thelic broke from his mission to reach Bandaar, his need to protect Maya undiminished despite her...death. He broke inside, dark wrath taking over in a new sort of possession.

Elkin and Keela collided with two of the guards as they approached, and Thelic slammed into another that had just reached Maya. The guard raised his blade, then flew back across the room as a sharp wind lifted him from his feet. Loki breezed onto Thelic's shoulder, snarling at the next soldier who broke from the battle at the sight of his comrades failing to recapture their prisoners.

Thelic gazed wide-eyed at the Finkel as it darted from his shoulder to latch on to the face of the approaching Esterbellian. Hope bloomed at the emergence of the sprite, and he spun to face Maya.

The Water Finkel and Pavinic's cat were by her side, their eyes closed and heads bowed towards her. As Thelic stepped back onto the stone circle, he watched as Maya's blood swept slowly back towards her in a cherry ripple, as if she were somehow turning back time. He knelt by her side and carefully pulled the spear from her chest, then rolled her onto her back.

The cat evaporated, disappearing back into its seal which grew to encompass her body in a tattoo of twisted swirls along her arms, neck, chest and exposed legs. Her body glowed as ghostly flames emerged from the markings.

Thelic leaned protectively over Maya as a deep rumble shook the very foundations of the Keep, the sharp smell of fire and sulphurous brimstone oozing from the chamber floor, with sparks of smoke and embers following quickly after. Soldiers gasped, pausing mid-battle to shrink back from the quickly forming mass, as a devilish creature appeared within the smoke.

With blazing horns and eyes of burning amber, the Gouram of fire regarded the humans with a snarl that seemed to resonate with their very souls. Composing himself, he looked to Maya. "I should have known it would come to this," Pavinic growled. "We have need of you yet, child. As I have never joined entirely with any creature, let us hope her body and spirit can take it." With those words, Pavinic disappeared in wisps of smoke.

Maya's body shook and Thelic cradled her head in his hand. "Maya?" he whispered, stroking her cheek. After several moments, she stilled, and Thelic's hope began to fade.

Maya's eyes snapped open, her irises as ruby as the bloody stains beneath them. The eyes of a God.

Sorry for the cliffhanger!!

Thank you so much for continuing on this journey with me. Your support means the world, and every page read goes a long way towards making an indie author's career!

If you have the time, a review would be super duper awesome too!

ALSO BY KATE CRAFT

The Chaos Covenant:
Chaos Forged a Fable
Chaos Deals in Death

ACKNOWLEDGMENTS

Thank you. Yes, I mean *you*, the person who has read so far as to reach these acknowledgements. I'm a writer and yet words fail to convey just how much you all mean to me. When you pick up a book, you not only immerse yourself in the worlds we painstakingly create, you contribute to an author's dream. So truly, I thank you.

Someone else who deserves all the love and gratitude I have to give, is Antony Walsh. Not only is he a best friend and family, he has been the most phenomenal editor a girl could ask for. Don't get me wrong, he's utterly brutal and it's a credit to my sanity that I haven't snapped as my manuscript is slowly picked apart. But with all of his notes and ideas and corrections, he has been truly invaluable on this journey, and I'm blessed to have him.

To my affianced, my other half, you are what makes this possible. You are my inspiration for Thelic, his kindness, loyalty and boundless courage…and his hunkyness too, obviously. Thank you for your unwavering belief, for pushing me to chase this dream and for standing beside me.

This book was written during a difficult time in my life. Everything is changing, much like it has with Maya, where I now face a new and uncertain world. One person in particular has helped me through this, she has taken some of my chaos so that I may stay afloat, and supported me wholeheartedly with my decision to write. Maria, thank you so much for all of your help and your unfounded faith in me, it means everything.

There are so many more I feel deserve to be acknowledged for their support. Mum, to whom this book is dedicated, for your endless encouragement and unconditional love. Cat and Gus, for your incredible friendship and for enduring my endless updates. Bodhi, for suffering the occasional shorter walk when deadlines loomed and for making me smile when I needed it the most. Edna, for being the best hype-woman and for going so far as to recommend my book to the Royal Family (bless her). Josh Plevey, for reducing me to howling laughter by enforcing chapter updates on my less than thrilled fiancé.

Thank you all so much.

STREET-TEAM

All my love and gratitude to these truly wonderful bookstagrammers who helped me along the way. I could not hope to dream without your support. Thank you.

Find them on Instagram:

a_reads_alot
amandaeredpandapaleo
readit.with.red
beastreader
bookishcharli
calmstitchread
life_tell.me.a.story
the_bookish_palss
reviewsbyrudra
book_dragon_gems
sunflowers.dragonflies
reading_to_the_last_page
booknerdy2020
the_introvertedreader
livingina_fantasy
j.g.writes
noteriasu
di_the_reader
carol_theavidreader
inked.eunoia
kyproff

madeby.mrym
talesfromthedragonslair
stewardofbooks
booking.with.janelle
nannersreads
booksyflowers
cindymariej
haywozreading
moonlight_libraryy
alohabooksandbujos
thebookwebb
rhyzkhua.reads
lost_spectre
jarjarbindings
book.lover005
amandaesworlds
erikas_reading_corner
through_coloradas_eyes
rockymountainreader
bri_serena_reads
sunshine_and_stories

ABOUT THE AUTHOR

Kate Craft is a British fantasy author who debuted in March 2022 with her first book in The Chaos Covenant series. Stepping into the world of indie publishing, she continues to chase her dream of weaving new tales filled with love and mayhem.

Born and raised travelling the world, Craft finally settled in the United Kingdom to complete a BSc in Psychology and Criminology, before joining the British Army in 2016. She is always eager to hear from readers and writers, so feel free to reach out!

facebook.com/KATECRAFT.Author
instagram.com/book.cove

Printed in Great Britain
by Amazon